Born and brought up in Islington, London, Susan Oudot worked in publishing for ten years before becoming a literary agent. From there she moved into the world of journalism, where she worked for various newspapers and magazines, before turning freelance. *Real Women*, her first novel and the sequel, *All That I Am*, were made into highly successful BBC TV dramas. Her second novel, *Virtual Love*, is currently in TV development. She lives in North London with her husband and four daughters.

Also by Susan Oudot

REAL WOMEN

VIRTUAL LOVE

ALL THAT I AM

Perfect

Susan Oudot

POCKET
BOOKS

LONDON · SYDNEY · NEW YORK · TOKYO · SINGAPORE · TORONTO

First published in Great Britain by Pocket Books, 2001
An imprint of Simon & Schuster UK Ltd
A Viacom Company

1 3 5 7 9 10 8 6 4 2

Simon & Schuster UK Ltd
Africa House
64–78 Kingsway
London WC2B 6AH

Simon & Schuster Australia
Sydney

A CIP catalogue record for this book is available from the British
Library

ISBN 0 671 01569 9

Typeset by SX Composing DTP, Rayleigh, Essex
Printed and bound in Great Britain by
Omnia Books Limited, Glasgow

For Debbie Shewell, in friendship and gratitude

Part One – Only Make-Believe

Chapter One

Fly Me To The Moon

The church hall was tiny, far too small for all the people who had crowded into it, let alone for the tables and chairs and, in one corner, up on a tiny stage, the four-piece band who, with their slicked-back hair and matching suits, looked like they'd come straight out of some other, distant era.

Right now they were playing an old Sinatra number, 'Fly Me To The Moon', and the makeshift dance floor was as packed as a tube carriage in the rush hour, mainly with older couples who, with their floral dresses and shiny suits, seemed to have come with the band, as part of a nostalgia package. This was their music, from their time, and for this brief moment they were back there, as if the years between had never passed.

Portsmouth on a rainy Saturday afternoon. The local team were playing, and two youths, distinct in their smart yet casual clothes, stood in a corner of the hall, a tiny radio held between them, as they craned to follow the match. Nearby, just beyond the edge of the milling crowd, the door to the loos opened and a woman stepped out, looking about her, taking in the scene, holding the train of her bridal dress in her right hand.

Julie's vividly blue eyes flicked from one face to another, then settled upon a youngish, dark-haired man who sat at a table on the far side of the hall, looking slightly awkward in the morning suit he was wearing, the chair beside him empty. Two men – twenty-somethings – stood just behind him, talking, emphasising each thing they said with an exaggerated movement of their beer-glasses. There was laughter, a friendly nudge, and then they moved away. For a moment the youngish man looked down at the table directly in front of him, as if deep in thought, then he looked up and across, and met her eyes.

Brian's smile was just the same as it had ever been, and as she smiled back at him and began to make her way across, Julie knew that she ought to be feeling nothing but happiness on this day of all days. But something was wrong. It had begun at the altar, even as the vicar had read aloud from his little book. She had glanced across at Brian standing there beside her, as nervous as a schoolboy, a sheen of perspiration on his brow, and had realised that she was already going off him – that whatever had brought them this far no longer had the power to take them further. It was as if she was in a boat, carried along by the wind, yet just as soon as she had made shore, the wind had died, and she had felt becalmed.

As she edged past the other guests, then sat, he reached out and, putting his arm about her shoulders, leaned close to kiss her cheek.

'You look beautiful, sweetheart. Really beautiful.'

She smiled and squeezed his arm, aware that everyone was watching her; that even the dancers out on the floor, swaying to the dying bars of the song, looked across at her from time to time and smiled. Smiled at how beautiful she looked; at how perfect a couple they so obviously were. No one saw the inner doubts, the sudden, almost giddying uncertainty she was feeling. And maybe that was a good thing, because she was sure she still loved Brian; sure she had done the right thing in marrying him. And she would make it work – she was determined to make it work – only . . .

Only what?

No. Whatever she was feeling at this minute, she would not let it affect their marriage. Brian was a good man, a nice man, and he deserved it of her. Yet as she looked about her once again, she saw how one of Brian's friends, Danny, was watching her from a nearby table, that same wistful expression on his face that she had often noticed, and, seeing it, she gave him a smile, looking down almost instantly and then back up again, as if to catch him out. And this once she did catch him – saw, in that brief instance, the longing in his eyes, and knew, without a shadow of a doubt, that the poor sap was half in love with her.

Julie turned to Brian and smiled. 'You wanna dance?'

He laughed. 'What? To this crap? Nah. Wait till they play something decent.'

'You don't mind if I do, do you?'

Brian shrugged.

'Say if you mind.'

But she knew he didn't. Brian hated dancing. At least, *proper* dancing. He'd jerk about a bit to some of the more modern stuff, but he wasn't a dancer. And that was a shame, because he didn't know what he was missing; didn't realise that a good dance – up close and pressed tight, his arms about you, yours at his neck – was like good sex, or, better still, like the promise of good sex.

Julie stood and, gathering up her dress, gestured towards Danny.

'Hey, Danny – fancy a quick twirl?'

And as she took Danny's hand and led him out on to the dance floor, she told herself, *Just this once. Just to let him know what he's missing*. But deep inside she felt a tiny thrill, and as his arm went about her waist, she knew that she liked this, liked the way he looked at her, the way each movement of his betrayed how much he wanted her.

Yes, just this once. And then I'll go back across to him.

After all, Brian's my husband now.

She had always tried her best to be a good girl. Only trying wasn't always good enough.

The music was coming from the old hi-fi in the corner, a real big box of a thing in walnut and padded leather with an illuminated radio dial on the front, that, as it heated up, gave out a distinct and reassuring smell. It was one of her step-father's LPs, one of the really early ones from the beginning of the Sixties, and as the singer's dreamy voice filled the living room, so she twirled about, as if in the arms of some handsome boy.

And as she danced, so she closed her eyes, imagining how they'd talk and then, afterwards, how they'd kiss, and how he'd put his arms about her back and—

Crash! She hit the sideboard with a thump and stumbled, throwing out an arm to save herself. But that only made it worse. As she went down, she knocked the sideboard again and one of the three big vases toppled and, seemingly in slow motion, bounced off the carpet and into the fire grate, where it shattered with a deafening smash.

For two bars the song went on. Then, in the ensuing silence, she heard footsteps thudding down the hall stairs and turned to see the door thrown open, her stepfather standing there in his shirtsleeves, half-shaved, taking in the scene.

He glared at her. 'You little cow!'

She saw him come at her as in a dream, one of his massive, workman's hands grabbing her left arm so tightly that afterwards the bruise came up large and yellow-black. But that was not the worst of it. She knew what was to come and struggled against it, squirming away from him as his free hand sought to tug down her knickers. And then, as she squealed and the tears came, he finally got them down and, pulling her towards him, brought his hand down, palm open across her bare buttocks.

It stung like hell, but not half as much as the words. 'You're a stupid, useless little cow!' And his hand fell again and again on her reddening cheeks, even as the strings played the opening bars of 'Fly Me To The Moon' and Frank Sinatra's silk-smooth voice filled the room.

She had always tried to be a good girl.

Julie woke suddenly, in darkness, the regular tick-tick-tick of the bedside clock beside her the only sound in the room. Her heart was hammering in her chest and her breathing was strangely laboured, as if she'd been running, yet of her dream she remembered little.

As her pulse slowed, so she became aware of someone in the bed beside her, and for a moment she thought it must be Brian.

Brian . . . *That's* who she was dreaming of. Brian and their wedding day. But it sure as hell wasn't Brian who lay next to her. She could smell the beer in his sweat, could see, in the half light, the long curve of his naked back as he lay on his side, facing away from her.

Karl.

Julie let out her breath, remembering now the argument they'd had last night. Karl thought he'd won it, because she'd gone all silent on him; but she'd not shut up because he was right, she'd shut up because she'd suddenly realised that it wasn't worth fighting any more. So she'd let him think he'd won. Whereas, in fact, he'd lost, big time.

She got up slowly, careful not to wake him, and tiptoed through into the bathroom. She was on days this week, but it wouldn't be too hard to get a morning off. The ward sister liked her, and she'd done her enough favours in her time, so she ought to be safe to ask one back.

Usually she showered, but she was loath to wake him and have him come in on her, so a brief wash-down sufficed. Besides, she could always have a proper shower at work later on. It took only a minute or two to get her uniform on, then she was in the kitchen, chewing on a slimming biscuit while she looked through the drawers for the building society book.

Brian. How strange that she'd dreamed of Brian. It was a good few years since she'd last seen him. He was a decent bloke, and he'd always treated her well. That was, until things went wrong. Until he blew all his money and got into debt and started thieving.

There was no sign of the book, but it didn't matter. She could look for it again tonight. She didn't need it today.

No. But she ought to sort out the rest of it. A few calls ought to do the trick. There was that young guy she'd met in the bar near the restaurant – the one who'd given her his address. He might help. And Sonia . . .

Julie hesitated a moment, wondering if she ought to phone Sonia and give her warning. The trouble was her Ricky. Ricky was one of Karl's best friends, and if he got wind of what she planned—

No. She'd just turn up at Sonia's and trust to her better nature. After all, she could only say no. Only she wouldn't. She was a mate, and mates never said no, even if they had doubts.

Julie smiled, then walked over to the mirror that was

propped up beside the bread bin and, leaning in, had a long hard look at her reflection.

Not bad, she thought. *Even at thirty-four, I've still got it.*

Not that Karl noticed, these days. Not that he paid one blind bit of notice whether she had make-up on or not, or whether she'd had her hair done or not. For all he cared, she could be wearing a cloth bag over her head.

No. Lately, the only time he noticed her at all was when he had a hard-on. And then it didn't matter how she looked, as long as she parted her legs for him.

Men!

Not that she really minded that part of it. And not that it really mattered any more; not now she'd decided.

Sometimes she would find herself remembering. How dark the stairs were; the smell of the cold linoleum underfoot; the echoing emptiness of the hallway with its umbrella stand that was never ever used, and the stained glass of the front door panels that lit up so cheerily whenever the sun shone, which was not often in that long and rainy childhood.

As she sat there on the top deck of the bus, heading in to work, her handbag in her lap, Julie could see it all vividly, as if the veil of years had fallen from her eyes.

It had been an old house in a curved and sloping street of red-brick terraced houses, and if you looked out from the top window you could see the long wall of the harbour, down there beyond the solid sheet of grey. It was an old and quiet house – quiet because her father had been dying. So long dying, in fact, that his silent presence lingered long after he had gone.

There had been a worn brown leather sofa in the front living room, the arms and cushions threadbare in places, a dark line scored into the wall where it had stood so long. Above it had hung a faded print, the painting so dark behind the undusted glass that one had to squint to make out the subject.

She remembered . . .

The tick of the old Victorian clock on the mantelpiece. The gatefold table in the corner with its chunky scrolled legs and its yellowing lace cloth. The repetitive floral pattern of the wallpaper. And upstairs, the almost Spartan feel of the bathroom, with its cold enamel bath, its high ceiling and the big wall-mounted boiler in the corner, that would rattle like it was alive and that she'd always been afraid of.

Beside the bathroom was her bedroom, just across the hall from her parents' room. A small room, big enough for her bed and a small chest of drawers and nothing else. More a cupboard than a room. At nights she had lain there, fearing the creak of that door across the way, the groan of the floorboards on the landing.

There had been good times too. She had gone to a mixed school, a comprehensive, up near the park. Close enough to walk and save the busfare for some fags. She'd always seemed older than the other girls anyway, and the shopkeepers had never questioned her. She had started smoking at thirteen. As for school, well, school itself was okay. She was bright enough to get by. But she was never very popular – not with the girls anyway. With the boys . . . that was a different matter. She could still recall how, aged fourteen, Billy Matthews and Steve McDonagh had fought over her behind the gym – a brief yet brutal contest, with blood spilled and Billy, the taller, lankier boy, the victor. And later, for his reward, Billy had pressed her against the wall of the changing rooms, his cock as stiff as a bicycle pump through his thin trousers as he rubbed himself up against her. There'd been a long kiss with tongues, and then, to his delight, she had let him feel her tits.

She smiled at the memory, then stood. ''Scuse me.'

This was her stop, two before the hospital. She always got off here. There was a baker's on the corner just up the way and she always stopped there to pick up a tuna mayonnaise sandwich and a coffee before making her way in.

She was early – at least twenty minutes early – and so she took her time, savouring the morning, enjoying this brief freedom from the daily grind. Not that she hated her job. Not at all. She liked nursing. It was the one thing that actually fulfilled her, and she was good at it. Even the exams hadn't put her off, for once. It had been hard, but she'd buckled down and done it.

Alice, the ward sister, was alone at the nurses' station as she walked in, hunched over the desk, preparing the list for the pharmacy. She glanced up, then, seeing who it was, sat back, smiling.

'Now aren't you the early bird?'

Julie grinned. 'I know. Look, can I have a word?'

The honeymoon had been awful, truly awful. Brian had booked a week in Teignmouth. He'd announced it to her in the car coming away from the reception, grinning at her as he said it, as though she was supposed to be thrilled, but she was a long way from being thrilled – a good thousand miles or so, to be truthful. She'd known he'd booked something, and she'd hoped for Ibiza, maybe, or Tenerife. But Teignmouth!

It might have been okay if it had been sunny, but it turned out to be the wettest May week in forty years, with a wind whipping off the seafront that could have pebble-dashed the whole damned town.

She should have known then – should have left him right there and then – only she had promised herself that she would make it work. She kept telling herself that it wasn't his fault that he'd got it wrong – that maybe he couldn't afford anything better – only try as she might she *did* blame him, and on the third night, when he reached across for her in bed, she rolled away, turning her back on him. And that was that.

Oh, they had sex after that. And it was alright. It was sex. Only – well, the spark wasn't there any more. It was *just* sex.

The rest was downhill. Two months into the marriage Brian had an accident in his van. It wasn't much of a prang and he wasn't injured, only he also wasn't taxed or insured. Word got out to his customers and that was that. Within a month he'd lost most of his delivery work, and when the police summons arrived, it seemed to send him into a terminal decline. He started drinking. And not just drinking . . .

Those had been hard times for her, living in a one-bedroom council flat, with no income and a husband who wasn't worth a shit. But she hadn't left him. Despite all provocation, she had stood by him till the last.

The day they'd come to arrest him was, perhaps, the strangest of all. It was late August by then and she had been sitting out on the balcony in her bikini, enjoying the brilliant weather. Brian had been indoors, sleeping off a late night, when the doorbell rang, so she had gone through to answer it, her eyes unaccustomed to the shadows as she drew the door back on the chain.

'Yeah?'

There were three of them. Uniforms. A sergeant, a very young-looking PC and a policewoman. It was the sergeant who answered her.

'Are you Mrs Carter?'

'Yes.'

'Is your husband at home, love?'

'Why? What's he done now?'

But she knew what he'd been up to. She'd seen the suitcase he kept beneath the bed, and had even looked into it. Not to speak of the video players she'd found in the bottom of the wardrobe. She knew alright.

She also saw how nervous the young PC was, and realised that this was probably his first arrest, and strangely she felt sorry for him. Even so, she kept the chain on.

'Well?'

The sergeant gave her the politest of smiles. 'Take the chain off and open the door, will you, love, and maybe we could talk about this properly.'

She saw the official-looking document he was holding and nodded towards it. 'You got a warrant?'

The sergeant held the warrant up with a degree of irritation.

She took off the chain, then stood back, conscious that she was still wearing her bikini. As she did, Brian called to her from the bedroom.

'Julie? Wha's up?'

She didn't answer, just met the eyes of the others as they came past her; the sergeant's polite little nod, the police-woman's tight smile of understanding, and the young PC's slightly anxious smile of thanks.

She closed the door then turned, just in time to see Brian

appear in the bedroom doorway, scratching at his beer gut, looking dishevelled and pathetic in his pants and vest. He blinked, then: 'What the fuck?'

The sergeant faced him solidly. 'Mr Carter? Mr Brian Geoffrey Carter?'

'Yeah?'

'I have a warrant for your arrest on a charge of burglary and possession of stolen goods. Anything you say will be . . .'

As the sergeant read those words, familiar from the cop shows, she watched Brian slump; saw the light die in his face and a look of animal resignation take its place. Another man might have fought them, maybe, or at least shown defiance, but not Brian. He gave up without the least little quiver of protest. If he'd trussed himself up and handed himself over on a plate, he'd not have surrendered so meekly.

And seeing it, she knew it was over. Finally and irrevocably. Because she couldn't stay hitched to such a loser. Such a *nothing* of a man. She might tell him that she'd wait – that she would be there for him when he came out – only she knew she wouldn't, because prison wouldn't change this man – not for the better. It would only confirm what was already apparent in him. If he was a loser now, he'd be a much bigger loser when he got out.

Besides, she was bored with him. Bored with this dull little lifestyle in this dull little flat. It was time to move on. Time to cut her losses and run.

She watched in silence as they handcuffed him and led him out, then went out on to the balcony and watched from four floors up as they took him across the concrete apron and put him in the back of the panda. And, looking about her, she realised that she was not alone. A good dozen or more of her neighbours were out on their balconies, watching her humiliation. And as she turned and caught the eye of one of them – that pinch-faced snooty cow from thirty-seven she had often shared the lift with, always in silence – she knew that that was it. Returning inside, she changed from her bikini.

You prat, she thought, thinking of Brian, of what a sad

bastard he'd looked as they'd taken him away. *You total fucking prat.*

'Nurse? Can you help me, please?'

Julie turned from where she was taking her elderly patient's blood pressure, then smiled good-naturedly, seeing what it was. Eric had spilled some juice on the floor beside his bed.

'Don't worry about it, my love. I'll be there in a tick. Just got to check that our Pete here's alright.'

She turned back, smiling at the grey-haired old dear, lowering her voice as she deflated the armband. 'That's fine, sweetheart. We'll have you out of here within the week, don't you worry.'

The words seemed to reassure the old man. But it was more than that. Like many of them, he positively glowed in her presence, as if her attentions breathed new life into him. The poor old sod was on his own now. Eighty-two and a widower. Not a good thing to be. At least she had most of her life ahead of her, not behind.

'Now,' she said, marking the chart, then slipping it into the slot at the end of the bed, 'let's tuck you in again, then we'll see what that troublemaker Eric is up to.'

Eric was the ward comedian. In his early fifties he was a good twenty years younger than the others in the ward, but the sad truth was that Eric was probably going to die before any of his fellows. He had cancer and there was nothing they could do about it. He'd left it too long before coming in for treatment, and now the most they could do was make him comfortable. Not that he ever complained. No, because Eric – cancer and all – was one of the cheeriest men Julie had ever met.

She walked across and looked down at the mess Eric had made, then shook her head in mock irritation and, crouching down, began to clear it up.

'I love watching you.'

She looked up and saw that he was looking at her, not the slightest sign of a smile on his lips. His sallow, yellowing face was dead serious for once.

'Yeah?'

He smiled. 'If I'd had a woman like you . . .'

'Yeah?' But she said it softly this time.

She slipped the sodden cloth into the bin beside the bed, then stood, wiping her hands on her apron. 'There must have been a woman.'

Eric smiled briefly. 'Plenty. But never one who really cared. Never one like you.'

'And you think I'd have really cared for you?'

Eric nodded, his watery grey eyes intent suddenly. 'Yeah. I can see it. You're like the bloody sun. Whatever you shine on grows.'

She smiled at him, touched. 'You think so?'

'Oh, I know so.' The corners of his mouth lifted as he pulled back the bedcovers.

'*Eric!*' She looked about her, embarrassed, but if any of the others had noticed, they gave no indication. Leaning across, she pulled the blanket back across him, covering him up.

Eric grinned. 'I can still shock you, then?'

She giggled. 'I could have you arrested.'

He sighed. 'Yeah, well I made my point. It's a man's delight and his downfall, his glory and his gaoler. If I'd had my time again, I'd have . . .'

'Chopped it off?'

'Nah. Used it more wisely. Like the gift it was. Found me a woman who would have treasured it.'

He looked away a moment, then back at her. 'Have I said too much?'

'No. It's just that I've never thought of it like that. I've always thought . . .'

'What?'

She was tempted. Tempted to tell him everything. But she wasn't going to. No, not even to a dying man who was trying to be honest with her.

'The trouble with you men is you think that thing makes you all strong and virile, but the truth is it's the biggest weakness you've got. Women can make you do anything. If they know how.'

'And you know how, eh?'

She grinned; then, more seriously: 'So what brings this on? Where's the ward joker today? Got the day off or something?'

He smiled. 'I heard you're off.'

'Off?'

'Leaving. I was going past the desk, heading for the loos, when you told sister.'

'Sorry. I would have told you.'

'Would you?'

She hesitated, then leaned forward and gave him a peck on the cheek. 'I'll come back and see you. I'm not going very far.'

'Then why . . .?'

Julie smiled thoughtfully, looking at him long and hard. 'I told Sister it was my mum. But it's not. It's man trouble. Know what I mean?'

Eric nodded. 'Yeah. I know. I *was* man trouble.'

And they both laughed. Laughed until the old men turned their heads, wondering what the hell was going on.

Julie stood in her kitchen, late night, the radio playing softly as she held the cordless phone to her ear, listening to the ringing tone. Beyond the window, the tiny square of garden was dark. She could hear the sound of the traffic on the main road and the noise of a dog barking somewhere on the estate.

'Hello? Two-oh-six-three.'

'Jake?'

'Yeah? Sorry, who is that?'

'Jake – it's Julie. You know, from the wine bar. You gave me your number.'

'Oh. Oh, right.' He sounded vague. 'How are you?'

'Fine, thanks. But look. I desperately need a favour and, well, I know it's a cheek, but you did say that if I ever needed a hand . . .'

'Yeah?'

'Well, I've got to move some stuff. It's all rather urgent and – well, if it were smaller . . .'

'When you gotta shift it by?'

'Tomorrow. First thing.'

'Early, like?'

'Not too early. Half nine. Ten, maybe.'

'And what about transport?'

'It's all taken care of. I've got a van. I just need a hand loading it.'

'Yeah. Yeah, okay.'

'Great! No, that's wonderful. You don't know how much of a help it'll be. You're a star.'

'Yeah, well maybe we can have a drink sometime?'

'Yeah – yeah, I'd like that.'

'So what's the address?'

She gave him the address, then said her goodbyes and put the phone down, feeling a little shaky now that it was done. She didn't have to be in work until one herself, so there'd be plenty of time to move everything.

She stood, then walked across the kitchen, looking out into the darkness of the garden. She wouldn't miss this place. She wouldn't miss it one damn bit. Only it was strange sometimes how the fear gripped you. Fear of change. Of digging yourself out of the mess you'd got into. But it wasn't as great as the fear of staying put.

Karl was out, at the pub with his post office mates. He'd not be back till late, unsteady on his feet. But she'd be in bed by then, asleep, or pretending to be, and by the time she woke again he'd already be gone – out at work again, pushing his little trolley and delivering his letters . . .

She smiled at the thought, then turned, looking back across the kitchen. Two years she'd lived here. It wasn't much when you thought about it. It was barely time enough to set down even the tiniest of roots. Not that she'd really liked it here. They'd talked about getting a bigger place, somewhere in the suburbs, but Karl had done bugger all about it. He was lazy like that. Unambitious. Besides, he didn't like to stray far from his local.

Well, sod him. He could keep his local and his drinking buddies. See if she cared.

The radio was still playing. Some old song from way back. Sinatra. She listened for a while, humming along with it, then reached out and switched it off.

No one was going to the moon. Not tonight, anyway. All flights were cancelled.

Julie looked about her, then, taking the building society book from where she'd left it on the table, she went over and switched off the light.

It was going to be a busy day tomorrow.

Chapter Two

Band Of Gold

Jake was there at nine, standing on her doorstep and grinning in at her, his dark hair slicked back, like he'd showered just ten minutes ago.

'Hi.'

'Hi. Thanks ever so much for coming.'

She acted coy, let him kiss her and embrace her briefly, then it was down to business. Strictly business. Karl had gone out at six, and she'd been up almost as soon as the door had slammed behind him, packing all of her personal stuff into the two new suitcases she'd bought yesterday. They stood in the living room against the wall. They'd be the last things to go on the van, which she had backed up on to the driveway. It was empty right now, but not for much longer.

'Okay,' she said, heading up the stairs. 'Big stuff first. The bed and the wardrobe. Then we'll put the sofa on.'

She saw the momentary query in his eyes, but he didn't say anything. As far as he knew she lived alone, and if this was a flit – to avoid paying the rent – then he wasn't going to blow the whistle on her. And she knew exactly why. He was like most men. He thought that a favour here, a favour there, and he might just stand a chance of shagging her. She would be grateful, after all, and a grateful woman . . .

Julie smiled to herself as they manoeuvered the mattress out of the room and on to the landing. She knew what he'd been thinking, seeing the double bed. He'd been hoping they might have a quick one before they got on with things, and on another day she might have let him, only she wanted him focused – didn't want to risk him sloping off just as soon as he'd got what he'd come for. No. She wanted the stuff in the van. Then, maybe, she'd consider how things stood.

Getting the big stuff in took the best part of an hour. Disconnecting the cooker and getting it up on to the van was the hardest. But by half ten it was all in there. All of her worldly goods. And Karl's, come to that. Only Karl didn't matter any more.

Jake wiped a hand across his brow, then turned to look at her. 'That everything?'

She met his eyes and smiled. 'Yup.'

'You need a hand the other end?'

'Nope.'

'Then . . .' He hesitated, not knowing how to play it.

She stepped past him and closed the back door and locked it, then turned and looked at him.

'You look hot.'

He still wasn't sure. She'd been so organised, after all. Not the least bit flirty.

'I'm going to take a shower.' She made her way to the foot of the stairs. Looking back over her shoulder she saw Jake standing there.

Why not? she was thinking. *I fancy him, after all.*

Only she didn't want to risk leaving the van on the driveway too much longer. What if one of Karl's mates saw it? She didn't want him coming back and discovering her. Even so . . .

'Well?' she said. 'You coming or not?'

He nodded eagerly.

She took his arm and led him across to the open doorway, closer to him suddenly than she'd been all morning. 'Just a quick one, mind.'

There was a girl at school called Rosie Bowyer, and Rosie Bowyer had hated her guts. That might have been fine, only she had a gang, and the gang did whatever Rosie Bowyer told them to do.

Normally she managed to elude them. She'd hang about with the boys, or wait to walk home, taking a variety of routes back, always avoiding the park, where she knew they liked to hang out. But one evening, in late November, they were waiting for her in the playground.

She had been kept behind for something or other. What it was she couldn't remember now, but one of Rosie's gang had been in the same detention group; and the others had hung on after school, waiting for her to be let out.

Julie hadn't even noticed them at first. She was too busy rehearsing in her head what she would say to her stepfather. He'd warned her against getting another detention, and she feared having to explain just why she'd been kept late again, but she was only halfway across the dimly lit playground when she saw the group of them standing by the gate, blocking her way.

She stopped, at a loss as to what to do. There was only one gate open this time of the evening. If she wanted to go home, she would have to go past them. She glanced back, to the lights of the big, square school building, then, deciding she would risk it, walked on, keeping her head down, determined to breeze past them and ignore their taunts. What could they do to her anyway? What could they say that hadn't been said already behind her back?

She was only three or four paces from them when Rosie Bowyer stepped out, directly into her path.

'Where d'you think you're going, *tart*?'

Julie swallowed. The girl was a good six to eight inches taller than her and packed a punch like a boy. She'd been roughed up once before by her, in the changing rooms after netball, and she didn't fancy facing that again.

She looked down, not meeting Rosie's eyes. 'I'm going home. I'm late.'

There was laughter, like she'd said something really funny.

'What? Late as in missed your period?'

Julie glanced up, then looked back down again. Her heart was racing now.

'Well, *tart*? Cat got your tongue? Or was it the cat's arse?'

Julie balled her fists, conscious that she was blushing now. Not that they'd see. In the light of the distant lamps, they could barely see the expression on each other's faces. But she knew that they were all grinning, enjoying her discomfort.

She stepped forward, making to pass, but Rosie pushed her back.

'Where the fuck do you think you're going? I ain't finished with you yet.'

Julie swallowed. The worst she could get was a beating, but maybe that would save her a beating when she got home.

'Let me go.'

There was more laughter, then Rosie stepped closer, breathing down into her face. 'Why? Why should I let you go, you little slag? We're going to have a little game, and you know what our game's called?'

Again she swallowed. By now her mouth was completely dry. She could barely talk '*No*,' she whispered.

'It's called "hunt the scrubber". And you know how you play it?'

Julie shook her head, fearing the very worst.

'Well, it's like this. You come along with us, to the park, and then we let you go.'

'You—?' But hope died instantly. She saw how the other girls had formed a circle now about her. A silent, threatening circle. Julie shook her head. 'You can't.'

'No?' Rosie sounded surprised. 'Now why's that? Are you going to stop us? Or maybe you're going to offer to shag us all, like you do all the boys. Only you know what the trouble is? We're not lezzies. Or common little tarts. And we don't like you. In fact, we hate your tarty little guts.'

She froze. For a moment she seemed to lapse out of herself. But as she came back, she realised she was still there, standing at the centre of that circle of hate, the very focus of all that nastiness and spite, and the realisation chilled her. It felt like something died in her at that moment. Yet even as she bowed to it, even as she let herself be taken by them, her arms grabbed, her bag ripped from her hand, she heard a voice, echoing across the playground.

'Oi! You girls! Stop right where you are!'

She squeezed her eyes tight shut, close to tears, as she heard the teacher's footsteps rapidly approach.

'Oh, I might have known it would be you, Rosie Bowyer. Wherever there's trouble, there you are at the centre of it!'

'Sir? I don't know what you mean. We was just talking to our mate Julie.'

'Talking, eh? It didn't look like talking from where I stood.'

'You calling me a liar, sir?'

There was a moment's silence, then: 'Would you like to continue this discussion in Mr Difford's office tomorrow morning?'

'No, sir.'

'Then get off home. And don't let me see you hanging around, okay?'

There were ooohs and mutterings, but when Julie opened her eyes again they were all gone. All, that is, except her saviour, Mr Williams.

'You alright?' he asked gently.

She nodded.

'You want to tell me what it was all about?'

She shook her head.

'Okay. Then would you like a lift home? I've got my car.'

She hesitated, then nodded silently.

'Good. Then come on. I can explain to your parents what happened, if you like.'

He'd not actually touched her, not then, but in her head she had imagined him putting an arm about her and taking her to his car, and later, to some lover or other, she had said that they'd had a 'thing', her and Mr Williams, only it wasn't true, he'd only ever been kind to her. Not that that had stopped her fantasising about him. Because, sitting in the car beside him that time, she had found herself enjoying being there – liking the smell of him, his air of calm authority, the simple confidence of the man. She liked the fact that he had come to her rescue, that he had stood up to her tormentors and scattered them with just a few words.

Yet when they stopped outside her house and he offered again to come in and explain to her stepdad just what had gone on, she shook her head, then said quietly 'No thanks. I'm fine now.' And even though she knew it would mean a beating, to her that was better than having him come in and actually meet her stepfather. No, she wanted him kept out of all that stuff. Wanted to keep him separate.

And as she watched him drive away, she knew also that Rosie Bowyer wasn't done with her. That she'd be even more determined to get her now. But somehow that didn't matter quite so much: not now that she had someone she could turn to.

And maybe that's where it began. Her obsession with older men. With father figures. For though she'd had her share of lovers of her own age, she'd always found herself happiest with older men. Men who wanted to look after her. Men who'd stand up to the world for her.

Schooldays. It was funny how often she went back to her schooldays.

Jake had gone, all pink and scrubbed and fresh with a grin on his face the size of the Cheshire Cat's. As Julie combed out her hair in the hall mirror, she smiled to herself, remembering the look of surprise on his face when she'd gone down on him. Well, he'd been a gem, and there was always the chance that she might need him to help out again sometime. Besides, he wasn't bad-looking, even if he wasn't really her type. A relationship was out of the question, but that didn't mean she couldn't see him from time to time. After all, a girl had her needs . . .

She turned from the mirror and glanced across at the living-room doorway. The last two suitcases rested there still, her overnight bag beside them, her toiletries and make-up bag on top of it. Going across, she packed the final few things, slipped her wallet into her handbag, then gathered up her keys.

She had just stepped out on to the doormat when someone whistled to her.

It was Karl's pal, Ricky, their local postman. Looking at him warily, she set the bags down.

'Alright, Ricky?'

He handed her her post, then reached out to take the bags. 'Need a hand?'

'No – no thanks. I'm fine. Cheers!'

He hesitated, the slightest frown on his face, then shrugged. 'Okay. See you.'

'See you.'

She took a long breath, watching him walk away, then looked down at the mail he'd handed her. Bills. Nothing but bills. She threw them down into the hallway, then stepped outside, pulling the door closed behind her.

Shit! she thought. *Why did I have to bump into him?* But it was okay. After all, it'd be a long time before Ricky got to speak to Karl, and by that time— She smiled. By that time, she would be long gone.

Julie hurried down the steps of the building society, looking about her in case a warden was hovering. The van was parked up on the pavement, on a yellow line, the hazard lights flashing. She glanced at her watch, then slipped the savings book and cash into her handbag. Yet as she turned, something caught her eye. There, two doors along, in the window of a clothing shop, was the most gorgeous dress she had seen in ages: a bright red clingy number that she knew would show off her figure to best effect. It was expensive, but for once that didn't matter. What mattered was how she'd look in it.

She glanced about her once again, wondering if she could take the risk, then, smiling to herself, she walked across and pushed open the heavy glass door.

If she got a ticket, she got a ticket. Besides, they'd have to find her first.

Standing there in the changing cubicle, she realised that it had been ages – a year at least – since she had bought herself anything new. Even for her birthday Karl had skimped. Not that she'd expected him to be inspired, only a new iron wasn't exactly every girl's dream present.

It was tight, but it was perfect. Turning side on, she patted the flatness of her stomach, pleased that she'd not let herself get out of shape. She knew plenty who had, even those who'd not had children, and no matter what they said about women's lib, the truth was that most men preferred a woman with a good figure, and in her experience, those who didn't were either gay or short-sighted. Nah, all that crap about the importance of a woman's personality was fine if you had a face like a wet weekend and a figure like a sack of potatoes, but first you had to get a man's attention; you had to turn his head, and to do that you had to give him what he wanted.

And what did he want? Sex, gift-wrapped. You had to tease him, give him a bit of a display.

Squeezing out of the dress, she slipped it back on the hanger, then quickly dressed again, feeling strange back in her nurse's uniform after wearing something so sleek and sexy. But she was happier now, her mood brightened, and as she took the dress over to the counter, she hummed softly to herself.

'Well now, *we're* in a good mood, aren't we?' said the assistant, a tall young man in his mid-twenties, balding and clearly gay.

'Yep,' she answered cheerily, giving him her sweetest smile. 'Won the lottery, didn't I?'

'*Really?*'

'Nah. But I live in hope.'

Sonia pulled down the garage door and turned to Julie.

'Are you sure you're gonna be alright?'

'Yeah.' But Julie's smile was unconvincing. 'Listen. I'd better go.'

Throwing her cigarette down, Julie stamped on it, then stepped across, giving Sonia a hug.

'Take care,' Sonia said, smiling at her.

'I'll write. And thanks. As soon as I'm settled, I'll come for it, alright?'

'Right.'

Julie smiled again, then went over to the van and climbed inside.

'See ya!'

'Bye!'

Yet as Julie drove away, Sonia wondered what Ricky would make of this once he knew. Not that she was going to tell him – not until she had to.

You owe me one, she thought, going back inside. But the truth was she didn't mind. Because Julie had been great to her that time she'd had the miscarriage. She'd been there for her in a way Ricky hadn't. She'd understood what she'd been going through, whereas Ricky had been totally insensitive. To him, it had been a bit of an inconvenience. But Julie – Julie had been blinding.

The vacuum cleaner was where she'd left it, in the middle of the living-room floor. Smiling to herself, she picked up the brush then kicked the red button on the side of the Hoover. At once the room was filled with sound. But Sonia was grinning now, imagining the look on Karl's face when he got home that night.

'Serve him right,' she said quietly, the words swallowed up by the noise from the vacuum cleaner.

It had rained most of the afternoon, but the sun had come out now, and inside the ward it was one of those peaceful lulls you sometimes get, when everything's done for a time and the patients are sleeping. Or trying to.

Julie, standing at the bedside of one of her patients, was singing to herself, totally unselfconscious as she checked the old man's chart – some old song from the Sixties that they often played on the radio. As she turned, she saw how the ward sister, Alice, was watching her, a smile on her face.

'What?'

Alice laughed. 'Holy Jesus! We'll be glad to see the back of you and that voice of yours.'

Julie looked down at the old guy in the bed and winked. 'You can tell she's upset, can't you?' Then, to Sister Alice, 'You're gonna miss me. You know you are.'

'Huh! Like a leaky bedpan!' Then, coming across, her voice quieter, 'So what's the news on your mum? How's she doing?'

Julie's face dropped. 'Not so good. Still, she might perk up a bit once I'm there.'

'Sure she will.'

Alice seemed to be about to say something more, when a nurse appeared in the doorway at the far end of the ward and indicated that she was wanted.

'Sorry. Duty calls.' And with a squeeze of Julie's arm she was gone.

Julie turned back, staring down at the old man, then reached out to gently adjust his oxygen mask

'You don't think anything's ever going to happen to your mum, do you?' she said quietly. 'It's like she's always going to be there for you. Still, a double dose of TLC will do the trick. We all need a bit of that, don't we?'

'Julie!'

She turned at the summons. One of the other nurses was standing there in the doorway.

'Yeah?'

'Sister wants you in the office.'

'Okay.'

She turned back, gently loosening the strap to the mask a little, making sure it wasn't hurting him, then smiled.

'Alright, sweetheart?'

The old man nodded. Satisfied, Julie turned away, making her way between the beds, towards the ward sister's office. She glanced at her watch. It was almost the end of her shift.

She paused at the foot of Eric's bed. He was sleeping, his thin face drawn and pained despite the drugs. He really ought to have been in a hospice, only no one was going to take the responsibility of discharging him. Not yet, anyway.

'See you,' she said softly, touched by his vulnerability.

As she pushed through the door into Sister's office there was a cheer and the sound of a cork popping as one of the other nurses opened up bottles of Buck's Fizz. The room was crowded with her workmates, all of them smiling at her.

Julie laughed, surprised and touched. 'Oh, you daft buggers!'

Sister Alice stepped across, hugging her, then stood back, gesturing to one of the others. 'Aw, come on. Give the girl a drink before she goes all soppy on us.'

One of the nurses held up a syringe, filled with wine, and squirted it into Julie's mouth as Alice raised her own glass in a toast.

'To Julie! Good luck!'

There was another cheer and a dozen glasses lifted into the air.

'To Julie!'

*

The Horse and Hounds was a fairly ordinary pub. A regular sort of place with two bars, no frills and only the smallest passing trade. Most of its customers came from the estate, and from the nearby sorting office. There was a jukebox in the corner, and Sky TV, and on Friday and Saturday nights there was a stall outside that sold seafood. In fact, it might have been any local in any part of the country.

Karl and Ricky stood at the bar, surrounded by several of their mates from the sorting office, one or two of them still in their work clothes. They'd been there since opening time, and some nights Karl was there until they chucked him out, but Ricky wasn't a big drinker. He reckoned he couldn't afford it, not with all the things Sonia was forever asking him for. Right now he downed the last of his pint and put the glass back on the bar.

Karl frowned. 'You ain't going already, are you?'

'I promised Sonia I wouldn't be late. Besides, I'm hungry. I only had a roll dinner-time.'

Karl reached out and held his arm. 'Look, give Sonia a bell. Tell her you've got some overtime.'

'Yeah, but—'

'Look, you can come back to my place. Julie won't mind. We'll have a bit of dinner then go up the Eagle for a couple.'

Ricky made a mime of considering it, then shook his head. 'Nah. I'd better shoot off.'

Karl turned, looking about him, making a gesture to indicate that Ricky was under his wife's thumb. There was laughter. Ricky looked sheepish a moment, then shrugged.

'Aw – go on, then.'

Grinning, Karl turned to the bar, beckoning to the barmaid at the far end. 'Hey, darling! Two more pints of your best, please, love.' Then, turning back to Ricky, 'So what d'you reckon? You think Sonia'd wanna make a foursome of it?'

Ricky shrugged. Karl was talking about a 'do' they'd been invited to. And though Sonia would have loved it, it was forty quid a ticket, and he hadn't got that sort of money to throw away. But Karl didn't understand that. Karl didn't have kids.

He only had himself and Julie to think about.

The thought made him open his mouth then close it again. Julie – what was it about Julie? Ricky thought about it a moment, then nodded to himself. Oh yeah – this morning. The suitcases. He'd been meaning to ask Karl all evening where she'd been off to, but if she was going to be there to cook them some dinner, then it didn't really matter, did it?

As Karl turned and handed him his pint, Ricky grinned. 'Cheers, mate!'

'Cheers! But look, you need to make your mind up soon. Those tickets are like gold dust, and if I don't tell Pete soon, they'll be gone.'

She'd almost been too late. The guy was pulling the wire gate across when she'd driven up, and only a flash of her nurse's uniform and her biggest, most flirtatious smile had persuaded him to see her. Now she stood there at the desk, signing the transfer documents, as he ogled her.

She knew what effect her nurse's uniform had on some men, and so she'd opened her coat to give him a good look. If it made him give her another fifty, then it was worth it – and she suspected that it had.

'There,' she said, looking up. 'That's done.'

He grinned at her. 'Is it true what they say about nurses?'

She knew what he meant, but she acted innocent. 'Yeah, course. We're all angels.'

And, smiling sweetly, she handed him the papers.

'Keep me wings in the bag, don't I?'

He laughed, then glanced down the form, checking she'd made it out okay.

'Looks alright to me,' he said, looking to her again, unable to keep from smiling. 'You got the keys?'

'Here,' she said, handing them over.

'And here you are, my darling.' And he handed her back a thick bundle of tenners.

She tipped her head towards the carrier bag by her feet. 'Thanks. Actually, you ain't got a ladies' I could use, have you?'

'Yeah, sure – just out the back there. Help yourself.'

He was standing there, chatting to one of his mates, when she emerged from the loo. As she walked across the courtyard, she could see their eyes trying to take in the transformation.

Yes, she thought. *I was right about this dress.*

She had gone into the loo a nurse and had come out as a vamp. Walking past them, she grinned. 'Bye . . . and thanks.' And she walked off down the street, enjoying the effect she was having on the pair, conscious of their eyes on her still as she posted the package at the letterbox on the corner, then turned to hail a cab.

It was an hour, maybe two hours later, when Ricky and Karl finally staggered back to Karl's place. The street was empty now, the sun gone down, all the kids indoors, except for a few of the older ones, who hung about on the corner like predatory young wolves. It was still warm, and as Karl felt for the keys in his pocket, he began to laugh, a low, drunken chortle.

''Ere, Ricky. Maybe she thought you was a rich pop star or something, only *disguised* as a postman!'

And he let out a roar of laughter.

Ricky looked down, unamused. He'd thought they'd dropped the subject long ago. They were talking about one of the women on Ricky's rounds who he thought fancied him.

He made a sour face at Karl. 'Yeah. Very funny! All I said was that she kept smiling at me.'

Karl's hand emerged with the keys. He stared at them a moment, then looked back at Ricky and grinned.

'Tell you what, mate. She'd have to be a bloody care in the community case to let you get your leg over! Care in the community!'

And he was off again, laughing his head off.

'Well?' Ricky asked, put out by this turn in the conversation. 'We going in or what? I'm bloody starving.'

Karl took a long breath, then looked at Ricky. 'You know what? I'm gonna say no to old Batesy.'

Ricky looked incredulous. 'What? At fourteen quid an hour? That's a good rate!'

Karl lowered his voice a touch, as if conscious that he might be overheard. 'Yeah, but she'd do her nut if I did any more overtime. She moans enough as it is.'

'Well, I reckon it'll come in handy. Sonia's talking about going to Spain for our holidays—'

'Spain!' Karl turned and slipped the key in the lock, a look of triumph on his face that he'd managed it first time. 'Sod working your arse off all year for just a coupla weeks in Torremolinos sitting by some poxy pool! Nah, mate. More hassle than it's worth, that. More hassle . . .'

His voice died. He had switched on the light and stepped into the hallway. Now he stood there, his jaw dropped, staring into the living room.

'What's up?' Ricky asked, coming alongside him. 'What the—?'

'Shit!' they both said as one.

The living room was empty. Without the furniture it looked three times as big as usual. Karl walked through and turned the light on. Beneath the glare of the bare bulb, it looked even worse. Karl turned full circle, his face shocked. Then, as if waking suddenly, he ran out of the room.

Ricky stood there a second, then blinked. The van that morning . . .

He heard Karl stomping about upstairs, then: 'Bastards! The fuckers have taken everything!'

Karl came back in and rushed over to the phone, which now rested on the floor, still plugged into the wall.

'The bastards have cleared me out! The bed, the wardrobe, the TV – even the sodding cooker!'

Karl slumped down on to the carpet and, picking up the handset, began to dial, but Ricky touched his shoulder. 'Hold up, mate.'

Karl looked up, to see Ricky pointing towards the mantelpiece.

He stood and walked across. Someone had placed the top tier of a wedding cake on the fake marble shelf. On top of the cake stood a tiny plastic model of the groom, but where the bride should have been there was only a tiny little hole in the icing. Beside it was a note, folded in half, the word 'Karl' written on it. He unfolded it and read, then threw it down and, picking up the cake, threw it against the far wall.

'The bitch! The fucking bitch!'

Julie sat in the window seat, looking out at the darkened fields and the backs of passing houses as the train rattled its way through the dark towards London. She had bought herself a book at the station – one of those Black Lace erotic things – but her mind wasn't really on it. She kept thinking about the first time she had travelled down to London, back in the early Eighties. That had been scary. She had been so young back then, and she hadn't really known anyone in London. What's more, everything had seemed so huge after the smallness of her home town. She'd had an address to go to, but she hadn't a clue how to get there, and the tube map on the wall of the Underground had been beyond her. In the end she had slept on the platform at Kings Cross, and had been woken by two transport policemen who had taken pity on her and given her the money to get a cab.

She had been back three times since then, but not for a good few years now. Not since she'd stayed with her friend Marie, and Christ alone knew if she was still in that flat.

She picked up the book and started reading again, but she had only got a few more pages further on when the door at the end of the carriage hissed open and a middle-aged man in a business suit with a small but smart overnight bag stepped through.

Julie looked back at the page, even as he set his bag down opposite her then sat beside it.

Not bad, she thought. *Keeps himself trim. Probably works out at a gym. And a good dress sense, too, right down to his soft leather shoes.*

She liked men who dressed well. Liked a man who looked well-groomed and smelled of cologne and body spray.

She looked up. The guy was watching her. He smiled, then looked away. All casual like. A nice smile. Pleasant. Unthreatening. Julie smiled to herself, then crossed her legs, showing a little more thigh, then turned back to her book.

*

His name was Charles and he was married with two young kids. But men like that were often the worst. They flirted a little and he gave her his work number, and then, because he saw her waiting in the cab queue, he gave her a lift, even though it was well out of his way.

He had a nice car, a Jag, and sitting beside him in the front seat she indulged herself in a little fantasy, that she was his fiancée and they were going home together after a weekend away. But all too soon they were there, and he was helping lift her cases out of the boot, and giving her a hug.

'I'll ring you,' she said, blowing him a kiss as he hovered by the open driver's door. 'I promise. We could meet up.'

But she was pretty sure they wouldn't. She had no ambitions to be a mistress. Still, he'd got her here.

She looked about her, frowning. It was a fairly old estate, but the council looked to have tarted the place up a bit, with new windows and new entryphones. But Marie's place – if she still lived there – was in one of the three big high-rises that dominated the centre of the estate. She looked across at it with a sense of foreboding, then, picking up her cases, began to walk across.

Karl was in such a state that Ricky thought he ought to go with him to the hospital. Half-cut or not, Karl had wanted to drive, but she'd taken the van too, so they'd got a minicab. Now Ricky stood there, looking on, embarrassed, wincing slightly as Karl had a go at the nurse on the desk.

'Don't give me that bollocks! Just go and bloody well get her!'

The flap doors at the far end of the ward opened and the ward sister appeared, accompanied by the nurse who'd been sent to fetch her. She walked briskly across and stood next to Karl at the desk. He turned to confront her.

'You in charge?'

But she wasn't having any of it. She shushed him like a schoolmarm, annoyed with him, yet totally in control.

'Will you *please* keep your voice down. We have sick people on this ward, and if you can't behave in a civilised manner, then I'm afraid you are going to have to leave. Now what's the problem?'

Karl bristled. 'I want to speak to Julie.'

'Yes, well, as you can see, this is a men's ward. Now if you'd like to—'

'Julie Mason. My wife.'

The sister did a double-take. 'Oh! Oh, but—'

It was Ricky's turn to speak. While Karl was confronting the sister, he'd had a quick word with the nurse on the station.

'She's gone to her mum's.'

Karl turned and stared at him. 'You what?'

'Her mum's. I didn't know her old lady had cancer. Maybe that's—'

Karl laughed, as if he were going slightly mad. '*Cancer?* What the fuck are you going on about?'

The sister spoke up. 'Julie's gone to look after her mother. Surely she—'

'Her *mother*? Her bloody mother's dead!'

Julie sat on her bags on the doorstep, looking fed up. The flat behind her was dark, and she was beginning to have misgivings about coming here. What if Marie had moved? Or what if she was out all night? It wasn't cold, and she wasn't going to get wet, but—

Just then, two people stepped out on to the balcony from the landing, a woman and her young daughter. They were talking quietly and laughing.

'No, I don't snore, you cheeky madam.'

'You *do*!' And the eight-year-old made snoring noises.

They took another half a dozen steps then stopped dead, staring at Julie perched on their doorstep, smiling up at them.

'Hiya! Long time no see.'

Marie looked uncertain, while the young girl looked up at her mother, as if for some kind of explanation.

Then realisation dawned in Marie's face. Her eyes flew open wide. 'Julie?'

Julie stood and grinned. 'Hi, babes, how you been?'

Chapter Three

Stepping Out

Marie stood with her back to the sink, smiling at Julie while she waited for the kettle to boil. She was the same age as her friend, but darker-haired and broader at the hips. Back in the past, blokes had often kidded them that they were sisters, but the resemblance was only passing. They weren't really that much alike.

Julie sat at the kitchen table, looking back at her. She looked tired now.

'Look,' she said, 'if it's any trouble I could always look for a B and B.'

Marie shook her head firmly, then uncrossed her arms, picking up the now-boiled kettle and pouring the steaming water into the pot. 'Oh no you don't! I won't hear of it. You're staying right here!'

Julie smiled, grateful. 'If you're sure, Marie. I know it's a bit of a cheek, me turning up like this out of the blue.'

'Don't be daft. Mind you, you'll have to make do with the settee. I've only got one bedroom, and—'

On cue, Ellie ran into the room, going straight to her mum and cuddling her legs.

'—and me and this little monkey have to share it as it is. My little hot water bottle, ain't you?'

Marie tickled her daughter, and the eight-year-old ran off again, giggling.

Julie stared after her a moment, then turned back to Marie. 'I can't believe it – a little girl! Look, the settee's great. But only if you're sure. I don't want to get in your way. Anyway, it won't be long. Just till I get myself sorted out.'

Marie poured her a cup, added milk, then handed it across.

'Its fine. As I said, you're welcome. So come on then, tell me – when did you get married?'

Julie looked down, as if abashed. 'A few years back. It was just a quiet do.'

'So what went wrong? You know, between you and—?'

'Karl. Huh, where d'you want me to start?'

'That bad?'

'Nah, in the beginning it was great, you know, all hearts and flowers and all that. He'd want to be out the whole time showing me off. Then, after a bit, it all started to change.'

'Real life kicked in, huh?'

Marie sat facing her across the table, cradling her own cup.

'Oh yeah, it did that alright. He started coming home later and later. Always full of excuses. Like a silly cow I fell for 'em at first, but – well, you just know, don't you? You know when something's up, whether you want to or not.'

'What was it, another woman?'

Avoiding eye contact, Julie nodded. She looked upset now, crestfallen.

Marie let out a long breath, indignant on her mate's behalf. 'What a bastard!'

Julie seemed close to tears. She rubbed at one eye. 'I really thought he was the one – you know?'

Marie stood, then came round the table and, kneeling, put her arm round Julie's shoulder, comforting her.

'So what's he say when you left?'

'What could he say? He denied it all, but . . . I knew. I bloody knew.'

'Bastard!'

Karl brought his clenched fist down on the counter and leaned in to the desk sergeant threateningly.

'Don't tell me to bloody calm down. I've got every right to be angry! That bitch has walked off with everything I sodding well own! The table, the chairs, the bed, the sofa, the fucking cooker, the lot!'

The desk sergeant looked over at two of his uniformed men, who were pissing themselves with laughter behind Karl's back, then, with an exaggerated calm, answered him.

'And I'm telling you to mind your language or I shall have to ask one of my officers to find you a nice cell. Now will you listen to me?'

Karl turned half away, a dark fury in his eyes. 'You're just not interested, are you? The bitch rips me off and you don't give a toss!'

The desk sergeant rolled his eyes to heaven in exasperation. 'As I said to you before, sir, this is a domestic dispute, between you and your wife. You need to talk to her, and—'

'Christ! I know that! But how the hell am I supposed to talk to her when I don't know where the bloody hell she's gone?'

'Well, if she wanted you to know, I imagine she would have put it in the note. But as she didn't—'

'Christ Almighty! You lot are about as bright as a torch without a fucking battery!'

The desk sergeant looked to his two officers. 'Jimmy, Steve – if you'd like to show this gentleman to our overnight accommodation—'

Karl stepped back, raising his hands, signalling that he was not to be touched. 'It's okay – I know when I'm not wanted. I'll go. But I'll be writing to my MP. I'll be letting him know what a fat lot of good you lot were when I needed help.'

'I'm sorry, sir, but—' The desk sergeant sighed, seeing the sudden pain in Karl's face, hoping to God the guy wasn't going to burst into tears. 'Look, if we hear anything—'

But Karl was backing away, shaking his head pathetically, his eyes distraught now that he saw it was no good – that there wasn't an easy answer. 'But I've got to find her. She's my wife. She's my wife . . .'

Julie lay in the darkened living room, on the sofa, a duvet over her. The door was open a crack and there was a faint light from the hallway. For a while she just lay there, staring into the shadows, then, like she'd just remembered it, her fingers found the ring on her left hand and, wiggling it about a moment, slid it off. She looked at it, her eyes expressionless, and then she let it drop on to the carpet. Tucking her hand back beneath the duvet she rolled over and closed her eyes. And dreamed . . .

Of Whitby when she was a child; of growing up in that narrow little town, perched on the edge of the cold North Sea. Most of the year it was cold. Even in high summer – even on the very warmest of days – there was the suggestion that tomorrow it might rain, or that later on a misty squall would come in over the sea from Scandinavia and blight the day. People often said how beautiful it was, what with the abbey and the cliffs and the harbour, yet its beauty never really touched her, only its smallness, the meanness of the lives surrounding her.

Things might have been better, only her upbringing had been a strict one. Her real father had died when she was six and she remembered him only vaguely. As for her stepfather, he had been a domineering man, not to be gainsaid, and when he was drunk he could have the most vicious of tempers. Equally, drunkenness could render him maudlin, even sentimental. She could recall how, sometimes, he would come back late at night after a long session in the local pub, singing at the top of his voice, not caring if he woke the neighbours. And always sentimental love songs. Songs like 'I've Got You Under My Skin' and 'Can't Take My Eyes Off Of You', 'Unchained Melody' and 'Unforgettable'. Songs that could still send a shiver up her spine whenever she heard them.

By contrast her mother had been quiet and careworn. In Julie's memory she never smiled. It was as if she had been born old, weighed down by life.

Of course, she couldn't wait to get out. Life in that northern town was so small, so constrained, so hopeless.

The incident with Rosie Bowyer and her gang hadn't helped, either, and though she had found a protector in the form of Mr Williams, she knew it was only a matter of time before Rosie sought her out. Yet for a week or two following the incident it seemed as if things might turn out okay.

That was wishful thinking, however, and it might have ended badly for her, but for pure chance.

She had gone down to the abbey with a couple of boys, two brothers, Nick and Barry, who were neighbours of hers. They were a lot younger than her and just friends. There was no chance that *they'd* be fighting over her.

It was a Sunday afternoon, and as ever the hours seemed to drag. Though it was the first week of December, it was strangely warm, and they sat around, among the ruins, talking for a bit. Then the boys had a kick-around between them on the grass, while Julie walked down the long grassy aisle of the ancient church, humming to herself. It was dull, but there was little else to do, not unless she went to the park, and that would mean risking bumping into Rosie and her gang, so she put up with the dullness, daydreaming of a time she could get away. As far away as possible.

It was getting on when the boys decided they had to get back for their tea.

'You coomin'?' Barry asked, red-faced from his exertions.

'Nah,' she answered. 'Ah'll hang about a bit.'

And so they left her, sitting in the shadows of the great stone arches, daydreaming and ignoring the stares of the respectably dressed tourists who wondered what a scruffy-looking girl like her was doing in that peaceful spot.

An hour passed and the shadows lengthened. It was time she got back. Her stepfather usually slept most of Sunday afternoon, but if she was too late there'd be hell to pay. Tea was on the table at five on the dot, and he didn't like to be kept waiting.

Julie didn't have a watch, but she could tell it was getting on towards four. She stood and brushed herself down, then began to walk across the grass towards the gate.

She didn't even see her at first. Walked straight past her without noticing. It was only when Rosie called out to her – telling her to hang about, tart! – that she realised the danger she was in.

Julie glanced back, then, without another thought, began to run, not left, towards the bridge and the town beyond where she'd have been safe, but right, towards the lifeboat station and the cliffs.

Years later, recalling that moment, she had wondered what in God's name she had been thinking of, making that choice. It was like her common sense had departed her, because it had been as good as running down a blind alley.

She had heard Rosie puffing and panting behind her as she ran to catch up, not wasting her breath to shout at her or threaten her, but conserving all her energies for catching Julie. The thought of being caught scared the living daylights out of her, because she knew that Rosie wasn't like most girls she knew; that there was something wrong in Rosie's head, and that if she caught up with her, she would be unrelenting; that there would be pain and blood, and maybe other humiliations. And so she ran, like she was running for her life, along past the lifeboat station and down the long cliff steps that led out on to the east pier, the jagged shapes of the rocks to her right.

She ran on, past clusters of elderly tourists who turned to watch, on past the fishermen and a strolling family, until she could run no further. And then she turned, facing her tormentor, afraid, yet not so afraid that she would beg for mercy.

Rosie had stopped, a dozen paces away, her whole body rising and falling with every heaving breath she took. Then, slowly, she began to approach.

'Where's your teacher now, *tart*? Where's little-willy Williams now you need him?'

Julie was trembling, but she wasn't going to look away. Nor was she going to call for help. Not this time. Clenching her fists, she took a step towards the bigger girl.

'Fuck off! Fuck off and leave me alone!'

Rosie laughed. 'You threatening me, you little slag? Ooooh, I'm so scared.'

Rosie took another step, enjoying this, a kind of leering delight in her face. 'Is that why he did it? Is that why he saved you that time? Word is you two do it in his car.'

Julie swallowed. Was that true? Was that what they were saying behind her back?

'It's a lie. He's just—'

'A *friend*?' Rosie sneered. 'A bloody good friend, if you ask me. You've been seen, tart. *Seen*.'

It wasn't true, but then she knew it didn't have to be true. It only had to be believed by enough people, and Rosie would make sure it was believed.

Julie swallowed. People were watching. They were standing on the pier, not thirty feet away, and watching. But no one was going to do anything; no one was even going to say a word. It was just two girls fighting, after all.

'So,' Rosie said, a sadistic gleam in her eyes. 'You ready?'

Yeah, she thought. *I'm ready*. And, turning, she climbed up on to the rail and jumped. Out into the blue, careering outward, falling down and down and down until she hit the solid sheet of water with a bone-jarring thud.

She learned later that a fisherman had saved her. That a small boat had been passing by not twenty yards from where she hit the surface, and that one of the crew – a young lad of twenty – had dived overboard into the ice-cold water and fished her out, unconscious, blood trickling from her mouth and ears.

And when her stepfather had come to visit her in the hospital, she remembered how he had stared at her, as if looking at a total stranger, unable to believe that she had done such a thing. It was in the local news. And when she went back to school, her fellow pupils looked at her differently, like they'd not known her before then, when all she had done was jump.

'You jumped?' Billy Matthews had asked, coming up to her after school. 'You *really* jumped?'

'Yeah,' she'd said, and shrugged, as if it was nothing. And he'd put his arm round her, like he was somehow proud of her.

'Shit – how did it feel?'

Only she never answered him – never answered any of them – because she was never quite sure how it had felt. She could remember jumping, and she could remember waking in the hospital bed. And between?

Nothing. Not a thing.

But that was when she'd decided. That was the moment she had known for certain. One day she was going to leave her home town. Leave it and never come back.

*

Sonia was at the sink, washing up the last few bits, when she saw Ricky's car turn the corner and come straight up the drive.

'Shit!'

She threw the unwashed pan down into the water, then wiped her hands hastily on her jeans and hurried out into the hallway.

As she reached for the latch, she could hear the car screech to a halt and the handbrake scrunch on. Panicking now, she threw the door open.

'Ricky, wait! I need to talk to you about—'

She fell silent. Ricky had walked round the front of the car and opened up the garage door. Now he stood there, staring in at the solid mass of furniture that filled the tiny space.

'What the—?'

She walked across and stood beside him, glancing at him sheepishly.

'Is this whose I think it is?' he asked, clearly recognising half the stuff.

'Yeah, but look, I can explain. I didn't know she was going to bring it here. And anyway—'

He looked at her angrily. 'Anyway, what? What the hell were you thinking of?'

'Before you start getting on your high horse—' she started, then smiled wanly. 'Look, come inside. I'll make some tea and tell you what happened.'

Karl lay on the living-room floor, a blanket thrown over him, six empty beer cans strewn across the carpet next to him. As the letterbox clattered in the hallway, he woke with a snort, then rolled on to his back, wondering where the hell he was. For a while he just lay there, his eyes half open, then he sat up.

Shit! So it was true. He hadn't dreamed it. Getting up, he padded out into the hallway then bent down to pick up the letters. He sorted through them blearily, then came suddenly awake, recognising Julie's handwriting on one of them. Absent-mindedly dropping the others on to the space where the hall stand had once stood, he walked back through, tearing the envelope open as he went.

And stopped dead, surprised to find himself staring at his building society savings book, and – more unexpectedly – a wad of cash. He counted it, then whistled. There was two hundred and fifty quid. He pocketed it, then opened the book.

'Christ!'

He looked away a moment, a tear welling in his eye, then looked back. The bitch had drawn out exactly half their cash. He groaned, then looked across the room at the remains of the cake where it lay smeared over the wall and on the floor, the tiny figure of the bridegroom half buried in the mess of cake and icing.

'Oh, shit! Shit!'

The words were pure pain, pure loss. He looked at the envelope, trying to get some clue from it as to where it was posted, but it was local. No doubt she'd posted it on her way in to work. Screwing it into a ball, he threw it down, then slumped on to the carpet, sitting there cross-legged, his head fallen forward into his hands as he sobbed.

Marie had gone to take Ellie's overnight bag to the friend's she was staying with that evening, and Ellie herself was at school, so Julie was alone in the flat for the first time. Normally she would have settled on the sofa with a magazine, but it was years since she had seen Marie and she was curious, so while Marie was gone, she wandered about the flat, looking at her bits and being nosey.

Not that there was that much to see. Marie wasn't a reader and she didn't keep a diary, and a quick peek into her drawers and cupboards seemed to confirm what she had already said. These days Marie lived for her kid, not for herself. Even so, Julie was surprised not to find a vibrator at the very least.

She'd once read – in *Cosmopolitan* or somewhere like that – that women bought over four million vibrators a year in the UK alone. That was a lot of loneliness.

One thing was for sure, however, Marie had a definite sentimental streak. There were framed pictures of babies everywhere – stylised, almost cherubic babies, rosy-cheeked little darlings in picture-postcard poses. The kind you buy in gift shops.

Julie let out a long, shivering breath, then wandered back out into the kitchen and switched on the kettle. Not that she really wanted another cup of tea – just that it was something to do. She was pouring when the front door banged shut and Marie walked in. Julie turned and smiled.

'Hi, babe. You okay?'

'Fine. You?'

'Great. Just making more tea. Want one?'

Marie grinned, then shook her head. 'Actually, I wouldn't mind something a bit stronger. D'you fancy a proper drink?'

'You're not kidding. D'you know a good place?'

'Know it? I work in it.'

'Hang on, I'll get my jacket.'

The Red Lion was only five minutes away. As they crossed the road facing it, Julie looked about her, taking in her new surroundings. The roads round these parts were narrow, the houses four or even five storeys tall, the brick dark with grime, so that the whole place had a kind of shadowy, Dickensian feel to it. That said, it wasn't the worst place she'd ever stayed. The roads weren't littered with glass and derelict motors, so she guessed it was probably okay. In fact, there were one or two nice cars about, now that she really looked, and the houses seemed in good repair.

The pub itself was neat yet unspectacular. It looked old-fashioned. There'd been no attempt to modernise or tart it up, but equally it wasn't a tip. The carpeted floor had been recently hoovered, the tables were clean, and there was a jukebox in the corner, the glass of which gleamed in the overhead lights.

As they stepped through, Marie waved to the girl at the bar, who waved back.

'That's Rita. She works here most days.'

They found a seat by the window, then Marie went across to get their drinks. As she stood there talking with the barmaid,

Julie slipped off her jacket then sat, looking about her again.

There was something about pubs. As soon as you walked into one, you could tell whether it was a good one or not. This one had a good atmosphere. It was well-lit and didn't smell like a crew of navvies had just vacated the place. She imagined the loos would be clean and tidy, too. All signs that the landlord – or landlady – was on top of their job.

Marie was back in a moment, a vodka and tonic in one hand and a pink Bacardi Breezer in the other.

'There,' she said, handing Julie the vodka. 'Get that down you. And cheers! It's lovely to see you again.'

Julie smiled back at her friend, then gave an apologetic shrug. 'I'm sorry. It's not that you mean to lose touch, it's just – well, things get in the way.'

'Yeah. Yeah, I know.' Marie clinked her bottle against Julie's glass. 'Anyway. Here's to the future, eh? Probably do you good not to have a fella hanging on your leg for a while.'

Julie grinned, then leaned forward, lowering her voice, as if confessing some dark and terrible secret.

'Truth is, though, I just ain't any good at being on my own.'

Marie looked about her as two men drifted into the bar, nodding to her familiarly.

'I know what you mean, but I'd sooner be on my own than— Well, anyway, Ellie's my priority right now.'

Julie looked down, trying not to show how envious she felt at that moment. Then, more cheerily, 'Yeah, but what about sex? Don't tell me you've become a nun!'

Marie grinned. 'I have my moments, don't you worry!'

'And there's always the spin cycle!'

Marie made a face. 'I go to the laundrette.'

'Ah, group sex!'

They both burst out laughing, and were still giggling as a man in his late twenties came in through the door on the far side of the pub. He nodded towards Marie, then went to the bar to get a drink. A minute or so later, he wandered over, carrying a pint and another bottle of pink Bacardi Breezer. Coming up behind Marie he leaned close, speaking to her ear.

'And how's my favourite barmaid?'

Marie gave a little jump, then turned, and as she did, he handed her the bottle.

'Alright, darling?'

Marie's voice held a mild trace of sarcasm. 'Thought you'd left the country.'

He smiled. 'Came back to see you, didn't I?'

He pulled out a chair and sat beside her, leaning in, his attention fully on her now.

Marie seemed to preen herself. 'Ooh, I'm honoured.'

'So you should be, sweetheart. You not working tonight?'

'No. Time off for good behaviour.'

'Well, we'll have to see what we can do about that, won't we?'

Marie giggled and, annoyed now by her exclusion, Julie took the chance to butt in.

'Don't mind me, will you?'

Marie turned, remembering suddenly. 'Oh sorry. Gary, this is my friend Julie.'

Julie smiled, but Gary merely nodded, turning his attention back to Marie almost immediately.

'So how've you been?'

Julie was about to stand up and walk over to the bar, when a guy – slim, but clearly late forties – appeared just behind Gary.

'Marie, do us a favour. Cath's phoned in sick and—'

'Oh, Dave, no – I'm sick of that bar.'

'Come on. You know what it's like. The lunch trade'll be here any minute and we'll be up to our eyes. Look, I'll make it worth your while.'

'I can't. I've got to get back for Ellie. I said I'd only be out for a bit.'

Julie made a face at Marie, but Marie seemed unrepentant. Disgruntled, Dave made his way back to the bar.

'Who was that?' Julie asked.

Marie glanced at her. 'That's Dave. He's the landlord here.'

Julie gave a nod, then fiddled with her empty glass. Gary looked at her a moment, then looked back at Marie. 'So what time you gotta be back for your kid?'

Marie leaned in to him, lowering her voice. 'That was just for his benefit. Actually she'll be out all night. Staying with a friend.'

Gary grinned. 'You don't say.'

Seeing the way things were going, Julie glanced over at the bar, then stood and made her way across. Already the place was filling up, more punters arriving by the moment.

'Dave, is it?'

The landlord looked up from where he was pouring a pint. 'Yeah?'

'I could give you a hand.'

He'd looked back down at the pint. Now he looked up again.

'I'm a mate of Marie's,' she quickly explained. 'I'm staying with her for a bit.'

She knew she looked good, but Dave's appreciative once-over made her feel even better.

'Done any bar work before?'

'A bit.'

'Whereabouts?'

'Oh, you know, all over the place.'

'I'll need you to come in again tonight.'

'Okay.'

'Oh, and we do a lot of cocktails,' he said, handing over the pint and taking the customer's money. 'D'you know how to—?'

'Look. Anything I don't know, I'll ask. Right? I've got a tongue in my head. Now have I got the job?'

Dave grinned, clearly liking her self-confidence, her *front*. 'Yeah. Yeah, why not?'

Chapter Four

All In The Game

She had left school at sixteen, right after her O'Levels. She'd done alright, as it happened, five passes – enough to get her into the sixth form if she'd wanted – but there was no way she was going to stay on. She wanted to get out, into the world. She wanted her own money and her own place. But it wasn't that easy.

She'd had jobs before then, but they'd all been part time, pocket money kind of jobs, filling in during the summer or over the Christmas holidays.

It was one of her mates, Stephanie, who she'd got pally with in the last year of school, who'd helped her find it. Steph was working in a baker's shop just down the road from the restaurant, and when she saw the 'Help Wanted' sign up in the window, she had gone out straight away and phoned Julie at home.

Her stepdad hadn't liked it, but she had stood her ground and gone in for an interview. The owners had liked her and had taken her on – on trial, as they said – and she had proved popular with the customers. It was a nice place, right up on the West Cliff, specialising in fish, and for the first time in years she felt like she fitted in somewhere.

She'd had such plans back then, had been so full of it, but he was always dragging her back, dragging her down. That first time she had brought home her pay packet he had insisted that she hand it over to him. She'd looked to her mother for support, praying that for once she would stand up to him, but she only looked away, then murmured something like, 'Your dad knows best,' and she had wanted to say, 'He isn't my dad. My dad's dead', only she knew she'd get a hiding if she said that, and so she kept quiet and did as he said. And later on, when he'd come to her bed, she had turned her face away from him and faced the wall, wanting to show somehow how angry she was with him. Not that it mattered. Not that it ever mattered.

She had thought about moving in with her mate, Stephanie. Steph had just got a flat with her boyfriend, Rob, and they had a spare room. But then the accident had happened and everything had changed, and next time she saw Steph it was eleven years later, in Manchester, and they had found it hard to talk, they were such different people.

But that was life. Some people you stayed in touch with, others just drifted away, and it was no one's fault. There just wasn't enough time to keep in touch with everyone. Yet some days she found herself wondering what this friend was doing, or that fella. Some days she wished she could hold a big party and invite them all and find out what they'd all done with their lives.

Pissed it away, probably, she thought, as she reached up to put away the glass she'd just wiped.

The evening session started in less than five minutes, and Dave was just finishing off wiping the tables over. Some pubs didn't close between sessions these days, but Dave made sure they had a break. And it made sense. If they hadn't, there'd have been no time to clear up and get straight again, and the place would have become a tip.

She had enjoyed the lunchtime session, busy as it was, and it hadn't taken her any time at all to get back into the flow of things. At first she'd noticed Dave hovering nearby, watching her, making sure she got things right, but then, about half an hour in he smiled at her and nodded, and after that she was on her own, looking after one end of the bar while Dave looked after the other.

But it wasn't just the work she enjoyed. She liked meeting new people, and what better place than at a bar? In no time at all she was chatting to the locals as if they were her oldest friends. She hadn't even minded when Marie had sneaked off with Gary without so much as a bye-bye and take care. Not that she blamed her.

Dave came across and stood there, staring at her. They'd not really talked since she'd started – it had been too busy – but now he seemed to want to say something.

'Well?' she asked, pre-empting him. 'Will I do?'

He smiled 'Yeah. And thanks for your help, Julie. You were great.' He paused awkwardly. 'I meant to ask – how do you know Marie?'

Julie shrugged. 'We trained together. I'm a nurse.'

'A *nurse*!'

She laughed. 'Why do men always say it like that? A nurse! It's like someone's handed them a copy of Playboy!'

Dave looked away, embarrassed. 'Nah, it's not that – it's just I didn't know Marie was . . .'

'She dropped out. Bedpan Alley's not everyone's cup of tea. Actually, I wouldn't mind having a bit of a change myself. Get away from sick people for a bit. Know what I mean?'

Dave nodded, staring at her thoughtfully. 'Well, if you fancy doing the odd shift here—'

Julie raised an eyebrow. 'I dunno. Some of your customers looked pretty sick to me.'

He looked a query at her, then saw she was teasing again and grinned.

'D'you mean it?' she asked.

'Yeah. I could use some more help.'

She beamed. 'Then thanks. I'd like that.'

Noticing the time suddenly, Dave turned and hurried over to the door, reaching up to take off the bolt. As he opened it, a number of Julie's afternoon customers stepped through and, seeing her at the bar, came straight across.

She smiled at them and nodded towards the pumps. 'Yes, babe. And what'll it be?'

As she poured, she looked along the bar, seeing Dave there again, busy drawing a pint, and as he looked up, she met his eye and smiled. And he smiled back, bashfully, like a man who wasn't quite sure yet why he was smiling.

It was after one and she couldn't sleep. Not surprising, really, since Gary and Marie had been going at it hammer and tongs the last half hour. Since she'd come in, in fact. And noisy wasn't the word. If Marie said 'yes' just one more bloody time—

Julie plumped up the pillow yet again, then, in desperation, covered her ears with it. But it didn't work. She could still hear them.

'Shit.'

She stood, then walked over to the window and, drawing the curtain back a little, stared down, out over the estate. There were kids down there of no older than eleven or twelve, still out at this time of night. Not that their parents gave a shit, but it wasn't right. It was no way to raise a child.

But then, what did she know?

The noise through the wall rose to a crescendo. For a moment it seemed almost like they were in the same room.

'Oh, Gary – Gary!'

There was a strange, almost strangled little noise, and then it went quiet. A moment later there was a giggle – female, clearly Marie – and then silence.

Thank Christ for that, she thought. But now she was feeling randy. Wanting what Marie had so very obviously got.

She lay down again, then, unable to help herself, eased down her knickers and began to touch herself, slowly, gently at first, fantasising, imagining that having satisfied Marie, Gary had slipped out of bed, naked, his cock still erect, still hot and hard as he stepped into the shadows of the room. She imagined him rolling her over without a word and taking her from behind, silently fucking her until—

She gave a little groan, pressing at herself with hard, almost angry movements of her fingers, until, with a huge shudder of release, she came.

Oh, Gary Gary . . .

Letting out a long sigh, she rolled over and closed her eyes.

Men. How she hated them sometimes.

Julie stood in the kitchen, looking out at the bright morning sky and humming to herself as the kettle boiled.

They were at it again, like two randy teenagers, and this time the noise was much worse than last night. It just wasn't fair.

She poured the teas, then added milk and sugar, still humming to herself. Then, the vaguest of smiles on her lips, she took them through, pushing the door open with her foot.

'Morning!'

Marie looked up past Gary's naked shoulder, astonishment in her eyes. But Julie didn't even look at her, just stepped across and placed the two mugs down on the bedside table.

'I didn't know if you took sugar or not, so I put it in but I ain't stirred either of 'em.'

She straightened up, smiled, then walked back out.

Back in the kitchen she sat down, grinning to herself. The noises had stopped. There was a moment's silence, then hushed voices and the sound of Gary dressing.

Julie sipped at her tea, then opened up the paper as if she was reading it, but she didn't take in a word. She was straining to listen – to hear what they were saying.

The bedroom door creaked open. There were footsteps, then a pause before Gary's voice came clear through the wall.

'See you around, babe.'

'Yeah, bye.' All plaintive, like she knew he wouldn't ring.

There was the sound of the front door closing. A moment later Marie came through. Julie sipped at her tea, pretended she was reading.

Marie hesitated, then walked over to the bread bin and took two slices from the wrapped loaf and dropped them into the toaster. She had her back to Julie. Her shoulders looked very, very tense.

'Marie—?'

'What?'

'Look, I'm really sorry about barging in like that. I didn't think you'd—'

Marie turned, looking back at Julie, her eyes cold, the words coming through gritted teeth. 'It's fine. But maybe next time you could knock.'

'Look, I didn't—'

But Marie didn't let her finish. Ignoring the toast, she walked straight past Julie, out into the hallway. 'Forget it,' she called back. 'I'm going to run a bath.'

Julie turned, sighing, then recalled the sight of Gary's bare buttocks, clenched in mid-air, hovering there between strokes as he realised that someone was standing next to him, and put her hand to her mouth to stifle a giggle.

You cruel bitch, she told herself. *Still, it served them right for being so bloody noisy.*

Yes, but even so—

She got up and, taking her tea across, poured it down the sink, then stood there, grinning to herself. He had a nice arse, Gary. Nice and firm.

Ricky had left the room briefly, leaving the two of them alone for the first time. Karl had been quiet so far – broodingly so – but now he looked across at Sonia.

'So you ain't heard from her?'

Sonia had been busying herself with the dinner, avoiding his eyes. Now she rounded on him testily.

'I told you! No!' She took a calming breath, then, more gently. 'How 'bout you?'

Karl shook his head. 'Not for three weeks now. Five hundred quid she let that van go for! Half its sodding value! I can't understand it. I mean, we had our arguments, but she never let on that there was anything.' He sighed heavily. 'To just take off like that. No chat. No nothing.'

Sonia glared at him. 'Maybe she just got fed up with—'

She stopped, not wanting to say more, but Karl was staring at her, his eyes half-lidded.

'With what? No, come on.'

Ricky came in, then looked from one to the other, sensing something was up. Sonia glanced at her husband, then, in a low voice, said what she was going to say.

'Maybe she got fed with being knocked about.'

Mortified, Ricky looked daggers at his wife. Karl just looked incredulous.

'*What?* Is that what she told you?'

Ricky stepped between them. 'Leave it, Sonia.'

'No,' Karl said, pushing him aside. 'I want to hear what she's got to say.'

Sonia was angry now; angry for her friend. 'There's plenty I could say.'

Ricky turned, putting his hand on Karl's arm. 'Listen, mate, what went on between you and Julie is your business.'

Karl shrugged off his hand. 'I don't fucking believe this!'

Sonia laughed sourly. 'There's no smoke without fire.'

'Bollocks! I never touched her! *Never!* So you can keep that sodding mouth of yours shut, alright?'

'Oi!' Ricky said angrily. 'You're bang out of order!'

Karl looked to his mate, then gave a little shrug. 'Look, I don't know what she told you, but I never laid a finger on her, and that's God's truth. Course we argued, but that's all. I never hurt her. Okay?'

And, looking from one to the other, he turned and left. Ricky watched him go, then rounded on his wife, tapping his nose.

'Keep that out! I told you, it's none of our fucking business.'

Then he rushed out, calling after Karl, hurrying to catch him up, leaving Sonia to stare down at the floor.

She sighed, then, going to the sink, emptied the dirty water out of the bowl. It was hard to know what to think. She didn't like Karl much – he was a bit of a mouthy sod at times – but she'd never known him to be violent.

And besides, she'd not *seen* any bruises . . .

Julie was at the far end of the bar, standing there, leaning across the counter as she talked to the little group of men who'd formed there. She'd not served a pint in a good five minutes, but her audience was rapt, hanging on to her every word.

'—so then he asks to have a word in private, and when the doctor pushes the curtain back, you could tell he was dying to laugh. Turns out the old boy was enjoying his bed baths so much, he didn't want to go home!'

There was a roar of laughter, and one or two lewd comments. Dave, washing up further down the bar, looked across.

'He was seventy-eight, bless him. Anyway, after that the

doctor reckoned I could dish 'em out on prescription for anyone needing a pick-me-up! Cheeky sod!'

Again, there was laughter. As it died, the door swung open and one of her regulars, Alan, walked in. Seeing him, Julie called across, reaching up for a glass as she did.

'Alright, Alan?'

She liked Alan, he was young and smart and made her laugh, but she wasn't really *interested* in him – not in that way – only she knew that when she flirted with him, something happened in Dave's eyes; an age-old response, that dated back to the Stone Age and beyond.

Alan smiled, then walked across. 'What have I missed? More confessions of a Florence Nightingale?'

Julie beamed at him, then leaned across the bar, as if Alan was suddenly the only male in the place. It was outrageous, but she knew what she was doing.

'You've heard all the best ones. Well, nearly all.' She winked. 'Your usual?'

'Yeah, thanks.'

But as she went to pour, Dave stepped up and took the glass from her. ''S alright. I'll get that. We could do with some crisps put out.'

'Crisps? But—'

Dave's look warned her that she had pushed him far enough. He didn't mind a little flirting, but enough was enough, and this *was* his pub.

She nodded, then gave Alan another smile.

'Yeah. Yeah, alright.'

But as she brushed past Dave and walked over to where the crisp boxes were stacked, she knew that it wasn't only Alan's eyes that were following her every movement, and that Dave knew it and hated it, and inside she smiled, enjoying the turmoil she was causing. It was an old game and she loved playing it. Loved the attention, the strange, almost hypnotic power she had over them. But most of all she loved the thought that they'd go home and still be thinking about her, fantasising maybe, imagining her there as they lay on their narrow beds in their lonely rooms, cock in hand.

Yes. Thinking of her. Imagining her there naked with them.

She pulled out a selection of different flavours, then turned abruptly, seeing how two or three of them – Alan among them – looked away quickly, embarrassed to be caught out watching her. But Dave stubbornly had his back to her, pouring pints, trying to ignore her. Even so, his shoulders were hunched and tense, because he, more than any of them, suffered from her games.

Marie groaned. It had been a shit day, all in all. She'd got a letter back, telling her she'd been turned down for the new job she'd gone for, and it had been one of those mornings when all the bills turn up at once. Nor did it help that Ellie kept going on about getting a new pair of trainers. So seeing the state of the living room was the last straw.

She stood there in the doorway, feeling real anger well up in her. There were items of Julie's clothing strewn everywhere, and bits of make-up littered the floor and the arm of the sofa.

Marie stepped inside and began gathering up whatever she could find, mumbling to herself angrily as she did.

'Soddin' mess! It's like a flippin' dosshouse!'

She scooped up the pillows and the duvet and turned, making for the bedroom, but ran into Ellie in the doorway.

'I thought I told you to get your shoes on! I'm going to be late for work as it is!'

Ellie gave her an aggrieved look. 'I think I left 'em in Auntie Julie's room.'

She snapped. 'It's *not* Auntie Julie's room! It's our living room!' She closed her eyes, forcing herself to be calm. 'I'm sorry. Just go and find them – there's a good girl.'

But the effort of calming herself was almost too much for her. She almost burst into tears. This wasn't how she'd imagined it. Living with Julie had been fun last time round. But they'd been younger then, and she'd not had Ellie. They'd both been a bit wild and carefree. But now . . .

'I'm getting old,' she moaned quietly, almost beneath her breath. 'Too bloody old to put up with all this, anyway.'

Marie took a deep breath, then nodded to herself. She'd have a word, tonight: make Julie understand just what she was feeling and why. Maybe suggest that it was time she found her own place. After all, she couldn't live here indefinitely.

Not if they were going to remain friends.

Marie's bad mood carried over into work. Julie sensed it and, guessing the reason, took her aside.

'Here,' she said, pressing fifty quid into her hand, 'towards my keep.'

'I can't,' Marie said, trying to give it back.

'But I want you to have it.'

Marie looked down, feeling awkward suddenly. 'No, I've told you. It's fine.'

Taking the money, she pushed it into Julie's hand and folded her fingers over it.

Julie sighed. 'Look, I don't expect you to put me up for nothing. I like to pay my way. Have it. Buy something for Ellie.'

'No. Really. If the arrangement was going to be long-term, I'd take it, but, well now that you're earning . . .'

She left it unsaid, but Julie cottoned on at once. Her face changed, her mouth opening in a tiny circle of surprise. 'Oh.'

Dave, who'd been watching from the far end of the bar, came across. 'Come on, Marie – you can't come in late and then just stand there gassing. There's customers to be served.'

Marie threw Dave a dirty look, then went over to the bar, smiling at the young guy who was standing there. 'Sorry, love, what can I get you?'

Julie stared Dave down, then turned away, fed up now. Alan was propped up against the far end of the bar. She went over to him, raising her voice so both Dave and Marie could hear.

'You ain't got a bed going spare, have you, Alan?'

Alan looked flustered; like she'd just made some lewd suggestion to him. 'Well, I've, er, got a sofabed in the front room. You'd be welcome—'

She grinned, then put her hand out to gently touch his chin. 'Ah, Alan, you're so sweet.'

Seeing the gesture, Dave came across at once. 'What's sweet?'

Julie nodded towards Marie. 'My landlady's just given me notice, but Alan's going to save me from the streets. He's offered me a bed.' She looked to Alan and winked. 'Thanks, Alan, I'll bear that in mind.'

Alan smiled shyly, then sipped at his pint, but Dave didn't seem quite so amused. He glared at Alan, then turned back to Julie. 'Give Marie a hand with the glasses, will you?'

Julie made a face behind Dave's back, then sauntered down the bar to where Marie was beginning to wash up some pint glasses. She glanced at Julie.

'I feel really rotten now.'

Julie put her hand on her arm and smiled. 'Don't be dopey. You're right. I need a place of my own. Anyway, I'm sure something will turn up.'

She turned, looking along the bar at Dave.

But Dave was purposefully not looking at her now. Even so, the stiffness of his gait, the very way he forced himself to look away from her, not at her, gave him away.

Julie smiled to herself. *Something will turn up.*

Julie stretched and yawned, then opened her eyes. The curtains were drawn, but it was light enough in the living room to see the mess that surrounded her. A copy of the local paper lay over the arm of the sofa beside her head, open at the 'Accommodation /To Let' pages, rings round several of the ads. But that was as far as she'd got. Feeling that she couldn't be bothered, she threw the paper across the room, then reached down for her fags, lighting one up.

Marie was right of course, and it wasn't fair on her. But it wasn't just that. You couldn't live on someone's sofa for the rest of your days, even if they'd let you. You needed your own space, your own things about you.

Julie brought her legs round and sat up, then reached across with her foot and hooked the strap of her handbag with her toes and dragged it over to her. She didn't keep much, and what she did keep was mainly to be found in her secret box, but she did keep one small token of the past on her. She took it out now and smiled.

It was a postcard. On the front was a picture of an old thatched cottage, a cherry tree in blossom in the front garden. On the back – and she turned it and read the familiar words once more – was a message from her aunt. Probably the only card she'd ever got – that summer when she'd had to stay with Aunt Jean, after she'd had the mumps. Back before her dad had died. Back before everything went wrong.

She turned it back over, staring at the cottage. For all her adult life it had been her ideal, to own a house like that, to have that cherry tree in blossom in her garden. If she closed her eyes she could imagine it; could see herself standing at the sink in her kitchen, looking out through its branches at the sunlit day. She could almost hear the birds singing in the branches.

She slipped the card back into her bag, then lay back, staring up at the shadowed ceiling. Aunt Jean had died not long after. That same winter. Julie sighed. Reality hit hard sometimes. Sometimes – well, it felt like someone was playing with her, dashing her hopes at every turn, raising her expectations, only to see it all come crashing down, time and time again. But then *someone* had to own that cottage, that cherry tree. So why not her? Why did she always have to put up with the shitty end of the stick?

She didn't have to get up just yet; not for another hour or so. Then again, she could always run a bath, tart herself up a bit. After all, Dave had been eyeing her up these last few days. Well, maybe it was time she gave him a bit of encouragement.

Smiling she stood up and, humming to herself, walked through into the bathroom. She put the plug in, then ran the taps, sitting on the edge of the bath as the water poured.

Maybe she'd nick a bit of Marie's *Obsession* while she was at it. It wouldn't hurt to swing the odds in her favour. And there was that new lace bra she'd bought last week. That was bound to help.

Grinning to herself, she sat there, finishing her fag.

Yeah. She'd been patiently fishing long enough. Now it was time to reel him in, hook, line and sinker. Time to draw him over to the bank and pop him in the net.

Poor old Dave, she thought, beginning to unbutton her top. *He won't know what's hit him.*

Things had been so busy that morning that Dave had not had a chance to look through his post, but now that the girls were in, he took the chance to go through to his office and do a bit of paperwork. As he sat there he could hear the noise from the bar outside – the chink of glasses, the chatter of the fruit machine, the sound of the music from the jukebox, all of it so familiar – the backdrop of his life, it sometimes seemed. And normally it would have made him happy enough, only things weren't so great right now.

He sorted through the envelopes, putting the five brown ones to one side, then slitting one of the three white ones open with his fingernail. It was only as he unfolded it that he realised what it was, and swore softly.

'Shit!'

Dave stared at the letter from the bank a moment, then screwed it into a ball and threw it in the bin. But the damage had been done. His day was ruined now. Even so, he'd put a brave face on things. He'd have to.

He went out into the bar. Julie was pulling a pint. She looked really nice today, and she smelled absolutely delightful. As she turned to put the money in the till, he smiled at her.

'No luck yet? With the flat, I mean.'

'Nah, not yet,' she said, concentrating on keying in the drinks right, then picking out the change. 'I tell you what, though, I can't wait to find somewhere. Oh, don't get me wrong, Marie's lovely, but she's – well, a bit messy, let's say. And I like a bit of order to things. I like to be *organised*. Know what I mean?'

She handed over the change, then turned back to Dave, disappointed by the distracted look in his eyes. 'It was like when my sister was killed. I did everything. Funeral, the lot. I had to have it all just so. It was beautiful, mind.'

'I'm sorry. How did she . . .?'

'Car crash.' Julie smiled bravely. 'You just have to get on with it, don't you?'

Dave nodded. 'I don't suppose—'

She had turned away to serve another customer, but now she turned back, smiling at him brightly. 'What?'

'Well, I was just thinking. If you didn't fancy staying in, I don't like to hang around this place when I've a night off, so I thought, maybe . . .' He hesitated, uncertain now he'd got this far. 'It's just that I was going to go out for a meal, and—'

'A date?'

He swallowed, then gave a nod.

Julie beamed. 'That'd be nice.'

Dave grinned back a her, a little ripple of pleasure passing through him. 'Great. I'll phone Rita then – get her to cover for you.'

'Okay.' She turned away, walking back up the bar, leaving him to watch her, elated now, his troubles momentarily forgotten.

In love? Nah, he wasn't in love. But then why did she make him feel so bloody gauche – like he was seventeen again?

Dave stood there a moment longer, then walked back through into his office and picked up the phone, dialling Rita's mobile number.

And even as he listened to the ringing at the other end, he found himself shaking his head, amazed.

She said yes. She bloody well said yes.

Chapter Five

Island Of Dreams

They were sitting at a table in the back corner of the restaurant – a local Italian Dave often went to, though usually alone – and it was late. They'd finished their meal a while back, but were lingering over coffee and brandies, enjoying each other's company, talking away the hours.

Dave was wearing a smart blue suit that made him look businesslike, distinguished even, while Julie had bought a new outfit that afternoon – a stunning thing in black that showed her figure to its best advantage. The nearby tables were empty now, the candle burning down. It would soon be time to leave. But still they talked.

'It was all a long time ago,' Dave said, staring down into his brandy glass. 'We were just bits of kids really.' He laughed softly. 'I should have listened to my mother.'

Julie was watching him all the while, her eyes encouraging him to talk. 'How long were you married?'

'Six years. Broke my bloody heart at the time. Don't suppose I'd even recognise her now.'

'Yeah, but there must have been others since then – good-looking fella like you.'

'You get used to your own company.' He looked up, smiled. 'How 'bout you?'

Julie shook her head. 'My mum always reckoned that any bloke who married me would have to be barmy.'

Dave laughed. Julie made a face.

'You're supposed to say she was talking rubbish and that I'd be a catch for any man.'

He grinned. 'Well, you've said it for me.'

Julie's smile changed subtly. 'How 'bout kids?'

'Nah. I wanted 'em, but – well, you think you've got all the time in the world when you're young, don't you? Well, you're still young. I meant—'

Julie reached across and put her hand over his. ''S okay. Age is a state of mind. Like everything else.' She smiled. 'Anyway, you look as though there's still a bit of life left in you.'

Dave went to answer, then noticed the waiter who'd come across. He looked to Julie. 'You want anything else? Another coffee or something?'

'Nah. Thought you might do me a cup of coffee. Back at your place.'

'Oh. Oh, right.' Dave turned back to the waiter. 'Just the bill, ta.'

Julie stood in the middle of Dave's living room, swaying to the music as she looked about her. It was nice, surprisingly tidy for a bachelor flat, and the furniture was tasteful, not the usual tat you found in single guys' flats. Dave was clearly a man who took care. He'd not let himself go like some of them did. All the more surprising, then, that he'd not found someone already.

As he came back into the room, she turned, smiling at him.

'Brandy.'

She took the glass, then chinked it against his. 'Nice place.'

He shrugged. 'Yeah. Not bad. I could have lived over the pub, only I like to get away from the place. Know what I mean?'

She nodded, conscious for the first time of just how nervous he was. It was sweet. He sipped at his brandy, then nodded towards the windows.

'I had the whole lot double-glazed a couple of years back. You can lie in bed and not hear a thing out front. It's like living in the sticks.'

'Yeah?'

Dave was silent a moment, awkward, like he wished he was somewhere else. Julie smiled, amused by his unease.

'It's too big for me really. But the people two doors up have done a loft conversion as well, so—'

'You wanna give me the tour?'

'The tour?'

'Yeah.' She smiled provocatively. 'You know, so I can see for myself.'

'Yeah – yeah, alright.'

He led her out into the hall and up the stairs, on to the landing. Straight ahead of them was a door. He went across and opened it.

'Bathroom.'

She wandered over and, grinning, looked inside. 'Nice.'

There were two more doors. He pushed open one of them. Rails of clothes ran along the far wall and a two-bed settee sat among empty suitcases and other rarely used items.

'It's the spare, but it's turned into a bit of a junk room.'

Julie grinned, closing the door. She turned towards the door opposite. 'And that one?'

Nervously he walked over and pushed the door open.

'This is my room.'

Julie stepped past him, walking about the room while he stood in the doorway watching her, running her fingers over the bed. She turned, looking across at him. He was more nervous than ever, but aroused now, his eyes following her every move.

Slowly, button by button, she undid the front of her dress and let it fall away, revealing a sexy black bra. Then, watching him all the while, she let the dress fall to the floor.

Dave's lips had parted now, his eyes were wide. And no wonder, for she was wearing the scantiest of undies, stockings and stilettos.

She smiled, then stretched out on the bed, patting the space beside her.

'Well?' she said softly, provocatively.

He hesitated, then, reaching behind him, pulled the door shut.

It was ten to nine when she got back to the flat, and she walked right into a full-blooded row between Marie and Ellie. Closing the door quietly behind her, she paused in the hallway, listening.

'. . . and I've already told you,' Marie was saying, 'your teacher said you don't have to have a leotard!'

'But Becky—'

'I don't give a sod about Becky!'

'Hi.' Julie stepped into the kitchen, smiling, but both Marie and Ellie ignored her.

The doorbell went, and Marie thrust Ellie's coat into her arms.

'Now wipe your mouth and get your coat on. I don't want to hear no more about it, hear me?'

Still ignoring Julie, Marie went to answer the door.

Julie looked to Ellie and whispered, '*What colour?*'

Ellie's eyes lit up. She whispered back, '*Pink.*'

'Ellie!'

Julie winked at Ellie, then followed her out into the hallway, where Marie was waiting beside another woman and her young girl. She watched as Marie gave her daughter a hug, then turned and went back into the kitchen, switching on the kettle then dropping a slice of bread into the toaster.

The front door banged shut. A moment later Marie came back into the kitchen.

Julie turned and smiled at her. 'You want a cuppa?'

Marie shook her head, her face hard. 'No, and listen, Julie. Don't you go getting her that leotard. She's starting to think she can have anything she wants, and I don't want her to end up spoiled.'

Marie sat, then looked up at her again. 'I don't suppose that ad was any good?'

'No. The place had gone.'

The toast popped up. Gingerly taking it from the toaster, Julie dropped it on to the work surface and began to butter it. Getting up from her seat, Marie snatched it away angrily, reaching up for a plate.

Shocked, Julie yelled at her. 'Oh my God, Marie! It's just a bit of toast! What the hell's wrong with you?'

Marie looked down. Then, quietly, 'I think I might be pregnant.'

They went in to work together. Rita let them in, and for a moment Julie thought that maybe Dave had taken the morning off, but then she saw him sitting in his office behind the bar. He saw her and looked down, embarrassed.

'Mornin'!' she said cheerfully, then walked over to the back of the bar to hang up her jacket, noting, in the mirror, how he stood and came out into the doorway to watch her.

She turned, looking straight at him and smiling. 'What's the matter? Cat got your tongue?'

Dave smiled awkwardly, then came right up to her, lowering his voice. 'I didn't know if – it's just I wasn't sure everything was . . . alright.'

'Why shouldn't it be?'

'It's just – I didn't know if it was alright for you last night.'

Julie smirked, letting her hand rest on his arm a moment. 'Yeah, it was alright for me. How about you?'

She took his hand and placed it on her breast, holding it there, while with her other hand she brushed against his thigh then covered the hardened length of his cock, squeezing it gently through the cloth. For a moment he seemed to resist, then, with a strange urgency, his hand began to fondle her breast and, leaning in to her, he kissed her, his tongue seeking hers.

It was late, but neither of them were going to get any sleep until this was resolved. Julie sat on the floor outside the bathroom, her back against the wall, waiting. It had been quiet for a long time. Too long, perhaps. She stood up, meaning to knock on the door and see how Marie was, but right then the door opened.

'Well?'

Marie's face crumpled. She dissolved into tears. 'How am I going to cope?'

Julie was aware that Ellie had come out and was standing in the doorway to her room, looking across at them, bewildered. She gave her a kindly smile, indicating that she should go back inside, then stepped across and put her arms around Marie.

'Shhh,' Julie said, smoothing Marie's back, trying her best to comfort her. 'Ssshhh, sweetheart. Everything's gonna be okay.'

But looking past her into the bathroom, Julie saw the

pregnancy test box, the tester with its unwelcome news and in an instant the idea was formed. It was going to be alright. It was all going to be just fine.

In her dream she had been arguing with her mother over a dress she had wanted to wear to a party. Her mother had said it was too 'modern', too revealing, and had threatened to take her scissors to it if she defied her and wore it. But Julie had worn it anyway, only to find herself standing there suddenly in a crowded room, wearing a dress of shredded cloth. And then she'd woken – woken with the image of her mother's face clearer than it had been in many a year. Her mother, Vera, who she'd not spoken to now in almost twenty years.

She lay there a moment, feeling strange, then remembered with a start just where she was. The warm, naked body next to her was Dave's.

For a time she lay there, remembering their lovemaking. He had been nervous at first, but eager. Too eager! Then later they'd made love again, and it was soft, comfortable. Not the best she'd had by far, but . . .

Feeling mischievous, she burrowed down beneath the blankets and, taking it in her fingers, began to coax it back to life, gently kissing it with wet little kisses A moment later, Dave woke with a grunt of surprise.

'What the—?'

'It's okay,' she said soothingly. 'Just lie back and let Nurse Julie see to you.'

The morning was bright and clear as Julie stepped out of the health centre. She was looking very pleased with herself, and as she stood there on the steps, wondering whether to walk down to the bus stop or wait for a taxi, she had the look of a woman who knew what she wanted and how to set about getting it.

She had her ante-natal appointment card in one hand, along with a clutch of pamphlets about pregnancy. Smiling to herself, she stuffed them into her handbag, then tottered down the steps. Her new shoes were pinching her a little, but they were worth it. She'd seen how Dave's eyes had lit up at the sight of the stilettos.

She giggled, remembering. It was obvious he hadn't had a woman in a while, which in a way made it even more exciting for her; his eagerness, his anxiety, giving her the sense of power and control she wanted.

Halfway down the high street she stopped, then turned side on to the window of a bakers, looking at herself, at the flatness of her stomach. The women serving inside saw what she was doing and nudged each other, but Julie just gave them a broad smile, patted her stomach, and walked on.

Dave didn't expect her back until four-thirty, so she had practically the whole day to herself. It was the kind of day you might wish you were a tourist, in the city for the first time, but sightseeing didn't appeal to her – not one tiny little bit.

Shopping. Yeah, she'd go 'Up West' and spend the day shopping. She'd go to Principles and Next, M&S and New Look, and maybe even a couple of the posher stores. It was a while since she'd really treated herself, and she felt she deserved it. Besides, what better way to stimulate Dave's interest than to flaunt it in a few new glad rags?

Turning, she looked up and down the street, then raised her arm, hailing an oncoming cab. As he squealed to a halt, she tugged gently at the waistband of her skirt, getting comfortable, then raised her eyes to find the cabbie watching her, the faintest grin on his lips.

He looked nice: young and well-groomed, with an earring in his left ear. She could tell at once that he was fun to be with. At any other time she might have flirted with him and seen where it led, only today she found she wasn't interested, and as she told him where she wanted to go and then climbed into the back, she wondered why that was.

Until she'd actually slept with Dave, it had been like she was just going through the motions – setting her cap at him simply because she could. But things had changed, and she found she rather liked the way Dave looked at her, the way he now paid her such attention. Of course, she had always liked the attentions of men, but that hadn't really been why she'd gone after Dave. Or not entirely.

Then why did you? she asked herself, staring out of the window at the passing streets, the cabbie forgotten.

Maybe because she'd seen something in him – that same hunger for love and romance she knew was in herself. And maybe because all of the younger men she'd been with these last ten years or so had proved so useless, had let her down when it came right down to it. For once she wanted a good man, a sensitive man – a man who was going to look after her.

And Dave would look after her. He was mature. He knew what he wanted. He couldn't get enough of her. She giggled at the thought then looked up to meet the cabbie's eyes in the mirror.

No, she thought. *Another time, maybe. But not today. Today I've got Dave.*

Chapter Six

Night And Day

Dave was sitting there, staring at the rough draft of his accounts, wondering how the hell he had got into such a mess. It wasn't that they didn't do a fair trade, it was just that, however hard he worked – whatever he did to try to generate new business – it was never quite enough. His expenses were always higher than his income. The loan didn't help, of course. He'd known that was a mistake right from the start. But it was either that or give up the pub, and he'd put too much time and effort into making things work for him to give up without a fight. Even so . . .

He stood, then walked through into the bar. Julie was standing at the far end, unusually quiet, staring away across the pub and chewing on a nail. He walked across and stood just behind her.

'You alright?'

She turned. 'Yeah, fine.' But she didn't sound fine.

'What's up?'

Julie shrugged. 'Nothing. I just feel a bit icky, that's all.'

'Yeah? Come here.'

He put his arms about her. She snuggled in to him, smiling, enjoying his embrace.

'Better?' he asked, looking into her face and smiling.

'A little.'

'Why don't you pop out for a bit of air? We'll be okay here for five minutes.'

Julie shook her head, then sighed. 'I feel as though I ain't got an ounce of energy.'

He studied her a moment, his eyes full of concern. 'Listen, I think the best thing'd be to get you checked out at the doctor's.'

'Nah. It's probably just something I ate.'

'Yeah, well, better safe than sorry.' Dave kissed her on the cheek. 'I'll call a cab to take you up the surgery. See what they say, yeah?'

Julie gave a pathetic little nod. 'Yeah. Yeah, alright.'

The cab was waiting for her in the side street. As she stepped out of the pub, Julie reached into her handbag and took out her ciggies. She lit up then, giving the cabbie her best smile, walked over and climbed into the back.

He looked at her in the driving mirror, clearly liking what he saw.

'Where to, darling?'

'Shopping centre, please.'

She wasn't sure about the shoes she'd bought. The top was fine, but maybe the shoes wouldn't go with her blue dress after all.

Julie turned, ignoring the other shoppers who filled the crowded pavement, wondering if she had the nerve to take them back after all the trouble she'd put the assistant through, then, deciding she couldn't be arsed – and that, anyway, she could always buy a dress to match the shoes – she turned back. And stopped dead, as church bells began to ring out and the doors of the church just across the way from her swung open, spilling out a wedding party.

Looking on, watching the white-dressed bride and her groom come down the steps, confetti filling the air from all sides, Julie felt her heart quicken with excitement. For a while she simply stood there, entranced by the couple's evident happiness, by the dream made real; this was their day, a day they would remember all their lives, but then, even as the cameras flashed, a cloud darkened the sky overhead and rain began to fall.

'Shit!'

Julie hurried across the pavement, into a shop entrance, then turned back, looking, but the couple had gone, the steps were empty. She had a glimpse of them in the big white car, and then that too was gone, and the church doors closed.

Even so, she had seen it, and it felt like a sign. Dave was a good man, a kind and loving man, and she liked being with him. So why not?

Three hours later she was sitting up in bed, naked beneath the duvet. Dave had come back to the house to see how she was, and she had enticed him beneath the sheets. But halfway through she'd had to stop.

Julie put her head back against the headboard and closed her eyes. She was like that when Dave came back into the room, in his dark blue dressing gown, carrying a glass of water. He came across and, sitting beside her, handed her the glass.

She opened her eyes and smiled weakly. 'Thanks.'

He smiled back at her indulgently. 'You should have said something. I wouldn't have started if I'd known you were still feeling ill.'

'I wasn't. I'm . . . alright. Really.'

Dave watched her face a moment then looked down. 'Is it me, then? Is it something I've done?'

'Nah.'

But Dave looked unconvinced. More than that, he looked upset now. She reached out and took his hand, making him look at her. 'No, you daft bugger. The thing is— Oh, Christ! There's no easy way to say this. I'm pregnant.'

'*Pregnant!*'

She reached down the side of the bed for her bag and pulled out the appointment card and a leaflet. She handed them across, but Dave just stared at them uncomprehendingly.

'I should have known by the sickness, I suppose,' she said.

Dave looked up at her again, his face a picture. The news had him gobsmacked.

'You sure?'

Julie nodded, but Dave still seemed in shock.

'Oh Christ!' she said, squeezing his hand now. 'Say something, for God's sake!'

He shook his head. 'I can't believe it. I just can't believe it.' Then, unexpectedly, he threw his arms about her and gave her a big hug. He was close to tears now, his voice trembling as he spoke.

'You'll never want for anything. Either of you. I promise.'

Beaming, Julie hugged him back, savouring the moment, loving the daft sod for his kindness, knowing, without a doubt, that this time it would work.

Dave had offered to come along with her and help her pack, but she'd said no. She didn't want Marie to feel put out. And she certainly didn't want to tell her about the pregnancy, and if Dave was there that might be difficult. In the end he dropped her there, on the estate, giving her the money for the cab back.

She'd made him stop at an off-licence on the way over so she could buy a bottle of wine. Now, travelling up in the lift, she rehearsed what she was going to say. Marie could be a bit of a funny cow sometimes, but she ought to be pleased for her, especially as it meant she was finally getting rid of her.

Marie frowned at her as she opened the door. 'You okay? I heard you weren't well.'

Julie followed her inside, playing it straight-faced for a moment. 'Nah, I'm fine.' Then, beaming. 'In fact, I'm more than fine. Dave's proposed! He's asked me to marry him!'

Marie had been walking across to the sink. She stopped and turned, a look of shock on her face.

'*Marriage?*'

Julie nodded, then, holding up the wine, 'Yeah, and I thought we'd celebrate!'

Marie looked stunned. She went over to the cupboard and took down two long-stemmed glasses, but she seemed in a daze.

'Are you sure?'

'Yeah. Well, as sure as I can be.'

'Yeah, but marriage! I mean, you don't really know him.'

Julie shrugged, a bit put out now. 'I know enough. I know he loves me.'

Incredulous, Marie shook her head. 'But Julie—'

The cork popped, and Julie filled the glasses

'I'm sorry, but I think you're bloody mad. I mean, it's a big step. You need to think about what you're doing. Make sure you're not just on the rebound from Karl. What's it been, a couple of months?'

Julie went to speak, but Marie interrupted her. 'Anyway, you ain't had your divorce through yet.'

'That's okay. I'm getting a quickie. It'll be through any time now.'

Marie made a face.

'Look,' Julie said, trying not to lose her patience, 'I know he's not your idea of Mr Right, but he is mine. I've made up my mind.' She grinned. 'Besides, I've seen a lovely dress. Oh, and I want you to be a witness, and I want Ellie to be a bridesmaid. She'd love that.'

'Julie! Just listen to yourself!'

'What?'

'What d'you mean, "What?" You sound like a lovesick kid. You've gotta think about this. It's a big decision.'

Julie bit back at her, irritated now. 'I *have*!'

'Yeah, but you ain't. I'm talking about – well, this is the man you're saying you want to spend the rest of your life with.'

'Look, what's your bloody problem? Why can't you just be happy for me? Or is it that you're jealous?'

Marie winced, hurt by the accusation. '*Jealous?*'

'Alright – look, I'm sorry. It's just – well, I want you to be happy for me. You're my best mate and – you *are* happy, ain't you?'

Marie sighed resignedly. 'If it's what you really want.'

'Yeah. Yeah it is. Oh, and listen, Marie. Do us a favour and don't mention Karl in front of Dave.'

'Dave does know about him?'

'Yeah. Course he does. It's just that he gets the hump when I talk about him.'

Julie made to refill Marie's glass but she put her hand over it.

'I'd better not.'

'Have you told Gary yet?'

Marie shook her head. 'No point.'

'How d'you know that? Maybe he'd want to give it a go. Marry you, even.'

'Marry me!' She laughed, clearly amazed by the suggestion. 'We only managed to sleep together once! Unlucky or what?'

Then, more quietly. 'Anyway, the thing is I wouldn't want to marry *him*, baby or no baby.'

'See, that's your trouble! You don't think things through. At least you'd have someone to look after you for a change. At least you'd have that.'

She could remember the evening when he'd first come round. She'd been seven by then and just getting used to the fact that her dad was dead and that her mother never seemed to stop crying. Only for a month or so beforehand, things had been different. Her mother had stopped crying; she had seemed a lot more cheerful, almost happy. Julie had not understood why, at first, and if she'd seen a bit more of her Aunt May than she was used to, it hadn't clicked at first that her mother was seeing anyone. Until she brought him home.

Julie had been sitting in the chair by the fire, watching some cowboy film or other, when the door opened and he walked into the room. She'd turned her head to look, surprised to see him, a stranger, standing there. Then she saw her mother, much smaller, frailer than him, standing there beside him, looking up into his face, a kind of weary hope in her eyes, and she knew something had happened.

When he spoke, it was in a soft yet uncompromising tone. 'Your mother has something to say to you. So turn the telly off and listen.'

As far as she remembered that was the last time her mother had ever made any kind of speech. From then on he was the mouthpiece, he the breadwinner and he the decision-maker in the house. In her dad's house. Whatever he said went. But that evening it was her mother who made the announcement.

'Julie,' she began, her cheeks flushing with embarrassment. 'Ted here's to be your new dad. We're going to get married.'

And that was it. Nothing more, and no explanations. Yet it had taken her years to understand just why she'd done it. So she'd not be alone. So she'd not have to cry her way through the nights until she died. And she thought she understood that finally, only Ted Wright had been a bastard from the start. There'd been no honeymoon. Right from the outset he'd been a nasty git. And later, when things were really bad, she had found herself wondering at her mother's desperation, that she should have taken on such a man out of choice. Only that was life, and theirs wasn't the only household in which such misery existed.

And the point was that part of her *had* understood, and part of her still did. To have a man – that was why God had put them here on earth, wasn't it? Even those Evolution professors agreed with that. Only it wasn't always the right man.

Not always. But that, too, was life. She understood that now.

The jeweller took the ring from the tray, polished it, then handed it to Julie. She slipped it on, then turned to Dave, beaming at him, her eyes wide with delight.

'Oh, Dave, look at that! It's beautiful. Ain't it beautiful?'

Dave smiled, trying to share her delight, but he seemed slightly anxious. He looked to the jeweller. 'How much?'

The jeweller discreetly handed the price tag to him. Dave winced. Handing back the tag, he ran his finger along the row of rings, then picked another, looked at the tag, then handed it to Julie.

'This one looks nice.'

Julie looked put out. Reluctantly she slipped off the first ring and handed it to the jeweller, then tried on the other.

'What d'you think?' Dave asked hopefully.

She turned her nose up. Tugging it off, she handed it back, then took back the more expensive ring and slipped it on again. For a moment she simply stared at it, admiring it, then she looked back at Dave, giving him her most winning smile.

'I really love it.'

Dave shook his head, then, smiling at her, wanting to please her, he took out his wallet and, sorting through his credit cards, handed one over to the jeweller. Delighted, Julie cuddled up to him.

'Thank you.'

He grinned, softening now, putting his arm about her. 'Yeah, well, nothing's too good for you.'

*

That night Dave's mum and dad were coming round. While Dave pottered about in the kitchen, Julie went back into the bedroom and stood there, looking at herself in the full-length mirror of the wardrobe.

She wasn't happy. This wasn't how she wanted to look for them. Taking off the dress she threw it on to the bed, on top of several others she had discarded, then rifled through the others hanging on the door.

Dave called to her from outside. 'D'you think this is enough carrots?'

He appeared in the doorway, holding out a pan filled with chopped carrots.

'I thought you were dressed,' he said, admiring how she looked in her skimpy underwear.

She turned to him and smiled. 'I want to look nice.'

'You look bloody wonderful.'

'Stay like this, shall I?'

'What, and give my old man a heart attack?'

Grinning, she came across and looked into the pan. 'Best do a few more.'

Dave reached out to caress her breast, but she playfully tapped it away. He grinned. 'It's only my family.'

'Yeah, but I want them to like me.'

Dave put an arm round her. 'I dunno why you're worrying, sweetheart. They're gonna love you.'

Dave's mum, his dad, his sister Barbara and her husband John stood in a line near the fireplace. The first three had slightly shocked looks on their faces, while John merely smirked, impressed despite himself.

Dave stood aside, putting an arm out as if he were presenting royalty. 'Mum, Dad – this is Julie.'

She had settled on something skimpy. Something that showed off her figure in its best light. Someone else might have called it tarty, but that was just because they were jealous, not having her figure. But it was like she'd read somewhere or other – if you've got it, flaunt it.

She said her hellos, shaking hands with each of them, then
stood back as Dave organised the seating arrangements.

'You have this one over here, Mum. Dad, you have that one.
And Barb, you and John have the sofa.'

John patted the old brown leather sofa fondly, like one
might pat a dog. 'About time you got this old thing put down,
mate.'

Dave laughed. 'Don't start!' He looked to Julie. 'John
manages a furniture shop.'

Julie looked to John and smiled. 'Really? That's handy.' She
touched Dave's arm. 'John's right, though. We ought to think
about getting a new one.'

Dave's mum spoke up. 'Settees today haven't got no guts in
'em. The first one me and your father had lasted us twenty-five
years. I tell you, it saw some ups and downs, that sofa.'

John grinned and Barbara nudged him, giving him a look
that said 'Behave!'

Dave turned, looking at his sister. 'Christ, d'you remember
that thing, Barb?'

Barbara giggled. 'In the summer you used to stick to it when
you sat down. It was made of this horrible plastic stuff—'

John made a farting noise, and everyone laughed except
Dave's mum.

'Dirty beggar!' she said. 'Anyway, it was all the rage back
then, Barbara.'

Barbara and Dave laughed, teasing their mum, but she
ignored them, turning instead to Julie.

'And where's your home, then, Julie?'

'Well, I come from up north, originally.'

'North?' John asked, suddenly interested. 'What part of the
North? I used to be a rep up there.'

Julie looked to Dave, but Dave was busying himself with the
cutlery, straightening it under his mother's watchful eye.

'Yorkshire,' she said finally. 'Just north of Leeds.'

'Yorkshire,' John said, grinning and nodding at the same
time. 'Well, I'm surprised. You've no trace of an accent and
most Yorkshire lasses—'

'It's been a while,' she said, smiling at him to soften the

interruption. 'I left there in my teens. I—'

Dave's mum cut in abruptly. 'Is that where your family lives, then?'

Julie glanced at Dave, then answered her. 'I don't have any family.'

A moment's silence fell. Dave smiled and rubbed his hands together. 'Right! Who's for bubbly?'

As Dave popped the champagne cork, Julie gave a little cheer, then held out two long-stemmed glasses.

'There you are,' she said a moment later, handing one to Barbara. 'Mum,' she added, turning to hand one to Dave's mum.

Dave poured another glass, then looked up, noting the brief eye contact between his mum and sister; seeing at the same time that Julie was oblivious to what was going on. He looked back down, concentrating on pouring another glass, then set the bottle down and carried the full glasses across, handing them to his dad and John.

John raised his, winking at his brother-in-law. 'Congratulations, mate! I'm really pleased for you!'

There was a muted murmur of agreement. Dave grinned, then, putting his arm round Julie's shoulders, looked to his mum.

'What d'you reckon then, Mum? She'll do, won't she?'

Dave's mum's smile was brief, non-committal, as if she'd not quite made up her mind just yet. But Julie didn't see it. Julie was looking up into Dave's face and beaming, enjoying the moment, enjoying basking in his attention, like a sunflower turned towards the sun, drinking it all in.

Julie stood in front of the bathroom mirror, smoothing cream into her skin. She called out to Dave, who was clearing up in the living room.

'D'you think they liked me?'

'Yeah,' he called back, 'they loved you.'

Hearing him coming through, she went over to the toilet and, lifting up the seat, knelt down, making heaving noises. Then, as he appeared in the doorway, she straightened up, flushing the cistern, affecting a weary expression.

Sympathetic, Dave came across and, crouching, rubbed her back. She closed her eyes, enjoying the attention.

'Can't you get one of the others to work tonight?'

'I can't.'

He put his arm about her and she leaned in, laying her head on his shoulder.

'Why don't you get an early night,' he said. 'I could get Marie to come in and do the lunchtime tomorrow, if you like.'

Julie gave a weak nod. 'Just tell her I've got a bit of a migraine.'

Dave reached down, cupping his hands over her tummy.

'I still can't take it in. You know what? I think I'd given up on the idea of ever being a dad. I thought—'

Julie smiled uncomfortably. 'Oh, I meant to tell you. I've found a place that hires out suits and top hats and all that, and I thought—'

She saw how he was looking and stopped.

'Listen, love, in view of . . .' He nodded towards her tummy. 'Well, I reckon we should keep it simple. Not get too carried away.'

She smiled. 'I'm not. I just want it to be nice, that's all.' She looked down, tearful suddenly. 'It's just it's my big day and I wanted it to be special.'

Dave softened. 'Yeah, yeah, I know you do, sweetheart.' He smiled, touching her cheek, wiping away the tears which, now that he looked, weren't actually there. 'So where's this place, then?'

Despite her reservations, Marie couldn't help smiling as she watched Julie lift the veil and head-dress from the Cellophane wrapping and put them on.

'Well?' she asked. 'What d'you think?'

They sat down in the living room, on the sofa – Julie's 'old bed' – and talked for a bit. Marie seemed more comfortable with the idea of Julie marrying Dave than she'd been before, even so, Julie didn't sense any kind of enthusiasm in her. Ellie, however, was a different matter. She woke and, hearing Julie's voice, came in. Marie made to scold her and send her back to bed, but Julie persuaded her to let her stay, and even let Ellie try on her veil and head-dress. They were sitting there, smiling, watching Ellie swan about the room, pretending she was dancing in the arms of her husband, when Julie stood up abruptly, the smile and all the colour vanished from her face.

'Get it off!' she screeched. 'I said get it off!'

Frightened, Ellie looked to her mother, who had stood and was staring in amazement at her friend; an amazement that quickly turned to anger.

'Who the bloody hell d'you think you're talking to?'

But Julie didn't seem to hear her. She reached out and snatched the head-dress off Ellie, who ran to her mother, dissolving into tears.

Marie hugged her daughter, glaring all the while at Julie, who just stood there, staring at the head-dress as if in a trance.

'It's alright,' she said softly, stroking her daughter's back. 'Go and watch telly in the bedroom for a bit, eh, darling?'

Ellie looked up at her, then gave a little shudder and nodded. As she sloped out, Marie turned to face Julie, who now looked back at her, as if waking; as if she didn't know what she had done.

'Look, I—'

But Marie just shook her head and, turning her back on her in disgust, went through to see if her daughter was okay.

It was late now and the table was strewn with half-eaten take-away cartons from the local Chinese. Ellie had gone back to bed, but there was still an underlying tension between the two women. Julie had opened a fresh bottle of champagne and poured a couple of glasses, but Marie had hardly touched hers. Nor had she spoken much since the incident with the veil. Julie studied her friend a moment, then, knowing she had to break the ice, spoke up.

'I'm sorry, Marie. Really I am. I—'

Marie rounded on her, her face hard. 'You don't do that to kids. Especially my kid. Maybe she shouldn't have messed about like that, but—'

'I know. I know. I'm so sorry. I'll go and—'

Julie went to get up, but Marie gestured for her to sit back down.

'No. Leave her for a bit.'

Julie looked down, pulling at her fingers agitatedly. 'It must be nerves.'

Marie nodded. She poked at one of the boxes half-heartedly, then put the fork down. 'What happens about the divorce, then?'

Julie eyed her warily. 'What d'you mean?'

'D'you have to give them the papers? Up the registry, I mean.'

'What? Oh, yeah. Yeah, it's all sorted.'

Marie's face softened a little. 'Dave must be pleased.'

'Yeah.' Julie stood, indicating the containers. 'You want any more of this?'

Marie shook her head, so Julie began to clear away.

'Just think,' she said. 'This time tomorrow! And I do love a good party. You know, a bit of a bop.'

Marie grunted. 'The way I feel I won't be bopping anywhere.'

Julie paused, staring at her, concerned. 'I take it you've decided about the abortion.'

Marie nodded, not looking at Julie at first, then she noticed Julie was watching her and grimaced.

'Don't look like that!'

'Like what?' Julie asked.

'Look, if I thought for a moment I could have this kid, I'd have it. But I can't.'

'But I know how much you love Ellie, and—'

Marie gave an exasperated sigh. 'Of course I love Ellie, but I can't do it again. Not on my own. It's just too hard. Unless you've done it you—'

Marie shook her head, tears welling in her eyes. 'I can't,' she said quietly. 'What a fucking mess.'

'There are plenty of couples who can't have kids. Maybe . . .'

'Oh yeah,' Marie said, irritated now by her friend's insensitivity, 'have it adopted and spend the rest of my sodding

life wondering where it is and what it looks like. I couldn't
handle that.'

'But what if . . .?'

Marie stood, her voice trembling now. 'Can't you understand? I couldn't carry a baby in my belly for nine months and
then just give it away!'

Julie stared at her a moment, shaken by her words, then
looked down, a strange little movement in her face. She was
about to say something when Ellie called from the bedroom.

'Mu-um!'

Marie went to the door, but stopped, looking back at Julie.
'I mean, how *could* I?'

And she went out, into the hallway, leaving Julie standing
there, feeling as though she had been slapped.

Chapter Seven

When I Fall In Love

The tiny room was silent as they waited for the female registrar to begin the proceedings. Alone on the front row sat the bride and groom, Julie excited and slightly overdressed in her frothy white dress, Dave nervous in his simple grey morning suit, while their witnesses and guests gathered in the adjoining room.

The registrar placed a pair of metal-framed glasses on her nose, then read through the forms in front of her. She looked across at them, then began, the almost incantatory drone of her voice filling the silence as she put the first of those questions she had by law to ask before the ceremony proper could begin.

'First the groom. Could you please tell me your full name.'

Dave cleared his throat. 'David John Freeman.'

'Are you or have you ever been known by any other name?'

'No.'

'How old are you today?'

'Forty-nine.'

'And have you ever been through any previous form of marriage in this or any other country?'

'Yes.'

'How did that marriage end?'

'In divorce.'

'Have you been married again since that divorce?'

'No.'

The registrar nodded, then turned to Julie, smiling once again. 'If I could ask you to confirm your name.'

Julie smiled, then answered, her voice clear, confident. 'Julie Vera Harding.'

'And how old are you today?'

'Thirty-four.'

'Are you known or have you ever been known by any other name?'

'No.'

'And have you been through any previous form of marriage in this country or any other country?'

'No.'

Dave looked at her and smiled. Reaching down, she took his hand and squeezed it, returning his smile, loving the way he looked at her today, as if she were some miracle, the whole thing some kind of dream.

'Okay,' the registrar said, smiling brightly at them both. 'That's it. We can call the guests in now.'

'Right,' Dave said, getting to his feet abruptly. Then he paused, looking down at Julie, his face softening once more. 'Right.'

There was a small door inset into one of the two bigger doors of the prison's gate, small enough to make an average-sized man stoop and duck his head as he went through into the daylight outside.

As Brian stepped out on to the road, he looked about him, but if he was expecting anyone, he was disappointed. The road was empty.

He was mid-thirties now and casually dressed, his hair shaved to a fine stubble, his cheeks clean shaven. Under his left arm was a bundle – the sum total of his possessions on this earth – and in his pocket he'd enough money to get him through the next couple of weeks. Beyond that he didn't know. They'd given him a card with an address on it and a telephone number, but he had no intention of using it.

He looked about him one last time, then, his head dropping, he began to walk. Home. He was going to go home.

'Well, *Mrs Freeman*?' Dave said, in a breathless moment on the steps of the Register Office, grinning into her face. 'Happy now?'

'Ecstatic, *Mr Freeman*.' And she giggled, then took his face in her hands and kissed him.

Cameras flashed, confetti formed a blizzard in the air about them. Everyone, it seemed, was grinning and laughing on every side. She looked about her, basking in their attention, then squeezed Dave's hand. Yeah. This was the best feeling ever. Better than sex.

Everywhere she looked there were friendly faces. Even Dave's sour-faced old mum was smiling for once. The only one who wasn't smiling was Marie, and Julie felt sorry for her.

'Love you,' Dave whispered in her ear as he put his arm about her and drew her close.

Julie smiled and kissed his cheek.

'I know.' And right then she felt it. Could feel the love flowing out of him for her. She beamed and he beamed back.

'Thank you.'

She stared at him, surprised. 'What for?'

'For this.'

She saw the tear form in the corner of his eye and leaned in to kiss each lid. Dave's mum saw the little gesture and smiled to herself, yet as her son and his new wife passed her, she could not help but feel a fleeting moment of anxiety for her son.

Don't let her hurt him. Please God, don't let her hurt him.

Brian stood outside the door of the flat, hesitating. He'd heard tales while he was inside – stories of women moving other men in while their fellas were locked away, like they were some kind of time-share. He didn't know whether he could handle that. Didn't really know how he'd feel after all this time. Only he hadn't seen her in a while.

He ran his hand across the top of his head, then reached for the knocker. And stopped. No. It was his flat, after all. He had a right to be here.

Brian pushed his hand into his right-hand pocket and fished out the bunch of keys. Fumbling for the right one, he slipped it in the lock and turned it.

There. Just like old times.

There was a strange smell in the air. A kind of musty, almost pissy smell. Maybe she'd got a cat—

He stopped a moment, frowning. He could hear the telly

through the living-room door at the far end of the shadowed hallway, but it wasn't that that had made him stop. He was just noticing things. Like the old-fashioned prints on the wall, the hideous patterned carpet underfoot.

Deciding that there was no point delaying any further, he walked straight down the hallway and threw the door open.

An elderly couple were sitting in identical armchairs to either side of the television. Like two strange, wizened puppets, they turned together, staring at him, startled to see him there in the doorway. The old man's voice trembled with fear as he challenged him.

'Who the hell are you? What do you want?'

Brian stared back at them, shocked to see his living room transformed into some museum for the elderly. 'I'm Brian,' he said, maybe a touch too belligerently. 'Who the fuck are you? And where's Julie?'

The old man made to rise, but gave up on it. 'Who?' he asked shakily.

'Julie! You deaf old git!'

And now the old fella did haul himself to his feet, his wizened-faced wife's mouth making silent shapes as if to warn him to take care.

'Sod off, before I call the police! Go on! Get out!'

He nodded to the phone on the table by his wife – 'Maisie!' – then turned back to confront Brian once more.

'Look, there ain't no Julie here. Julie who?'

But Brian could see now what had happened. She'd gone. Fucked off without a word. Even so, he answered the old fella, sorry now that he'd yelled at him, his tone softer, quieter than before.

'Julie Carter. She used to live here. She's my wife.'

'Ah.' And it was like the old man saw it all at a glance, saw it and – sympathised. But Brian didn't want sympathy. He didn't want an old man's understanding. He wanted Julie. He wanted back the life he'd lost – the life she'd promised him.

Turning, he stormed out, slamming the door behind him, his heavy footsteps echoing on the stairs as he took them in twos and threes, hurrying to get away.

*

Dave's brother-in-law John looked about him at the packed room – at faces which were still laughing from his last crack – then raised his glass in a toast. At once, the air was filled with wavering champagne glasses.

'To Julie and Dave!'

The toast was deafening. 'Julie and Dave!'

Seated beside John, Dave and Julie both wore beaming smiles. Dave looked at his new wife and reached out to take her hand, his eyes resting on the band of gold about her third finger. He put his arm around her and gave her a cuddle, then sat back, grinning like a drunkard as he looked about him at that little sea of smiling faces.

But he was not about to get off lightly. There were calls for a speech from the groom, scattered at first, but then they became a kind of chant.

'Speech! Speech! Speech! Speech!'

Dave stood, nodding shyly, and the room fell silent.

'First of all,' he began, 'I want to thank you all for coming. It means a lot to me and my wife.'

'Where's her white stick?' someone shouted from the back.

Dave nodded, waiting for the laughter to die down. 'And you know what? That's not something I thought I'd ever say again. *My wife*.' He turned, looking down at Julie, smiling gently, then went on. 'I know you all thought I was going to end up a sad, lonely old man. Yeah, well, I thought so myself at times, I can tell you. Then I met Julie, and I realised I'd been looking for this woman all my life.'

There was an 'ahh' from all the women at that, but Dave raised a hand.

'But then I thought, hold up, Dave, women like her don't fall for blokes like you. Only for some reason she did. And when I asked her to marry me she said yes.'

Dave stopped a moment, clearly choked, then, after clearing his throat, went on.

'She's good, she's kind, she's beautiful, and I know I don't deserve her, but I will look after her, and when our baby's born, I'll be the happiest man alive.'

There was a collective intake of breath at that, as if they'd misheard, but Dave was grinning now and nodding his head.

'Yeah. That's right We're going to have a baby.'

There were whoops as well as looks of stunned amazement. Dave himself was grinning like he might split his face open, while Julie was looking down, smiling coyly. Marie just stared, utterly gobsmacked by the news, one hand pressed to her stomach. But Dave's mum's eyes were narrowed with suspicion.

After a moment, everyone was crowding round, offering congratulations.

Dave, still grinning, looked down at Julie, who narrowed her eyes in mock annoyance.

'I know,' he said. 'I know you didn't want to say anything yet, but—'

'It's just that it's so early.'

'I know, but I just couldn't help it.'

Julie reached out and took his hand. 'You're like a big kid. Go on, you'd better open some more bubbly.'

His smile softened. 'Better do what the missus says.'

As Dave made his way across to the bar to get some more champagne, Alan squeezed through the crowd. Seeing him, Julie stood.

'Congratulations!'

Julie smiled. 'Thanks. Don't the bride get a kiss?'

Smiling awkwardly, Alan moved closer, meaning to kiss Julie on the cheek, but she drew back a little, then, as he looked at her, confused, kissed him on the lips.

'Well?' she said, flirting with him now. 'What d'you think?' And she did a slow twirl, taking care not to knock the cake.

Alan couldn't take his eyes off her now. There was a colour at his neck, and he seemed a little flustered as he spoke.

'You look beautiful. He's – he's very lucky.' Alan glanced across, seeing Dave coming back with two glasses of bubbly held out before him. 'I expect Dave'll be getting the sign changed now you're married.'

Julie looked confused. 'Sign?'

Dave edged through and, handing Julie one of the glasses,

placed a proprietorial arm about her shoulders. 'What's that?'

Alan tried to look at Dave, but his eyes kept on flitting to Julie. 'I was just saying. You'll be getting the sign changed. You know, above the pub. Mr and *Mrs* Freeman.'

But Dave shook his head. 'No need for her to work now she's married. Like I said, I'm going to look after her.'

Surprised, Julie looked up at Dave, but she was enjoying being cossetted. He gave her a brief kiss.

'Back in a tick.'

As Dave walked off, Alan looked back at Julie. 'So! A baby!'

Julie grinned. 'Yeah.'

She took a half swig of her champagne then, as she half-turned, looking about her, glimpsed Ellie being dragged towards the door by Marie. Marie looked like she'd been crying.

Julie touched Alan's arm. 'Hang on a sec.' Then, squeezing between people, she hastened across.

'Marie!' Then, louder. '*Marie!*'

Julie was almost at the door when Dave's mum stopped her.

'I thought we might have heard before anyone else.'

Julie looked past the old woman, wanting to ignore her and go after Marie, but knowing she couldn't, not without causing a row.

'Yeah,' she said. 'I'm sorry.'

'Accounts for the rush.'

Julie ignored the barb. 'Yeah, well, you know what men are like.'

'I know what my son's like!'

But right then the music started up again – Nat King Cole, singing 'When I Fall In Love', one of her all-time favourites. And there, on cue at her side, was Dave. He put his arm about Julie, then looked to his mum and smiled.

'Don't mind, do you, Mum, I'd like to dance with my wife.'

A space cleared as people moved back, and as the song filled the air, the newlyweds moved out on to the tiny dance floor, in a slow romantic waltz that drew 'ahhs' from all around.

All, that is, except from one quarter. Dave's mum, clutching her handbag, stood there, watching them dance, knowing in her guts that her son was in trouble, whether he realised it or not, and that there was nothing – not a single thing – she could do about it.

Chapter Eight

Cryin'

A fortnight passed before she next saw Marie. They had made the arrangement before the wedding, but Marie clearly hadn't expected her to remember, and as she stepped out of her flat that morning, she stopped dead, surprised to see Julie standing there.

'Alright?'

Marie gave a curt nod. She looked down a moment, then met Julie's eyes, angry still.

'Christ, Julie, I can't believe you didn't tell me you were pregnant!'

'I wanted to, but—'

'But what? You just decided to sit there, did you, feeling smug?'

Julie looked stung. 'No – don't be stupid. I didn't tell you, cos I knew you didn't—'

Marie held up her hand. 'It doesn't matter. I've got to go.'

'I know, but—'

Marie brushed past her, heading for the stairs. Julie stood there a moment, then hurried after her.

'Marie! . . . *Marie*!'

Marie stopped on the stairs, waiting for her.

'I'm sorry, Marie. I— Look, I'd never hurt you. You're my friend.'

Marie turned. There were tears in her eyes, but whether they were for friendship or for her own sad state Julie couldn't tell. She went across and gently took Marie's arm.

'Let me come with you. Please, Marie. I want to.'

Marie took a long, shuddering breath, then nodded.

It was a cold, cheerless room. The walls were a pale cream, the chairs late Eighties IKEA. Marie and Julie sat in the far corner, next to a low table piled with women's magazines, but no one wanted to read. Though every chair in the waiting room was occupied, there was a tense silence in the room. Everyone kept themselves to themselves, not wanting to meet anyone else's eyes.

Marie was one of the oldest women there, though not the oldest. That was a hefty-looking woman in her forties who sat broodingly alone across from them. But most of the patients were young – one of them seemingly under-age, there with her mum, hunched forward in her seat, her face hidden behind a veil of dark hair, clearly finding all of this a terrible ordeal.

As indeed it was.

The door opened and the nurse stepped into the room, a folder of notes under her arm.

'Kylie McFadden?'

The young girl looked up, startled almost to hear her name, then nodded. The nurse smiled, waiting for her and her mum to gather their belongings, then led them through.

The doors flapped shut behind them.

Julie glanced at Marie; saw how nervous, how *disturbed* she was by all of this. She leaned in to her, speaking in a low whisper.

'It's not too late.'

Marie glanced at her, but said nothing.

Julie took a long breath, then leaned close once more. 'I just – well, I just don't want you to do something you'll regret.'

Marie gave an ironic laugh. 'Oh, I'll regret it. But better that than have it and regret it. This way I'm only hurting me.'

'But I know—'

Marie turned to face her, her voice raised now, as if they were alone in the room. 'Listen, Julie. I don't want this child. Can't you understand? Christ Almighty! I've prayed every day that I'd miscarry! What kind of mother love is that?'

Julie looked down, conscious of everyone listening.

'It's different for you,' Marie went on. 'You've got Dave and you both *want* your baby.'

There was an awkward pause, and then the door opened

again. It was the older of the two nurses this time. She glanced down at the name on the folder, then looked about her.

'Marie Talbot?'

Marie jumped up, then followed the nurse as she turned away. But at the door she paused, looking back at Julie, a strange look in her eyes.

'*Good luck*,' Julie mouthed, but Marie didn't seem to see, it was like she was in a daze. She hesitated a moment, then turned and walked through, closing the door behind her.

Ellie was waiting at the school gates when Julie got there.

'Sorry I'm late, sweetheart,' she said, smiling cheerfully, 'only I forgot what the time was.'

'Where's Mum?'

Julie put her hand on Ellie's shoulder, then turned to check the road. 'She's having a bit of a lie-down. She wasn't feeling well.'

They crossed, then went through the gates into the park. Ellie was silent a moment, thoughtful, then she looked up at Julie again. 'Why don't she feel well?'

Julie smiled. 'She's just got a bit of an upset tummy, is all. She'll be fine once she's had a rest.'

Again Ellie brooded a moment, then: 'Is Mum going to have a baby?'

Julie stopped, giving a little laugh, taken aback by the question. She hadn't thought Ellie had known. 'What makes you say that?'

Ellie shrugged.

'No,' Julie said, beginning to walk on. 'No, she's not.'

'Julie?'

'Yes, love?'

'If you have a girl, it can have some of my dolls.' She looked up at Julie. 'I hope it is a girl.'

Embarrassed, Julie smiled weakly. But Ellie was grinning now.

'I can pretend like I'm her big sister, and when I'm older I could babysit, couldn't I?'

Julie looked away, unable to meet Ellie's eyes. 'We'll see.'

But Ellie wasn't finished. 'If I had a little girl, I'd called her Kalina. What are you going to call your baby?'

There was a look of pain in Julie's eyes now. 'I'm not sure.'

'Will it have its own bedroom?'

'I—'

'Can I help you choose the stuff for it? Mum says I'm good at that. If I had my own bedroom I'd paint it red. Bright red. But I'd still want to sleep with Mummy.' Ellie looked up at her again, the smile becoming a frown once more. 'Is she really going to be alright?'

Julie smiled and took her hand. 'Yeah. Yeah, she'll be fine. So, what d'you reckon? Big Mac or Kentucky Fried?'

Dave was in the kitchen, washing up the dinner things, while Julie stretched out on the sofa, watching TV and slowly munching her way through a box of chocolates. Dave had bought her flowers, too, and cooked her a special meal – steak with all the trimmings.

He came into the living room now, wiping his hands on a tea towel, grinning at her.

'All done!'

Julie smiled up at him, then reached for the remote, turning down the volume on the telly. Dave came over and squeezed into the space on the sofa next to her.

'I've put the kettle on.'

He began to massage her feet. Julie laid her head back, closing her eyes.

'Ooh, that's nice.'

Dave smiled. 'I was chatting to some woman in the pub and—'

Julie opened her eyes, teasing him with a raised eyebrow.

'Not like that! Anyway, this woman was saying that when she was pregnant she used to have these massage sessions, you know, on her belly. She reckons it helped with the birth.'

'Yeah?'

Dave grinned. 'Well? What d'you reckon?' And, leaning closer, he lifted her top slightly and placed his hands gently on her stomach, smoothing them over the naked flesh, a kind of awe in his eyes at the thought of what lay within.

Seeing that look, Julie had to look away. She forced a laugh. 'You wanna stick to feet!'

And she sat up a little, forcing his hands from her belly.

'Well, what happened to that cuppa? I'm gasping!'

'Oh right – course.'

Dave jumped up, a confused, apologetic look on his face, like he'd done something wrong, only he didn't know quite what. And as he walked through to make her tea, which she didn't really want, Julie covered up her stomach, only too aware of its flatness.

It was hard to sleep that night. Hard for her to know quite what to do. Listening to Dave sleeping contentedly beside her, she knew she couldn't possibly tell him the truth. Not now. So maybe it was just best, after all, to wait. To put it from her mind until it became an issue.

She gave a little groan, then rolled over, her back to Dave. And as she did he reached out and wrapped his arm about her, his hand resting on the bare flesh of her upper thigh, his body pressed in close suddenly.

'You okay?'

'I thought you were asleep.'

He gave a soft laugh. 'I was, but—'

Dave pressed in to her, as if to make his point.

'Alright,' she said softly. 'But from behind, and be gentle. Remember my condition.'

He hesitated a little at the reminder. 'Are you sure, love?'

She patted his hand. 'Yeah – yeah, it'll be nice.' And, to make sure he didn't mistake her meaning, she eased her knickers down. 'Now come on before I fall asleep.'

Dave pressed his body closer and, with what sounded like a contented sigh, he began to make love to her.

It was Dave's idea. An old mate of his who was in the business had said he'd look after the running of the pub while they were gone, so there were no excuses. They packed a case, put it in the boot of the car, and they were off.

'Have you got any idea where we're heading?' she asked, as he accelerated into the fast lane of the M4.

'Cornwall,' he said, smiling like the mystery man. 'A little place me mum and dad used to take us when we were kids. It's magic, I tell you.'

'So you've booked us somewhere, then?'

Dave nodded. 'A little B and B, overlooking the harbour. You'll love it.'

Julie wasn't so sure, remembering Teignmouth and that disastrous week with Brian, but at least they were going somewhere.

'So this is, like, a kind of honeymoon?'

He glanced at her, like he hadn't thought of that at all, then grinned again. 'I guess so. I mean—'

She leaned across and kissed him on the cheek. 'You're a sweetheart, you know that?'

'Yeah.' And he laughed. 'I know that.'

As it turned out, the place was perfect. They got there just as the sun was going down, and, as she stepped into their room, she saw how their window opened out over the harbour, giving a breath-taking view of the setting sun, its last light casting a great golden glow across the sea.

'Oh, Dave!'

She turned and went into his arms, kissing him long and passionately, until, with a little laugh of surprise, he broke from her.

His eyes were bright with lust. 'You better let me close the door, eh?'

Julie looked past him, seeing that the door was open, their case resting there where he'd put it down. She giggled. 'Alright, but I want you to have me here, right by the window.'

He blinked, once more surprised by her, then, grinning, turned and went across to shut the door.

Turning her back on him, she rested her hands on the sill, staring out into that wonderful golden light as Dave returned. She pushed back against him as his hands felt beneath her skirt, then roughly tugged her knickers down, exposing her to him.

She heard the rip as he pulled his zipper down, then, suddenly, he was inside her, pushing up so far that she caught her breath and almost cried out.

There were people just below, on the harbour front, families strolling along in the last rays of the sunlight, stopping to admire the view, and she knew that if they turned and raised their eyes they would see her; would see her face as Dave fucked her, his thrusts so strong, so urgent, that she had to grip the sill tightly so as not to fall forward. And as he came, so she pressed back into him, grinding herself against him so that he gave a little groan and gripped her shoulders hard, forcing his seed into her, once, twice, a third time, his whole body shuddering against hers.

Slowly he relaxed. Slowly he slipped from her.

Julie turned, facing him again, her hair corona'd by the golden light. She smiled, then gently laughed. 'Well, Mr Freeman – will I do?'

It was a golden week. Though it was late in the season, the weather was magnificent, and Dave made sure she saw the best of that south Cornish coast. There were delightful little pubs, and lonely little beaches where, if you were careful, you could have it off beyond the sight of prying eyes.

Dave had been reluctant at first, making love outdoors being outside his experience, but he quickly caught on, and the one time they almost got caught – on a cliff top next to an old ruined tin mine – had been at his instigation. They'd scrambled back to the car, half-naked, then sat there side by side in the front, giggling like two naughty schoolchildren.

That was when he'd said it. He'd looked across at her and his face had changed.

'You know what?'

'What?'

'I don't think I could love anyone more than I love you. And when our child—'

Dave broke off, looking down, swallowing back the emotion, then looked back at her.

'When our baby comes, I—'

She took his head in her hands and caressed it; held it in her lap and stroked his hair for a long time after that. And as she did, she wondered why it couldn't always be like this. Why things always had to change.

It was on the last day of their holiday that they came upon the cottage. It wasn't *the* cottage, of course – the one in the postcard – but it was as close as made no difference, right down to the cherry tree in the front garden. Dave had wanted to walk on, down to the bay, but Julie had stopped dead, staring at it across the low slate wall, until he'd come back and asked her what the matter was.

She took the postcard from her handbag and handed it to him. He looked at the picture, faded now, then flipped it over and read the words – looked up at her, a sudden understanding in his eyes – then, finally, took in the date on the postal franking that covered the old mauve stamp.

Dave handed her back the card, then put an arm about her shoulders.

'It's pretty.'

She shivered, then shook her head. 'No, Dave. It's perfect. Look at it. It's like a dream.'

'Yeah, but—'

She turned her head to look at him. 'But what?'

'Well, it looks nice right now with the sun shining, but in the dead of winter— No, babe, give me a city any day. All this open space gives me the heebie-jeebies.'

Julie was quiet a moment, then, on impulse, she slipped out from under his arm and, walking to the gate, opened it and began to make her way down the path.

'Julie—'

He followed, meaning to stop her, but even as he caught up with her she stopped abruptly.

'Look!' she said, pointing.

He looked. There, just beyond the cherry tree, stuck into the earth beside the porch, was an estate agent's sign, with FOR SALE on it.

Looking back at her, Dave's mouth went dry. The look in

her face was strange; she was smiling, but it was also like she was haunted.

'Babe, let's—'

She brushed off his arm and, like a sleepwalker, stepped up to the door and knocked.

'*Julie.*'

She turned and looked at him, that strange, disturbing look still on her features, barely recognising him, it seemed. For a moment he thought there'd be no answer – that the house would be empty, thank God – but then, as she went to knock again, the door creaked open and an elderly-looking woman stepped out.

'Yes?'

'Julie! We've got to go—'

But Julie ignored him. Smiling at the woman, she began to ask about the cottage, as if she was seriously interested in buying it. Dave stepped up to her, putting his hand lightly on her arm, but once again she shrugged him off.

'You want to come in, my dear?' the old woman asked, looking strangely at Dave. 'Have a look around?'

'If I could.'

Dave went to speak, then closed his mouth. What was the harm, after all? They couldn't buy the place, even if they wanted to. Even if he sold the flat and settled all his debts, they'd barely have enough to buy a bike shed, let alone a cottage, and what would he do for a living out here in the sticks?

Run a pub, she'd say, but that was easier said than done. It took time to get in with the local brewers, and besides, you didn't just swan in to a job as manager of a pub in these parts. The locals didn't like that. You had to be part of the community, and he knew – without a shred of doubt – that he'd never fit in out here. He was a townie, through and through.

Yeah, but he didn't feel good about this. He'd seen the look on her face and he didn't like it, especially after that trick with the postcard.

The cottage was small and dark and cramped, and though it

had its own charm, Dave could tell from experience just how much work would have to be done to make it properly habitable – at least to the standards he was used to. Yet as they came down the narrow twist of stairs, Julie reached out and, taking his arm, leaned in to him.

'This is it, Dave. This is what I've always wanted. It's—'

It's crap, he wanted to say, *and I can't afford it*. But this was his Julie, and they'd had such a good week, so he just shrugged and said, 'We'll see.'

But that wasn't enough for her. 'Dave – we've got to buy it. We could make a new life down here. You could find a pub—'

He wanted to tell her the truth – that it wasn't going to happen; that it was all just make-believe in her head – but he couldn't. Looking at her – at that strange need in her – he found himself saying: 'I'll look into it, hon. Give them a ring. See what they say.' As if those words would be enough for her, and, when they got back home, she'd forget about it all. And as they walked away, Julie pressed into his side, her arm locked in his, he felt awful, knowing that her present happiness was an illusion that at some stage he'd have to pop like pricking a soap bubble.

That cottage. That fucking cottage.

Julie and Barbara were bustling about the kitchen, clearing up after Sunday lunch. Iris, Dave's mum, stood by the kettle, waiting to make a pot of tea. She was sounding off as usual, her pompous, toneless voice making Julie's nerves grate.

'Yes, well, I'm afraid in my book there's no such thing as an accident as far as pregnancy's concerned. And you a nurse!'

'Which hospital are you under?' Barbara asked.

'Er – St Anthony's.'

'I was in there for my bowel – d'you remember, Barbara?'

Barbara nodded, then returned her attention to Julie. 'How many weeks are you?'

'Twelve.'

Even as she said it, she was conscious of Iris staring at her flat stomach.

'You should be showing soon,' the older woman said sourly.

'They give you scans early these days, don't they?' Barbara chipped in quickly. 'To pick up any – you know . . .'

'You want to make sure you have one of those,' Iris said pointedly. 'Have you booked in?'

'Yeah. Yeah, I've got one next Tuesday.'

Dave had entered the kitchen unnoticed. 'One what?'

Julie jerked round.

'A scan,' Barbara said.

Dave looked to Julie, his eyes bright with excitement. 'You didn't tell me.'

'No, well, I know what you're like. You'd have gone on and on about it. I was going to tell you tonight. A surprise.'

'Aw, sorry.'

He stepped across and laid a hand on Julie's tummy, grinning. 'It's amazing. I can't believe I'm actually going to see my baby. It'll be bloody brilliant, won't it, love?'

'Yeah,' Julie said, an awful sinking feeling gripping her even as she smiled weakly. 'Yeah, it will.'

It was raining – that kind of cold drizzle that is like misery itself. Dave had turned his collar up, but still the rain kept running down his neck.

'Look, so I'll owe you for two deliveries. What's the problem? I always pay.'

The driver was an old fella, in his late fifties, and usually he and Dave got on brilliantly, but today – perhaps because the weather was so awful – he seemed out of sorts. Or maybe he'd had a bollocking from his boss.

The brewery's delivery lorry stood in the middle of the road, blocking the side-turning, its awning pulled across.

'Listen, mate,' the driver said impatiently, 'it's no good giving me grief. I'm only passing on the message. You hand me a cheque, and everyone'll be happy. But till you pay up, I don't unload. Simple as that.'

There was a flash of anger in Dave's eyes. 'I'm gonna speak to Reynolds.'

The driver leaned back a little. 'It was Mr Reynolds gave me the message.'

'Yeah, but—'

Dave stopped. Marie had appeared in the nearby doorway. She was holding out the cordless phone.

'Dave—'

Dave held up a hand, then turned back to the driver. 'What kind of tuppeny ha'penny outfit is it that—'

'*Dave!*'

He stopped and turned, surprised by the urgency – the insistence – in Marie's voice.

'What?'

'It's Julie. She sounds a bit—' She mouthed the last bit. '*—upset*'.

Dave walked across and took the phone, shaking the rain from his hair as he did.

'Julie?'

Marie watched him from an arm's length away. Saw how his face crumpled. He looked desperate, panic-stricken. He almost threw the phone at Marie, then made straight for his car.

Worried, Marie ran out after him. 'Dave? *Dave!* What's wrong?'

The driver, seeing him about to drive off, came storming across. 'Hey! You want this lot or not?'

Dave hesitated, his car door half open, then gestured to Marie. 'Pay him!'

Then, climbing in, he slammed the door shut, revved up the engine and was off.

Dave sat there on the sofa, comforting Julie as she dissolved into another flood of tears. As he'd walked through the door earlier, she had burst into tears. Now, it seemed, she couldn't stop crying. As for Dave, he sat there, stone-faced, trying to be strong, but inside he was aching.

'Sweetheart, let me call the doctor.'

Julie sobbed. 'What's the point?'

'Maybe he should examine you. Just to check.' His voice caught in his throat. 'You know, see whether the—'

Julie turned her tearful eyes on him and he fell silent, looking down. This was all too much.

'The baby's gone. It's gone.'

Dave winced. He didn't want to hear.

'Why me?' she sobbed. 'I didn't do nothing wrong. *Why me?*'

Dave stroked her back, trying to hold himself together, even as he held her. 'Ssshhh. It's alright.'

But Julie pushed away. She stood up, then turned to face him, wailing now, real distress in her voice. 'I want my baby. I *want* my baby!'

She lay there, alone in the big double bed, on her side, listening to Dave crying in the other room. She could almost picture him, sitting there on the sofa, a bottle of scotch open on the table before him, a half-full tumbler in his hand, the tears rolling down his cheeks. But for once she could do nothing for him. This once she couldn't comfort him. Because there'd been no other choice for her. It was do this or be found out. And she couldn't be found out. Besides, maybe it was for the best that he got the hurt out of his system now, before he invested too much hope – too much love – in the little fantasy she'd cooked up for him. And he'd get over it soon enough.

Julie sighed and rolled over, remembering how it had been, back home in Whitby, that time, after she'd been ill – that time when she'd jumped off the east pier and nearly drowned. Well, that was how she felt right now. Exhausted – emotionally exhausted – but alive. Once more she had come through. The worst was past. She could face the world again.

Or could if he'd only stop crying. If only Dave would stop fucking crying.

It was dark and it was cold and he had nowhere to stay. For a time he'd thought of maybe going back to the flat and asking the old couple if he could kip on their sofa for the night, but he knew that wouldn't really have been on. They'd have been on to the police like a shot, and where'd he have been then?

But even a cell would have been comfortable on a night like this. Only he didn't want to take that kind of step. Not on his first night out. So, finding a suitably dark shop doorway, he settled down, his back against the shutters, his feet stretched out in front of him, and tried to doze.

Julie. All day long he'd been thinking about Julie. Wondering where she was and what she was doing. Julie – the only woman he'd ever been happy with. His wife.

Only Julie had buggered off without a word. She'd upped and left, almost as soon as he'd gone inside. She'd visited for a couple of weeks, and then it had stopped with not a card, not even a single, solitary letter from her.

Brian shivered, then pulled his coat collar up about his neck against the cold.

Julie. He'd give her some fucking grief when he found her.

Closing time had come and gone, but still the three men sat at the bar, the last customers to go, as, all about them, the bar staff cleared tables and swept up. For a time their murmured conversation drifted on. Then, as if even they knew they were outstaying their welcome, two of them stood and, pulling on their jackets, made their way over to the door, where one of the barmen undid the bolt, let them out, then slid the bolt again.

Karl sat there a moment longer, staring down into his empty glass, then looked up to find the landlord there on the other side of the counter.

'Alright, Karl?'

Karl sniffed. 'Nah. But that ain't the point, is it?'

He'd drunk a lot. Enough normally to make him pissed. But somehow he couldn't get really drunk these days. It was like something wouldn't let him. He must have knocked back twelve, maybe fourteen pints, but he still felt stone-cold sober. Well, maybe not sober, but not drunk. Not fall-down-and-pass-out drunk.

'So what is the point, mate?'

'Eh?' He met the landlord's eyes, trying to work out if the guy was taking the piss. But he seemed genuine enough. The bastard wasn't smiling, anyway.

'I miss her,' he said. 'I miss my wife. She ran off—'

'I know. You've told me.'

'Yeah, well.'

He stood, then turned a full circle, trying to locate his jacket. It was on the floor. He stooped and picked it up, then draped it over his shoulder, not bothering to attempt to put it on. He looked at the landlord again.

'It's just – I go home and there's no one there. No one. Not a fucking dicky-bird.'

'I'm sorry, mate. It must be hard.'

'Yeah. 'S hard. Fucking 'ard. But you know what?'

'What?'

'I've got one consolation.'

All the others had stopped their clearing up and were listening now.

'Go on,' the landlord said. 'Tell me.'

'I know I ain't the only bastard she's gonna screw over. You can bet your life on that.'

Dave was fast asleep on the sofa, cradling the empty bottle, all cried out. For tonight, anyway. It was after two, and as Julie tiptoed back to the bedroom, she couldn't help but stop and look at him, his face empty now, his features aged and lined, like he'd put on twenty years in a single evening.

Her fault. Or maybe not. After all, life was a bitch. It was no good investing all of your hopes, all of your tiny share of trust and love, in one person. She had learned that much over the years. People let you down. They promised one thing and gave you another. Like Dave with the cottage. Well, that was the way of the world, and there was no point crying over it.

Only people did.

Closing the bedroom door behind her, she went over to her wardrobe. Dresses, coats, skirts and trousers were packed tight, with yet more folded and stored away beneath the hanging garments. But underneath all that was a drawer, and in the drawer she kept all of her bits – her belts, scarves and other accessories – gloves and things.

And a locked box. A small, wooden box with a big brass combination lock.

Wary of Dave waking and coming in on her, she pushed aside the clutter and lifted the box out, placing it on the floor beside the wardrobe. Then, kneeling beside it, she manipulated the tumblers on the lock until they gave her birth year and clicked it open.

Inside were all kinds of things: letters and papers, and a number of photos. It was one of these that she now drew from amidst the others and, sitting back on her heels, stared at for a while.

A photo of a baby girl.

For a long, long time she sat there, staring, not saying a word, barely – it seemed – breathing. Then, with the tiniest of shudders, she put it back and, clicking the lock shut, rolled the tumblers.

Lifting the box, she returned it to the drawer, covering it over with stockings and gloves and a few other bits, then closed the wardrobe door. Her life.

Yeah, well, it was like she'd said: life was a bitch. Life was—

Julie turned, looking across at the mirror of the dressing table, then sat down on the bed, wiping away the tear that had dribbled down her cheek.

Chapter Nine

For No One

Julie was bustling about the kitchen, making breakfast for herself, constantly having to avoid bumping into Dave, who followed her about, tidying away after her.

'What I don't understand,' he was saying, 'is why you should want to go back to work.'

She turned, facing him. 'Why? Because I'm going barmy stuck here on my own all day.'

He looked puzzled. 'I get back as soon as I can. You know that.' Dave reached out, trying to take her hand, but she pulled it back. He sighed, exasperated. 'Look, what if I get the girls to cover a few more shifts? That way I could spend more time—'

'Oh yeah! And how long'll that last? Five minutes!'

'But I thought you liked not having to work.'

'Yeah, and now I don't.'

Dave looked about him, then looked back at her. He lowered his voice, trying to say this next thing gently, so it didn't hurt her.

'Maybe it's just that you've got too much time on your hands to think. You know, since the— Well, since the baby. We can try again and then—'

'Try again! What am I, a bloody production line?'

'Not straight away. I realise that. But I thought that once you'd got over it we could—'

'So me wanting a job suddenly turns into me wanting a baby?'

She looked angry now. Aggrieved. But Dave didn't heed the signs.

'I want it too. When you—'

'Leave it, Dave! I don't even want to think about it!'

'But all I meant was—'

'I said leave it!'

And she turned and, ignoring her breakfast, stormed out of the room, leaving Dave to stare after her, wondering just what he'd said.

They still weren't talking two hours later when Dave had to go. Julie was sprawled out on the sofa, flicking through the channels with the remote, when Dave came into the room, pulling on his jacket.

'See you later.'

She nodded, not even bothering to turn and look at him. For a moment he stood there, just staring at her, then he turned and left. A moment later the front door slammed.

Julie watched the TV for a few moments, looking bored, distracted, then clicked it off and, throwing the remote on to the floor, grabbed her jacket and bag.

It was time she did something. Time she sorted out her life.

Dave had been in a funny mood since he'd first arrived; kind of cold and distracted. Watching him now, Marie knew that something had happened at home, something on top of the miscarriage. He was talking to Cathy right now, handing her an envelope and talking in a low, urgent voice. Cathy stared at the envelope, not understanding for a moment, and then she glared at Dave.

'Yeah, well, fuck you!' And, grabbing her bag and coat, she stormed out, looking furious.

Marie walked across. 'Where's she going?'

Dave turned, looking sheepish now. 'I've laid her off.'

'You've—' Marie shook her head slowly. 'You're not going to—'

'No. No, you're fine, Marie. We're just a bit quiet, that's all.'

'Dave. If things are tight—'

He snapped back at her. 'Things are fine.'

'Right. But you could always get Julie back to help out. I reckon she'd—'

The phone began to ring in Dave's office. He went through and answered it.

'Hello? Yes. Who's that? Oh – er, no, sorry. I'm a bit busy this afternoon. Perhaps— Oh, I see. Yeah, okay then. Three o'clock.'

He slammed down the phone, then stood there for a moment, lost in his thoughts, chewing at a thumbnail. Then, abruptly, he became aware of Marie there, watching him. He turned to her belligerently. '*What?*'

'Keep your hair on,' she said, turning away.

But she knew something was wrong. Seriously, badly wrong.

Julie walked slowly down the High Street, for once oblivious of the shop windows, her mind set, determined. Dave was like all the rest of them. They talked about looking after you, when what they really meant was controlling you. Well, she wasn't playing his game any more. She wasn't going to be the compliant little woman that he seemed to want. If she wanted to work, she'd work – and not just on his terms.

Besides, she'd missed the job. Missed the company and the banter with her patients. Missed being needed by them.

The woman from the agency looked up from her desk as Julie entered and, giving her a beaming smile, indicated the empty chair in front of her. Julie went across and sat.

'So how can I help you?'

Julie rummaged in her bag and produced the large brown envelope that contained all of her nursing stuff – qualifications, letters of recommendation, previous employment records – and slid them across the desk.

'I want a job, and I can start tomorrow.'

The woman emptied out the envelope and, after a moment or two looking through the various documents, looked back at Julie and smiled. 'Tomorrow, you said?'

Dave came down the three broad steps, then stood there on the pavement, looking about him at the crowded High Street. It was a sunny day, and everywhere he looked people seemed to be smiling, enjoying the weather, but he was in the foulest of black moods.

The bastards, he thought. *They always kick you when you're down.*

And not just a gentle tap, but a right fucking toe-punt, repeated until you got the message.

He turned one hundred and eighty degrees, trying to remember where he'd left the car, tempted, for the first time in his life, to simply walk away. But that wasn't his way. He was a fighter. He always had been. There *had* to be a way out of this. Trouble was, he couldn't see one. Oh, there were people he could borrow the money from – you couldn't be in his trade and not run across them – only they were even bigger trouble than the banks. At least the banks only wanted their interest. Some of those guys weren't happy unless they had their pound of flesh too. And literally. Or so he'd heard.

What worried him most was how Julie would react. That's why he'd said nothing to her. He'd not wanted to bother her with his money worries, so he'd said nothing, not even when that last gold card bill came in. Going off about that would really have put the kibosh on things, and to be frank things weren't that good between them right now.

Dave walked through to the side street where he'd left the car, then sat there for a while, the engine idling.

He could sell up. Only the market wasn't good right now, and there was the risk that he'd not raise enough to cover the bank loan, let alone have anything left to start anew. Besides, what would Julie say? She'd be right to be angry. He'd told her he'd look after her. He'd *promised* her.

Resting his forehead on the steering wheel, Dave groaned. How the hell had he got himself in this mess? And how the hell was he going to get out of it?

Maybe it was for the best that their baby hadn't been born. After all, what kind of father would he have made? A failure. A bankrupt. No, it wasn't even worth contemplating. Only . . . Dave sighed, a long, deep sigh. *Only I wanted it. I wanted it so much.*

And, sitting there, in that back street with the engine idling, he began to cry.

It had been hard work at first, but she had not minded that. At the end of each week she got her wages slip and it was hers, and, if she didn't like the place, she could move on. That was the great thing about being an agency nurse. You weren't tied to the same old place, week in, week out. That didn't mean you didn't get some shit jobs at times, oh and some shit people to work for, but it did mean that if you'd had enough you could leave. There were always nursing jobs to be had, wherever you went. Like barmaids, they were never out of work.

So it was that she was in a good frame of mind when she got home that teatime. Dave wasn't in yet, so she busied herself clearing out the old dead flowers from the vases, and arranging the lilies she had bought on her way home.

She was still doing this as the front door opened and Dave came in.

'Julie?'

'In here.'

He came through, then stood there in the doorway, one hand on the edge of the door, watching her. She knew he had something to say. She could always tell.

Dave stepped into the room, filled the kettle and flicked on the switch. Resting his back against the worktop, he watched her in silence for a moment.

'I've been thinking,' he began.

'Yeah? What about?'

'About what you said. About going back to work.'

Refusing to look at him, Julie raised her eyes, waiting for him to say '*but*'.

'Well, I was thinking. You're right. You should.'

Surprised, she looked up. 'What brought this on?'

'Nothing. I just – I can see you're bored at home. And with me being out most evenings— The thing is, you wouldn't have to work as many shifts as before. Just when the pub's busy, you know—'

She looked back down, busying herself with the lilies again. 'Sorry. Can't do it.'

'What d'you mean? I thought that's what you wanted.'

'It was. Only I can't now because I've already got a job. Up St Thomas's.'

'What, nursing? But you said—'

'I fancied a change.'

Dave was silent a moment. Then, like he was issuing an ultimatum, he said, 'I want you to come back to the pub.'

Julie glanced at him. 'I told you. I can't!'

His shout surprised her. 'Sod it! You're *my* wife! I want you in *my* pub!'

She yelled back at him. 'And I told you, I'm taking that job!'

They glared at each other, then Dave turned and left the room. Julie took a long, calming breath, then, picking up the old dead flowers, carried them across and dropped them in the bin.

'Here we are, Nancy. Look, I'll put them here so you can see them properly. Alright?'

Julie carried the flowers over and placed the vase on the bedside table next to the elderly woman, who smiled her thanks. Pausing, Julie straightened Nancy's covers, then turned away, busying herself. She was singing now, not softly, but quite loudly, like she was alone in her own room and not in the middle of a ward of twenty elderly female patients. But there were no complaints. It was a lovely sunny day. Besides, Julie had a nice voice, and the song was an old one, cloyingly romantic. Listening to it, more than one of the women smiled to herself wistfully.

In the end he'd rung the number on the card and the social worker had agreed to see him that afternoon. She was a middle-aged woman, well-meaning but clearly out of touch, like most of her kind. Her office was nice, orderly, with tiny little pot plants scattered all over. It was sunny, but Brian was sure she'd keep the plants well watered. She looked the type. Homely. In charge of her life.

He was talking; telling her about things; about Julie and what had gone wrong.

'First few weeks or so she came down regular. Then it got to every now and again. She said the fare was too much. She had to get a bus then a train then a cab. I told her to get the coach but she said it made her feel sick.'

'She didn't write?'

'Now and then. A card or something. Then it all stopped. Nothing. One of my mates said the same thing had happened with his bird. She'd played around a bit while he was banged up. But I thought, well, even if she's been with another bloke, we could – you know – have another go.'

'So how long ago did she leave the flat?'

'I dunno really. Two years, I guess. I'm not sure.'

'And you still want to get back with her?'

Brian hesitated, then nodded. 'Yeah,' he said. 'She's my wife, ain't she. She's all I've got.'

It was gone nine when she got home. Closing the door, she paused, listening, then called out.

'Dave!'

No answer. She walked through into the kitchen, wincing at the sight of the dirty dishes from that morning still in the sink where she'd left them. Going over to the kettle she switched it on, then noticed the note. She picked it up and read.

Had to go in early. Back about midnight. Dave.

The fridge was almost empty. That was another thing she'd meant to do. For a moment she stood there, her forehead pressed to the edge of the fridge door, then she closed it and, picking up her bag and coat, walked out, even as the kettle started to boil.

'Christ! It's you!'

Julie stood there, outside Marie's front door, a bottle of wine in one hand, take-away pizzas in the other.

'Stuffed crust pepperoni with olives, right?'

'Thought you'd forgotten where we lived!'

There was an edge to Marie's voice and Julie was relieved when Ellie ran out into the hallway.

'Ju-lie!'

Julie grinned. 'Hello, darling.'

Marie opened the door wider, letting Julie pass. 'So,' she began, 'what's been happening?'

Julie put the pizzas down, gave Ellie a big hug, then walked across and took the opener from the drawer, prising the cork out and pouring two glasses before she answered.

'I've just started a new job.'

'A job?'

'Yeah. Didn't Dave tell you?'

Marie shook her head. 'Mind you, he's a right moody bugger these days.'

'You're telling me.'

They clinked glasses.

'So what're you doing?'

'Nursing. At St Thomas's.'

Marie nodded, impressed. Then, noting that the pizzas were getting cold, she gestured towards them. 'Can we tuck in?'

Julie nodded, then smiled. 'That's what they're there for.'

'There you are,' Julie said, handing Ellie the one-pound coin she had just taken from her purse and placing it in Ellie's palm, next to her tooth. 'And if you put that under your pillow, I bet the tooth fairy will bring you another one.'

Ellie grinned, showing the new gap in her teeth, then let Julie give her a good-night hug. 'Night, sweetheart.'

The ruins of the take-away were scattered all about the table between them, their wine glasses empty.

Ellie went round the table, then hugged and kissed her mum. 'Night, Mum.'

'Night, babe.'

Marie looked to Julie, watching her as she in turn watched Ellie leave the room, a wistfulness in her eyes. Thus far they had steered away from serious topics, mainly because Ellie was still up and she had a habit of asking awkward questions.

'So, how are you feeling? Really.'

Julie turned to her and smiled gently. 'I'm fine. *Really*.'

'Christ! When I think of dragging you to that bloody abortion clinic!'

'You didn't drag me anywhere. I went because you're my friend.'

'Dave's taking it hard.'

'He'll get over it.'

Marie looked up, taken aback by Julie's off-handedness.

'Did he tell you he's laid Cathy off?'

Julie's surprised look said it all.

'It's all them wine bars opening up,' Marie went on quickly. 'Buggers up the local pub trade. I think he was hoping you might come back.'

'Yeah, well.'

Again it seemed hard, and Marie found herself goaded into commenting.

'Listen, Julie. I know it's been hard on you, losing the baby and all . . .'

Marie hesitated, waiting for Julie to say something, but Julie just stared at her.

'. . . but at least you've got someone who really loves you. You could try again and maybe—'

This time Julie didn't let her finish. Irritated now, she interrupted.

'You've obviously been talking to my husband. Look, I've lost my baby. I don't want another one. Okay?'

She pretended she was asleep. She lay there, her eyes tightly shut, wondering if he'd come across and try to make it up with her, or whether he'd just leave her alone. Men were strange like that. You could never tell what they were going to do. Especially guys like Dave. They knew what they felt like doing, only they weren't sure how to behave. They wanted to act like cavemen and take their women back, only that wasn't how they were made emotionally. They were too sensitive for their own good. So they waited. And sometimes that was the worst thing you could do.

The door clicked shut. It was dark in the room again. From the living room she heard the telly come on, blaring for a moment, then quieter as he turned the volume down.

She knew what he'd be doing. He'd have brought a bottle of scotch home from the pub and he'd be opening it now, unscrewing the cap and pouring himself half a tumbler full.

It was his way of coping. Of keeping his demons quiet. Only they weren't. He only had to look at her these days and she could hear them screaming out, wanting things from her, *demanding* them.

She stretched out, enjoying the luxury of having the bed all to herself.

Julie was doing her ward round, taking the blood pressure and temperature of her patients and marking their charts. She'd got as far as Molly, a pale, small, mousy woman with almost see-through grey hair. She was propping her up, making her comfortable.

'You'll find it'll help your breathing if you're up a bit higher, Molly. That's it. Comfy now?'

Molly nodded, the very faintest of smiles appearing at the corners of her mouth.

'Good. I'll come and check on you later. Make sure you're alright.'

And with a smile she turned away, moving on to the next bed.

'Ah, here she is!'

It was Nancy who addressed her. And today, sitting by her side, was a man in his late twenties, early thirties. He moved back a little as Julie edged past him and reached down to take Nancy's arm.

'Sorry, Nancy. I know you hate all this.'

But Nancy didn't fuss for once. She seemed keen, rather, to introduce her visitor.

'This is my son, Michael.'

Julie half-turned, even as she expertly checked Nancy's blood pressure. 'Get away,' she said, grinning at him. 'I thought he was your boyfriend!'

He smiled awkwardly. 'Hi.'

'It was Michael who sent me the flowers.'

'Yeah?' She looked at him again, her eyes appraising him this time. 'They're beautiful.'

Leaning forward a little, Nancy spoke to her son. 'She's the one I was telling you about. Always singing.'

Julie gave a little laugh. 'That's just to get you lot home quicker.' And she winked at Michael, then popped the thermometer into Nancy's mouth.

'Do you have far to come?'

It took him a second or two to realise it was him she'd spoken to. 'Er, no. Not too far. How long do you think they'll be keeping her in for?'

Julie looked to Nancy as she answered, smiling down at her reassuringly. 'At least a week or so, I should think. We need to get her blood pressure down a bit first.'

She took the thermometer out of Nancy's mouth, read it, then jotted down the reading on the chart.

'Okay, Nancy, you're done. See you, Michael.'

But as she moved away, he called out to her. 'It's Mike, actually. Only Mum calls me Michael.'

Julie turned back, smiling broadly. 'Okay, Mike.'

Ricky was sitting at the kitchen table, reading the evening paper, while Sonia pottered about at the stove, preparing dinner. Karl had been upstairs, playing with the kids, but now he came in, a big grin on his face.

'The kids are bloody blinding on that computer, ain't they?'

Sonia half-turned from where she was mashing the potato and looked to Ricky. 'Get 'em off it, will you, Ricky? And get 'em to wash their hands.'

Ricky folded his paper and stood. He winked at Karl, then went.

Karl stood there watching as Sonia began to dish up the food. 'This is good of you, Sonia. I appreciate it.'

'That's alright.'

'I never was much of a cook. I bought a new microwave, but stuff just don't taste the same when it's done in one of them things.'

Sonia turned, a filled plate in one hand. 'Sit yourself down. So you never heard from Julie?'

Karl shook his head, then sat. 'Don't s'pose I will now.'

She placed the plate in front of him. 'Don't wait for the others or it'll go cold. It's murder dragging 'em away from that bloody machine!'

Karl looked up at her and smiled. 'Cheers!'

Watching Karl tuck into his food, Sonia softened towards him. Now that she knew him a bit better, he didn't seem too bad – but you could never tell.

She tried to imagine it, then gave up. What people did in private often beggared belief, only there usually were small signs in the way they behaved in public. Little things. Only Karl didn't seem like a wife-beater.

Ricky reappeared. 'They're coming down. Two minutes. They've got to save the game or something.'

Sonia smiled, then turned back, beginning to fill a plate for her husband.

Nancy was sitting in the chair beside the bed while Julie changed the sheets.

'He was the baby of the family,' she said. 'A bit of an afterthought, I suppose. Have you got brothers and sisters?'

Julie shook her head. 'Only child.'

'Ooh. Spoiled, I expect?'

Julie just shrugged. 'How about the older two?'

Nancy shook her head. 'Rita's in Canada. I've got two grandchildren as well, you know. And Peter's up in Northampton, but he doesn't get down much. Very busy, you see. And his wife's a bit awkward. I miss Rita though. It's a bit different with a daughter.'

'Oh?'

'You have more in common, don't you? We talk about things. Oh, nothing important. You know, food, the garden, my aches and pains. And the children, of course. Bless them. Boys can't be bothered with any of that. Don't get me wrong. I love both of them, but, well, a daughter's rather precious.'

Julie looked wistful. Nancy noticed it and frowned. 'Do you see much of your family?'

'Nah. Dad died when I was a kid. And I lost Mum when I was sixteen.'

'Oh, I'm sorry.'

Julie smiled bravely. 'Yeah. But you've gotta get on with life, haven't you? You can't let it beat you. If you do—'

She turned over the cover, then stood back, admiring her work. 'There. Nice and comfy for you.'

Nancy smiled. 'Thank you, dear.'

They'd finished the meal a while back, and now, while Karl was upstairs with the kids, they had the chance to talk. As Sonia washed and Ricky dried, they spoke in low, hushed tones.

For a moment Ricky's voice rose, a hint of incredulity in it. 'Give her the benefit of the doubt!'

'Shhh.'

Ricky lowered his voice to almost a whisper. 'Yeah, well, she buggers off, taking his home with her—'

'It was her stuff too!'

'Well, she can't want it that much, can she? It's still in our bloody garage! If you ask me, she was just being a bloody-minded bitch!'

Sonia looked down, annoyed. 'Maybe she's still trying to find a place.'

'What, after all this time?' He gave a sarcastic laugh. 'Anyway, we don't know, do we? She ain't bloody been in touch, has she? I'm telling you, she's taken us for a right pair of mugs, and if it weren't for landing meself in the shit, I'd clear that garage out and give it all back to him.'

They fell quiet, hearing footsteps on the stairs. A moment later Karl came in.

'I've just been thrashed on PlayStation.'

Ricky and Sonia smiled falsely. Putting down the tea towel, Ricky placed a hand on Karl's shoulder 'You fit, mate?'

'Yeah.'

Ricky turned to Sonia. 'See you later, love.'

'See you.'

Karl smiled at her. 'Bye. And thanks for dinner.'

She watched through the window as the two men went down past the garage and round the corner, and wondered what Karl would have said if he'd known he'd been walking past all his furniture these past few months. She looked down into the sudsy water, feeling suddenly uneasy. Ricky was right. She had no proof. Nothing but Julie's word.

Yeah, well, maybe she could find something. Maybe there was something among her stuff.

Wiping her hands, she went across and called up the stairs.

'Katie! Answer the phone if it rings! I'm just popping out to the garage for a bit!'

'A'right, Mum!'

It was pitch-black in the garage. The bulb had gone a while back, and Ricky had never bothered to replace it. Not that it mattered; she had a torch. Switching it on, she pointed it here and there, picking out this item and that, trying to recall where she'd seen what she was looking for. Squeezing through between the sofa and the cooker, she climbed over some bits and pieces, then stood there, getting her breath while she moved the beam of the torch across the nearby objects.

There! That was it! She climbed across, then, propping the torch next to her, reached down and lifted it up.

It was a small trunk, a kind of travelling case, a small bicycle lock securing it. Sonia tugged at it a moment, then, picking up the torch, clambered back to where she knew Ricky kept his tools. She searched a moment, then went back.

The cutters snipped through the arm of the lock like a knife through warm butter. She set them aside, then, lifting the torch so that it illuminated the contents, opened the trunk.

Sonia nodded to herself. Yes, here it all was; all of Julie's personal stuff. Photos and school certificates, a small tatty doll, some old 45 records, some faded schoolbooks and more, much more.

For a moment she hesitated. She didn't like doing this, but she had to know. Had to be sure. A bit further down the trunk was a photo album. She opened it, then smiled. It was a wedding album. Pictures of Karl and Julie – Karl looking good in a morning suit, Julie looking lovely in a full white dress – filling the pages. She put it aside, then dug further, unearthing another album.

Her brow furrowed as she stared at the first page. It was another wedding album. But this time a stranger was standing next to Julie. Some dark-haired guy, slimmer than Karl and a good bit taller. She hungrily turned the pages. There were the same predictable wedding images, the same posed shots that everyone had on their wedding day, but they seemed wrong without Karl in them. Sonia flicked through to the front page and read the two names that were written inside the stylised heart: 'Julie and Brian'.

She set the album down, beside the other one, then searched some more. There was an old fob-watch, what looked like a doll's pink cardigan, and finally, at the very bottom of the trunk, a third photo album.

Sonia opened it, then shook her head. Once again, there was Julie, much younger and dressed in bridal white, standing in the doorway to a church, confetti strewing the path beneath her feet. But beside her was yet another man, his hair slicked back, his body smartly adorned in a light grey morning suit as he grinned back at the camera on that most perfect of days.

Once more she flicked through to the front. Once more she read the names entwined within the heart, then shook her head, her eyes as wide as saucers.

'*Duncan?* Who the bloody hell is Duncan?'

Chapter Ten

Almost Tomorrow

Julie was standing at the nurses' station, catching up on some paperwork, when she caught sight of Mike coming into the ward, a basket of fruit in one hand. He didn't seem to notice her, but went straight over to where his mother lay and, placing the basket on the side, sat, looking down tenderly at her sleeping figure.

Julie finished her notes, then closed the file and, capping her pen, got up. She wasn't due to check on Nancy for a while, but it wouldn't hurt to do it now, before her break.

Mike glanced up as she approached. 'Hi.'

'Hi.'

She stood there a moment, smiling at him. Once again he seemed shy, at a loss as to what to say. He made the vaguest gesture towards his mother.

'It's difficult to know what to do. I don't like to wake her.'

'Ah, she'll be upset though if she finds out you've been and gone.'

Mike nodded, giving her the faintest of smiles, then looked at his watch. 'I'll give it a bit longer.'

Making her way round to his side of the bed, Julie brushed past him, reaching across to take down the thermometer. She knew his eyes were on her as she shook the thin glass tube, as if to check it was still functioning.

'She's very lucky to have you, you know.'

Mike looked down, a genuine modesty in his actions. 'Not really. She's my mum.'

Julie turned, looking down at him. 'Well, it can't be easy. I mean, with your brother and sister not around to help you out and you— Well, sometimes it's a bit unfair on the one who's left.'

Mike's look showed that he felt the unfairness of it. Julie glanced at her watch, then looked down at Nancy once again.

'She looks out for the count. I'm on my break in two minutes if you fancy having a cup of tea.'

He looked up at her, a brief, almost startled expression in his eyes. Then he nodded. 'Yes – yes, I'd like that.'

It was one of those days when there was a lot of cloud about, and one minute it was sunny, the next dull. Out in the courtyard of the hospital, you could observe the cloud shadow moving across the concrete and the flowerbeds, and as Mike and Julie sat there, drinking their tea from plastic cups, so the sun made a sudden reappearance, brightening the space between the buildings.

Mike was talking, his left hand making tiny movements as he did, as if to emphasise certain words. It could have been irritating, but Julie found she rather liked it. It was very much a part of who he was, slightly innocent, naïve even. It wasn't just that he was shy, which appealed to her, it was like he was almost – well, *virginal*. And that was strange, because he was a good-looking bloke. It had flashed through her mind that he might be gay, but then he gave no sign of being gay.

'I paid two months rent in advance,' he said, 'but then she had the fall and, well, I couldn't really leave. She was a bit nervous about being on her own, I s'pose.'

'Yeah, but nothing's to stop you moving out once she's up and about.'

He shrugged. 'We'll see.'

Julie looked down into her cup. 'Must be a bit difficult with girlfriends and that.'

Mike smiled awkwardly, and she knew she'd guessed right.

'Sorry,' she said. 'I'm a right nosey cow, ain't I? Better be getting back.'

Julie stood, throwing the cup into the nearby bin. He was looking at her, all nervous suddenly.

'Actually, I was wondering if you'd like to – you know – come for a drink or something. After work. After you've finished.'

'Sorry. I can't.'

Mike looked crestfallen, like he'd gambled all his chips on black and it had come up red.

'How 'bout tomorrow?'

His head had dropped, now it came up again. He was beaming.

'Yeah. Great.'

She grinned back at him. 'Okay. Pick me up from the ward. I finish at eight.'

Going home that evening, she managed to avoid Dave. He was out already, and by the time he finally got in she was in bed, 'asleep', rolled over on her side, her back to him, in that posture which was as good as a 'No Entry' road sign. But the morning was different. He was up before her, and though she dressed slowly, he was waiting for her as she went out into the kitchen, a kind of weary sourness in his face that had become his standard expression. She knew she had to tell him sometime, so why not get it over with.

There was bread in the toaster, and the kettle was coming to the boil.

'You want tea?' he asked.

'Nah.' She sat, looking across at him. 'I'm gonna be late tonight. They've asked me to work an extra shift.'

'*What?*' He had turned away to butter some toast, now he turned back. 'What d'you wanna go doing that for?'

She stiffened. 'Well, you won't even be here, so what's the problem?'

'I just don't want you having to do— Look, I just don't like it.'

'Oh, don't start that again! If you think I'm gonna sit around here waiting for you to come home at God knows what time—'

'I *have* to be there! You know that!' He took a breath, then spoke more calmly. 'Why don't you come up the pub and wait for me? Have a drink. You could see Marie. She's been—'

'No. I can't. I've told them I'll do the shift. I can't let them down.'

Dave turned away, sulky now. He made to butter the toast,

then threw the knife down angrily. Julie gave it a second or two, then spoke again, her voice all sweetness and light.

'I was gonna pop out during my lunch break and do a bit of shopping. There's this dress I saw and—'

Exasperated, Dave raised his eyes to the ceiling.

'What? I'm not asking you to buy it for me. I'll pay you back just as soon as my wages come through.'

'It's not just the money, Julie. You've got two wardrobes full of clothes already.'

She stood, angry now. 'So what does that mean? Because I've got clothes I can't ever have anything new?'

'I'm not saying that. It's just that you wear your uniform at work and as you said yourself, we're not exactly going out a lot.'

Her look was scathing. 'Huh! So much for you looking after me! What a bloody joke!'

She grabbed her coat and bag.

'Julie, can't we—?'

'No! And you can stick your bloody money!'

She turned, sweeping from the room. A moment later the front door slammed. Dave slumped, closing his eyes, real pain, real defeat in his face.

'Shit,' he said softly. 'Shit, shit, shit.'

Julie waited in the queue, the skirt and top and the black silk underwear over her arm. It was a Friday lunchtime and they were busier than usual, but it didn't matter. Waiting there, she smiled to herself, imagining his eyes when he saw her in these.

The smile became a grin as the customer in front of her was served and she stepped up to the till.

'Good afternoon!'

'Hi.'

Julie handed across the clothes, then waited as the assistant ran the little laser-thingy over each of the price codes. Finished, the assistant looked up at her again and smiled.

'And how would you like to pay?'

With the slightest hesitation, Julie held up the cheque book she had taken from her bag.

'Thank you. The machine will print it for you.'

Julie handed over the blank cheque and watched with some anxiety as it was fed into the cash register

'Check the amount, then sign the cheque, please.'

Julie glanced at the girl, then, accepting the pen from her, quickly signed her name. She handed back the cheque and the banker's card she held tightly in her hand.

'Thank you.'

The young girl wrote down the card details, rang up the cheque and popped the receipt in the bag, handing it across the counter to Julie. 'Have a good day!'

Julie smiled. *Oh, I will*, she thought. *I will*.

Alan was loitering outside the pub, along with a little group of customers. Dave was late opening today – almost ten minutes late. Irritable, Alan turned and, balling his hand into a fist, banged loudly on the door. Glancing at his watch, he put it to his ear, then, looking decidedly grumpy, he banged again.

A guy in the van across the road stopped reading his newspaper a moment, then, a knowing smirk on his face, looked back at the page.

Dave stood with Marie, his back to the bar, looking on as the bailiff, clipboard in hand, wrote down items on his sheet of paper as they were piled up in the middle of the pub.

His helpers were two huge, burly-looking guys, professional removal men. It was their van which was parked outside.

Exasperated, Dave spoke to the bailiff.

'This is mad. I mean, what's the point of taking away the only means I've got of making money? Where's the sense in that?'

The bailiff didn't answer. His two helpers walked across and began to lift a heavy arcade game.

'Oi!' Dave barked. 'That's hired!'

The bailiff looked across and nodded to the two men, who set the machine down, then came across to Dave, offering him the clipboard and a pen.

'I'm only doing my job, mate. Sign there, will you?'

Reluctantly, Dave signed, then watched, a hint of despair in his eyes, as the two removal men opened the outer doors and began to carry things out.

As they took their first load out to the van, Alan and several of the punters stepped inside.

'You open?' Alan asked, surprised to see everything piled up that way.

But Dave barely heard him. He turned, looking to Marie, his voice breaking.

'I've fucked it all up. How the hell am I gonna tell Julie?'

Julie was standing before the patient board, briefing some of the night shift. She was off in five minutes, but there was still no sign of him. Well, maybe he'd had second thoughts, or maybe he'd just chickened out.

As the group about the board began to break up, Julie turned to one of the younger nurses.

'And don't forget to check the dressing again tonight. It looked a bit weepy. We need to keep it clean and dry.'

The nurse nodded, then turned away. As she did, Julie noticed Mike, standing by the door. Calling across to the desk, Julie gave the nurses there a big smile. 'Okay? See you!'

She walked over to Mike, still smiling, pleased he'd turned up after all. 'You not popping in to see your mum?'

'No. Better not.'

It was why she'd thought he wasn't coming. She had been sure he'd come early, to see Nancy. She nodded.

'I've just got to change into my civvies. Okay?'

Mike nodded and Julie began to walk away. Seeing that he wasn't following her, she put an arm out, gesturing to him to hurry.

'You coming?'

Julie was on one side of the divided changing area, while Mike waited on the other. She was wearing the short skirt she had bought earlier and her new black bra. Glancing over the divider, she noted where Mike was, then walked over to stand before the full-length mirror. From where he stood he could see her now, even though she pretended not to notice him there. For a moment she stood there, side on, admiring herself, smoothing her hands down her stomach, then, provocatively, she pulled on her skimpy new top.

Turning from the mirror, she went round to his side of the divider.

'Alright?'

But though Mike nodded, she knew he was far from alright. He was quite clearly aroused. Smiling, she took his arm and led him out.

'I know this great place.'

He nodded, then found his voice again. 'Yeah? Okay.'

'Good. You're gonna love it.'

Lights pulsed out on the dance floor, the beat of the music pounding like a power hammer, its insistent rhythm working the dancers into a frenzy of arms and legs and twisting, perspiring bodies. For a time Julie lost herself in the sound, the simple ecstasy of the dance, but then, as the bass rhythm died and the electronic burble tweedled into a low-pitched whine, she found herself facing Mike again.

Mike had tried his best. At first he'd just stood there, unable to comprehend just what it was he was supposed to be doing with his body, but as the evening had worn on and he'd got a drink or two inside him, he'd relaxed more and let himself go a little. Even so, he looked ill at ease out there, and he knew it.

'God!' Julie said into the sudden silence. 'I'm gasping! Let's get a top-up!'

She took Mike's arm and led him off the floor, joining the throng at the long bar. It was a pretty tacky place, but Julie seemed unaware of it, attracted by its energy and superficial gloss.

'It's great, ain't it?' she said, as Mike waved a tenner at the barman, vainly trying to get his attention. 'A couple of the girls from work come here.'

Mike nodded distractedly, then looked back at her. 'It's just – well, I'm not a very good dancer.'

She looked at him as if he were mad. 'Don't be daft! You're fine!'

'Yeah?' His face changed slightly. 'You're amazing.'

Pleased with herself, Julie grinned. They'd taken off the ambient stuff now and were playing a smoochy love song. Hearing it, Julie reached out and took Mike's hand.

'Come and dance with me.'

She led him out on to the floor once more, but this time they danced close, his arms about her, her body pressed close, moving against his sensuously, arousing him. She could feel how hard he was and, putting her hands up to his neck, rested her chin on his shoulder, her mouth almost touching the side of his neck so that he could feel her breath on his skin. When the song ended and their faces moved apart, she could see in his eyes that he was excited, that he wanted her.

Well, that was the idea, wasn't it? That was what dancing was all about, after all. But there was time, lots of time, for that.

'Come on,' she said, smiling mischievously at him. 'Let's go and get that drink you promised me.'

Dave paced the floor of the living room, back and forth, measuring out the distance between the door and the sofa countless times until, anger and frustration mounting within him, he went out into the kitchen and, finally succumbing, took the spare bottle of Laphroaig from the top cupboard, over the larder.

The pub was gone – or good as – but it wasn't enough. He'd have to sell the house.

He uncapped it and drank straight from the bottle, letting the fifteen-year-old malt course down his throat, then set it down by the sink, wiping his mouth with the back of his hand.

Dave looked about him, half squinting, seeing Julie everywhere he looked, in her nurse's uniform that morning, or in a skimpy dress after an evening out, in her dressing gown, or – and he almost groaned at the thought – in her underwear.

Damn her! he thought. *Damn her for picking this day of all days to work an extra shift!* And yet there was a part of him that was glad that the moment he would have to confess his failure was delayed, though he knew it couldn't be for long. He still had to tell her: still had to explain just how he'd got into this mess.

He sat, leaning on the kitchen table, one hand cupping his brow.

It was like death, this. It was like he was trapped and had nowhere to turn. Nowhere to go. Oh, if she were only here, then maybe she'd hold him, comfort him, tell him it didn't matter and that they'd work something out.

But she wasn't.

Feeling like a condemned man, Dave pushed through the double doors and into the ward. It was late, and he didn't like the idea of a scene, but he had to tell her. It was no good keeping it to himself any longer. She would have to know.

Most of the patients were asleep now, and as he stepped up to the desk, he noted the look of irritation on the ward sister's face.

'You shouldn't be here,' she said quietly but firmly. 'Visiting finished four hours back.'

'I know, I— Look, can you tell me where I'd find Julie . . . Harding?'

'Julie? I'm afraid you've missed her.'

Dave shook his head. 'No – no, she's working the night shift.'

The woman looked at Dave strangely. 'Not tonight, she's not. I was here when she left. All glammed up.'

Dave stared. 'She can't have—'

'Look, I'm sorry. Who shall I say called?'

But Dave just turned on his heel and left. *Gone?* he thought. *She can't have gone!*

Only she had.

Mike had parked his car in the street outside his mother's house. It was dark, the nearest street lamp a good forty or fifty feet away, and as they kissed, his hands were all over her, touching her breasts, her thighs— Not that Julie was behaving herself. As her right hand smoothed his neck, so her left cupped his balls through the cloth of his trousers, her thumb tracing the length of his aroused cock.

Suddenly his hand moved beneath her skirt. Julie stiffened.

'We can't,' she whispered, moving her face away from his. 'Not here.'

'Yes we can.'

'I can't.'

But the fingers of her left hand were giving off a different message. Slowly she caressed the whole length of his penis, pushing down against it, making him groan with pleasure.

'Inside,' she said. 'Let's go inside.'

His hands pawed at her, reluctant to let her go even for a moment, his eyes on fire with need. Then, with a little shudder, he moved back. 'Okay,' he said, as if it hurt to say so. 'Okay, let's go inside.'

He could barely keep his hands off her. Closing the door behind him, he turned, then pulled her to him, kissing her, his hands fondling her breasts and thighs. If he could he would have taken her there, in the hallway but, breaking from him, she shook her head, smiling.

'Upstairs.'

She went first, his hands stroking her back, tracing the curves of her buttocks as they climbed the stairs. There was a small landing at the top with three doors leading off. They stood there a moment, kissing passionately, grappling with each other, their bodies pressed close, then, abruptly, he grabbed her hand and started pulling her towards the door on the right.

'God, Julie, I really—'

She stopped dead, pulling back even as he pushed open the door to Nancy's room. It was furnished in a Fifties fashion, a double divan dominating the room, its white satin cover looking almost new.

'I couldn't. Not in her bed.'

She gestured towards the door across the landing.

He looked at her a moment then took her hand and led her

across the landing into his own room, the single bed a mocking symbol of childhood.

'It's sweet,' Julie said, walking across to stand beside it.

'Julie—'

Her mouth curved into a smile. Her eyes held his. Unbuttoning her top, she let it fall, waiting a moment before slowly unfastening her bra.

Her breasts were firm and taut, the nipples hard with arousal. Seeing them, Mike's lips parted in wonder. His eyes were wide, amazed at the sight of her, there in his room. She watched him, loving the look on his face as she moved closer; excited by the fear and longing she saw in his eyes, and knew she had him.

Chapter Eleven

No Regrets

Ricky was at the bar of the Rose and Crown, their first customer, fresh from finishing his round. He'd been enjoying his pint and a joke with the young Aussie barman, when Karl burst in and came straight across to him.

'Ricky, mate! Listen! I need you to cover for me!'

Ricky laughed with disbelief. 'Piss off. I've only just finished!'

'No, listen. I've gotta go up the police station.'

Karl thrust the bank statement into Ricky's hands. Ricky stared at it blankly.

'*And?*'

'I've got her! Julie! I know where she is!'

Ricky shook his head. 'Look, mate . . .'

'Well?' Karl said, a look of desperation in his face. 'Come on, mate.'

Ricky stared at his pint fondly, then, with a resigned little shrug: 'Yeah, alright. But you owe me one, Karl.'

'Great! Thanks, mate!' And, tearing the statement from Ricky's hand, Karl turned and practically ran from the pub.

Ricky sat there a moment, staring after him, then he picked up his pint once more and looked to the barman.

'His wife, is it?' the barman asked, with a knowing smile.

'Yeah. Stupid bastard. Still—'

No. He couldn't criticise Karl. Not if he was honest, because it was what he would have done, if Sonia had run out on him. He'd have wanted to know why. That before anything else. Just *why*.

Dave woke just after eight with a blinding headache and a sense that something was wrong. Well, something *was* wrong:

his whole bleeding life was going down the tubes.

He made coffee – black, two sugars – then sat there, staring into the air.

Where the fuck was she? Who the fuck had she been with all this time?

He'd kill her. He'd fucking kill her.

Dave groaned and buried his head in his hands. What kind of idiot had he been, thinking he could make it work? But it was like he'd had no choice. He'd fallen for her, and when she'd said she was carrying his kid . . .

The letterbox clattered. He stood and went out into the hallway.

'Julie?'

But it wasn't her. Walking across, he saw the two brown envelopes on the mat. Looking defeated, he picked them up and, without bothering to open them, went back to the kitchen and threw them in the bin.

He sat again, cradling his coffee between his hands, thinking. Maybe if they'd bought that cottage after all – maybe if he'd sold up and done what she'd wanted then everything would have been okay. Only he didn't think so. Running away wasn't the answer. But then, what was? It was like he couldn't win. He'd done his best but it wasn't enough.

Closing his eyes, he let out a long, low groan.

'The bitch. How could she fucking do this to me?'

They lay in the small, single bed, naked, kissing, Mike's right hand stroking her breast gently, tenderly. They had hardly slept, and when they had, it was to wake and make love yet again, even as the sun came up outside the drawn curtains.

Breaking from the kiss, Julie slipped from beneath the sheets, heading for the bathroom. Watching her go, Mike put his hands behind his head and grinned, like the cat who'd got the cream. She was beautiful. Her back, her shoulders, that lovely little arse.

He gave a little shiver, but it wasn't from tension. He felt relaxed; more relaxed than he had ever been, possibly. It felt so right.

She was back in a moment, standing there in the doorway, just the sight of her making his cock go stiff. He smiled at her and pulled back the cover.

Julie smiled, then slowly walked across. 'Alright. But then I've got to go. I promised a friend—'

But Mike was barely listening. Reaching up, he pulled her down and, pushing her on to her back, climbed above her again, entering her almost at once, crying out, his movements urgent, Julie's voice, as she, too, groaned with pleasure, enflaming him, making him want to pin her to the bed.

'Oh, God – oh Christ! Oh, Mike – yes!'

Karl was sitting in the interview room, across the table from the sergeant who was silently studying the bank statement. He looked up and sniffed, then handed it back.

'You say you asked the bank to cancel the card?'

'Yeah. I phoned them just as soon as she'd gone, but according to this she's used the bloody thing five times in the past two weeks. Someone's obviously made a cock-up. But at least we know where she is now, so you can—'

But the sergeant was one step ahead of Karl. 'The thing is, Mr Mason, there's not a lot we can do. If it was a joint account and your wife's card was still valid, then—'

'But I *phoned* them!'

The sergeant sat back, smiling apologetically. 'I'm sorry, sir, but that's something you'll have to take up with the bank. As far as I can see, your wife hasn't committed any crime.'

'Yeah, but—'

'No buts, I'm afraid. Cock-up it may be. Crime, no. I'm sorry, but we can't investigate this, even if we wanted to.'

Karl stared at the statement for a second or two longer, then he stood, throwing back his chair, and stormed from the room.

Dave heard the front door slam, then her footsteps in the hall-way. As she came into the kitchen, she was clearly surprised to see him sitting there at the table, but her momentary surprise was quickly covered by a smile.

'Oh. Alright?'

She walked across and flicked the kettle on, then turned, looking back at him.

'You're late going in.'

His face, like his voice, was expressionless. 'Wanted to make sure you got back okay. How was work?'

'Alright. I'm just gonna run a bath.'

She didn't miss a beat. There was not a flicker in her face. Seeing it, Dave felt something die inside him. He looked down, trying to keep his emotions in check. For a time he sat there, listening to the bathwater run, to her singing to herself as she pottered about. Then the kettle boiled and clicked, and he stood, going over to make a cup of tea.

Julie was standing at the mirror, wearing just her bathrobe, when he went into the bathroom. The bathwater was still running, the bath half full. Dave held out the mug to her, and she turned and smiled.

'Thanks.'

He watched her a while, then reached up and began to caress her shoulder, then moved closer, kissing her neck, then running his hand down under her breast. Yet as he did she leaned forward, away from him, affecting to test the bathwater. Undeterred, Dave ran his hand down the length of her back.

'I love you.'

Ignoring the comment, Julie straightened up, but as Dave nuzzled into her neck she pulled away abruptly, turning to face him.

'You need a shave.'

Almost absent-mindedly he felt his cheek. She was watching him now, her eyes half-lidded. 'Better do it before you go to work,' she said.

He reached into the cabinet for the shaving foam. Angrily, he squeezed some of it into his left hand and rubbed it into the right side of his face. Then, picking up the razor, he drew it sharply down his cheek, cutting himself.

'Careful!' But as she reached up to cover the wound with her hand, he grabbed her wrist, pushing her hand into his cheek, then pulling it down to his lips and kissing it hard.

'Dave!'

Julie eased her hand from his grasp, then handed him a towel. She looked a little shocked, but her voice was calm, practical.

'Wipe that and I'll clean it for you.'

Dave's voice seemed to sneer at her. 'My wife, the nurse!'

She glanced at him curiously, but let it pass.

'So how was it last night?' he asked. 'Work, I mean?'

'Busy. I feel knackered.'

'Were you on Jackson Baker, then?'

She had been looking for a plaster, but now she turned back. 'Yeah. Course. A couple of patients were brought in from Casualty, then it was murder cos it woke everyone else up. I didn't even get a proper break.'

'Which sister was on? Was it Pat?'

She reached over and turned off the taps. 'Pat? Yeah. Moanin' on as usual, she—'

'You're lying.'

She blinked, amazed by the sudden anger in his voice.

'*What?*'

'I spoke to her. You didn't work last night.'

Julie stared at him as if he were stupid. 'What are you talking about? Of course I worked. When did you speak to her?'

'Don't lie to me. I *went* there.'

'I'm not lying. You must have gone to the wrong ward.'

Dave shook his head, astonished that she could still deny it. The wrong ward? There was a look of contempt on his face now.

'You're seeing someone. Who is he?'

'What? I don't know what you're talking about.'

'Just tell me who he is.'

'You're talking rubbish! There ain't no one!'

'Is it Alan? Are you sleeping with Alan?'

'*Alan?*' She laughed, but Dave was just about hanging on to his self-control. He spoke slowly, but there was a hint of threat in his voice now.

'Don't laugh. Don't fucking laugh.'

'What else d'you expect me to do? You stand there like the

lord and bloody master! If I was to find someone it'd be because I don't get what I need from you. You go out—'

He yelled, a dark fury in his face suddenly. 'I go to work! Who d'you think I do it all for? How d'you think I keep a roof over our heads?'

'Yeah, and that's about all you can do! I want a husband, not a bloody landlord! I want sex! I don't want to go to bed with some old man who does it cos he wants a baby.'

'But I love you.'

'So what.'

His slap took them both by surprise. As Julie crumpled to the floor, Dave stared at her, horrified by what he'd done. He looked at his hand, like it wasn't his, then, turning about, he stumbled from the room.

Julie sat there, the stinging in her cheek making her close her eyes against the pain. It wasn't the first time she'd been hit, but she hadn't thought Dave capable. Shocked, she listened to the banging noises coming from the bedroom. There was a moment's silence and then the front door slammed.

It took her a moment to get up. She was trembling and her legs were like jelly. Even so, she pulled herself up against the bath, then slowly made her way through.

The bedroom was a wreck. Clothes were pulled from the wardrobe, drawers emptied out. Julie stood there a second, shocked by the sight, then, worried lest her precious box had been disturbed, she rushed across and, delving beneath a pile of clothes, was relieved to find it there, unopened.

There, amidst the wreckage of the room, she sat and, placing the box in her lap, opened it. She reached in and took out a photo of a baby. And as she looked down at the photo, so the tears finally came, running down her cheeks one after another in an unending stream.

The young woman, a fresh-faced eighteen with long dark hair, sat staring at a photograph of a baby while the official finished writing.

Finally, the older woman looked up and smiled kindly. 'I don't suppose you've seen that before?'

Charlotte shook her head, reluctant to take her eyes away from the photograph. Reaching into the file, the official produced a birth certificate and handed it across.

Charlotte studied the document, her eyes wide, then read the name aloud.

'Julie Vera Harding.'

She looked over at the adoption worker. 'So my real name's Harding?'

'That was your birth mother's name, yes.'

Charlotte looked back at the certificate, struggling to take it in. Then, softly, almost to herself, she repeated it again.

'Julie Vera Harding.'

Part Two – Cry Me A River

Chapter Twelve

Always Something There
To Remind Me

Church bells filled the air as the wedding party spilled out into the sunlight at the top of the steps. Turning, Julie grinned at Mike, then leaned across and kissed him full on the lips.

'Well?' she asked, her eyes seeking his. 'D'you believe it now?'

'Yeah,' he said, smiling like he'd split his face. 'Yeah, I do.'

Everything was perfect. The sun was shining, the bells ringing out, and she was dressed in white, the train of the wedding dress held up by two of Mike's nieces, who had been recruited as bridesmaids. Guests threw handfuls of confetti into the air, while across from them, just beyond the old lych-gate, a white Rolls idled, its driver leaning across the front seat to watch them as they emerged, a smile on his face.

The Rolls had been Mike's idea, and though he could barely afford it, he'd been insistent. 'I'm only gonna do this once, so I'm gonna do it proper,' he'd said. And she'd not argued. In fact, the only disappointment was the honeymoon. They weren't going to have one. But in the end that had been at her suggestion. She'd persuaded him that they could do it when Nancy was a bit better. They'd only spend the whole time worrying, after all. So until then, they'd make do. Besides, as long as they had each other, what did it matter where they were tonight?

She beamed for the photographer, her hand squeezing Mike's tightly, then turned to kiss him once again as the cameras flashed.

Mike's mum, Nancy, came up and stood at Julie's side.

'You look lovely, dear.'

Mike grinned, looking at her. 'I could hear you having a little cry.'

Nancy reached across Julie to tap her son playfully. Julie smiled, enjoying their mutual fondness.

'We girls are allowed to, ain't we, Nancy? Or is it alright to call you Mum now?'

Nancy looked down, clearly moved.

'You'll start her off again,' Mike said, laughing now.

'Yeah, well.' Gently, Julie took Nancy's arm and pulled her across until she stood between her and Mike.

'Come on – one for the album.'

Nancy looked up at her gratefully, then looked ahead, smiling for the photographer, a tear trickling down her powdered cheek as the camera flashed.

As Mike opened the door to the Rolls for her, and she climbed across that broad leather seat, Julie felt a little shiver pass right through her, and as Mike clambered in beside her, she leaned close, running her hand over the soft leather and whispering to his ear.

He half turned to stare at her, shocked. '*Julie!*'

'What?' And, nodding towards the driver, 'I bet he's seen worse. Anyway, I'm only saying.'

But there was a mischievous smile on her lips now, and despite himself, Mike grinned. She leaned closer, gently placing her hand on his knee and slowly, deliberately running her fingertips lightly up the inside of his thigh. Turning into him a little, she whispered in his ear again.

'We could always stop off at your mum's on the way. Say we had to freshen up.'

Mike swallowed, then nodded. 'Okay.'

Julie looked down, smiling at the sight of the bulge in his trousers, then turned and, waving through the window, blew Nancy a kiss.

Sonia stood in front of the garage, looking on as Karl and Ricky carried Karl's sofa across from the garage and into the back of the hired van.

Karl had been totally pissed off at first. He'd called her and Ricky every name under the sun. But then, when he'd calmed down a bit, he'd seen how hard it had been for her. Anita had helped, of course. She'd made him see just what kind of dilemma Julie had put Sonia in, and after f'ing and blinding for a wee bit longer, Karl had finally come round.

It was a conversation over dinner two nights back that had finally swung it. Karl had been talking about setting up home with Anita and what a shame it was that that cow – Julie – had run off with all his stuff. Feeling guilty, Sonia had met Ricky's eyes across the table, and he had shrugged and – bless him – bitten the bullet, telling Karl everything.

When Karl had finally calmed down, they'd gone out in the dark and, opening up the garage, had shown him. Karl had stood there, one arm around Anita's shoulders, shaking his head in amazement.

'And it's been right *here*, all this time? Well, fuck me!'

They were taking it all – all, that was, except the bed. Anita had made it clear that, whatever else they kept, she was *never* going to sleep in any bed that that bitch had slept in, and Karl – whilst ruing the fact that he'd have to pay out at least five hundred for a comparable bed – had thought it sensible not to fight her over that one.

There were only one or two pieces of furniture left to load now. Anita had gone back inside the house; now she came out again, carrying a couple of opened beers.

She grinned at Sonia, then nodded towards Karl. 'It's like he's won the bleedin' pools, you know that?'

'Yeah, I can see.' But it was her Ricky she was happiest for. He'd hated keeping things secret, and now it was like a massive burden had lifted from him. Him and Karl couldn't stop grinning at each other and slapping each other across the back, like they were in some American buddy movie.

'It must have been hard for you, though,' Anita said, lingering next to her. 'I mean, I know she was your mate.'

Was. But that was only half true. Julie still was her mate, and a little bit of her felt guilty about all this. But then, Ricky was right – she should have rung. She should have been in touch. It wasn't right to use people the way Julie used them.

Besides, she wasn't so sure she knew her friend any more.

After all, who else did she know that had not one but three wedding albums?

The box was upstairs, in the loft, safe from the kids' prying eyes. Nor had they mentioned it to Karl. But then, why should they have? The furniture – well, that was Karl's and he had as much right to it as she had, but if Julie did turn up one of these days, Sonia wanted to have a clear conscience about things. She wanted to be able to give Julie something.

Yeah, and if the truth be known, she wanted to ask her old friend a few questions. Like why she'd never mentioned all those other fellas.

But that could wait. Right now everything was fine and, watching Anita walk across and hand the guys their beers, Sonia couldn't help but smile.

'Charlotte? Are you okay?'

It was her mother, calling up to her from the foot of the stairs. Standing, Charlotte walked over to the doorway and, pushing it open a crack, called back to her.

'I'm fine.'

'Do you want anything to eat?'

'I did something earlier.'

It was a lie, but if she didn't say that, her mother would do something anyway, then bring it up to her, and the last thing she wanted right now was a heart-to-heart.

'Okay – well, then, look, darling, I'm off. I doubt I'll be back until about seven. Management meeting. If Dad's back first, try and muster supper between you, would you?'

'Okay.'

She stood there, waiting until she heard the front door shut, then, closing the bedroom door, she went back across and sat there once more on the edge of her bed, staring down at the birth certificate and the tiny, full-colour photograph of her as a baby. It was not a lot, but it was more than she'd had only a week ago. And now she had an address. Up north. How strange that was. She'd never thought of herself as being born up north.

She picked the photo up and stared at it a while, then put it down and picked up the certificate, re-reading the details line by line. It didn't say here who her father was, but then that wasn't surprising, according to the lady social worker. A lot of young girls were too ashamed to tell their parents who the father was, and even if they knew for sure, the Registry couldn't agree to put the name on the certificate unless the father gave his written consent. And that was true for a lot of adopted babies. There were a lot of accidents; a lot of children born when they weren't wanted. The homes were full of them. But she'd been lucky. Or luckier than most. She had a loving family. Only it wasn't her blood. And now that she knew who her birth mother was, she had to make a decision: whether to know just this much, or whether to take the next step.

And if she needed another reason to want to know, she felt she had one now.

Charlotte stood, then turned side on to the mirror, wondering if it was just her, or whether she really was beginning to show.

She looked about her. There was a portable TV/video on the dressing table, a stereo on the shelf among her books and CDs. Beneath her feet was a plush new carpet, while at the far end of the room was a built-in wardrobe with all her coats and dresses in. It was more than most children had. Yet suddenly, inexplicably, it wasn't enough.

She turned from the mirror, letting the certificate fall from her fingers, then lay back on the bed and closed her eyes, forming the words quietly:

'Julie Vera Harding.'

How strange that name still sounded, even now that she'd said it a hundred times.

'Julie Vera Harding. My mother.'

The three-tiered wedding cake stood in the centre of the table, a plastic bride and groom atop the snow-white icing of the upper layer. On the far side of the hall the real bride and groom were cuddling up, like lovesick teenagers, their voices raised so as to be heard above the music that boomed out from the DJ in the corner.

'Happy?' Mike asked.

Julie beamed. 'Yeah. You?'

'Couldn't be happier. Oh, and thanks.'

'What for?'

'For looking after Mum so well. Look at her! Three months back I'd have never dreamed she'd ever look this happy again.'

'Just like her son, eh?' Julie said, reaching up to gently touch his cheek.

He took her hand and kissed it. 'I love you, you know.'

'Yeah, well, you'd better do. You're married to me now.'

As Karl turned from giving his order, Ricky shook his head in mock despair.

'I tell you what, mate. You're a bleedin' glutton for punishment.'

Karl shrugged exaggeratedly. 'What can I do? She wants to get married.'

'I just thought it'd be a case of once bitten, twice shy. I'm telling you, if me and Son ever split up, there's no way I'd get dragged up the aisle again.'

'Yeah, well, if I can't get hold of Julie, I'm gonna have to wait five years anyway.'

Ricky frowned. 'Why's that?'

'For the divorce, wally!'

'Ah. Yeah, well, if I was you, mate, I wouldn't be looking too hard.'

Karl shook his head. 'You're a cynical bastard, d'you know that, Ricky?'

Just then the barmaid returned with their pints. Karl took one and handed it to Ricky, then lifted his own in a toast, grinning. 'You do know what cynical means?'

Ricky went to say something, then shook his head and took a long sup of his pint. If that was what Karl wanted, then fine. Besides, Anita seemed nice enough. Softer than Julie and less demanding, even if she was insistent on marriage.

'You know what?' he said, after a moment.

Karl looked to him. 'What?'

'I was just thinking, maybe *she'll* come looking for *you*.'

'Who?'

'Julie. I mean, if she meets another fella, then— Well, *she* might want a divorce. You thought of that?'

'Yeah, but I ain't countin' on it. Nah, I reckon I'm gonna have to find her. And I will. Trust me.'

Julie set down the mug of hot cocoa on the bedside table, careful not to spill any down her wedding dress, then, reaching behind Nancy, plumped up her pillow. She stood back a little, surveying her handiwork, then smiled down at Nancy, who was looking up at her with smiling eyes.

'There you go, Mum,' she said, picking up the mug again and carefully handing it to her. 'Nice and milky.'

'You're a good girl. And I bet your mum would've been proud of you today. You look lovely.'

Julie smiled weakly, then, bending down, she gave Nancy a kiss on the cheek. 'Sleep tight.'

'And you, my love.'

Back in the front room, Mike was waiting for her. He had brought out two old candlesticks from the cupboard and blown off the dust. As Julie came in he was placing them on the dining table, where he'd laid two place settings.

Julie pulled the door closed, then went across, smiling at him, her voice teasing: 'What's the matter? You trying to save on electricity?'

Mike grabbed hold of her and they tussled a moment, play-fighting. Then Mike moved back sharply, pretending he was hurt.

'Ow.'

She looked at him uncertainly. 'What? What is it?'

'I think I need a nurse.'

Realising he was having her on, she went to move away, but Mike grabbed her hand.

'I've had this ache all evening.'

Julie grinned. 'Let me guess.'

Pulling her hand down, he placed it over his crotch.

'Mmm,' he said. 'Feels better already.'

'Good. Then let's eat. I'm starving.'

But Mike wasn't letting her go. 'The only thing I'm hungry for right now is you.'

'Well, you can have either a starter or a pudding.'

Mike's grin broadened. 'I can manage both. I'm a growing boy.'

She giggled. 'So I see!'

'Well?'

Julie shivered, then slowly unzipped him and took him in her hand, her eyes on his all the while.

'You're insatiable, d'you know that?'

'Yeah,' he said, 'well whose fault's that? Besides, it's our wedding night. You're supposed to do it on your wedding night.'

She laughed. 'Yeah, and on your wedding morning and wedding afternoon, eh?'

He shrugged. 'I cant help it if I can't keep my hands off you! You complaining?'

She shook her head, her eyes suddenly serious. 'No. Only let's do it on the sofa this time, eh? I don't wanna get no carpet burns.'

They had bought coffees from one of the kiosks and now stood there, an awkward little party of three, not quite knowing what to say to each other now that the time had come.

If anything, Charlotte seemed the least bothered by what was happening. She seemed detached today, distant, her small black travel bag wedged between her feet as she stood there looking across at the Departures board. She looked what she was, a young woman, well-groomed and well-educated, quite clearly middle-class, a fact which her well-dressed parents, standing to either side of her, emphasised.

Imogen, her mother, was the most disturbed by all this. She had wrestled with her feelings this last week, trying hard to do what her husband, Richard, asked and see it from Charlotte's viewpoint, yet now that the moment had come, she felt only an unworded dread at the thought of what lay ahead. This was her little girl, just as surely as if she had issued her from her womb. It was she who had raised her, nurtured her, made her the young woman she was, not this stranger, this *birth mother* who her daughter now set out to find.

Imogen was fifty-two this year, and suddenly it seemed old. When they'd adopted Charlotte, she had been thirty-four, Richard thirty-six, and they'd seen Charlotte as their last chance to have what they'd always wanted – a family. Nine years of heartache had preceded that decision; nine barren years that had taken their toll on their marriage. But then Charlotte had come into their lives, and everything had changed. It was a cliché, but it was true: suddenly the sun had shone on her and Richard, and they had been as happy as it was possible to be. Everything had fallen into place, and Charlotte had been the key.

Now, however, she was forced to hide her unhappiness, to bite back the words that sometimes flooded her head. As Richard had said, this was something Charlotte had to do, and until she did it she would not be at peace, and so *they* would not be at peace. And so she endured this torment, standing with her daughter, knowing in her heart of hearts that she was in danger of losing her to a woman who had cared so little she had given her away without a thought.

Yes, that was the toughest part: not saying that to Charlotte; not expressing all the hurt, the bitterness she felt. Try as she might, she could not feel this but as a betrayal, as some monstrous ingratitude on Charlotte's part – *after all they had done*.

They had been quiet for some time now. Charlotte had been watching the board. Now she looked back at them.

'That's my train. I'd better go.'

Picking up her travel bag, she began walking towards the barrier.

Imogen looked to her husband, a kind of panic gripping her, yet he seemed calm, controlled. His smile, as ever, was tolerant, understanding. Catching up with Charlotte, he reached out, touching his daughter's arm.

'Let me come with you.'

'I wish you would, darling,' Imogen said breathlessly. 'I'd feel a lot happier if Daddy were there.'

'I'll be fine.'

'But you don't even know if—'

'Mum, I'll be fine.'

They walked on. There was no guard at the barrier to check her ticket, but Charlotte turned to face them, as if some invisible line lay just behind her. Again it was Richard who spoke first.

'Shall we come through? See you on board?'

Charlotte's smile, her little shake of the head, were enough to set Imogen off, but still she controlled herself. She would not let the mask slip. Not yet. Not while Charlotte could see it. As Richard had said to her, it wasn't fair.

'No, it's okay,' Charlotte said. 'I'll walk up to the end of the train. It'll be emptier.'

She set her bag down a moment, then embraced them, her father first and then Imogen, kissing them, as if she were heading off to college.

They stood back.

'Bye, darling,' Richard said.

'Yes,' Imogen chipped in. 'Phone us just as soon as you've—'

But Charlotte had already turned away. She called back to them over her shoulder. 'I will. Bye.'

They stood there, watching her figure diminish as she walked further and further up the platform, and as it did, so that sense of dread – of sheer, unadulterated fear – threatened to overwhelm Imogen, but then Richard reached out and took her hand, squeezing it reassuringly, and when she looked at him she saw how he was smiling at her – not a bland, unfeeling smile, but a smile of sympathy, of total understanding.

'She'll be okay,' he said. 'She's a sensible girl.'

Imogen swallowed, then nodded. 'I know, but—'

He stepped closer, then held her, as if suddenly he were the parent, she the child. 'Hey, you, it's okay. She'll come back. You're her mum, remember?'

Charlotte had packed a book, but she had barely looked at it. Most of the time she had just stared out of the window, watching the landscape change as the miles flew past. She had never been north, not even on holiday, so that it felt like she was travelling into some foreign country, far stranger in its ways and customs than those she had visited with her parents – Switzerland, France, America and Greece. Those places had seemed to welcome her, to involve her in their strangeness, but this – the greyness of it, the unrelenting dourness – seemed to exclude her, to shut her out.

Or maybe that was just her state of mind.

Charlotte looked down, into her lap. She was on the last leg of her journey now, rattling through the bleak North Yorkshire Moors. The day itself was grey, rain streaking the soot-smeared windows of the carriage, and for the first time since she'd set out, she began to wonder if this were not some huge mistake.

She had run through all of the various scenarios. Her birth mother could be dead, or ill, or mad. Or maybe – and this might be the worst – she might be embarrassed by this physical reminder of her past. She might be happily married now, to a man who knew nothing of her past, and Charlotte's untimely arrival might prove the unravelling of her happiness. Against which was the possibility – the hope – that she had missed the daughter she had had to give away; that each day of her life had been filled with an aching regret for what she'd done.

Part of the trouble was that the birth certificate gave her so very little information. Where the father's name should have been was a straight horizontal line, likewise where his occupation should have been given. There was no mention of the mother's age, nor of her circumstances, and the adoption people had nothing on their records to enlighten her, so all she had was a name and an address.

The train dipped. For a moment the skies ahead lightened. There was a glimpse of something bright and shimmering in the distance, and after a moment she realised what it was. The sea.

Her heart was racing suddenly, her mouth dry. All along she had been calm about this, but now that she was so close, she found herself suddenly afraid of what she was doing. There had to be a reason why her mother had given her away. People didn't just give away babies.

The woman sitting opposite her noticed her sudden distress and leaned forward, touching her knee, then spoke in the broadest of Yorkshire accents. 'Are you alright, love?'

Charlotte nodded, smiling gratefully, then found her voice again. 'Yes, I'm fine, I just felt a bit faint, that's all. I've been travelling all day.'

'Ah.'

For a moment she feared the woman would start up a conversation; would force her to confide just what she was doing all this way from home, but she seemed content to leave it there.

Relieved, Charlotte sat back. Opening the book again she tried to focus on the words, then, relenting, she looked back out again, watching the land dip away, seeing how the sea was spread out like a cloak of grey ahead of her, the small town sprawled on the rocks above it, and felt her stomach tighten once again.

The past lay ahead of her. She had only to go up to the door and knock.

She tried the house, but the woman there said that they'd moved, three years back. She had a forwarding address though and, after a bit of persuading, agreed to give it to Charlotte. Now Charlotte stood there, on the third landing of the small council block, trying to get up the nerve to knock a second time.

There was no knocker as such, just a letterbox on a stiff spring hinge. Pushing at it, she let it bang shut twice.

Nothing. Only the sound of the lift from down below. Charlotte waited, her heart beating, then pushed at the flap again, letting it bang shut.

This time she heard a sound from inside; a door opening, footsteps, and then the front door opened a fraction on the chain.

The woman was elderly, probably late sixties, distinctly working-class, with a worn, pinched face.

'Yes?'

'Oh, I er—'

'If you're selling anything, dear, I don't want any. I'm a pensioner.'

'Oh, no. I'm not selling, I'm—' She took a deep breath. 'I'm looking for Julie Harding and I was told this is where she lives.'

The old woman's eyes changed. They were wary now, suspicious. 'Julie?'

'Yes. Julie Harding. Does she live here?'

'Where you from? The Social?'

Charlotte gave a small laugh. 'No. No, I'm trying to—' She crinkled up her eyes. 'Are you Mrs Harding?'

The woman looked taken aback. She hesitated, then took the door off the chain and stepped out into the light of the hallway. She was a small, neat woman with short grey hair.

'I was. That was my first husband's name. Who – *are* you?'

'I'm Charlotte. Julie's daughter.'

Chapter Thirteen

You'll Never Know

Charlotte was sitting in an old armchair by the unlit fire. It was raining outside, and the room was filled with the day's grey light as if everything had been washed in that dreary colour. The old woman – Vera – was busying herself about the room, dusting, unable to rest with Charlotte there, unable to meet her eyes for more than the briefest moment.

'I told you,' she was saying, 'I ain't seen her since she left home.'

'How old was she?'

'Sixteen.'

Charlotte blinked. The answer shocked her; reverberated through her like a plucked string. For a moment she lost what she was going to say. Then, collecting herself:

'But you *must* have heard from her?'

Vera stopped dusting, shook her head. There was a strange little movement in her face, then she resumed her activity.

Charlotte's eyes wandered about the room, confirming what she already knew. There was nothing new in this room; nothing from the last few decades, anyway. Every stick of furniture, every last piece of furnishing, was from the Sixties, as if the whole flat had been preserved in a time warp.

'Is there anyone else who might know where she is? Any other relatives?'

Vera stopped and faced her. She seemed angry suddenly.

'No. I've *told* you. We don't know where you can find her. She left and never came back, and that's all there is to it.'

'But you must have looked for her. She's your daughter. Don't you want to know that she's alright?'

'If she ain't been in touch, it's cos *she* don't want us to know.'

'What about my father?'

Again there was a movement in Vera's face. She turned away, dusting again, her thin, liver-spotted hands moving quickly, nervously.

'I don't know nothing about that.'

Vera stopped suddenly, then glanced at Charlotte. 'Look! The first thing I knew about her being— she was nearly seven months gone. Could have been anyone.'

Charlotte looked down, crestfallen. 'I'm sorry, I—'

'You'd better go.'

She looked up, nodded, then followed Vera through to the front door. As Vera held it open for her, they faced each other. It was a strange, awkward moment. They were blood, but they were also strangers. They lived in different worlds. Briefly she met her grandmother's eyes, saw the strange, frightened look there, quickly hidden, and gave a little nod, her own face unexpressive. But inside she wanted to cry. Inside she was aching for the waste of it all. Yet as she was about to turn away, her grandmother spoke again.

'What are they like, the people who – you know, the ones who took you in?'

Charlotte smiled. 'They're great.'

'Good.' Vera nodded. 'That's good.'

Again, that awkwardness, and neither of them able to breach the gap between them. Then Charlotte was struck by a thought. Reaching into her bag she brought out her notebook.

'Can I leave you my address and number so that—?'

'Oh, I don't think—'

'Please. Just in case. You might— Well, you never know.'

Quickly she wrote it down; her name, and then the address and phone number, then tore the page out and offered it. Vera took it reluctantly, her eyes fastening on what was written there.

'I'll leave you now. I—' But Charlotte could see she had exhausted her. She was slumped now, her back against the wall. 'I – I'll let myself out.'

Yet as she pulled the door closed behind her, she felt a huge emptiness inside that had not been there before, an unfathomable well of loss. *Sixteen. She'd only been sixteen.*

*

The old man paused on the bottom step, getting his breath. The shopping bag was heavy, and it was three floors up, but he didn't like using the lift. Those yobbos from the top floor used the lift, and besides, it stunk of piss and other even less savoury smells.

He was about to carry on, when a young woman came hurrying down the stairs and past him. He had only a glimpse of her, but he could see she was crying, and that made him turn to watch her as she half ran, half stumbled across the forecourt and out on to the main road.

Well-dressed, she'd been. And her hair – her hair had been nice. Not like the local girls. Tarts, all of them! Done up like little prostitutes!

But she'd been crying.

Ted turned, looking up the stairwell, then frowned. Ah well, it was none of his business, after all and, lifting the bag, he began the long climb to the third floor.

Vera stood at the window, the scrap of paper in one hand, a photograph in the other. It was a small, square, coloured photo with a white border and the date it was developed printed on the back. Ted had had an old Kodak back then, and they had asked a passing holidaymaker to take the snap. Ted was in the middle, tall and upright, even though he was in his late forties back then. He was grinning like he'd won the pools. A big, tanned man with slicked-back black hair. She was beside him, to his right, her hand in his, almost grimacing into camera. Forty-two she'd been that year. Making up the family portrait was Julie, ten years old, standing to Ted's left, holding his hand, her face closed, miserable.

Hearing the front door closing, she hurriedly slipped the photograph into a drawer, then turned as Ted came into the room.

'I'm gasping.'

She nodded, then pushed the piece of paper into her apron pocket. 'I'll put the kettle on.'

Vera made to leave the room, but his voice stopped her.

'There was this girl on the stairs. She was crying.'

She waited, her back to him. 'Yes?'

'I just wondered if you'd heard anything, that's all. Well-dressed young lass. Not from round here, you can be sure.'

'Mmmm.' But she said no more. She went out and switched on the kettle. And as the kettle began to rattle and steam, she took the slip of paper out once more and stared at the address.

Mike stood in the doorway, looking in at Julie. She had spread a cloth on the bare floor and laid out two places, as if it was a table top. Now she was lighting candles. Noticing him there, she turned slightly, looking up at him.

'You okay?'

Mike shrugged. 'I was just thinking about Mum.'

Julie made a sympathetic face, then came across to him, holding him a moment. 'She'll be fine. Sure she will. She's been looking after herself all her life. And we're not far away here. If she needs us she can phone, and you'll be over there in five minutes. So don't worry.'

Mike smiled and kissed the crown of her head. 'I s'pose so.'

'I know so. It'll do her the world of good to stand on her own two feet.'

'Yeah?'

Julie squeezed past him into the kitchen, then returned with two wine glasses. She handed one to Mike, then raised her own, smiling.

'To us!'

He looked back at her, smiling, clearly in love, then chinked his glass against hers. 'To us!'

Imogen brought through the dish of potatoes and set it down in the middle of the table. Since Charlotte had got back it had all been very awkward. She'd told them what had happened, but it didn't seem to account for the mood she was in. Oh, Charlotte could be moody – she always had been – but this was somehow different. It was like she was shutting her and Richard out – *excluding* them.

As she dished up, she looked from her daughter to her

husband, noting how they sat there, Charlotte with her head down, refusing to make eye contact, Richard watching his daughter, that calm sympathy of his making her want to hug him for being so nice. She wished *she* could feel that way, only she couldn't. All of this business simply annoyed her, made her feel she'd been wasting her time all these years. She had tried and tried to understand, but when it came down to it, she couldn't argue with her feelings. If the woman had wanted her, she'd have kept her. It was as simple as that. They weren't living in Victorian times, after all. These days the Social Services made anything possible. There'd been lots of stuff in the papers about how young girls only had to fall pregnant and they'd get a two-bedroom flat on a new estate. So why hadn't she kept her? Why?

But she couldn't say any of this. She didn't dare. And so she left it to Richard, with his infinite patience to wheedle it out of her bit by bit, while she looked on and suffered.

She filled Charlotte's plate and put it on the table before her, then loaded up Richard's and put it in front of him. But neither of them seemed the least bit interested in their food. Richard watched her, his brown eyes filled with concern, his lips parted a fraction.

'Maybe—' he began. 'Maybe if you went back to Social Services.'

Charlotte shook her head. 'That's the only address they had.'

'Then what about the Inland Revenue?' Imogen asked, unable to help herself.

Richard looked to her kindly. 'She couldn't. They're not allowed to give out that kind of information.'

Charlotte stared at her untouched dinner a moment, then stood.

'Where are you going?'

Charlotte glanced at her. 'I'm going to write to Vera.'

'But darling, Vera doesn't know where she is. She told you that.'

'I know. But she might have remembered something.'

Imogen closed her eyes, biting back the urge she had to tell her to leave it all alone. But she knew she wasn't going to. This thing had Charlotte in its grip, and Charlotte could be obsessive about things when she wanted to be.

As Charlotte left the room, Imogen pushed her own meal aside, then looked across at her husband. She kept her voice low, whispering almost.

'What are we going to do?'

He sighed, then shook his head. 'Nothing. There's really nothing we can do.'

Ted sat in the old armchair by the fire, straight-backed, the opened envelope resting on his knee, three of his long, spatulate fingers lying stiffly across the pure white vellum. It was late morning, but the day outside was grim, grey cloud filled the sky. The flat was shadowy silent, the tick of the clock on the mantelpiece the only sound as he waited. His heavily-lined face was set, his eyes like the day outside, grey and miserable.

For a long time there was nothing, then there was the sound of the key in the latch, of Vera's footsteps on the hallway lino, the front door closing behind her.

She came in, a bag of food shopping in one hand, a news-paper in the other, talking as she entered.

'One counter they had open in that post office, Ted! Just one! More than twenty minutes I had to queue.'

Vera put the newspaper on the table next to him and made for the kitchen.

'You want a cup of tea?'

There was no answer. Turning, she looked at him. Saw, in that dim light, the anger in his face and felt herself go cold.

'What's the matter?'

He threw the envelope at her. Shaken, she bent down and picked it up. It was addressed to her; even so, he had opened it. She looked up at him and saw the anger there, but she too was angry now.

'What is this?'

His voice was as hard as nails. 'Just read it.'

She took out the letter and unfolded it. It was from Charlotte. She felt her breath constrict, her pulse begin to race.

'You don't answer it,' Ted said, standing up and snatching at his jacket angrily. 'D'you understand?'

She swallowed. 'It was addressed to me.'

He whirled about, his face dark now, threatening.

'But Ted—'

He took a step towards her, the newspaper raised. 'I'm *telling* you. You don't answer it.'

She nodded, then watched him turn and go over to the door. A moment later the front door slammed behind him.

Vera stood there a moment, her hands trembling, shaken by the anger she had seen in him, the fury in his eyes. Then, steadying herself, she went over to the window and, taking her glasses from her pocket, began to read.

It had been a long shift, and she was tired. Sometimes she changed at work, but today she had left her uniform on, and as she stood at the bus stop, she put her hand to her mouth to shield a yawn.

'Tired?'

The voice made her jump. She turned to see Dave sitting there, in his car, not ten paces away, looking out at her, his face unreadable. He was wearing dark glasses.

She walked across.

'What're you doing here?'

'Waiting for you.'

Still no expression. She couldn't see his eyes.

'How are you?'

'Better than when you last saw me,' she said, not bothering to hide the bitterness from her voice.

Dave looked away, unable to meet her gaze.

She counted to ten in her head, then shrugged. 'Well?'

'I wanted to talk.'

'What about? We've got nothing to say.'

'We have. *I* have.'

'So?'

Dave took a deep breath. 'Not a day's gone by when I ain't thought about you.'

'Yeah, well, that's nice for you. But you left me, remember?

I had bailiffs, the lot. Oh, and let's not forget the black eye.'

Dave dropped his head.

Julie looked round at the bus stop, aware suddenly of the people behind her in the queue, eagerly devouring every word.

'I want you to go,' she said quietly.

'But you're still my wife.' He nodded towards her left hand. 'You're still wearing my ring.'

Julie guiltily fingered the tiny band of gold on her third finger, then pushed her hand deep into her pocket.

'I thought—' His voice softened. 'I thought we might go for a drink.'

'A *drink*?' She laughed. Then, relenting, seeing how hurt he suddenly looked, she shrugged. 'Where?'

They found a little bar just off the High Street and took a table in the far corner. Julie rested her back against the padded wall, staring across at him as he ordered their drinks. Dave had never really got the fashion thing: he always looked comfortable rather than sharp, but he'd lost some weight and he looked a lot better for it.

They'd not talked much in the car, but now, even as he set the drinks down between them, he launched in straight away, as if he sensed he only had so much of her time.

'I've been thinking about you a lot lately.'

She didn't respond.

'Today wasn't the first time I've waited for you after work.' 'What?'

He'd removed the dark glasses now and she could see how troubled his eyes were; how sad his expression.

'Oh, I don't wanna sound like some kind of sad-fuck stalker, but – I just had to see you. And the times before – well, I didn't have the courage to call out. But today, seeing you like that in your uniform, tired I . . .'

She couldn't speak, though clearly he expected a response.

'It's just I've missed you so much.'

He fell silent, his eyes on her, waiting.

'You don't hurt people you love. You look after them,' she said finally.

Head bowed, he nodded in agreement. 'I thought you was having an affair.'

'Well, I wasn't.'

He looked up suddenly, the relief only too evident in his face. 'I wouldn't have blamed you.'

There was such a look of earnestness about Dave at that moment that something in her melted. She could see, suddenly, just why she'd fallen for him. Reaching out, she took his hand.

His fingers squeezed hers, warm, their pressure familiar.

She stood, freeing her hand. 'Look, I've got to go. I—'

'But you ain't touched your drink.'

'I know, but—'

Rummaging in his wallet, he pulled out a card and handed it to her. It was a business card: smart, neatly printed.

She took it, studied it a moment, then looked back at him.

'I'm just the manager this time,' he said. 'So no money worries. I live above the pub. It's not as big as the last place, but—'

'Good. I'm pleased for you. I—'

'Don't go.'

'I have to. I've moved on. You've got to do the same.'

'I can't. I—'

'You must. It's over.'

She slipped away from the table and made her way to the door. Without looking back, she pushed it open and stepped out on to the rain-washed street, hurrying to get home to Mike.

Nancy was sitting in the big armchair in the corner of the living room, engrossed in a Harry Bowling novel. Across from her, Mike was busy stuffing his football kit into an old Adidas sports bag. He picked up a yellow sports shirt – an old Arsenal away strip – and gave it a sniff, making a face before he added it to the rest. He looked about him a moment, as if wondering whether there was anything else he'd forgotten, then looked across at Nancy and smiled. He was about to pick the bag up again when the front door banged shut.

'Hiya!' Julie called cheerfully from the hallway.

'Hi!' he called back, going over to the door to greet her. Nancy looked up as Julie appeared in the doorway, still wearing her nurse's uniform, a plastic carrier bag in one hand. She smiled as Mike gave Julie a kiss.

'Good day?' he asked.

'Mmm. Not bad.'

Julie stepped past him and began unloading the carrier bag on to the table. There were two bottles of wine and a couple of beers.

'And,' Julie said, 'to go with it . . .'

Pleased with herself, she held up the copy of *The Matrix* she'd hired from the video shop.

'I thought you said you hated it.'

'What I said was, I didn't understand it. Thought you could explain it to me. Over a glass or two of vino . . .'

Julie raised her eyebrows suggestively, but Mike was suddenly looking very sheepish. Julie frowned, then, her eyes widening, she saw the sports bag.

'What's that?'

Mike walked across and patted the bag as if it were an old familiar friend. 'The blokes at work asked me if I wanted to go football training with them.' He smiled weakly. 'Must be desperate.'

'What, tonight?'

'You don't mind, do you?'

Julie's face, her voice, were suddenly much harder. 'Mind? Why should I mind? I mean, I've only wasted an hour buying this lot and—'

Mike took a step toward her. 'It ain't wasted, is it? We can watch it tomorrow. And the wine'll keep.'

'Oh, I see. I get fitted in whenever you feel like it, but when your mates say jump you jump. If I'm starting to bore you, you only have to say.'

Mike laughed, then took another step. 'You ain't boring me. We're married, not joined at the bloody hip. Look, it's football training, not lap dancing.'

'And suddenly you're a football fanatic?'

Mike stopped. His eyes now had a faintly stunned look of

disbelief. 'No. But it is the football season. Christ almighty, Julie, this is ridiculous!'

He turned and picked up his bag, then looked back at her.

'Look! If it'll make you happy, I won't go to the pub after.'

'No. You go if you want to. I don't care.'

He stared at her a moment, then stepped closer, trying to kiss her, to try and reconcile things before he went, but she drew back. Shrugging, he walked over to his mum and bent down, kissing her on the cheek.

'Bye, Mum. See you later.'

As the front door closed, Julie glanced over at Nancy, expecting a disapproving look, but Nancy was concentrating on her book. There was an awkward silence, and then Nancy laid the book aside.

'It was motorbikes with his dad. I said to him one day, "You love them bloody things more than you love me".' Nancy looked up. 'Michael thinks the world of you. You know that.'

Julie no longer looked angry; now she looked vulnerable. 'Yeah. Yeah, I know.'

She glanced across, making the briefest eye contact with Nancy before she turned and, sad now, left the room.

Vera had waited until Ted had gone out to his club, then sat at the kitchen table and wrote out her reply. Now she stood there on the corner by the postbox, hoping no one would see her there and mention it to Ted.

The envelope was in her pocket, and though she only had to take it out and pop it into the slot, it seemed to be the hardest thing she had ever done. All her life she had taken the easy option, walking the path of least resistance, trying to keep her head down and stay out of the firing line. But now, suddenly, something had woken in her. Perhaps it was the mention of Julie's name – Julie, her only child, who she had tried hard to forget these past eighteen years. Or maybe it was something in the girl herself – something she'd seen and recognised. Whatever, it had made her wake up after years of drifting along, doing nothing.

Ted would be furious if he knew. He'd rage and storm. But

that wasn't why she hesitated. She was afraid. Afraid to wake up all of those feelings, all those memories and emotions. It was like they'd all been sleeping, dormant in her, all these years, until the girl had come and knocked on her door, dragging the past along with her.

Slowly, she turned full circle, taking in the bleakness of the estate, the awfulness of the day. In an hour it would be dark, and the sea, in the distance, seemed like a sheet of melted lead.

Go on, Vera, she told herself. *Do it. You've done the hard bit.* But that wasn't true. She could still back out. She could still walk home and, tearing the letter up, burn it in a saucer. And then no one would know. Not a solitary soul.

She closed her eyes, counting to ten, then pushed her hand deep into her coat pocket and fished out the letter. Like a sleepwalker, she found the slot and thrust the letter deep into the box, almost wedging her hand in the narrow gap.

Opening her eyes again, she stared at her knuckles, where she'd just grazed them, then, surprised by the violence of what she was feeling, turned and hurried across the open ground towards the flats, afraid yet exalted now. Strangely exalted.

Chapter Fourteen

No Other Love

As the doorbell rang, Imogen looked up from where she sat at the kitchen table, listening to see if anyone else was going to answer it. She was halfway through her report and really didn't want to be disturbed, but from the silence in the hallway and on the stairs, it looked like she was going to have to.

'Damn it,' she murmured under her breath, then, pushing the chair back, got up and went out into the hallway.

She knew who it was at once, from the shape of the shadowed form behind the coloured glass of the door. Tall, gangly, his head bent forward, like he was forever slouched. Jack.

Imogen pulled the door open wide and smiled pleasantly at the young man. 'Hello, stranger. Long time no see.'

Jack moved his head a little, like it was difficult even to speak, then gave a little shrug. 'Is Charlotte in? I need to speak to her.'

The hesitant tone warned her. Something was up. And now, come to think of it, she realised that Jack really had become something of a stranger these past few weeks.

'Hold on,' she said sympathetically. 'I'll see if she's in.'

The truth was, she knew Charlotte was in, but she also knew better than to say so if Charlotte didn't want to see Jack. Maybe they'd had a row. Or maybe – just maybe – Charlotte had found somebody else. If so, it was strange that she hadn't said. She wasn't usually so secretive about such things. Besides, Jack was a nice lad, intelligent *and* handsome – and polite too, which was quite something these days – and she'd been sure Charlotte was keen on him.

She pulled the door over, then turned and hurried up the stairs, stopping outside Charlotte's door.

She knocked gently. 'Lottie—?'

No answer. There was the sound of the stereo, muted yet distinct. Taking a breath, Imogen eased the handle down and slowly pushed the door open.

'Charlotte?'

Charlotte lay on her back on the bed, staring up at the ceiling. 'What?'

'You've got a visitor . . . Jack.'

Charlotte didn't say a word, just nodded.

'Shall I ask him in?'

'No. I'll come down.'

Charlotte got up, snatched a jacket from the side, then brushed past her. As she went out on to the landing again, Imogen caught a flash of her daughter's back in the hallway, then the front door slammed.

She closed her eyes. Why was everything so difficult? Why couldn't things just work out like they were supposed to? Why couldn't Jack and Charlotte fall in love and marry and have kids and live happily ever after? Why was it so bloody hard just to be happy? Why were there always obstacles?

Nothing ever seemed to run smoothly, the way it was supposed to. Then she thought of Richard and his kindness and his infinite patience, and for a moment she was on the verge of tears. What would she have done all these years without him? What in God's name would her life have been like?

They walked down to the park in a silence that was both awkward and tense. Then, finally, as they came up on to the bridge that crossed the ornamental pond, Jack turned to her. The hurt in his face was visible. It was like he was angry with her and yet at the same time he wanted to cry.

'If you didn't want to see me any more, you should have had the guts to tell me to my face.'

She looked away, unable to answer him.

'Is there somebody else?'

Charlotte hesitated, then shook her head.

'Well, what is it then? I thought things were cool with us.'

'Things change.'

She met his eyes as she said the words and saw the shock in them. But shock quickly turned to anger.

'You were the one who did the running, remember? So tell me, what's changed between now and when you were shagging me senseless two weeks ago?'

That word angered her. *Shagging*.

'Well, if it was just a shag, I don't know why you're so bothered.'

Jack shook his head, amazed at the way she was deliberately twisting his words. 'If it *was* just a shag, I wouldn't be.'

Charlotte looked down, a sadness in her face suddenly. For a moment she seemed close to saying something, then she met his eyes again.

'I'll give you back your CDs.'

Jack shook his head angrily, amazed by her. 'I don't give a shit about the CDs. Do you know what it's been like? You don't want to talk to me, you don't want to see me. You don't even want to touch me. I love you, and you said you loved me, and now you're telling me that that means nothing.'

His words unhinged her. Reaching out, she let the words escape her, like a yelp of pain. 'I'm pregnant, alright? I'm fucking pregnant.'

Jack stared at her, shocked.

'So now you know why it's over.'

And, turning, she ran. Away from him. Away from all the happiness he'd brought. Leaving him shell-shocked and despairing. Eighteen and wounded.

Julie stretched across the bed, pulling the fresh, white sheet smoothly along the mattress and efficiently tucking under the corners. Normally she resented performing these more menial tasks, believing her nursing skills could be more usefully employed, but today she welcomed the tedium.

Last night had been a restless one. When Mike got home after football training she had pretended to be asleep. She lay on her side, turned away from him, listening to the sounds of his clothes falling to the floor, the tinkle of the coins in his pocket, and was careful not to move. She'd braced herself against his advances, but she had smelled the beer on him and he'd dropped off quickly. All well and good, only she had lain there for hours afterwards, unable to sleep, Mike's snores filling the room even as her mind buzzed with details from her meeting with Dave.

In the time she'd been married to Mike she had, in all honesty, hardly thought about Dave, pushing his memory into her past – a place rarely visited and never consciously so. But seeing him again had reminded her of what a good person he was and why she'd been attracted to him in the first place. Apart from those last few weeks, Dave had been nice, and life with him had been good.

Thinking about it, Julie threw the bedcover over the mattress and secured it under the bottom corners before turning down the top sheet. It was the last of them. But as she reached down to pick up a pillow from the chair, she glanced along the ward and stopped dead in her tracks.

There, at the nurses' station, stood Dave, a huge bouquet of roses in one hand. He was watching her, a look of uncertainty in his eyes.

She walked across, her anger matched by a strange pleasure at seeing him there.

'You can't just come here like this,' she said quietly. 'I'm working.'

'What did you expect?' Dave answered, offering her the flowers. 'I couldn't leave it like that, could I?'

Julie took the flowers and laid them on the desk, then looked about her, conscious that people – including some of her colleagues – were watching. 'I don't know what you want from me.'

'Yes you do.'

She shook her head and made to turn away, but Dave reached out and touched her arm. 'It'd be different this time. No money worries. And I've got the flat—'

'I don't want to know.'

But Dave wasn't giving up. 'Remember the wedding? When I told everyone how I was gonna take care of you? I know. I fucked up, but that's all I want to do. Julie, please.'

She glanced at him. 'It's too late.' But her voice was less certain now.

Then, as if she couldn't face it any more, she turned and hurried away, out through the door that led into the courtyard. Dave ran after her.

· 'It's not too late,' he called, slowing as he saw her standing there. 'How can it be? We're still married.'

She didn't look at him, just stared down at the ground. 'It just is.'

Dave came closer until he was only an arm's length away. 'If you want me to beg, I will.'

Julie shook her head. She didn't know what she wanted. She needed time to think. Turning away from him, she walked across the courtyard towards the fountain that stood in its centre. She stared at the water as it cascaded down the dark grey stone, her head pounding.

'What can I do? Tell me. I'll do anything.'

He was standing so close now that they were almost touching.

'Ain't you ever wanted something so much you'd do anything to keep it?' he said, his voice low but intense. 'Well, that's how I feel. I want you so much.'

Dave stared at her for a moment, trying to gauge what she was thinking, then, as if he'd noticed it for the first time, he looked at the fountain. He glanced back at her, then, as if it were a perfectly natural thing to do, climbed over the lip of the fountain and into the water.

'Is this what you want?' he asked, as the water splashed over him, soaking his suit. '"Man drowns himself over lost love." Is *this* what it takes?'

Julie clasped a hand over her mouth. 'Dave! Oh my God! You're gonna get pneumonia!'

Dave shook his head, water drops spraying out from his hair. 'I don't care. Not if I ain't got you.' He stopped, a look of surprise on his face. 'I must have heard that in a song.'

Julie was grinning now, unable to help herself. How could she not be touched by such an act? Seeing her smile, Dave's face broke into a grin also. He stepped out, standing before her, his hands held out.

'No one's ever going to love you as much as I do. You know that.'

Her lip quivered and she gave a brief nod, aware at that moment that he was probably speaking the truth.

He stepped closer, his sodden clothes leaving a puddle under him. Even so, when he made to kiss her, Julie didn't draw away, and when he put his hands around her back, their dampness leaving wet imprints on her dress, she didn't even seem to notice.

Imogen was standing by the fax, feeding in the last few sheets of the report, when she heard the front door bang. Turning, she caught a fleeting glimpse of Charlotte, hurrying up the stairs.

'Charlotte—'

But she was too late. She heard the bathroom door slam shut upstairs and winced. By the look of things, it hadn't gone well with Jack.

She stood there, patiently feeding the last sheet into the machine, then, with a little sigh of relief, picked up the letter from the table and went out.

The bathroom door was locked. From inside she could hear the sound of running water. She knocked, then called out.

'Charlotte!'

She waited a moment and was about to call again, when Charlotte answered her.

'What?'

'There's a letter for you. It came second post, while you were out.'

Richard had come out from his study and now stood beside her. He looked to the letter in her hand and raised an eyebrow. They both knew what this was, if only from the Whitby postmark.

There was a moment's delay, and then the door opened. Charlotte stood there, her face pale, every trace of make-up removed from it. From her reddened eyes it appeared that she'd been crying.

'Here,' Imogen said, handing her the envelope.

Charlotte took it, frowned at the unfamiliar writing, and then her eyes widened as she took in the name on the postal franking over the stamp. She looked to them, meeting their eyes briefly, then went back inside and shut the door behind her.

Richard reached out, putting his arm about his wife's waist. 'Let's leave her for a bit,' he said quietly. 'Come on, I'll make you a cup of tea. If she wants us, she'll know where we are.'

Waiting was the hardest thing, but eventually Charlotte came down again, scrubbed, her wet hair wrapped up in a towel, the opened letter in one hand. Taking a chair at the breakfast table, she looked up and smiled as Richard placed a fresh cup of tea in front of her.

'Thanks.'

'Everything alright?' he asked, seating himself across from her, beside Imogen.

She looked very young just then, and her eyes, while excited, also seemed confused. Fishing in the envelope, she brought out a photograph and handed it across.

'She's fifteen in that one.'

Curiosity getting the better of her, Imogen looked at the photo in Richard's hand. For a moment she just stared, then she looked back at her daughter.

'You have her eyes.'

Charlotte reached across for the photograph, then stared at it again.

'Oh, and there's something else. She's married. To a sailor.'

Mike looked up as she came into the room and smiled at her. 'You okay, hon?'

'Great.' She dropped her bag on the chair, then threw her coat down over it.

Mike patted the space on the sofa beside him. She hesitated, then went across. Leaning into her, Mike planted a long, slow kiss on her lips. At first she didn't want it, but as it went on, so she became strangely aroused by it, until, as they broke, she wondered what was happening to her.

'What's got into you?'

'Nothing,' he answered. 'Just felt like kissing you, that's all.'

'Just kissing?'

His lecherous grin made her insides melt. 'I'll run a bath, if you like.'

'Alright,' she said, liking the idea.

She reached out and gently touched his chin, stroking the smooth, shaved surfaces of skin, then drew his face towards her, kissing him again.

'Go on,' she said, 'but be quick – I'm not a patient woman.'

Yet even as he stood, she reached out and placed her hand on his thigh, stopping him, teasing him a moment as she ran her fingers lightly over his crotch, then playfully tapped his buttocks and sent him on towards the bathroom.

It was late. They had opened a bottle of wine, and now they sat there in the lounge, Imogen, Richard and Charlotte, three people – so Imogen had realised with a start – totally unconnected by blood.

Blood. That was what usually connected families, making two strangers into one through their children. But that wasn't the case here. However much love was in this room, it wasn't blood that linked the three of them.

They had been talking, circling the matter as if afraid to mention it, but now Richard shifted the conversation, bravely, gently raising the subject.

'Maybe they fell out.'

'What?' Charlotte looked to him and frowned.

'Your real mum and dad. Maybe they fell out.'

'What, over me, you mean?'

'Well, she was only sixteen, and single. And Whitby's a quiet seaside town. People can be very intolerant.'

'And if they did fall out because she got pregnant,' Imogen went on, jumping in, now that it was permitted, 'well, that's not your fault.'

Charlotte was quiet a moment, then she looked back at Imogen. 'But people don't not speak to one another for eighteen years over something like that. I mean, it's not as though they had to look after me or anything.'

'Yes, but it was still quite a while back, sweetie. Forget all of that permissive rubbish. Women still had a crappy deal, especially in the provinces.'

'But it was like she wasn't even curious about me. She just didn't want to know.'

Richard smiled at her. 'Give Vera time, Lottie. It must have been a real shock, you turning up like that out of the blue.'

'Maybe.' Charlotte was thoughtful a moment, then nodded to herself. 'I'm going to write to her. I don't believe she doesn't know where Julie is.'

Imogen groaned inwardly. 'Darling, I think Daddy's right. I think you need to give her time to get used to the idea. After all, she's got your address and—'

'But I don't want to just sit around and wait. If she knows where my mother is I have a right to know too. She's got no right to keep it from me.'

'Darling, I—'

But Charlotte had stood up and was gone. Imogen closed her eyes, overwhelmed by the pain, the sheer frustration she was feeling. Richard reached across and, taking her hand, gently squeezed it.

'I know. But we've got to be there for her, now more than ever. If she thinks we're fighting her over this, she'll hate us for it. But if we let her do this, if we help her—'

Imogen opened her eyes and stared at him.

'Don't think I don't know how difficult this is for you. But we've got to think now what's best for her. That's our job. We're her parents. That's what we took on when we decided to bring her home and keep her, remember?'

It was the thought of that – of the day when they'd brought her back from the hospital, Richard cradling that tiny bundle like she was a basket full of diamonds – that did it. Yet even as the tears coursed down her face, she knew he was right. This *was* what they'd taken on, even if they'd not known it was going to be this hard. Because love – real love – wasn't just about taking, love was about giving, too. Was about being responsible and, as Richard said, *being there* when you were needed.

'Okay' she said, letting him wipe away her tears. 'Okay. But

I don't want to meet her. I think that would be too much for me.'

'I know,' Richard said, turning to her, taking her in his arms. 'I know.'

It was a quarter after one. The pub doors were locked, the blinds down, but the place was packed. An old pot man went from table to table, gathering up beer glasses in precarious stacks which he then deposited on the end of the bar, while the two young Aussie barmen busied themselves filling the dishwasher and taking orders. The lounge bar was filled with smoke and conversation. The TVs had been switched off an hour back, together with the juke box, and at their table near the door, Karl, Ricky and Sonia sat drinking. Anita was at the hospital, acting as birth partner for her sister. She'd said she might catch them later, but it didn't really matter. Tomorrow was a Saturday and no one was in any hurry to go home. Not yet, anyway.

As ever on these occasions, their talk had turned to Julie.

'It's only now,' Karl was saying, 'that I realise how bloody little I knew about her.'

'Yeah,' Sonia agreed. 'I remember her saying she was brought up in Brighton or Eastbourne, or somewhere like that.'

Ricky laughed. 'Good one, Sonia. That narrows it down.'

Karl finished off one of the pints that were lined up in front of him, then wiped his mouth. 'You know what – it's like looking for a fart in a fog. Everyone you ask, it's like, "Sorry, sir, but we're not able to give out confidential information." I've tried the banks, the Inland Revenue. I went back to the hospital to see if they'd heard from her—'

'And?' Ricky asked.

'What d'you think? Not a fucking dicky-bird. You'd think I was a bleedin' stalker, not her husband!'

Just then, there was a hammering on the door behind them. The bouncer raised the blind a fraction, then, seeing who it was, reached up and unbolted the door. It was Anita.

She came across, Karl standing to let her past and giving her a peck on the cheek.

'Alright, babe? How'd it go?'

Anita beamed. 'She had a little boy. Seven pounds six. Aw, he was so beautiful.'

Ricky raised his eyes, but Karl ignored him. Anita could do no wrong in his book, and if she was pleased, he was pleased.

'Sit down, babe,' he said. 'I'll get you a drink.'

Anita edged into her seat. 'Her husband's useless,' she said, looking about her. 'He passed out when she had her Courtney.'

Karl was about to go over to the bar, when Anita reached out and held his arm, remembering something.

'Oh, I was talking to one of the nurses and telling her about your wife doing a runner.'

'Oh, thanks – so now the whole bloody place knows our business!'

'No. It's just that she was saying that all nurses have to register with some kind of organisation.'

She rifled through her handbag and brought out a scrap of paper.

'Here are! The United Kingdom Central Council.' She looked up at Karl, who was staring at her now with delighted surprise. 'Anyway, she reckons that if Julie's still nursing then they might be able to tell you where she works.' She paused, then smiled broadly. 'Go on, then. Mine's a vodka and cranberry.'

Chapter Fifteen

Let It Be Me

Nancy was sitting up in her bed, watching as Julie, sitting in a chair nearby, struggled with the knitting needles. After a moment, she lowered them, smiling exasperatedly at her mother-in-law.

'I'm never going to get the hang of it!'

Nancy smiled encouragingly. 'When Michael was little I used to knit all of his jumpers and cardigans. Oh, and I dread to think how many football scarves I've made. I used to watch him go off up the road with his dad to the match, the two of them with matching hats and scarves. It used to make me roar with laughter.'

Julie grinned. 'At this rate I'll be lucky to manage a pot holder.'

'It's like everything, dear, you have to persevere.'

Julie held up her knitting, revealing several dropped stitches, both of them laughing at the sorry sight.

'Here – give that to me.'

Julie handed it over, watching as Nancy's strangely nimble fingers took up the task as if it were the most natural thing in the world for a pair of hands to be doing. Leaning across, she kissed Nancy's forehead affectionately. Nancy looked up at her, surprised and clearly touched.

'I'll make us a cuppa.'

'Julie. Would you do something for me first?'

'Course.'

'Would you give me that box over?'

Julie turned and looked, then took the box from the dressing table. Nancy patted a space on the bed beside her. Julie sat.

Nancy smiled at her. 'I can't tell you what a relief it is for me to see Michael settled. I used to lie awake at night worrying about what was going to happen to him when – well, when I wasn't around any more.'

'You daft thing.'

'Mothers can't help it. We spend our lives worrying about whether our children are alright. He might be a grown man, but to me he'll always be my little boy. You'll be the same.'

Julie smiled, then watched as Nancy opened the box and brought out a necklace. She handed it to Julie.

'I want you to have this.'

Julie stared at the beautiful object, for once truly surprised. 'Nancy! I can't! What about your daughter?'

'Oh, there'll be plenty for her when I've gone. No. I want you to have it. Michael's dad bought it for me.'

Julie gave a tiny, shivering sigh. 'It's beautiful – thank you.'

Then, because she could think of nothing else to say, she leaned forward and gave Nancy a hug.

'Lottie? Are you awake?'

Richard peered around the door into the darkness of his daughter's room. From somewhere among the shadows, there was a distinct grunt and the sound of a body turning over beneath the sheets.

'Whaaa—?'

The half-formed word turned into a yawn.

Richard smiled. 'It's alright. You don't have to get up or anything. It's just that I've been talking to an old friend of mine, in the Navy. He's given me an address.'

He heard her sit up. 'What?'

'Oh, don't get too excited. It's not your mother's. No, it's just that the Navy has a department that deals with this kind of thing. I thought maybe it could help.'

He heard as much as saw her throw back the covers and come across to him. She took the piece of paper he was holding and looked at it, before putting her arms about Richard's neck.

'Thanks, Dad.'

It was a very different Charlotte who came down for a belated breakfast. Gone was the sour-faced, moody teenager; in her place was an excited young woman. Imogen stared at her daughter, surprised, then looked to Richard for an explanation.

'I got a pal to give me a contact in the Navy,' he said. 'They might be able to give her a lead.'

'Ah.' Imogen turned away, pretending to carry on with the washing up, but again she felt knocked back. How long was this going to go on for? And what was going to happen if and when she met this woman – her birth mother?

'There can't be that many Julie Hardings married to sailors, can there? And even if we have to track them down one by one—'

'Whoa, slow down there, Lottie,' Richard said. 'Let's take it a step at a time, eh, sweetheart?'

Charlotte stopped, seeing suddenly how Imogen stood there, stock-still, just staring down into the washing-up bowl. Slowly she got up and went across, standing beside Imogen so that their shoulders touched.

'I'll do that,' she said.

Imogen looked up into her daughter's face and, although her heart ached, she managed the ghost of a smile. 'Thanks.'

Anita sat at the kitchen table, looking on as Karl paced about, speaking into the telephone handset.

'I've told you her name. If I knew what her address was I wouldn't be phoning you, would I?'

He turned and looked to Anita, raising his eyes.

'Yes, I do know how many nurses there are in this country. A lot.' Karl turned, looking out through the kitchen window at the afternoon traffic. 'Fifth of August nineteen sixty-six. Yeah – yeah, I'm positive that she's a registered nurse. What I'm asking you to tell me is where she's working right now.'

He paused, his head tilted slightly to one side as he waited, then there was an angry little movement of his shoulders. 'Yeah. Yeah, well thanks for nothing!'

He slammed the phone down on the drainer then turned to face Anita again.

'Yes she's registered, but they can't tell me where she's

working. Can you believe it? I'm her bloody husband!'

Anita sighed, then shook her head, her face all sympathy. 'Well, babe, you're just going to have to think of something else.'

'Yeah but – *what*?' He huffed, then shook his head, real frustration in his face. 'I mean, just how hard is it to find someone in this bloody country?'

Anita grinned. 'Depends on how hard they're trying not to be found.'

They decided to go over to Mike's mum's for dinner. Mike phoned to let her know, telling her they'd pick up some fish and chips on the way.

It was while they were standing there, waiting for the fish to fry, that Julie suddenly remembered.

'Oh, shit!'

Mike looked to her. 'What?'

Julie looked down. 'Nothing.'

'Didn't sound like nothing.'

'I forgot something, that's all.'

The truth was she'd forgotten that she'd promised Dave she'd see him tonight. Only there was no way she could tell Mike that.

'It's just that I said I'd do a shift this week – maybe even tonight . . . and I said I'd phone the ward sister back about it.'

'Well, do it round Mum's. She won't mind.' He turned away a moment, then looked back at her. 'You don't really need to do extra shifts, do you?'

Julie shrugged. 'It's not that I want to, only they're short-staffed right now and anyway, I thought the extra money would come in handy. We could put it away for Christmas. Make it really nice.'

Walking from the fish shop to Nancy's, she wondered if maybe it wasn't a good thing she'd forgotten. After all, things were good with Mike right now, and getting back with Dave might prove more trouble than it was worth. Yet the memory of him standing there, dripping wet, declaring his love for her, filled her with a sense of belonging.

While Mike was taking the fish suppers out of the paper and putting them on plates, she closed the door and went into the passage where the phone was. Dialling Directory Enquiries, she quickly asked for the number of the Fox and Fiddle. She listened once, then let it play again, so that she was sure she'd got it firm in mind. Then, putting her finger on the cut-off, she quickly dialled again.

It rang and rang and rang, and she was just about to put the phone down when a familiar voice said, 'Hello – who's that?'

'It's me,' she said quietly, turning to stare at the closed door to the kitchen. 'Look, I'm sorry I couldn't make it tonight, only something came up.'

'Oh.' Dave was silent a moment, then, 'I guess I—'

'No, listen,' she said quickly, hearing that despairing tone in his voice. 'I can make it on Monday. Eight o'clock. I'll meet you there, at the pub, if you like. Yeah?'

'Yeah. Yeah, that'd be nice.'

'Good. See you then. And Dave—'

'Yeah?'

'I'm sorry about tonight, okay?'

''S alright.' But she could hear an edge of disappointment still.

'Anyway. Gotta go. See you Monday, eh?'

'Yeah. See you then.'

She put down the phone.

'Done?' Mike asked her as she came back into the kitchen.

'Yeah,' she said, avoiding meeting his eyes. 'Hmmm, that smells great!'

'Yeah,' he said, and, pecking her cheek, he picked up two of the plates and began to carry them through into the living room.

Mike had cleared away the plates a while back. Now the three of them sat there, the TV turned low, talking. Nancy had been reminiscing about the old days, while Mike was teasing her good-naturedly.

'I wouldn't mind,' he said, 'but she'd been yakking to it for a good five minutes before she realised it was a cardboard cut-out!'

Julie smiled, while beside her, Nancy took the joke in good humour.

'You're going to get old too one day, my lad. I just hope your children aren't as wicked to you. That's why, when I used to be able to get out on my own, I'd buy that magazine. That Big – what's it called?'

'Issue?' Julie offered.

'Yes. That's it. I used to get it off the young man outside the supermarket, because there but for the grace of God—'

'Mum.'

'No, it's true. It's all well and good thinking that kind of thing happens to other people, but it can happen to anyone. All those people out on the streets. I don't suppose they chose to be there.'

'We get them sometimes, on the wards. Poor sods. And they've all got a story.'

'Yeah,' Mike said, 'and it's never their fault.'

'That's unfair, Michael,' Nancy said. 'Sometimes life isn't kind, you know.'

'Yeah, but you say "there but for the grace of God", only I don't think it's true. Only a certain type ends up on the street. If you're strong you get on with things. Pick yourself up.'

'And you're one of the strong ones, are you?' Nancy said, eyeing her son with a mixture of amusement and concern. But before Mike could answer, Julie spoke, her voice tight, controlled. 'I don't think you can say how you'd react. Not in any situation. Not unless you've been there.'

A wind had blown up this past hour, throwing bits of waste paper and flecks of dust into the air, so that you had to turn your back against it from time to time or it went in your eyes. That said, it was warm and the rain had held off, so things weren't so bad.

Brian stopped at the corner bin, sorting through the wrappers and Coke tins, looking for something, anything he might eat. Sometimes you found the remains of a kebab, or a chip packet with a few left in the bottom. That was the good thing about the consumer society; people didn't eat everything they bought. There was a lot of wastage.

He hadn't liked doing it at first, but you got used to it. And it was better than begging. He hated begging. Hated the way some of those smug bastards apologised that they had no change, when they'd no intention of giving anything. That and the majority who just walked on, ignoring you, like you didn't exist. No, it was better not to beg unless you had to. Better to steal than to beg. Only he knew better than to do that. Bad as this was, he didn't want to go back inside. Not after what he'd suffered there.

He pushed the memory of it away. Best not think of that. Of what some of those bastards got up to. They weren't fully human, half of them.

He shuffled on, head down, avoiding eye contact. At first he'd been defiant, but a few beatings had changed that. You learned not to push things on the streets. Learned to be humble, whatever you felt on the inside. It didn't pay to be pushy.

Brian stopped, looking up at the sky. The park was just down the way, and maybe he'd get away with kipping on one of the benches tonight, if the weather held out.

Yeah, why not?

He shuffled through the gates and on, finding a bench halfway round, just past the pond. There he sat, putting down the tiny bundle of possessions he carried – among them his razor and a change of underwear – then taking from it the handwritten notice he'd made up the other day, setting it down beside the tiny plastic yoghurt carton. Only then did he stretch out on the bench, closing his eyes on the world.

Unlucky in love, it read. *Please help.*

Chapter Sixteen

Monday, Monday

As they pulled up at the lights, Imogen leaned over from the back seat and gave Charlotte a peck on the cheek.

'I'll jump out here. Good luck, you two. Phone me and let me know when you'll be back.'

As the back door clunked shut, Richard waved farewell, then looked back at his daughter.

'You okay?'

Charlotte smiled. 'I'm fine.'

Richard put the car into gear, tried to concentrate on driving, but there was something he wanted to say, and the best time to say it was now, before they took this any further.

'Look, Lottie, there's something you really ought to consider. About your mother. About Imogen, that is.'

'Imogen?'

'Yes. You ought to know that this whole thing – well, she finds it hard. Very hard. She tries not to show it, but—'

'Hard? Why should *she* find it hard?'

Richard stared straight ahead, a slight colour in his face now. 'Because she fears she's going to lose you. To this other woman.'

Charlotte was quiet a moment, then she shook her head. 'But that's—'

'Daft? Not at all.' He glanced at her. 'You're her child. And now – now it feels to her like she's going to lose you.'

'Why didn't she say?'

'If she'd have said something, you'd have ended up arguing. You always do these days. You can't help it, either of you.'

'She judges me – makes demands. Things she wants me to live up to.'

'Don't all parents?'

'No. You don't. You just encourage. The best I can do, that's always been good enough for you. But Mummy—'

'She's still Mummy then?'

Charlotte nodded. 'Yes. And she always will be, whatever happens.'

Jack swigged from the small, quarter bottle of whiskey, then tucked it away in his jacket pocket. He didn't usually drink at this hour of the day, but this once he felt the need. Dutch courage. Because if he was going to speak to her—

His legs felt wooden, like they weren't his. He had to force them to move, as if all of his reluctance, his fear, had focused itself in them.

He was afraid – shit-scared, if he was honest with himself – but he was going to do this, even if he regretted it later on, because it was the right thing to do.

The *right* thing, not the *only* thing. He'd gone through it all in his head these past four days. There were other options. He could deny it – say it was someone else's child. Or he could leg it, before Charlotte's dad came knocking at the door. But in both cases there was a problem.

I wouldn't like myself. Couldn't live with myself.

The letter was in the back pocket of his jeans. It explained everything. But it was really only a back-up, something to give her if she wouldn't listen and, knowing Charlotte, that was a distinct possibility. She was a stubborn cow, sometimes.

Jack almost smiled, picturing her, seeing the obstinacy in her face. He liked that about her; liked that she knew her own mind. But it could be problematic. Like now.

He had come to the end of her road. Two rows of identical-looking semi-detached houses stretched away on either side, each with its own garage, its own well-tended front garden.

They had talked about getting away from all this; from suburbia and well-kept lawns and brightly polished cars, from the *sameness* of it all, the predictability. Only they hadn't counted on complications. Hadn't counted on a baby.

He kept walking, pace after pace, until he stood at the front gate of her house. He was trembling now, shaking really badly.

For a moment he considered taking another sip of whiskey, only it wouldn't look good, especially if her mother was looking from the window.

Go on, he told himself. *Up the path and ring the bloody bell.*

Only he couldn't move. He'd got this far, but he couldn't take another step.

Jack closed his eyes and thought of her, recalled how desperate she'd looked when she had told him, and felt his strength of purpose return. Opening his eyes, he pushed open the gate and walked deliberately down the path. It was quiet. Not a murmur. Not even the distant sound of traffic. For a moment it seemed like the world itself had stopped. Then he rang the bell.

His heart was pounding now, like he'd just finished an eight-mile run, or – and the thought disturbed him now – as it had after he had made love to her, thumping away like it was trying to get out of his chest.

He waited, then, before courage failed him, rang again, giving the knocker two loud bangs just for good measure.

Nothing. A minute passed and still there was no sign of life from the house. He stepped back a couple of paces, staring up at the first-floor windows, but there was no twitch of curtains, no sign of a face.

Jack turned, meaning to walk away, then remembered the letter. It wasn't meant for this purpose. She'd think him a coward if she just read the letter – think he didn't have the guts to face her – only it was better than saying nothing, and he wasn't sure he had the strength to go through this ordeal twice.

He took it from his pocket and stared at it a moment. It had her name on the front in his best hand. Her name and a tiny X, signifying a kiss. He tapped it against his thigh a moment, then, almost impulsively, walked over to the door and stuffed it through the letterbox.

And turned, and ran, before someone came, before he'd have to do it all again.

'Charlotte Matthews?'

Charlotte looked up, surprised to see that the naval officer who'd summoned her was female; a neat woman in her late twenties or early thirties, with bobbed black hair and a pleasant smile. She wore the uniform of a lieutenant.

'Please, take a seat both of you,' she said, as she ushered them into her office then closed the door behind her. 'My name is Lucy Fielding, and I'll be dealing with your enquiry.' She sat across the desk from them and smiled. 'I understand you spoke to the Vice-Admiral himself.'

'He's an old schoolfriend,' Richard explained, a faint flush creeping into his face. 'We play golf together sometimes—'

Charlotte would have smiled at the old boy act, only she was too nervous.

'Right, I understand that you're trying to trace someone – a naval wife – is that right?'

'Yes,' Charlotte said, and realised that her father had said it at precisely the same time. He looked to her and smiled nervously, indicating that she should answer.

'Yes,' Charlotte said again. 'Her name is Julie Harding.'

'Okay.' The woman nodded, then typed something on her keyboard and looked at her screen. 'And her husband's Christian name?'

'I don't know. That's what I've come to find out.'

The woman looked up at her. 'But that's her married name, right?'

Charlotte shook her head.

'Hmmm, then we have a problem. The thing is, if we had the seaman's name then it would be relatively easy to check. But without it—'

'But there must be some way of doing it. You must have the names of sailors' wives!'

Lieutenant Fielding suppressed a smile. 'If they're married then generally speaking we're dealing with them by their married name.'

Charlotte looked crestfallen.

'I'm sorry,' the lieutenant went on. 'But really, unless you can come up with a name for your seaman, we really would be looking for a needle in a haystack.'

Seeing that this was the signal for them to leave, Richard

stood. 'Well, thanks for your help anyway. Do you think I could leave our details, just in case?'

The woman smiled. 'Of course. And here's my card, just in case you come up with a name.'

Outside, Charlotte turned to her father, letting him hold her a moment. 'I don't think I'm ever going to find her. It's like the woman said, it's like looking for a needle in a haystack.'

'Hey, it's not that bad. We've only just started.'

'No?' Her tone was sharp, angry, then she relented. 'I know – it's just—'

But she didn't have to say what it was. He knew.

Imogen nudged the gate-pen with her hip, then struggled up the path, three bags of shopping in each hand, the keys dangling from her mouth. It had been a good day. Her boss, Mr Kramer, had called her in and praised her for the work she'd done on the Obermann case, then had asked her if she'd like to take on something new. She'd jumped at the chance, knowing that it could lead to a promotion within the firm. The only trouble was that it would mean a much heavier workload, and what with Charlotte—

Well, she'd cross that bridge as and when. Right now she felt like celebrating. She would cook a meal for them all, with nice wine and cheeses afterwards.

She put down the bags and, taking the keys from her mouth, slipped the Yale into the lock. As she did, the phone began to ring inside.

'Shit!' she murmured, noting the letter on the mat. Bending down, she quickly picked it up, then hurried through, leaving the bags on the doorstep.

It was Charlotte, phoning on the mobile from the car.

'Hi, darling. Any luck?'

She said it lightly, but that wasn't how she felt.

'No,' Charlotte said despondently. 'We need the husband's name.'

'Oh – I am sorry.' And she was, only she also felt relieved. Distractedly, she placed the letter on the shelf beside the phone, not bothering to see who it was for. 'How long will you be?'

Yet as she listened, Imogen closed her eyes, calming herself, realising that she was close to getting into a state. Why was it so hard? Why did every little thing set her off like this? She wasn't a teenager, after all. Only recently it had felt like she wasn't in control any more – like it needed only the smallest emotional nudge and she would be in tears.

Charlotte said goodbye. The phone went dead. Imogen placed it back on the cradle then looked about her, as though she were somewhere strange, as though, suddenly, she had stepped right off the map.

A dog was barking further down the street. With a start she realised that she had left the door wide open, the shopping on the doorstep.

'Christ!' she said, hurrying through. 'Get a grip on yourself, woman!'

'Sister, have you got a second?'

The ward sister looked up from her desk and smiled.

Julie stepped inside and closed the door behind her. 'This is awkward. You see my husband, Mike, has this do with his firm tonight, and he was insistent that I go.'

'But you're not supposed to be on shift this evening, are you?'

'No, and that's the point. I told him I was – to get out of it.'

The ward sister frowned.

'Oh, it's deathly,' Julie went on. 'A whole room full of cable layers. I'm telling you, I'd rather have my teeth pulled than go to another of their do's. So if he phones, and asks if I'm here, could you tell him I am?'

'And what if he asks to talk to you?'

'Then tell him I've gone to escort a patient to another hospital. In the ambulance. Not that he'll phone. Only he'd kill me if he knew.'

'This is straight, Julie?'

'Oh, Girl Guide's honour!' And she made a little salute, making the ward sister giggle.

'Alright. This once. But don't make a habit of it, okay?'

'I won't. And thanks. Whenever you want a bedpan emptied—'

Stepping back into the corridor, Julie grinned. There! Easy-peasy. She wasn't going to get caught out twice. Not that Mike would call. He took her word on everything. Even so, it didn't harm to be careful. Especially if—

She thought of it – for the first time began to imagine it – she and Dave in bed again . . .

Imogen was stirring the goulash, lifting the wooden spoon to her mouth to sample a tiny bit of it, when the front door slammed. Putting the pan back on the hob, she turned the gas down, then hurried out into the hallway, but Charlotte had already gone. She had a fleeting glimpse of her back, dis-appearing into her room, and then the door banged shut.

She turned, looking to Richard, who was hanging his jacket on the peg by the door.

'Well?' she asked quietly.

'Not good,' he whispered back to her, gesturing towards the kitchen.

Inside, he closed the door behind him, then sighed. 'I reckon that's it. If we've not got the husband's name, then we can't trace the wife.'

'So what can we do?'

'Nothing. Just hope this all blows over.'

Imogen turned away. 'God, this is worse than knowing. She's been bad enough as it is—'

'Hey,' Richard said, 'it's not her fault. All this – it was done to her. She didn't have a choice. But now she wants to sort it all out, make sense of it. You can't blame her for that.'

'I don't blame her for that. I just wish—'

'Why don't you go up to her? Talk to her about it.'

'But the dinner—'

'I'll finish the dinner. You just go and see to your daughter. She needs you.'

Imogen looked to him fearfully. 'You think so?'

'Damn it, I know so. Now go!'

*

She knocked on the door. Then, when there was no answer, she pushed it open. The room was in darkness. Melancholy music was playing in the background; the kind of thing young girls seemed to thrive on these days.

'Lottie – what are you doing, sitting there in the dark?'

Imogen walked across and switched on the bedside lamp, then straightened up, looking down at her adopted daughter.

'Darling, I wish there was something I could do to make everything alright, but—'

'I'm fine.'

'Maybe we could hire somebody. You know, to trace her.'

'It's fine. I'll find her.' The tone was resentful – almost hateful.

Imogen rolled her eyes. This was hard. She sat down on the edge of the bed, then tried another tack.

'I saw Jess and Sophie today. In the High Street. They wondered why they hadn't seen you for a while.'

Charlotte looked up for the first time. 'And what did you say?'

'What could I say?' She reached out to take Charlotte's hand, but she drew it back. 'Do you want to talk about it?'

Charlotte was silent a moment, then she looked at her again. 'Why couldn't you have children?'

Imogen stared at her, taken aback by the bluntness of the question. Then, slowly, she began to answer her. 'I got pregnant. Twice. But I had two ectopics. Lost a tube each time. Just bad luck.'

She reached for her daughter's hand again; this time there was no resistance.

'Lottie, never doubt how much Daddy and I love you. To us you were a miracle we never expected to happen. When you adopt a child you – well, that child is very, very special.'

'But I never wanted to be special. I wanted to be normal, like all the other kids. I wanted to know who I looked like, where I came from. And I wanted to know just why she didn't want me.' She laughed bleakly. 'There was this boy at school. He used to say, "You're a Dopted," like it was a breed or I was an alien or something. It was like, "You're a freak".'

Imogen smiled through the pain she was feeling. 'Don't hate us for loving you, Lottie.'

She patted Charlotte's leg, then stood up and went over to the door. Charlotte looked up.

'Mum, I—'

But Imogen had already gone; the door closing behind her.

Julie had dressed up for the occasion, but it was Dave, for once, who caught the eye. As he sat there, he looked almost handsome in his smart suit, his silk tie and his Charles Church shoes. They were sitting in the corner, enjoying an Italian meal, a bottle of the house red on the table between them. Dave was talking, leaning towards Julie, emphasising words with little movements of his knife as always.

Julie had forgotten that habit. Not that she minded. No, Dave looked good, and thus far she felt comfortable in his company.

'I stayed with John and Barbara for a bit,' he said. 'Just while I got myself straight.'

'Not your mum's, then.'

Dave smiled at the slight hint of sarcasm. He knew what Julie thought of his mum. 'Nah. Mind you, at least then I could've had my old bed. Babs put me up in the boys' bunk beds. It was like being a kid again.' He laughed. 'If I slept on the bottom bunk I banged my head every time I got up, but if I slept on the top I'd fall out every time I got a little pissed.'

'Did that a lot, did you?'

'It stopped me thinking about you.'

'What did you think about?'

'Things that stuck in my mind. The first time I saw you, with Marie. And I thought about this place, too. D'you remember we came here on our first date?'

She didn't, but she smiled as if she did.

'Yeah, and about the first time you came back to my place . . .'

'Da-ave . . .'

Dave shrugged. 'I just want everything to be the way it was before. We're still married. You could—'

But Julie was shaking her head. 'You promised we could take this a step at a time.'

'I know. And I'm sorry. It's just – I want you so much.'

The way he looked at her made her weaken. 'Alright. Maybe a coffee. But don't rush me, Dave. I need time.'

Maybe it was something she'd said, when they were arguing that last time, just before they'd broken up – something about him being boring in bed, about not being adventurous enough – but halfway through their lovemaking, Dave took her completely by surprise by turning her round and then taking her from behind.

Mike was always wanting to try something new and had her moving about the bed like a gymnast, but Dave wasn't usually like that. The change seemed to work for them both, and what had, until then, been only satisfactory, suddenly became interesting, even enjoyable.

As he came, he seemed to wrap himself about her, pressing his body close and tight about hers, kissing her neck from behind, soft wet little kisses that made her tremble, and as they snuggled afterwards, she felt a real warmth towards him that surprised her.

'You happy?' he asked, beaming into her face.

'Yeah,' she answered, and it wasn't a lie. Right then she couldn't have been happier.

Chapter Seventeen

No Other Love

There were less than a dozen of them at the graveside as the coffin, sailor's cap atop, was slowly lowered into the hole. Among that sprinkling of naval personnel, Lucy Fielding was probably the only one who'd never met the man in life. She stood there, slightly back from all the rest, looking on. Then, when the ceremony was finished, and the hole filled with earth, she went across and, crouching down, read the cards on the floral tributes, looking for one name in particular.

It wasn't there, but then, she hadn't really thought it would be. It was just a long shot on her part.

Later, back in her office, she took out the cardboard box containing all that remained of the dead man's effects, and spread the contents out on the floor, kneeling down to sort through them, looking, once again, for something – anything – that might give a clue.

There were medals and documents, official letters and various odd pieces of paper and, at the very bottom of the pile, a wedding certificate.

Unfolding it, she read it through, then nodded to herself. Back at her desk she took out the official form she had been filling in and, alongside Next of Kin, wrote in the name on the certificate:

Julie Harding.

She paused, wondering why that name should ring a bell, then, with a shrug, dropped the certificate back into the box.

Marie and Julie were sitting at the bar of the Fox and Fiddle, having a drink and a chat. The pub would be opening for the evening in twenty minutes, and Dave was busy at the far end of the bar, getting things ready, but for the moment the two girls relaxed, enjoying a breather.

Marie leaned towards her, speaking quietly, confidentially. 'I'm glad you and Dave got things sorted out. He's like a dog with two dicks.'

Julie laughed. 'If only!'

'So when are you gonna move back in with him – only he's driving me mad going on about it.'

Julie's good humour seemed to evaporate at once. 'If it ain't broke, don't fix it.'

'Yeah, but you're married already. And besides, it's stupid you paying rent when you could be living here for free.'

Julie looked away. 'As it goes, I'm alright. The old lady I keep an eye on? You know, Nancy? I look after her, and in return I get my board and lodging free. It suits both of us.'

'Yeah, but you can't go on like that long-term, can you?'

Avoiding giving an answer, Julie smiled at Dave further along the bar. He grinned back at her.

'Anyway,' Marie went on, 'how'd you come to get that job?'

Julie turned, meeting her eyes. 'One of the women from the nursing home I worked in after me and Dave – well, she was looking for someone to live in with her mother-in-law. They knew I was looking for a place of my own, so . . .'

'That was lucky.'

'Yeah,' Julie smiled, then raised her glass to her lips, looking along the bar once again to find Dave staring at her adoringly. Looking back at Marie, she grinned. 'So when am I going to see that daughter of yours?'

Mike was dressing for work, snarling as he pulled on his trousers, almost pushing his foot through the material in his angry haste.

'Unreasonable! How am I being unreasonable? You worked two extra shifts last week and three the week before that.'

Julie was standing in front of the mirror, in her nurse's uniform, pinning up her hair. 'You say it as though I was doing it for my own benefit.'

'Well, it ain't for mine!'

She glared at him in the mirror. 'God, you're so selfish. I told you. I wanted to make a bit extra for Christmas. What's wrong with that?

Mike met her eyes, answering her sarcastically. 'At this rate you'll be able to own your own bleeding turkey farm.' He huffed, then straightened up. 'I'm going to work. I'll see you when I see you.'

And with that he stormed from the room, the front door slamming a moment later. Julie closed her eyes. She was tired of this. Tired of the rows and the black looks and the silences. Tired of having to explain herself the whole time. It was her own fault, of course, but that didn't make it any easier to put up with.

The sound of the phone ringing forced her out of the dark mood she could feel herself slipping into. Sighing, she picked it up.

'Hello?'

Slowly her face broke into a smile, and there was warmth in her voice when she next spoke.

'Nancy! I'm really glad you called!'

Vera was sitting in the kitchen, having a cuppa and reading the morning paper, when she heard the letterbox go. Stepping out into the hallway, she squinted into the half-dark. There, on the mat, was a single white envelope.

She walked across and, stooping down, picked it up and studied the writing. She didn't recognise the handwriting, yet something about it was familiar. The postmark was Portsmouth, and that too rang a bell, though for the life of her she couldn't think why.

Going back into the kitchen she sat again, then, putting on her reading glasses, she slit the envelope open and took out the letter.

She blinked, then smiled to herself. It was from Marge, who'd lived three doors up from them when they still had the house. She had moved down to Portsmouth five years back, and though she didn't write that often, she still sent them Christmas and birthday cards.

Unfolding the single sheet, she straightened it out and began to read. She was halfway down the page when, with a start, she realised what it was about and, turning the paper over, saw the advert that Marge had sellotaped to the back. It was cut out of her local paper down in Portsmouth and read as follows:

'JULIE CARMICHAEL
(nee Harding)
The Royal Navy seeks to locate the
whereabouts of the above-named with
regard to her husband, Ian Carmichael.
Anyone with information should contact
Lucy Fielding on . . .'

And it gave an address and telephone number.

Vera sat back, her heart racing, feeling suddenly very short of breath. So it was true, after all, Julie *had* married a sailor. And quickly, on the back of that thought, came another. She ought to let the girl, Charlotte, know. It was only fair.

She straightened up, hearing the sound of Ted's cough out in the corridor outside the front door. Panicking, she quickly folded the letter, slipped it into the envelope and stuffed it deep into her apron pocket. Reaching for the newspaper, she hurriedly opened it, pretending to be engrossed in one of the stories even as Ted came into the room.

'Bastard buses!' he murmured grumpily as he walked past her and, picking up the kettle, took it over to the sink to fill.

She got the phone call just after eleven.

'Hi, babe,' Dave said. 'Look, I know this is short notice, but can you meet me lunchtime?'

'Yeah, I can pop out for a bit, why?'

'I thought – well, maybe we could have a spot of lunch at that Italian restaurant you like.'

'But I'm seeing you tonight.'

'Nah. That's just it. I can't make it tonight. The guy who owns the pub – he needs to see me and, well, I can't really put him off, can I?'

'Oh.' In that one simple word she managed to convey every ounce of the resentment she was feeling.

'You know I wouldn't do this unless it was really important. Besides, there's something I want to tell you, and it can't wait.'

Intrigued, she agreed to meet him, telling the sister she had to go out on a personal matter. Thus, at twelve o'clock, she was waiting outside the restaurant, wearing her civvies, as Dave hurried towards her.

'Christ!' Dave said, pecking her cheek. 'They've got the roads up every-bleeding-where, ain't they?'

And it was true. Half of the High Street was dug up, and the traffic was crawling slowly between the rows of cones. There was a constant noise of jack hammers and drills.

They went inside.

Throughout the meal, Dave seemed quieter than normal, and Julie began to think that maybe there was something wrong at work. Maybe this meeting tonight was bad news and he didn't know how to break it to her. But she didn't ask. If Dave wanted to tell her, he'd tell her.

Finally, unable to bear it much longer, she reached across and covered his hand with her own. 'Dave? What was it you wanted to tell me?'

He looked up at her and gave a tense half-smile. 'I've done something.'

'Oh?'

'Yeah. The thing is, I always thought you felt a bit cheated, us not getting married in church, and I reckoned with the way things are going, you know, with us – well I've fixed up for us to get blessed.'

'Blessed?'

'Yeah. It's like a proper wedding, in church and everything, except you say different words.' He looked at her expectantly, then. 'Well? What d'you think?'

Julie stared back at him, speechless.

'Well?' Dave asked, apprehensive now. 'Say something.'

'I don't know what to say.'

'I know it's the right thing to do. I love you, you know that—'

Julie nodded.

'—and things have been going great. The same feelings are there. I know they are. We're good together, you and me.'

'But why don't—'

Dave interrupted. 'We're man and wife, Julie. Nothing's going to change that. This is just—' He shrugged. 'This'd just be like – well, a fresh start.'

Julie still looked worried, but she was wavering now. The thought of it was playing on her mind. Like a real church wedding. She liked the sound of that.

Dave was staring at her now, trying to work her out. 'You do still love me?'

At that moment he looked so vulnerable that Julie found herself moved. Solemnly, she nodded.

Dave blinked, and then his face broke into a great beam of a smile. He leaned across the table and kissed Julie full on the lips. Then, reaching for the wine bottle, he poured two glasses and handed one to her, raising his own in a toast.

'To us!'

Julie grinned, and mouthed the words. Not that it would have made much difference, for at that moment the noise outside started up again.

On the far side of the restaurant, the manager threw up his hands, then hurried outside to argue with the workmen, gesticulating furiously. Julie watched him a moment, amused, then looked back at Dave.

'Well?' she half-shouted. 'When's our big day?'

'Next Saturday.'

Julie grinned. 'You're a dark horse, you!'

'It'll work this time, Julie. I promise.'

'Maybe.' Her mobile began to ring. As she fished for it in her handbag, Dave stood, looking across to where the manager was still arguing with one of the workmen.

'I'll get the bill. Get away from this racket.'

Julie nodded, watching him walk off, then put the phone to her ear. 'Hello?'

With a shock, she realised it was Mike.

'Hiya, sweetheart,' he said. 'I thought I might just catch you on your lunchbreak.'

'I'm just going back in the hospital,' she said, looking about the room.

'Oh. Oh, okay. Look, I'm really sorry about this morning. And well, I thought we could go out to dinner. Tomorrow, I mean. Make up for me being a prat.'

'Tonight,' she said, straining to speak over the noise, but looking at the same time to make sure Dave didn't hear her. 'Why don't you take me out tonight?'

'But I thought—'

'They don't need me. They've already got cover.'

'That's great. If you like we could go to this place I know—'

'Yeah, okay, fine, but I've got to switch this off now. I'm—'

She stopped dead, shocked to find that she was staring through the window at Mike. He was standing there, right beside where the restaurant manager and the workman were arguing, watching them while he spoke on his mobile.

'Oh shit!'

'What?'

She had to think quickly. 'No, it's okay. I tripped, that's all. But I've got to get back now, so—'

She turned, seeing that Dave was coming back across.

'Look, gotta go. See you later. Bye.'

Switching off the phone she stuffed it into her bag then turned to Dave, smiling.

'That was the ward sister – seems they've had a bit of an emergency, need me back there.'

Dave was all sympathy. 'You want me to drop you off?'

Julie glanced at Mike on the other side of the window, and realised they'd be unable to leave without being seen.

'Nah. It's okay. I can walk. But let's have a brandy first, eh?'

'But I thought you said—'

'Sister said twenty minutes. It'll take me ten to walk, so—'

Dave shrugged. 'Alright, I'll go order a couple of brandies for us.'

'Okay, I—' Again she stopped dead. Mike had gone. No – shit! He was *inside*!

Julie looked about her desperately, prepared, if necessary, to dive under the table. To make things worse, Dave had now joined Mike at the bar, where the pair of them were chatting. Julie turned her back on them, hiding her face. In a lull in the drilling, their voices drifted across to her.

'Two brandies, Augusto,' she heard Dave say. Then, to Mike. 'Don't s'pose you lot'd like to take a tea break till me and the missus have finished our drinks, would you?'

Mike's voice was chillingly familiar. 'Sorry, mate. Wish we could. But we're s'posed to be finished here before the rush-hour traffic begins.' He paused, then, 'What's the food like here?'

'Good, as it goes . . .'

The noise from outside drowned out the rest. A moment later, Dave sat down beside her, handing her a large glass of brandy. He clinked his own against it.

'So what d'you reckon? Is it alright to start telling people about the do?'

Distracted, Julie stared at him blankly. 'What? Er, yeah. Yeah, fine.' She gave Dave a little smile, but all the while she was watching Mike as he crossed the road and went into the café opposite. Realising she needed to take advantage of the opportunity, she stood up smartly.

'Actually, I'd better get back. Just in case.'

'But you said—' Dave looked stunned. 'What about your brandy?'

Julie took the glass and, to his astonishment, downed it in one. Then, seizing Dave's, she downed that also.

'Right,' Dave said, more amazed by the minute. 'Guess I'll pay the bill then.'

Fuck this for a lark, Mike thought, as he punched in his boss's number. *What kind of arsehole is it thinks you can dig up a road without making a bit of noise?*

True, but this one ran a rather nice restaurant, and he'd said that if Mike did *him* a favour . . .

The phone rang, twice, then cut out.

'Shit!' The bloody thing kept losing its signal.

He went to the doorway and tried again, looking up and down the high street as he waited for McDonagh to answer. Some woman in a garish red dress hurried out of the restaurant opposite, her back turned towards him and half ran, half walked down the street. She looked a little bit like Julie, only tartier. One of Mike's workmen gave her a wolf whistle as she passed. Mike laughed. She looked vaguely familiar, but before he could work out where he'd seen her, McDonagh was on the line.

He gave a bit of a spiel about complications, and having to shut things down for an hour or so to get things straightened out, then, mission accomplished, he switched the mobile off.

Satisfied, he wandered back across the road and into the restaurant.

'Hey, Augusto! Can I have a word please, mate.'

Karl stood by the window, waiting patiently as the girl on the other end of the phone went through her records. On the coffee table next to him was a telephone directory, open at the Nurses' Agencies section. Several entries had already been crossed through.

Seeing Anita coming along the pavement outside, carrying the shopping, he gave her a brief wave and a smile, then, as the girl came back on the line, switched his attention back.

'Yeah yeah, okay love. But thanks for checking.'

He cut the connection and switched the phone off, then hurried through, greeting Anita by the door and taking the heavy bags off her.

'No luck?' she asked.

Karl shrugged. 'It's early days yet. Got a lot more to try.'

Anita kissed his cheek, then followed him through. 'There's a couple of beers in one of them bags. I'll get an opener, eh?'

Karl set the bags down on the kitchen table, then turned and grinned at her. 'Don't s'pose you went in the chemist's while you were at it, did you?'

Anita smiled despite herself. 'Might've done, but you've got a few more calls to make before the agencies close for the day.'

Karl sighed. 'Yeah. I guess so. I'll just have to settle for a beer.'

Anita stepped across and hugged him a moment.

Smiling again, Karl went back through and, crouching beside the phone book, began to punch in the next number on the list.

He straightened, turning to smile at Anita as she came into the room with his beer. 'Hello? Is that the Alliance Nursing Agency?'

Charlotte closed the door quietly behind her, then tiptoed down the hall. The house was silent, and there was no sign of the car outside, but even so . . .

The kitchen was empty. She sighed with relief, then went through and, setting her shoulder bag down on the table, walked over to the sink and poured herself a glass of water.

She had spent the whole day at the Family Records Center, over near the Angel in Islington, working her way patiently, laboriously through the bright green Marriages files, trying to find some trace of her mother. The trouble was, there were an awful lot of Hardings, and an awful lot of files to work through. Even working on the basis that her mother hadn't been married before she'd had her, that still left eighteen years of files – and with four files to a year, that meant she'd had to trawl through more than seventy files in total. She felt exhausted.

What made it worse, was that she hadn't a clue where or when her mother had been married. When she'd finally given up – halfway through – she had already noted down the marriage details of more than sixty Julie Hardings. If she wanted to take it any further, she'd have to order up copies of the marriage certificates, and as they cost £6.50 a time, that wasn't very likely.

Charlotte finished the water, then turned, looking back across the room at her handbag. As she did, she noticed that there was an unopened letter on the work surface, beside the bread bin.

She walked across. Seeing her name on it and recognising the handwriting, she grabbed at it eagerly and tore it open, fumbling at the letter in her haste to read it. It was from Vera. For a moment, she mouthed the words to herself. Then, with a laugh of delight, she read the name aloud.

'Carmichael. His name was Ian Carmichael!'

For a moment she felt faint, giddy. Then she laughed again, even as the front door banged shut and her mother walked along the hall and into the room.

Imogen stopped dead, surprised to see her daughter grinning and laughing for once. 'Charlotte? Are you okay?'

Charlotte beamed, then thrust the letter at Imogen. 'It's from Vera. I know who my father is!'

Mike was waiting for her in the car as she came off shift. As she climbed into the passenger seat, he grinned, then leaned across to kiss her.

'Had a good day?'

Julie smiled. 'Yeah, not bad. You?'

He started the car, put it into gear, then nodded. 'Not bad, as it happens. You wanna eat straight away?'

Julie thought of the meal she'd had at lunch time – she wasn't sure she could eat another so soon afterwards – but she didn't want to spoil Mike's night.

'Yeah. That'd be nice.'

'There's this place I know. As a matter of fact, I did the guy a favour . . .'

But as they drew up outside Augusto's, Julie looked anything but pleased. 'We're not going in there, are we?'

'Yeah, why not? The food's supposed to be good, and the owner's a bit of a character, and as I was saying—'

'No,' Julie said quickly. 'I don't fancy it. Let's go to that Chinese we liked. Or that pasta place further down the High Street.'

Mike looked dismayed. 'Hang on. I thought this'd make a change. You're always having a go about me not taking you places. I thought this'd be something different.'

Julie's voice hardened. 'I just don't fancy it, *alright*?'

Mike was taken aback. 'Okay,' he said, putting his hands up

defensively. 'Okay, let's go.' And to Julie's relief, he turned and walked off up the street.

As it turned out, they had a really pleasant evening. When Mike finally worked out that she wasn't really hungry, he took her to a wine bar instead, and they ended up leaving there well after midnight, the car abandoned, the two of them giggling as they staggered down the pavement, arm in arm, heading home.

Mike was too drunk to make love, but it didn't matter; she didn't feel like sex, she just wanted to be held for once, so he held her, and after a while he fell asleep. Hearing his soft snores, she got another fit of giggles and lay there, her head spinning, wondering just how she'd got herself into this mess.

She should have been in Dave's bed right then, making love to Dave. But here she was, with Mike.

Julie lifted the covers and looked at Mike's trim, muscular body, smiling to herself as she saw how small his penis looked when he was asleep, like a tiny little hibernating mouse. Another time she might have burrowed down and kissed it, waking him up, but right now she didn't have the energy. No, looking after two men wasn't all it was cracked up to be. A woman might have her needs, but as far as sex was concerned, one man was really quite enough.

Julie stretched, then closed her eyes; felt Mike move, then roll away from her. She yawned, then rolled over herself, her back to his. In less than a minute she too was fast asleep.

Charlotte was up at the crack of dawn, dressed and out, before Imogen and Richard had even stirred. Standing there, on the crowded, early-morning tube, she found herself wondering why Lucy Fielding hadn't contacted her directly. Not only that, but the name Carmichael hadn't been on her list. Even so she was excited. At last she was getting somewhere!

She had to wait almost an hour for Lucy Fielding to see her, and even when she finally did, the news the woman had for her was unexpected.

'I'm afraid he's dead. There'll be an inquiry, of course, but according to reports it seems it was a tragic accident. We tried to contact your mother, as she's still listed as next of kin, but it seems they split up quite a while ago.'

Charlotte was quiet a moment, stunned, devastated, even. Then she looked up again. 'But *how* have you tried?' she asked quietly. 'Surely there must have been an address?'

Lucy Fielding shook her head. 'Nothing, I'm afraid. We've contacted the local council, the DSS, the UKCC—'

'The UKCC?'

'She worked as a nurse at the forces hospital for a time.'

Charlotte stared at her, surprised. 'She's a *nurse*?'

The woman closed the file, gave Charlotte a smile. 'How about you? You said that you'd been in touch with her family.'

Charlotte nodded. 'Yes, but they don't know where she is. My grandmother knew about – well, she knew Julie had married a sailor, but—' She gave a small, shivering sigh. 'Do you have . . . anything of his that I could keep? A photo or something?'

'I'm afraid it's against . . .'

Seeing the disappointment in the young woman's face, the older woman hesitated, then, fishing in the box beside her, brought out a photograph and handed it to Charlotte.

Charlotte studied it wistfully. 'He looks so young. How old was he when he died?'

'Twenty-eight. That was taken shortly before the accident.'

'Twenty-eight!' Charlotte looked shocked now. Realisation hit her. 'Then – but I thought—'

'Oh. Oh, I see. Look, I'm sorry. I'm really sorry. If I find out anything more, I'll let you know, okay?'

Charlotte nodded, but her face was closed now, her eyes disappointed.

That week seemed to fly for Julie. Before she knew it, it was Saturday.

Mike was in a mood. He sat in the armchair, flicking the remote control, moving between channels without even looking what was on them.

'I still don't see why I can't go,' he said grumpily. 'It seems bloody funny that husbands can't go along with their wives.'

Julie came into the room, wearing a smart outdoor coat. She looked all dolled up and glamorous. 'I know, but maybe she's got too many people.'

Mike turned to her and grimaced. 'Well, I reckon it's a bit off.'

Julie made a face. 'Well, I can't help that, can I?'

Outside, a car horn sounded. Julie went to the window and waved.

'Look, I gotta go. My cab's here. I'll see you tomorrow.'

'Tomorrow?'

'Yeah. I told you. It's in Kent. You wouldn't want me coming home on my own, would you? You know what them trains are like.'

'Well, who are you staying with?'

'Her mum and dad. It's all above board.'

Mike didn't look happy. Julie bent forward and kissed his neck, whispering into his ear, despite there being no one else to hear. 'I'll make it up to you when I'm back.'

His face softened a little. Julie straightened, smoothing her hands down her coat.

'Oh, and don't forget Nancy's tablets. Two of the yellow and one of the blue, and *before* she eats, alright?

Mike nodded grudgingly. 'Have a nice time.'

Julie looked at him, but Mike was staring at the TV fixedly now, refusing to even look at her.

Julie was almost in the shadows of the great stone doorway when the vicar stepped out, one hand extended, to greet her.

Shit, she thought, recognising him from the last ceremony.

There was a tiny movement in his face as the smile of greeting became a look of puzzlement.

'Have we met before?'

Julie smiled nervously. 'I don't think so. Mind you, someone else said that to me the other day, so I reckon I must have a double. They say everyone's got one, don't they?'

The vicar smiled uncertainly, then, as the music started up inside, gave her a second, briefer smile and hurried inside. As he did, Marie stepped out, Ellie next to her.

'You okay?' Marie asked. 'You look white as a sheet.'

Julie nodded, then smiled back at her. 'You look beautiful. Both of you.'

'So do you,' Ellie said, her eyes sparkling.

'Good,' Julie said, nervous again suddenly. 'Well, let's go in.'

Imogen was sitting at the kitchen table, her work spread out in front of her, when Charlotte came into the room. There had been a palpable tension between the two of them these last few days, ever since she had got back from the naval offices, in fact, but suddenly, it seemed, that mood had blown over. Leaning close, Charlotte kissed Imogen's right temple, then, stepping over to the kettle, asked brightly, 'Would you like tea?'

She didn't actually want one – she had already drunk too much coffee – but she didn't want to reject this rare display of generosity, and so, smiling, she said, 'Thanks. That'd be nice.'

Charlotte lifted the kettle, weighing it in her hand, then took it over to the tap to fill. 'Where's Dad?' she asked, glancing round at Imogen.

'Squash. He should be back soon, though.'

Charlotte nodded, then quickly made the tea, handing a cup to Imogen, who received it with a smile. It was only then that she noticed how, under the sunny exterior, Charlotte seemed nervous. She got that way, sometimes, when she wanted to ask a favour, or when she'd done something she wanted to own up to – but it had been some time since she had done either.

Charlotte sat, cradling her own tea, as if summoning up the courage to speak. And then she did.

'I've made a decision.'

Imogen put her work down to one side. 'Oh? What about?'

'I've decided that I'm not going to take up my place at university.'

Despite herself, Imogen found she was shocked, yes, and disappointed too. Even so, she tried to keep her cool.

'I see. So, do you know what you *are* going to do?'

'Not yet.'

Imogen nodded, then, rather than lose her temper, looked back at her work. But Charlotte hadn't finished.

'And there's something else.'

Imogen looked up. 'Oh?'

'I'm pregnant.'

Imogen's eyes widened in purest shock. 'Pregnant!' Then she saw how young Charlotte suddenly looked, how vulnerable, how close to tears, and jumped up. Hurrying round the table, she knelt beside Charlotte, holding her as her daughter's face crumpled and she began to sob.

'Sshh, sshh. Everything's going to be fine. I promise.'

Charlotte took a shuddering breath, then, through her tears, asked, 'Am I going to be like her?'

'Sshh,' Imogen said, barely holding it together herself now. 'It's going to be fine. It is. It really is.'

Chapter Eighteen

Wooden Heart

Mike was sitting on the sofa, patiently unscrewing and testing each of the tiny bulbs, trying to discover which of them wasn't working. It was frustrating work, and as Julie came into the room, he looked up at her, a pleading expression on his face.

'Do I *have* to do this? Can't we just go to Woolies and buy a new set?'

'What? Twenty quid! No . . . Anyway, it won't take you a minute.'

The tree in the corner looked a bit forlorn. Nancy had had a few decorations, but only enough for the small plastic tree she usually used. But Julie had wanted a real tree for Christmas, and real trees cost money – especially when you added in the decorations.

Mike looked down again, getting on with things. But he wasn't happy. Christmas was becoming a bit of a chore as far as he was concerned.

'Does it really matter?' he'd asked earlier. 'We could have made do with the small tree. I mean, it's not as if we've got kids.'

But Julie had insisted. She wanted everything just so for Nancy.

Nancy hadn't been well, and while she didn't say so to Mike, Julie wondered whether she'd live to see another Christmas. That was why she'd moved back in with them. She was looking frail and old suddenly, and her long illness had made her susceptible to every cold and virus that came along. That was also why this Christmas was so important. And Julie would have done a lot more to make things perfect for her, only Nancy and Mike weren't her only consideration.

She glanced at her watch. *Shit! Was that the time already?*

'Look,' she said, scooping up her handbag and her jacket, 'I've got to go and do the shopping. You got some money?'

Mike looked up at her, then threw the string of lightbulbs down angrily. 'What happened to that thirty quid I gave you yesterday?'

'Blimey, Mike! Thirty quid don't go anywhere! Not at Christmas! I spent that on bits and pieces.'

'Well, they're bits and pieces we can't afford.' He stood and took out his wallet, then peeled off two ten-pound notes and handed them across.

Julie stared at them disdainfully. 'Is that all you got?'

'Well, what about all that extra money you were earning off of your extra shifts? I thought this was what you were doing them for.'

'I told you. I'm paying for the food. And anyway, I don't get most of that till January. In the meantime . . .'

Grudgingly, Mike took another tenner from his front pocket and handed it over. But she could see he wasn't pleased. 'I was gonna have a beer with that,' he said moodily. 'With the blokes from work.'

Mike was still playing five-a-side each Tuesday night – another bone of contention between them.

'Well, you'll have to go without, won't you?'

'Yeah, but . . .' He gave up the argument, sat down again. But everything about him said he wasn't happy, and not just about the money – but that wasn't her problem, that was his.

'Okay,' she said breezily. 'I gotta go. I'll just say bye to your mum.'

Nancy was still asleep. Seeing that, Julie went across and arranged her covers about her, making sure she was comfortable. Then, feeling a real warmth for her, she leaned across and gently kissed her brow.

'See you later, Mum.'

Then, hurrying now, knowing she was late, she went down the hallway and out, pulling the door to quietly behind her.

Dave looked up from where he stood at the bar, wiping glasses, and grinned at her. 'You're late, babe. Everything alright?'

'Yeah.' She came across and let him lean across the bar to kiss her. 'Listen, I'm going to nip out to get the shopping, and I want to get a few bits and bobs. Something for Marie and Ellie. Can you pay for that?'

'I've already done Marie,' Dave said, reaching up to place a glass on the top shelf. 'I thought she'd probably want the money. And I thought you said you had Ellie's. Skates or something, you said.'

She'd forgotten she'd said that. 'Oh yeah yeah, I forgot.'

'And look,' he added gently, almost fatherly. 'I know you're sorting out the food, but I don't want you to go too mad. Mum and Barb'll help.'

'I don't want them to help. *I* want to do it.'

Just then a customer arrived at the bar. Dave turned to him and smiled. 'Yes, mate?'

Julie stood there a moment, stymied, not knowing what to do. Then, without another word, she turned and hurried out, leaving Dave standing there frowning, wondering what the hell that was all about.

Lucy Fielding sat at her desk in the almost empty Navy building. It was gone twelve and she really ought to have been going. Everyone else in her department had left. But she had these last few things to do, and she really didn't want to come back from the holidays to a full in-tray. Even so, as she sat there, her mind was half on what she was going to cook for Christmas dinner. Her dad was coming up from Bath, and her sister and her kids. Bill had said he might come too, but knowing Bill he'd phone an hour or two before he was due to say he couldn't make it. Her brother was like that. And there were still a couple of presents to get. She could do that before she got the train, but right now—

She pressed ENTER on the keyboard, then closed the paper file and dropped it, with a little sigh of relief, into the out-tray.

'Last one,' she said quietly. 'Ian Carmichael.'

Lucy pulled the box across to her and, opening it, lifted out the photograph of the young sailor. She studied it a moment, feeling a vague sadness, then noticed the handwritten note that the young woman, Charlotte, had left her.

There! That was it! That was what she couldn't remember last time she'd looked at the file.

For a moment she hesitated, then, 'What the hell.' It was Christmas, after all. Maybe she'd have one more look, see what she could find.

She brought up the enquiry box, then typed in the name. It was only when she had pressed ENTER that she realised she had put in the woman's maiden name.

'Julie Harding? Oh, stupid girl, Lucy. It's Carmichael!'

She moved her hand back to the keypad, about to delete and re-type, when she realised from the page that had come up on the screen that there was a Julie Harding listed, only this one was married to a naval rating by the name of Tony Holloway.

Beneath the bride's name was an address and a date of birth. She read it aloud.

'Fifth of August nineteen sixty-six.'

Turning to the box, she searched through it until she found the wedding certificate, placing the pale green document in front of her.

There! Coincidence or what? She read the birth date aloud.

'Fifth of August nineteen sixty-six.'

Lucy blinked, then gave a surprised laugh. 'No. It couldn't be.'

Nancy was dozing in bed, when she heard a sound from the next room.

'Michael?'

There was no answer.

'Who's that?' she called, concerned now.

The door opened and Julie popped her head round. 'Sorry – just had to pop back for something. You alright?'

Nancy nodded, relieved that it was Julie. Julie smiled, then noticed her crumpled hankie and came across.

'Here, I'll get you a clean hankie.'

She walked over to the chest of drawers and, her back to Nancy, opened the top drawer. The folded hankies were to the

left, clean undies to the right. And there, in the centre, was
Nancy's jewellery box.

'Your mum would have been very proud of you, you know,'
Nancy said, a real warmth in her voice.

Julie quickly took a hankie and pushed the drawer shut. She
turned and smiled.

'Oh, I don't know about that.'

Nancy shook her head, gently chiding her. 'You shouldn't
have such a low opinion of yourself. You're a lovely girl.'

The words touched something in Julie. For once her answer
was brutally honest. 'I dunno. I wonder sometimes.'

'Nonsense,' Nancy said, lifting herself a little on her pillow.
'You are. But you know what they say – you've got to like
yourself if you want other people to like you.'

Julie thought about that then, giving Nancy her sweetest
smile, handed her the hankie. She leaned across her, kissing
Nancy on the forehead.

'I'll see you later.'

Back in her own room, Julie sat there, trembling slightly,
amazed by just how close she had come to taking Nancy's
jewellery. To have even thought about doing it! For a moment
she just sat there, her head lowered, her hands pressed
together. Then, straightening up, she nodded to herself and,
going over to her wardrobe, brought out her old memories box
from where it lay beneath a pile of summer tops.

Sitting on the edge of the bed, she rummaged through the
box. She was pretty sure she'd seen it in here, but for a moment
she couldn't find it.

'Shi-it,' she said, quietly but in a pained voice. 'Where the
hell is it?'

Julie picked up an old brown envelope full of Valentine's
cards and shook the contents out on to the bed, then hurriedly
sorted through them with her fingers, but it wasn't there either.

She closed her eyes, trying to calm herself. If she didn't find
it she'd be in big trouble – the kind she mightn't be able to talk
her way out of.

'*Think*,' she told herself. 'It *has* to be here. It *must* be.'

She looked again, taking each item out and shaking it gently, then putting it aside, going through the box methodically, until she found it, caught up in the sleeve of one of her old 45s.

It was odd seeing his name on the book beside hers. It scarcely seemed possible now that she had lived with him. But she had.

She looked at the card, then sighed with relief. It was still valid for another two months. There were only two cheques left in the chequebook, but it would probably be enough for what she needed.

Gathering up all her things, she quickly but carefully placed them back in the box and locked it, putting it back at the bottom of the wardrobe. She looked about her, checking that everything had been put away, then stuffed the chequebook into her handbag and hurried from the flat.

Though it was her job, Lucy Fielding didn't always like going on board ship. Some of the smaller ships were like tiny, floating villages, hostile to all outsiders, the crew regarding any newcomer as a potential enemy, or at best a nuisance, to be dealt with and got rid of ASAP.

She wondered if this was what months at sea did to people – a kind of mental hothousing process that turned ordinary sociable young men into sociopaths.

Of a kind.

Tony Holloway was one such. He sat there, opposite her in the captain's cabin, his face set, almost sulky. She could see from the way his eyes glanced quickly up at her, then looked away again immediately, that he thought he was in trouble – of what kind she couldn't guess – but his whole body language, his palpable discomfort, gave away the fact that *something* was troubling him. Normally, she might have taken her time and found out what it was, but this once she wasn't interested. It was none of her business. She was here about Julie Harding, his wife.

'Tony, are you married?'

The question was clearly unexpected. He frowned, then, 'I *was*.'

'You're divorced, then? Only, on your file—'

'No, not divorced exactly. Just – well, I haven't seen her for a while. A long while, if you want to know the truth.'

Lucy looked up, surprised. Tony had the slightest Birmingham accent. He was very different from Ian Carmichael. Shorter and fairer than the other man – almost stocky, whereas Carmichael had been slim and svelte.

'So you're separated?'

'Yeah. As in, I haven't a bloody clue where the woman is.'

'Ah, right. That was my next question. But you were married for—?'

'Four months.'

Lucy looked up from what she was writing. 'Four months? Is that how long your marriage lasted?'

'Yep. My first posting after we'd got hitched, it was. I was at sea fourteen weeks. And when I came back she was gone.'

'Did you talk to anyone about this?'

'No, why?'

Lucy shrugged. 'No matter. But look – have you got a picture of her? A wedding picture, maybe?'

Tony Holloway was staring at her directly now. 'Nope. Not a thing. She took all that kind of stuff when she left. Me ma might have a picture or two, but – well, once she'd buggered off I wasn't that keen on being reminded of her. Know what I mean?'

'Do you think your mother could get us a copy of one of those photos?'

'Why? Is she in trouble?'

Yes, Lucy thought, *she is.* But she wasn't going to tell him what it was. Not yet, anyway. She wanted *all* the facts before she took any action.

'Sorry.'

Julie gave a cringing smile to the old lady she had shunted into the shelves, then slowly pulled the trolley back into the centre of the aisle. It was Christmas Eve, the very worst time to be doing your supermarket shopping, but having two trolleys didn't help much either. She had to push one and pull the other, and what with all these little old ladies nipping in and nipping out to get some last little item to place in their baskets, it was a wonder she hadn't filled a casualty ward by herself.

Already she was getting worried. Catering for one family was bad enough, but for two . . .

Julie glanced down at the contents of each trolley. But for an item or two they were identical: a large box of crackers, a turkey, a big bag of Brussels, an even bigger bag of spuds, a Christmas pud, a packet of red and green serviettes, a bag of assorted nuts, some tangerines, a packet of mince pies, some after-dinner chocolates, a tin of custard, a boiling ham, several tins of fruit, and a dozen or more other items. Where they differed at all, it was in the most minor of ways. Dave liked tomato ketchup, Mike brown sauce. Mike liked pickled onions, Dave gherkins.

She paused, looking about her, then, putting the trolleys side by side, wandered over to the nearest shelf-filler, a cheery West Indian lady who was humming to herself as she worked.

'You don't do clothes, do you?'

The woman turned and smiled. 'No, darling. I'm sorry. But have a nice Christmas, eh?'

'Yeah, thanks – and you.'

Julie turned back, to find a thirty-something male – balding, all tweeds and trendy Gucci glasses – scowling at her, unable to pass with his trolley because hers were blocking the way.

'Sorry,' she said, but she felt a lot less sorry than she sounded.

'Merry Christmas,' she said under her breath. But as she moved back, one of her trolleys collided with yet another little old lady who had tried – unsuccessfully – to dash between Julie and the shelves.

'Sorry.'

Karl grinned, then drew Anita towards him, placing a long, lingering kiss on her lips.

'What was *that* for?' she asked, surprised by the sudden ardour of his embrace.

'You know. For everything.'

She smiled. 'Shouldn't be so irresistible, should you?'

He grinned. 'I thought this was going to be a shit Christmas, what with – well, you know what. But then you came along.'

'Yeah? And?'

He hesitated. 'And I love you—'

She looked up at him, surprised but delighted, her heart pounding in her chest.

'—and I want to marry you.'

She could barely breathe. 'But you're married,' she managed finally, hating herself for spoiling the moment and hating Julie for making her.

'I'll find her. We'll get a divorce.'

She allowed him to pull her to him and could feel the warmth of his breath as he whispered into her hair. 'I'll find her. I promise.'

Julie stood at the head of the queue, conscious that there were half a dozen impatient shoppers behind her as she packed away the last of the items into the second trolley.

The check-out girl looked up at her, bored, then handed her the bill and a pen.

Julie looked at the final total and winced, then dug into her handbag and pulled out the chequebook.

'Can I give you a cheque?'

The girl nodded, then looked at the next shopper, as if to say, 'Well, what can you do?' She watched as Julie painstakingly wrote out the total in words, put the number in the box, dated it, then scrawled her signature. Digging into the handbag again, she found the cheque card and, placing it with the cheque, handed both across.

Julie watched, nervously, as the girl studied the card, checked the signature on the cheque against the card, then handed the latter back, turning to press a button to make a copy of the receipt.

Taking it, Julie felt a wave of relief break over her. But she wasn't home and dry yet. As she steered the two trolleys out through the automatic door and into the parking lot, she hoped to God she wasn't too late. If Mike was already home—

There were two taxis in the lot. Banging on the window of

the first, she got the driver to get out and help her load the bags into the back.

'Christ!' he said, seeing the two trolleys. 'What are you doin' – feedin' the five thousand?'

'Feels like it,' she said, then, 'No, keep 'em separate if you can. That lot's for my mother-in-law. She had a fall two weeks back. Can't get out. I said I'd do her shopping for her.'

'Good girl,' the cabbie said, giving her a smile. 'Most women wouldn't give their mother-in-laws the time of day. I know mine's a right cow, she—'

And he was off, not stopping until she drew up at Mike's. And even then he kept it up, even as he helped her indoors with the first lot of stuff. Julie piled it all up on the kitchen table, then quickly wrote Mike a note and, popping her head round the door to see that Nancy was okay, hurried out to the cab again.

'Thanks,' she said breathlessly, as she climbed back in. 'To be honest I'll be glad when it's all over.'

'Nah, don't say that. It's the best time of the year. Like everyone's had a shot of the old happy juice. Even the most miserable old bastards like Christmas.'

'Well, it's a bit too much like hard work for my liking,' Julie said, but she grinned as she said it. 'You got your family at home this Christmas?'

'Nah, going up to me sister's, ain't we? We take turns. She lives Watford way. Only takes an hour or so. Means I can work right up to the last minute.'

'You like working, then?'

'Love it! It's the people, see. Can't beat this job for meeting people.'

And off he went, talking ten-to-the-dozen right up until he stopped outside the Fox and Fiddle.

'This your place?' he asked, as he helped her carry the bags across to the doorway.

'Nah, but my husband manages it.'

'Nice. Bet you have a few parties, eh?'

'Yeah.' But the thought of Dave throwing a party hadn't really occurred to her before that moment.

She turned, smiling at the cabbie. 'Thanks. What do I owe you?'

'Seven fifty,' he said.

Julie reached into her handbag and brought out her purse. It was only then that she realised she didn't have a brass farthing in it!

'Oh, shit. Hang on a minute. I'll just go and ask Dave for the fare.'

While he waited, she went inside. Dave was cleaning tables. He looked up a her and beamed. 'Alright, babe?'

'Dave – I've got a cab waiting outside. I went to pay him and found I ain't got a penny in my purse. I must have dropped it somewhere, while I was shopping.'

Dave gave her a sympathetic smile, then fished in his pocket and pulled out a small wad of notes. 'How much d'you need?'

'It's twelve fifty, and a tip – so give us a twenty.'

He peeled off a mauve twenty and handed it to her. In return she gave him a peck on the cheek and, turning about, hurried outside again.

The cabbie gave her a big smile as she emerged.

'You got change?' she asked.

'Sure.'

'Take ten,' she said, 'for your trouble.'

'Thanks. That's nice of you.' He handed her back a ten. 'Have a great Christmas, eh? And watch those brandies.'

'I will – and you!'

Julie stood there a moment, watching him go, then, stuffing the tenner into her purse, she picked up a couple of bags of shopping and went back inside.

Charlotte lay on the trolley, her top rolled up as the radiographer smoothed the gel over her exposed belly.

'Not too cold, I hope,' the woman said kindly.

'No. It's okay.'

Charlotte glanced nervously at the monitor screen, then back at the woman.

'Just keep watching,' the woman said. 'It doesn't hurt at all.'

Charlotte looked back at the screen as the woman ran the

scanner over her stomach. At first there was just a swirl of grey and black, but then it came into focus.

'There,' the radiographer said, leaning across to touch the screen and trace the shape with her finger. 'That's it.'

It was so small, so very, very tiny, but she could see the frantic little pulse of its heartbeat and felt her mouth go dry. A tear formed in the corner of her eye and ran down her cheek.

'That's beautiful . . .'

'Yes—' the woman touched the screen '— here, there'. A line formed momentarily. 'That'll give us the measurement from head to toe. From that we can calculate how far along you are, and give you a due date.' The woman looked up at her. 'That is . . .'

'Oh yes,' Charlotte said, unable to keep her eyes from the ultrasound image. 'Oh, definitely yes.'

Julie was working behind the bar, pulling a pint for a customer. Marie's daughter, Ellie, sat on a bar stool just across from her, watching her, a mischievous sparkle in her eyes.

'Well?' she asked, when Julie didn't answer her question. '*Have* you got me one?'

Marie, further down the bar, overheard. 'Ellie!'

Julie handed the punter his pint, then turned to Ellie, laughing. 'You'll have to wait and see, missie. Anyway, Father Christmas won't bring you nothing if you don't get to bed early.'

Ellie shrugged. 'I'm staying with my nan, and she don't believe in Father Christmas. She says it's a load of rubbish.'

Marie rolled her eyes, but Julie just grinned. 'You lot are too smart for your own good,' she said. Then, turning back to the punter, she asked, 'Anything else?'

'No.'

'That'll be two eighty please, darling.'

The man handed her a tenner. As she took it, Julie glanced along the bar. Dave was nowhere to be seen, and Marie was busy serving another customer. Ringing the sale up on the till, Julie took out the change, then, with another glance around to check no one was looking, snatched a handful of notes from the drawer and stuffed them into her pocket.

Nervously, she turned back to the punter, counting the change out into his hand. 'That's three, four, five, and five makes ten.'

He smiled and turned away. Julie watched him go, then glanced along the bar at Marie, but Marie had seen nothing.

Julie swallowed, then looked to Ellie again. 'And by the way, Father Christmas does exist. That's only something adults say to wind you lot up.'

'You mean my nan's been lying?'

Julie smiled. 'I didn't say that. But sometimes adults like to tease.'

Ellie considered that, then leaned forward to sip her lemonade through the straw. That done, she fixed Julie with a serious stare. 'Yeah, well, if he does, then how does he manage to visit *all* of the houses in one night, then?'

The room was beautifully decorated for Christmas. The scent of pine filled the air. Tree lights winked brightly in the late afternoon gloom as Charlotte sat at the table, wrapping up the last of her presents. Richard sat on the sofa nearby, using the remote to switch channels, his face visible in the glow from the fire.

Everything was warm and cosy, and as Imogen stepped back into the room, she smiled to herself. She had been shopping all afternoon up the West End. The bags she'd brought back rested on the sofa, where she'd dropped them ten minutes back. She went across and slumped down beside them, giving an exaggerated sigh.

'I know I say this every year, but there's something to be said for shopping by post. It was madness up there.' She grinned. 'Still, I did get this . . .'

Picking up a Gap bag, Imogen lifted out the most divine-looking baby outfit and held it up. Charlotte turned distractedly, then, seeing what it was, stood up and came across, taking the outfit from Imogen and holding it up. She smiled.

Imogen looked on, delighted. 'Isn't it gorgeous?'

Charlotte's smile became a grin. She looked to her adoptive mother. 'Yeah. Thanks.'

Imogen glanced at Richard, saw his smile of pleasure, and looked down. 'Lottie, can I have a word?'

Charlotte looked back at her distractedly, then nodded. 'Sure.'

'Not here,' Imogen said, feeling awkward now. 'In the kitchen, maybe.'

The slightest cloud crossed Charlotte's face, then, setting the baby outfit down, she nodded and followed her mother through.

'Blue or green?' Julie asked herself as she stood there, staring down at the identical-looking shirts.

'I'd go for the blue, myself,' the assistant said, her voice betraying the slightest trace of impatience. 'You can't go wrong with blue.'

'Nah, I guess you can't. Okay, two in the blue.'

The assistant smiled fixedly, then turned to get down another of the shirts in blue. 'Same size, or different?'

'Same size, ta.'

Good, she thought, *that's that done.* Only one more thing remained.

Taking out her mobile, she tapped in the number of the hospital. She waited a moment, then, when the receptionist answered, quickly asked for Sister O'Halloran on Gifford Ward.

'Hello, Mary? Yes, it's Julie here. Julie Harding. Yes, yes, I'm fine, thanks.'

She listened a moment, then laughed. 'Well, that's why I'm phoning actually. To do you a favour. I know I said I couldn't work over the holidays, but it seems now that I can. Yeah, just one shift, but if it'll help?'

She turned, grinning at the assistant, who stared back at her in a bored fashion. 'No. No, that'd be great. Yeah, that'd be perfect for me. Okay, see you then.'

Julie switched off the mobile, dropped it back in her bag, then took out her purse. 'So what's the damage?'

*

Charlotte put the letter down then sat back, a tear running down her face. 'Did you read it?'

Imogen nodded.

For a moment Charlotte said nothing, simply stared into the air, her eyes, her whole face a tissue of misery.

'And you say he's gone away?'

Again Imogen nodded, but this time she felt compelled to say something more. 'If I'd known how important it was – it's just the phone was ringing and I was bringing in the shopping, and I—'

Charlotte reached across and took her hand and squeezed it. 'It's alright,' she said gently. 'It's not your fault.'

It was such a mature thing to say that Imogen almost burst into tears. It was usually her forgiving Charlotte.

'Have you spoken to Jack's mum?'

Imogen swallowed. It was suddenly very hard to speak. 'She's had a postcard or two. From Manchester.'

Charlotte looked up. 'Manchester?'

'Oh God, what a mess. And it's all my fault—'

'No.' Again Charlotte squeezed her hand. 'But he's probably thinking now that I don't want to see him.'

'That's what I mean – and all because—'

Charlotte spoke firmly this time. 'No, Mum. It isn't your fault. In fact, if I'd got this when he meant me to get it, I'd probably have ignored it. But now that I've had time to think . . .'

Her voice trailed off. Imogen stared at her a moment, then, very gently, 'So what *do* you want? Do you want Jack back?'

Charlotte turned her head, looking at her, and smiled. 'I'm not sure. But I might know when I see him again. That is, if he wants to come back.'

She paused, then, brightening, got up. 'Which reminds me. I've got something to show *you*.'

Imogen waited while Charlotte went back into the living room. She was back in a moment, holding out a small piece of paper.

'What is—?' Imogen began, and then she caught her breath, her eyes changing as she took in the blurred ultrasound image. Then she began to cry.

Charlotte knelt beside her, putting her arm about her shoulders, but she too was tearful now. 'I knew you'd blub.'

Richard, who had seen the picture earlier, now stood in the doorway, looking on and smiling. 'At least we know there's only one in there.'

The doorbell rang. Richard smiled once more, then went to answer it.

Imogen looked to her daughter. 'And everything's alright?'

Charlotte nodded. 'As far as they can tell. There are tests they can do, but—'

Richard was back in the doorway. He cleared his throat, then, 'Er, Lottie . . .'

Charlotte looked up, then stood, her eyes wide with surprise. A figure stood just behind Richard, in full naval uniform, her cap in one hand.

'Hello, again,' she said, stepping forward into the light.

Dave sat at his desk in the back room, counting the takings for a second time, his face the picture of concern. As he did, Marie appeared in the doorway, her coat on, ready to go.

'Night, Dave!'

Distracted, Dave answered her. 'Night.' Then, looking up sharply, 'Marie?'

Marie turned. 'Yes?'

Dave stared at her, then shook his head. 'Nothing. Merry Christmas.'

Marie grinned. 'Merry Christmas!'

But Dave felt anything but merry. The money was short. Over a hundred and fifty short, to be precise.

Chapter Nineteen

Mistletoe And Wine

'Here, do you remember when it used to be that Leslie Crowther on the box Christmas morning – you know, visiting all the kids' wards in the hospitals?'

Mike was buttoning up his new shirt. On the bedside table next to him was a Christmas card, which read *To My Darling Husband.*

'Great Ormond Street,' he said. 'That's where it was.'

'Yeah, that's right. Christ, the smiles that used to be on those kids' faces.' Julie sighed wistfully. 'Whatever happened to him?'

'He died,' Mike said.

'Oh, shame – he used to do that Blue Peter, didn't he?'

'Crackerjack,' Mike corrected her.

'Well, whatever – it was before my time.'

Mike grinned, then did a little twirl for her. He was wearing no pants, but Julie barely seemed to notice. 'Yeah,' she said, 'it looks nice. I ordered you something else, but it hasn't come yet.'

'That's alright,' Mike said cheerfully. 'This is great. Besides, I rather hoped you'd give me another little pressie . . .'

Julie raised an eyebrow. 'If you mean nookie, you're gonna have to wait, mate.'

Mike shrugged, as if for once he didn't mind. 'You gonna open yours, then?'

'You want me to? I thought I'd save it for later so Nancy could see.'

Mike made a face. 'I think you'd better open it now.'

'Oh, I see!' And, excitedly, she picked up the soft, rectangular package and began to unwrap it. As she saw what it was, her eyes opened wide with delight.

'You like it?'

Julie held up the cream silk lingerie. 'It's lovely. Oh, Mike!'

'You could put it on if you like. Show me how much you like it.'

Julie playfully pushed him away. Mike's disappointment was written all over his face. 'Can't you phone in sick?'

'No, I can't. Anyway, it's only fair that those with kids get the day off.'

Mike grinned. 'We're going to have to keep on practising then.'

Avoiding eye contact, Julie began to get dressed. As she did, she gave Mike his instructions.

'Now, listen. I've prepared everything, and I've written down what goes on when.'

'Right little Delia Smith, ain't you?'

'Yeah, well, Mum's helped me a bit, but I want it to be nice, so don't go forgetting anything.'

Mike was amused. 'I won't. What time d'you want picking up?'

Julie looked up, then looked back down again. She seemed a bit flustered by the question. 'Oh I'll get that, um, Clare round the corner to drop me off.'

Mike frowned. 'How come she's working? I thought she had a couple of kids.'

'Yeah, she has, but she's separated. Her husband's got them today.'

Mike nodded. 'Whatever.'

Pulling on her nurse's outfit, she gave Mike a big grin. 'You couldn't make us a quick cuppa, could you? I'll take one in to Mum before I go.'

'Yeah.'

As Mike left, Julie felt relieved. It was hard having to think on your feet all the time, and she was sure she was going to get tripped up at some point. But so far, so good.

Rummaging through her underwear drawer, she brought out a packet of contraceptive pills and popped one in her mouth, then secreted them away again.

She turned back, pausing a moment to pick up and look at the beautiful silk underwear again.

'Shame,' she said softly, feeling the softness of the silk against her cheek. 'It would have been nice to start the day with a bang.'

Dave's front room was adorned with Christmas decorations; with streamers and glittering coloured balls, and – covering the tree like a fall of silver – endless pieces of tinsel. Dave's family sat at the table while, out in the kitchen, Julie served up.

They had just pulled the crackers, and John, paper hat on head, was launching into the jokes, unfurling the tiny bits of paper one at a time and reading them out. Seeing what was written, he put on a fake Chinese accent:

'Chinese proverb say passionate kiss like spider's web, soon lead to undoing of fly.'

Dave's mum frowned, not understanding the joke, but knowing it was smutty, while the rest of them chuckled.

Out in the kitchen, however, Julie wasn't laughing. The potatoes had been on for just that bit too long and half of them were stuck – *welded*, it seemed! – to the bottom of the baking tray. She had to dig away at them, like she was unearthing nuggets of coal, which one or two of them resembled, and occasionally, as now, one would go flying out of the tray and skid across the floor.

'Shit!'

She pursued it and, picking it up gingerly, hastened to place it on the big plate that held the turkey.

'Shit, shit, shit.' She blew on her fingers to cool them, then looked about her. The turkey looked mouth-wateringly gorgeous, despite the condition of one or two of the potatoes heaped around it. The carrots and brussels were already in dishes. Julie mopped her brow and then grinned. 'There! That'd show Iris!'

John was into another joke by now—

'Here we are, another Chinese proverb.' He put on his fake Chinese accent. 'It take many nails to build baby crib, but only one screw to fill it.'

'Dave!' Barbara said, looking to her brother. 'Where on earth did you get these crackers?'

'That shop in the High Street. You know, it does all sorts.'

'Well, no wonder . . .'

But John was enjoying himself. This time he screwed up his eyes in best Fu Manchu fashion. 'Foolish man give wife grand piano; wise man give wife upright organ.'

Iris tutted. 'Dirty beggar.'

Just then Julie walked into the room, carrying the turkey, and, edging round Dave, put it down in the centre of the table.

'Here we are, then. Sorry it's taken so long. Get the stuffing, will you, Dave?'

Iris stared at the turkey without expression, then glanced at Julie as if to say that she was far from impressed.

Barbara, meanwhile, had anticipated Dave and got up to bring the two foil containers of shop-bought stuffing from the side. As she placed them beside the turkey, she looked across at Julie.

'You should've said. I could've given you a recipe for a lovely stuffing.'

John grinned. 'She never says that to me!'

There was laughter, but Julie was looking down, deflated. Seeing it, Dave felt sorry for her.

'I wasn't sure about quantities,' Julie said. 'I'm only used to cooking for two.'

Iris was on her in a flash. 'From what *I* hear, you eat out most of the time.'

John looked at Barbara, as if asking her to intervene, but she looked away. Julie, however, had to bite her lip, the urge to tell the old cow to stuff it was right there on the tip of her tongue.

There was a moment's silence and then John spoke again.

'So, Julie? What did the mean git get you, then? New dartboard? A soap on a rope?'

Grinning, Julie showed off her ring.

'Very nice,' Barbara said, but her mother's voice almost drowned her out.

'Eternity ring – huh!'

Dave closed his eyes a moment, then opened them again, a fixed smile now on his lips. He raised his glass in a toast.

'Merry Christmas, everybody!'

The others, all looking thoroughly miserable now, raised their glasses to echo the toast.

'Merry Christmas.'

The club was packed, the music poundingly loud. Even through the wall you could feel the bone-shuddering vibration of that pulse. As he dialled, Jack moved his head to the beat. Nervous as he was, the rhythm carried him, pushed him along, like a leaf in the flood.

It was two months now since that day in the park, since the last time they had spoken. There'd been the letter, but she'd ignored that. And maybe that was it – maybe she really didn't want to see him again – but it was Christmas, and besides, he couldn't help himself. He had to speak to her.

He was trembling now. Not a lot, but enough to make him conscious of how big a step this was. He had tried to forget her; tried to get into this other life up here. But it was no good. Every girl he met seemed to remind him of what he had lost. Every smile reminded him of her smile.

The number bleeped through. There was a pause, and then it began to ring.

'Come on! Answer, damn you, *answer*!'

But it just rang and rang.

Jack smashed it down, angry now, almost in tears. 'Shit! Fucking, fucking shit!'

'You okay, Jack?'

He turned. It was the girl. Hayley, was that her name? She must have followed him out.

Jack swallowed back the hurt, then nodded. 'Yeah – yeah, I'm fine.'

But he wasn't fine. He wasn't even close to fine. In fact, he wasn't sure he'd ever be fine again. She reached out and took his hand.

'Come on,' she said. 'Let's go and get rat-arsed!'

*

'Well?' Imogen asked, 'who was it?'

The front door was still open. Richard was parking the car in the garage, and both Imogen and Charlotte were still wearing their coats.

'They hung up,' Charlotte said, putting the phone back on the hook. 'Shall I do a 1-4-7-1?'

Imogen put her bag down, then nodded. They'd been out to the carol service – the first time they'd been out as a family for a long time – but for all she'd joined in with the singing, Charlotte had still remained distant somehow, like only part of her was present.

She went across and switched on the kettle, turning to watch Charlotte.

'*Well*?' she mouthed.

Charlotte shrugged. 'I don't recognise the number.' She pressed three, for phone back, then smiled at Imogen.

The front door banged. A moment later Richard appeared in the doorway. 'Who is it?' he asked.

'We don't know. Lottie's phoning back.'

'Ah.'

After a moment, Charlotte put the phone down. She looked across and shrugged again. 'No one's answering.'

'What was the number?' Richard asked.

'Dunno,' Charlotte answered. 'Didn't recognise it.'

'Ah.' Richard looked to Imogen and smiled. 'You making tea?'

'And mince pies?'

'Lovely.'

He walked across and, gathering up his wife and his daughter under each arm, he cuddled them both. 'Merry Christmas, you two.'

'Merry Christmas,' Charlotte echoed, but her eyes seemed elsewhere.

Dave's family had gone home hours back. Dave and Julie had curled up on the sofa to have a cuddle and watch a bit of TV, but the late nights and early mornings had taken their toll and both of them had fallen asleep. Now, as the daylight drained away outside, Julie woke with a start and, staring at her watch, let out a little shriek of panic.

Dave blinked himself awake as Julie jumped up from the sofa.

'Shit!' she said. 'Why didn't you wake me?'

Dave rubbed at his eyes. He wasn't with it at all. 'What?'

Julie rolled her eyes. 'Never mind. Listen, I'm gonna have to get my skates on.'

Sitting, she pulled on her shoes, then dashed about the room, getting her bits and pieces together.

'I'll drop you,' Dave began, sitting up, all bleary-eyed and tired-looking.

Julie glanced at him, then shook her head. 'No. You're probably still over the limit. I'll get a mini-cab round the corner.'

'I'll be fine,' Dave said, trying to get up and failing first time. 'Just give me—'

'No,' Julie said sharply. Then, more calmly, 'I just don't want you to risk it, alright?'

She looked across at the table. The debris from their Christmas dinner still littered it.

'Christ!' she said. 'Look at this lot!'

'I'll sort it. You shoot off.'

Julie smiled. 'Great. But remember, I'm doing a double shift. So I'll see you tomorrow night, okay?'

She had got to the door now, but Dave called her back. 'Oi! Ain't you forgotten something?'

Turning, she rushed back and gave him a big kiss.

Dave beamed up at her. 'That's nice, but I meant your uniform.'

Flustered, Julie gave her head a little shake. 'Oh yeah . . . nah, I've got one at the hospital.'

Dave nodded. 'See ya then, babe.'

Julie nodded, then, turning on her heel, almost ran out of the door.

Julie glanced across the table to where Mike was about to carve the turkey. There was a palpable tension in the air as he dragged the big serrated knife across the breast of the dry and overcooked bird. He and Nancy looked mightily fed up, though Nancy was clearly determined to act as normally as possible.

'Just a little bit for me,' Julie said, her voice quiet.

Mike didn't look at her. 'The potatoes are like bullets.'

Julie looked to Nancy. 'I am sorry. You wouldn't have thought we'd have to wait that long for the AA.'

Nancy gave her the smallest of smiles. 'Because it's Christmas, I expect.'

Mike's voice was hard, however. 'You should've phoned. We've been sitting here starving.'

Julie spoke to Nancy again. 'I'm sorry.'

Nancy reached out and patted Julie's hand. 'It's just such a shame after you put in so much work.'

Mike finished dishing out the filled plates, then sat down to eat his own. He stabbed at a potato with his fork, but it was too hard to penetrate. He tried again and failed, then threw his fork down in disgust.

'I can't eat this!'

Upset, Julie stood and left the table, walking out into the kitchen. Tying the yellow plastic handles on the bin liner into a knot, she carried the rubbish out to the front of the house. Nancy looked to her son, appealing to him with her eyes. 'The girl did her best, Michael. She said she's sorry.'

Mike looked across to where Julie had been sitting, her food resting there untouched. Rising out of his seat he left the room and followed her out on to the front step. She stood in front of the dustbin, where she had deposited the sack, her body tense, rigid almost.

He stepped across and put his arms about her waist, snuggling into her back.

'I'm sorry.'

Julie sniffed. 'I wanted it to be perfect.'

He leaned closer, brushing her neck with his lips. 'I know.'

She softened her stance, letting her cheek rest against his shoulder, then turned her head slightly, and stretched up to kiss him.

*

Marie yawned, then looked back out of the window at the passing streets. A big bag of presents sat next to her on the back seat of the mini-cab. She planned to drop them off at her mum's, have a quick cup of tea there, then get on over to the Fox and Fiddle. She hadn't really wanted to work Christmas Day, but Dave had offered her a bonus, and things were tight, so she'd agreed.

As the mini-cab slowed to turn left, Marie saw a front door open, just across from her, and a woman step out, a black rubbish bin in one hand. She dropped it beside the overflowing bins, then stood there, even as a man stepped out on to the doorstep.

As Marie turned in her seat to watch, the man embraced the woman, and after a moment she turned and gave him a long, slow kiss, her right hand going up to his neck.

Marie turned back, facing the front again, a look of pure shock on her face.

Julie. It had been Julie!

Ted had gone down the pub with a couple of his cronies, leaving her to clear up the dinner things. In the old days he would have stayed and watched the Queen's speech with her, and maybe 'Fools and Horses', but these days he couldn't wait to get away.

She'd finished the washing-up and scoured the pans, now she took off her rubber gloves and, slumping down in the arm-chair, relaxed for the first time that afternoon.

Christmas – it was supposed to be a special time, a time for family, but Ted was all the family she had these days, and Ted had no time for her any more. Oh, she was of use to him – she cooked his meals and cleaned his clothes – but there was no love lost between them. And that had been okay, she hadn't really expected more, until the girl had come back into her life. Until the past had been made real to her.

Vera sat there a moment, just staring into the air, a faint wistfulness on her face, then she got up.

The photo album was in the bottom drawer, under the spare

tablecloths. She took it out and, making a space on the table, set it down and sat. She hadn't looked at it in years – not until recently, that was – but now she found herself drawn to it, looking at it at least once a day.

Ted wouldn't like it, but then she hadn't wanted to share it with Ted. As far as he knew, the album hadn't been touched for years.

She opened it now, her fingers tracing the familiar figures. Most of the early pictures were in black and white: her with her mum; her and her two sisters, both dead now, on holiday in Scarborough. And there, in a rare shot, her dad.

She turned the page, and there, suddenly, was Bill, tall and dark-haired, in his twenties then, a fine figure of a man, long before he caught the illness that would slowly kill him.

And there – Vera swallowed – was Julie, not four when that was taken, on a merry-go-round down on Whitby seafront, grinning back at the camera, her father half obscured in the background.

For years she'd been unable to look at these. It was like – well, like they were accusing her of something. Something she didn't want to know about; something she didn't want to face.

Vera closed the album, resting both hands flat on the cover. You could shut out the past – it was as easy as doing this. You could deny that anything had happened. But then something would happen. Someone would come along and open it all up again, as if it had only happened yesterday.

Vera reached up and touched her cheek, realising she had been crying.

'You silly—'

She stood and went across, placing the album back beneath the tablecloths, and closed the drawer.

Straightening up, she went over to the window and looked out. The day was grey and bleak, and if there hadn't been so many trees and decorations in her neighbours' windows, you might easily have thought it just another day. Vera sighed, then, taking her hankie from her apron pocket, wiped the tears from her face.

'Merry Christmas, Julie,' she said quietly. 'Wherever you are.'

Chapter Twenty

Finger Of Suspicion

'Lottie? Lottie, are you awake?'

Charlotte rolled over and stretched and yawned. Opening her eyes, she focused on the alarm clock, then sat up abruptly.

Christ! Was that the time?

'I'm coming!' She yawned again, then reached over to switch on the bedside lamp.

She had found it hard to go to sleep last night, knowing that this was the day, but at some point she must have drifted off, because it was gone ten now.

Her clothes were on top of the chest of drawers, where she'd left them last night. She had chosen them carefully, so as to try to give the right impression. Even so, now that the moment was upon her, she began to have doubts. What if they made her look too staid? Too middle-class? What if—?

'Get a grip!' she told herself sternly, staring at herself in the mirror, wondering, for the thousandth time, what Julie would make of her. But it was hard to get a grip. After all, it wasn't every day you got to meet your birth mother for the first time.

Imogen was waiting for her downstairs in the kitchen. As she sat at the table, Imogen came across and handed her a plate loaded with egg and bacon and mushrooms. Normally it was her favourite, but today she couldn't face it.

'I'm sorry, Mum, I—'

Imogen shook her head and smiled sympathetically. 'It's okay.' She paused, then, 'You still want me to drive you there?'

Charlotte nodded.

Imogen glanced at Richard, who sat nearby, his newspaper forgotten.

'Course.'

Charlotte looked down, then looked back at her adoptive

mother. 'I just want to say thanks for putting up with me these last few months, and for – well, for everything.'

Imogen smiled again. 'Just don't expect too much, eh?'

Charlotte nodded. She knew what Imogen meant, but it was hard not to have expectations; hard not to fantasise about this meeting. After all, she had imagined it so many times.

She looked to Richard. 'You're sure she'll be there?'

Richard nodded. 'That's what the ward sister said. She gets on shift at two and works through till ten. Unless she's taken sick, she'll be there.'

Charlotte nodded. She rubbed her hands together nervously, feeling how damp her palms were, then looked back at Imogen.

'Has Lucy Fielding called again?'

'No, love.'

'Oh.' Charlotte seemed disappointed. Lucy had hoped to get a picture to her, but so far she'd not had any luck.

'Maybe I should phone Vera? Tell her I've found her?'

'I wouldn't just yet,' Richard said gently. 'Wait till you've met her. Then you'll have something to say.'

Charlotte nodded, then, in an almost child-like voice, she wailed: 'Oh God I'm so nervous. I haven't got a clue what I'll say to her.'

Imogen came round and knelt beside her, using all her strength to hold back the tears she felt would choke her at any moment. 'You'll be fine.'

'But what if she doesn't want to talk to me? What if she rejects me again?'

Imogen was about to say something, but Richard interrupted her. 'You know you won't rest until you at least find out,' he said. 'And just remember. We love you.'

Anita was in the upstairs bathroom, in her undies, putting on her make-up, when she heard Karl's whoop of delight from downstairs. Going to the door, she shouted down to him. 'Karl? What is it?'

He turned, grinning, and waved a piece of paper at her. 'I've got her!'

'Sorry?'

'Julie. She's written some cheques from an old joint account. Now I know where she is!'

He came up the stairs and showed the returned cheques to Anita. At the top of each, 'REFER TO DRAWER – ACCOUNT CLOSED' was written in red biro.

Anita shrugged. 'I wouldn't get your hopes up too much. Maybe she don't live in that area.'

But Karl was adamant. 'You don't buy that much food if you don't live nearby, do you? No, this is a result! I can feel it!'

'So what are you going to do?'

'I'm going up there, to London. Find out where the nearest nursing agencies are and make a few calls.'

She smiled. 'I'm really pleased for you.'

'For both of us.' He smiled back at her, then stepped closer. 'Wish me luck?'

She held him close, giving him a long, slow kiss. Breaking from it, Karl was clearly aroused. He laughed gently. 'I'd better go.'

Anita smiled. 'I'll be waiting for you.'

He grinned back at her. 'You'd better be.'

Imogen sat beside Charlotte in the car as they waited for the traffic to get moving again. Tomorrow was New Year's Eve, and you'd have thought everybody would be at home still, sleeping off their festive over-indulgence, but half of London seemed to have taken to the roads.

The two of them sat in silence. Charlotte seemed lost in her own thoughts, not tense so much as distant. Looking across at her, Imogen smiled, then reached across and laid her hand gently on her daughter's slightly swollen stomach. Charlotte looked down at Imogen's hand and smiled also.

'Still frightened?' Imogen asked.

'Apprehensive.'

'Me, too.'

Charlotte glanced at her. 'What I keep thinking is that she doesn't know – you know, that I'm coming to see her. And I keep wondering if she's thought about me at all. Whether she's ever thought about me, or—'

'Lottie.'

'Yes?'

'Whatever happens, you've got to remember that none of this has anything to do with you and whether you're this kind of person or that kind of person. It's to do with Julie.'

A half-smile flickered across Charlotte's lips, then she pointed through the windscreen. 'You'd better go. It's green.'

'Bloody traffic,' Imogen said, putting the car into gear. But Charlotte, sitting beside her, was strangely glad for the delay.

Julie took the dead flowers from the vase and, after letting the ends of the stalks drip back into the greenish water, gave them one final shake and dropped them into the bin. She was singing to herself, oblivious of the male patients in the nearby beds, who, without exception, were watching her every movement.

She looked up, smiling, and saw that there was someone at the nurses' station – a young woman – but Sister was there and dealing with it, so she looked back down again, picking up the vase and carrying it over to the sink. She was pouring fresh water into it when she sensed someone behind her.

Julie turned, smiling. It was the young woman.

'Can I help you?'

The girl was staring at her strangely, an odd intensity in her eyes, her mouth slightly open. She seemed tense, frightened even.

'Are you alright?' Julie took a step closer. 'Was it me you wanted?'

The young woman blinked. 'Did you have a baby eighteen years ago?'

'Did I—?' Julie's eyes widened with shock. 'Oh God . . . *Charlotte?*'

Charlotte nodded, her eyes filling with tears. Stunned, Julie stepped back, bumping into the sink, then, abruptly, she turned and began to retch into the bowl.

'What are they like, the people who—?'

Julie stopped, embarrassed. They were walking in the court-yard, careful not to touch one another.

'They're great,' Charlotte answered. 'I'm very lucky.'

There was an awkward moment. Charlotte glanced at Julie, then: 'I brought some photos. I thought you might like to . . .'

They sat, side by side on the long, wooden bench. Reaching into her handbag, Charlotte brought out the photos.

'Do I—' She swallowed, trying to be as casual as possible. 'Do I have any brothers or sisters I don't know about?'

'No. There's only you.'

Charlotte handed her the photos, then watched as Julie slowly went through them. She seemed moved by them.

'You're married?'

Julie handed back the photos. 'Widowed.'

'I'm sorry.'

Julie smiled sadly. 'That's why I like nursing, I s'pose. Sometimes you think you can help people who are suffering.' She reached across and tapped the top photo – one of Charlotte when she was six. 'I remember a picture of me about that age.'

Charlotte stared a moment, then fished in her bag again and brought out the photo Vera had sent her only two days ago. Julie stared at it, taken aback.

'Where did you get that?'

'Vera.' Charlotte smiled. 'It'd just be too weird to call her Grandma.'

Julie looked away. 'Yes. It would. When did you see her?' she asked anxiously.

'Hers was the only address I had for you.' Charlotte looked away a moment, hesitating before she spoke. 'Do you mind? Me coming, I mean?'

Julie shook her head.

'Did you ever think about trying to find me?'

She nodded. 'Yeah, but I didn't think it would be fair.'

'Fair!' There was a sudden edge to Charlotte's voice that made Julie look up and meet her eyes. 'Fair on who?' Then, more calmly, 'Why did you give me up?'

'It was complicated. It just wasn't possible for me to keep you.'

'But how is it possible to give birth to a baby and then give it away, just like that?'

Julie looked stung by the question. She handed the photo back.

'I had you for eight days before they came and took you – you know that? And you were in my arms the whole time.'

Charlotte was crying now. Julie tentatively placed her arm round Charlotte's shoulders and hugged her.

'I was so frightened,' Charlotte said, through her tears. 'When I got pregnant I thought I wouldn't be able to love my baby, that I'd be like you. Except I knew I couldn't give it away. I knew I'd have to keep it.'

Julie nodded, her own tears beginning to fall. 'If you love that baby half as much as I loved you, it'll be a very lucky child. And it will be, cos you're going to be a great mum.'

Charlotte smiled. But Julie was struggling now to keep control. She stood. 'I have to get back. Will you be alright?'

Charlotte nodded. 'Yes. Mum's waiting for me in the car.'

The word 'Mum' cut through Julie like a knife. But Charlotte didn't seem to notice. 'Can we meet again? There's so much I want to ask you.'

Julie looked at her a moment, then, 'Tomorrow? Here at about half past two?'

Charlotte grinned, then scribbled on a scrap of paper and handed it to Julie.

'That's my number. Just in case.'

Julie took the piece of paper and stared at the writing, the sight of Charlotte's name familiar yet so strange to her.

There was an awkward moment, then Charlotte jumped to her feet and gave Julie a hug. There was pain now in Julie's face and as Charlotte turned to walk away, she was barely holding on to her emotions. Watching her go, she called after her.

'Charlotte!'

Charlotte turned.

She hesitated. There was so much she wanted to say. 'See you tomorrow.'

Charlotte smiled, then walked on.

Julie raised her hand, gave the ghost of a wave. 'Bye,' she said quietly, repeating the words she had said so many times since they had taken her, all those years ago. 'I love you.'

*

Karl was in a mood. As he joined the queue for a taxi at the station, he wondered if this were some kind of sign. It wasn't just that he'd missed the train he'd planned to catch by just two minutes – and that bastard in the lorry had been very lucky not to have his teeth put down his throat – but the one he *had* caught had practically limped along the line, stopping every ten minutes or so for no apparent reason, like some geriatric runner who had to pause for breath every few miles.

Now it was twenty-five to five, and unless he was very lucky the nursing agencies would be closed by the time he got to them.

There were only five people in the queue ahead of him, but as there were no taxis – and no sign of any coming – things didn't look good. For a moment he considered taking the Underground, but he knew that the moment he stepped out of the queue – and there were five, no six people behind him now – a couple of cabs would come along.

He persevered, gritting his teeth. If the worst came to the worst he could hire a room somewhere; start his search in the morning. He'd phone Anita, let her know what was going on. She wouldn't mind. After all, it was her he was doing this for.

And for me, he thought, wondering for the first time what precisely he would say to Julie when he finally caught up with her. The thing was, he wasn't angry with her any more. Hurt? Yes, a little. But not angry. After all, if she'd not left him, he'd never have got things together with Anita, and that, right now, was the most important thing in his life.

Yeah, but he didn't want to thank her. What he really wanted to know was *why*?

A taxi drew up, and then another. He shuffled forward a little, conscious that he had no overnight bag, no change of clothes. *Never mind*, he thought. *I can buy what I need.*

And now – now that his mood had changed – a whole fleet of taxis turned one by one into the station and began drawing up at the rank.

Bloody typical, Karl thought, giving the taxi driver the address of the supermarket Julie had used, then climbing into the back. And for the first time in hours, he smiled, knowing for certain now that he was going to find her.

Julie was polishing the glass panels over the top of the bar, her movements distracted, her mind filled with the meeting earlier that day with Charlotte, when there was a knock on the door. Dave was in the cellar, doing a stock check, so she went across.

Through the misted glass she could see it was Marie, and as she unbolted the door and pulled it back, she gave her a cheery welcome.

'Hiya! You feeling better now?'

Marie had been off sick these past three days, and Julie hadn't really been expecting her; even so, her silent scowl was unexpected.

'What?' Julie asked.

Marie looked about her, checking that Dave wasn't there, then, 'I want a word with you.'

'What?'

'I said I want a word. About Christmas Day.'

Julie looked confused.

'You're playing around, ain't you?'

'Playing around? You're mad.'

'I saw you. You and that fella. Christmas Day, it was. I was going over to my mum's. I drove right past you. Saw the kiss you gave him.'

Julie made a face of pure disbelief. 'I don't know what you *think* you saw, Marie, but you're bloody well mistaken!'

'Come off it! You were all over him like a rash!'

Julie gave an exasperated sigh. 'You've gone without for too long. You're starting to hallucinate!'

She made to walk past her, but Marie grabbed her arm.

'Take the piss out of me, fine, but don't you dare take it out of Dave. He's a decent bloke and he don't deserve it!'

Julie freed her arm, her face sneering now, anger in her eyes. 'What's the matter? You got so desperate that you're after my old man now?'

Marie tapped her head angrily. 'There's something wrong with you. Well, I'm telling you, knock it on the head with this other bloke or else I'm gonna tell Dave. Oh yeah, and I know for a fact that this other bloke's married. But then, I s'pose you don't give a shit. But I'll be round there, an' all. You know I will.'

And with that, Marie turned and walked away. As she hung up her coat behind the bar, Dave re-emerged from down below.

'Oh hello, love – you feeling better?'

Marie looked to Dave and smiled. 'Yeah. Lots better, thanks.'

Dave turned to Julie. 'Sweetheart, I—'

But Julie turned on her heels and, without a backward glance, disappeared up the stairs, slamming the door behind her.

Dave looked to Marie. 'Christ! What's up with her?'

Stony-faced, Marie shrugged. 'Dunno. Maybe New Year depresses her.'

Upstairs, Julie stamped about the flat, throwing cushions and generally venting her frustration. She hadn't thought anyone would see her, but that had been naïve. You couldn't have two husbands just three miles apart and not have *someone* put two and two together. The shame was that it had been Marie.

'Bloody bitch!'

And, picking up a china ornament – one of Dave's mum's presents to them – she let fly. As it smashed against the wall, so something gave in her, and she sank to her knees, feeling suddenly drained, as though she had no energy left to fight.

For a while she allowed herself to wallow in self-pity, but then, as she calmed, so she began to think again. It was no good letting things slide; she had to act, and act now.

Standing, Julie wiped at her face with the back of her hand, then, taking her overnight bag from the wardrobe, began to pack.

The station was quiet, with a kind of expectant hush. The New Year was hours off yet, and though there were already one or two drunks about making a nuisance of themselves, the streets were relatively quiet. It was after midnight that the real fun would begin.

Sitting at his desk, Detective Inspector Barry Clements looked up from his newspaper to find the duty sergeant standing there, an incident sheet in his hand.

'What've you got?' he asked, putting out his hand.

Taking the form, D.I. Clements turned it round and scanned it, then looked back at the sergeant, a look of total incredulity on his face.

'A bigamist! Come on, Harry! Someone's having a fucking joke, ain't they?'

Part Three – Sea of Heartbreak

Chapter Twenty-One

All In The Game

Matthew Parker sat at his desk in the high-rise offices of the *National Star*, staring at the screen in dismay. He'd been working on this story for the past three weeks, almost to the exclusion of everything else, but now it had all gone pear-shaped. One of his rivals on the *Sun* had got a tip-off, and as a result, Matthew's chief source had dried up and was refusing to say another word. She claimed she'd had a change of heart – a 'moral awakening', as she'd put it on the phone – but Matthew was pretty sure that it was a nice fat cheque that had actually done the trick.

Some days he got so paranoid, he began to believe someone was bugging his terminal, reading his every last word and having a bloody good laugh about it. It was just the kind of thing some of those bastards would do, rather than actually go out there and do the footwork themselves.

Matthew was proud of his work, proud of his ability to nose out the details of a story and flesh it out. He was good – in his own opinion one of the best – but lately he hadn't been having a lot of luck.

With a grunt of exasperation he closed the file, then sat back, scratching his beer belly, a look midway between constipation and puzzlement on his face. He had to come up with something new, and fast. There were other, younger reporters on staff who'd shaft their own grannies if it meant they could have his job.

The trouble was, he'd promised Harry something. He'd said he was on to something really big. And he had been. Only now the fucking *Sun* had both his story and his chief source. Oh, he could do a spoiler, sure – and maybe he would, just to buy himself time – but it wouldn't be the big exclusive he'd promised Harry.

He glanced at his watch. It was coming up to eleven. The pubs would be open in a bit. But first, he'd do the rounds; visit a few of the local nicks and see if they had anything interesting to tell him.

That was something that those arseholes from the other nationals didn't do. They relied on picking up stories from the local press. But Matthew knew better. Some of his best stories had come from chatting with a duty sergeant over a cup of piss-weak tea.

Besides, his doctor had told him to cut down. Either that or book in for an operation on his liver.

Pushing his chair back, he hauled himself up and, lifting his jacket, slipped it on.

'You off, then, Matt?'

Matthew looked across to where Harry sat in his office, glued to the chair like he never left it – which was not far from the truth – and nodded.

'Just popping out to check a few details,' he called back. 'I'll be back tea-time.'

'Sure. And mine's a double.'

He ignored the comment. It wasn't true, anyway. Not nowadays. But it was hard to do this job without having a *few* whiskies now and then. You had to put people at their ease, and a pub was always – *always* – the best place to do that, not least of all because alcohol loosened the tongue. Indiscretion was his meat and drink. Other people's indiscretions. And if that meant giving his liver a bit of a battering, then that was a price he was willing to pay. For journalism, for the truth, and in order to keep his job.

Karl woke and stretched, turning over to reach out for Anita. And promptly fell out of bed. Groaning, he got up off his hands and knees and sat on the edge of the mattress, holding his head.

Christ, he had a hangover! And not surprising. He must have sunk at least a dozen pints last night – twice what he usually drank of an evening. And it wasn't really even his fault. If he hadn't bumped into that young couple, he'd have probably called it a night after just two or three. As it was, the girl had turned out to be a nurse, and though she'd given it up for a better-paid office job, she'd been able to give him a list of all the local agencies, and had marked on his A–Z just where they were and which he ought to visit first.

It had been a major break, and he'd felt so grateful that he'd bought them both a round. Then they, of course, had bought him one back, and so on, until he'd forgotten exactly why he'd come up to London in the first place, enamoured as he was of his new friends.

But now he remembered why he'd come and, staggering over to the closet-like en-suite bathroom, he slipped out of his pants and stepped into the shower.

The water ran tepidly warm, but that was okay. He needed waking up, not lulling back to sleep. Coffee – a gallon of it – was called for. Then he would start to tackle the agencies.

Today was the day he'd find her again. Today he was going to nail that bitch!

Julie yawned, then looked to Dave and laughed.

'Sorry.'

'Nah,' he said, coming down the bar to her. 'You must be knackered, all them shifts you've been working.'

'Yeah, still – it'll help us pay for Christmas, eh?'

Dave smiled, but there was a slight shadow behind the smile.

'Did Marie say why she had to go?'

Dave shrugged. 'Some show Ellie's in. She's working tonight though so don't worry.' He squeezed her hand. 'Look, I'm just going to get some mixers while we're quiet.'

Quiet was not the word for it. It was early yet, but there wasn't a customer in the place. But from what Dave had told her about last night, it wasn't surprising some of them hadn't surfaced yet. It'd be a wonder if they got up for the following weekend, the amount they'd put away. Still, it had been a good night, even if she'd had to run about like a lunatic to keep both her fellas happy.

She'd spent the New Year with Mike and Nancy, of course,

having told Dave that she had to work a shift at the hospital. At midnight she had kissed Mike, hugged Nancy and then – because she'd promised Dave – had dashed out into the back garden and given him a ring on her mobile, keeping her voice down so that Mike and Nancy didn't hear. She'd told Mike she was phoning the girls at work, and he'd no reason not to believe her.

It's too bloody much, she thought, wondering when she was going to get a full night's sleep. What made it worse was that she was due on shift – for real – in just under an hour.

Julie looked about her. The place was like a tomb. Smelled like one, too, after last night. She could hear Dave downstairs in the cellar, jingling crates of empty mixer bottles, as he sorted things out down there.

She glanced at the till. He must have noticed. Must have. But he'd said nothing. Hadn't even mentioned it. She swallowed, then, her pulse quickening, stepped over to the till and rang up 'No sale'.

She knew Dave's habits. He cleared the larger notes out of the tills halfway through the evening and again at closing time – at eleven. But last night they'd had an extension, and though he'd cleared them twice, there was still money from the lock-in.

Julie picked up the bundle of tens and flicked through. There had to be three or four hundred quid there alone, and about the same in twenties. Quickly, before Dave had a chance to come back upstairs, she peeled off ten notes and slipped them into the cleavage of her bra, then eased the till drawer shut.

She needed the money – knew Dave was doing well and could afford it – even so, she felt guilty. Picking up a cloth she began to wipe the top of the bar. No, she didn't like dipping in the till, even if it was necessary. It made her feel unclean.

'Alright, babe?'

She jumped as Dave reappeared at the end of the bar, carrying a crate of assorted juices.

'Christ, Dave!' she said, a trace of annoyance in her voice. 'Don't do that. You scared the bloody daylights out of me!'

'Sorry, babe.' He put the crate down and came over and held

her, his face gentle, smiling. 'Hey, if it's this quiet, maybe we could have an early night tonight.'

'Maybe,' she said, but she had no intention of an early night. Not with Dave, anyway.

It had been a subdued New Year, with just the three of them and the telly. Imogen had wanted to go out somewhere – which was not her usual thing – but Charlotte had been against the idea and so they'd stayed home. Richard had tried to cheer things up with a bottle of champagne – to celebrate the year ahead – but even that had fallen somewhat flat.

Charlotte hadn't talked much after the meeting with her birth mother. She had been silent in the car coming back and Imogen had feared to press her. Since then they had fallen into a kind of awkwardness, with each of them seemingly afraid to raise the subject lest they'd somehow hurt or offend the other, but Imogen had to know.

When Charlotte finally emerged for breakfast, Imogen made her tea and toast; then, settling opposite her, asked, 'Can we talk about it?'

Charlotte looked up. It was clear from her eyes that she hadn't had much sleep. She shrugged.

Imogen smiled encouragingly. 'Please?'

Charlotte drew her tea towards her and stared down into it. She began slowly, falteringly almost.

'It was – well, funny seeing her standing there in a nurse's uniform. I . . . couldn't speak or anything.'

'Did she know it was you?'

'No, no, she – she probably thought I was a visitor who'd lost their way. Then I asked her if she'd had a baby, and—'

'Did you like her?'

Charlotte looked up, meeting her eyes. 'Yeah. She seemed nice.'

'Nicer than me, I expect,' Imogen answered, the lightness of her tone disguising the weight of the question.

'No. Course not.'

A pause, then, 'Did you ask about the father?'

Charlotte shook her head, drew the tea closer. 'No. I thought

I should take it slowly. I felt a bit sorry for her, actually. Divorced. Widowed.'

'And what did she think about becoming a grandmother?'

Charlotte shrugged. 'The thing is, I don't really know her yet.'

'But you'd like to?'

It was said innocuously, but Charlotte sensed how loaded the question was. She met her eyes firmly, keeping contact as she spoke.

'Mum, it's not going to change anything between you and me. You and Dad are my parents. You always will be.'

With a suddenness that took Charlotte by surprise, Imogen burst into tears. Charlotte went across to comfort her.

'This is so stupid,' Imogen said, wiping at her tears. 'I'm supposed to be the grown-up. It's just that I love you so much.'

'And I love you, Mum. Nothing's ever going to change that. But I have to give her a chance.'

Imogen nodded, smiling now through her tears.

'Are you going to see her again?'

Charlotte nodded, then looked up at the clock on the wall. 'In fact, I need to get going.'

'Today?'

Charlotte nodded.

Imogen forced a weak smile, determined not to allow her fears to surface. 'Want a lift?'

'You don't have to.'

'I know. But I want to. You are my daughter, after all.'

Julie looked about the room, checking she hadn't forgotten anything, then picked up the heavy holdall and eased it on to her shoulder. She meant to slip away quietly, without saying goodbye, but Dave was waiting for her at the bottom of the stairs. He smiled.

'You off, love?'

She nodded, feeling a sudden sadness and a genuine affection for him. He didn't know she was leaving him, but she was.

He leaned close and kissed her neck. 'Take care.'

'Yeah, you too,' she said, moving past him. But at the door

she turned, looking back at him one last time before stepping out into the chill air and closing the door behind her.

With Julie gone, Dave walked back through into the bar, then gestured to Marie.

'Can I have a word?' He carried on walking through to the office at the back of the bar.

She was slow coming.

'What?' she asked, almost belligerently, not budging from the doorway. It riled him.

'I want to talk about the missing money.'

Marie came across, standing over him at the desk. 'Missing money?'

'Oh, come on. There's a hundred missing from last night's takings. And it ain't the first time. A hundred and fifty went missing Christmas Eve.'

'Why didn't you say something, then?'

Dave sighed. 'Look, Marie, if you needed a bit extra, you should've asked. I've always tried to be—'

'Hold up! You think *I* took your money?'

'We were the only two people on. What the hell am I supposed to think?'

'Bollocks! I wouldn't take your poxy money! Think what the bloody hell you like! I don't take nothing that don't belong to me and if you don't know that I tell you what, Dave, you can stick your bleedin' job up your arse!'

Marie turned furiously, but she had only got as far as the door when she turned back. 'And for your information, we weren't the only two working them days.'

Dave looked puzzled, so she spelled it out for him.

'Julie. Yeah, your loving wife.'

Dave looked stunned. 'You call yourself a friend?'

She came back across, leaned across the desk, almost spitting the words into his face now. 'Grow up, will you? If she can shag someone behind your back, she can sure as hell pinch your bloody money!'

Dave was mortified. He almost whispered his answer. 'You're lying.'

Marie straightened up, then shook her head. 'There's no fool
like an old fool.'

Dave looked hurt. Seeing that, Marie took pity.

'I'm sorry. I shouldn't have—'

'Who?'

'Dave, just—'

Angry now, he stood. 'Who is it?'

It was on the tip of her tongue, but even now she felt some
last, small vestige of loyalty to Julie.

'Marie! Tell me!'

Karl had drawn blanks with the first three agencies he'd
visited, but he wasn't about to give up. As he checked the name
of the road he was in against the list the girl had written out for
him, a group of sullen yet noisy teenagers looked on from the
street corner.

He turned, looking about him, then spotted the agency, just
across the way. He checked the traffic, then hurried across the
road.

As he stepped into the agency, the woman at the desk looked
up, her welcoming smile turning to a look of puzzlement and
vague suspicion. Karl clearly didn't look the nursing type, but
he'd got the spiel down perfectly by now. He knew none of
them were keen on answering his questions, but with a little
flattery . . .

'Can I help you?'

Karl sat, giving her his most pleasant smile. 'I hope so. You
see, I'm trying to find someone. I lost touch, and—'

The woman stiffened. 'I'm sorry, but we're a recruitment
agency, not private investigators.'

'I know that,' trying his best not to rise to the bait and tell
her what a stupid stuck-up cow she was. 'Only it's really
important that I get in touch with her.'

The woman smiled coldly. 'I'm very sorry, but it's company
policy not to give any information about our clients to the
general public. If you want to trace her, I'd suggest you visit the
police.'

Karl nodded, as if he understood, but he'd only just begun.

The trick was to wear them down, so that they'd want to tell you just to get rid of you.

'Look, the thing is, she's my sister. There was a bit of a family bust-up but – well, it's our mum. They reckon she's only got a couple of days. Julie wouldn't forgive me if I didn't try and—' Karl broke off, his head going down as he feigned real hurt and bewilderment. 'I'm sorry—'

The woman, he sensed, was wavering. 'What's the name?'

'Julie. Julie Harding.'

The woman turned to her computer and tapped in the name. There was a moment's hesitation, then she looked at Karl again. 'What if I give her a call? If she says it's okay, then I'll give you her number.'

Karl's mouth was dry. He knew that Julie's address, her telephone number, were on that screen. 'I – look, the thing is, I'd really like to tell her myself. Her and Mum—'

The woman cut through what he was saying. 'I understand that, Mr Harding. All that I'll say is that you need to speak to her urgently. What's your Christian name?'

'Karl.' He cleared his throat nervously. 'It's Karl, but look—'

He tried to think of something else to say, to persuade her, but his mind was a blank. The woman had just picked up the phone and had begun to dial when there was a loud bang against the plate-glass window at the front of the shop. Karl turned, surprised, to see the gang of teenagers outside. They'd been messing about and one of them had fallen against the window.

Putting down the phone, the woman stood and stormed across to the door.

'Oi, you!' she yelled. 'Stop it right now, before I call the police! You'll go straight through the glass, you stupid boy!'

Karl, meanwhile, leaned across the desk. There was a phone number, but he wasn't interested in phoning Julie. What he wanted was the address of the hospital where she worked, and there it was! He almost laughed with delight.

The woman came back. 'I'm sorry,' she said. 'They haven't the sense they were born with, half of them. Now where were we?'

Karl stood. 'Look, I've been thinking. I don't want to get you in trouble, and I just remembered a cousin of ours she might be staying with. I'll try her, see what she knows, and if I draw a blank I'll come back, eh?'

'But—'

'No. I'm grateful, but – thanks.'

And, turning, trying not to whoop for joy, Karl hurried from the shop.

Dave's face was red with anger. His shirt collar was open and as he banged on the door, so the sweat flew from his brow in tiny droplets. Unable to start the car, he had run round to the address Marie had given him, and now, furious, sweating heavily, he growled as he smashed his fist time and again against the wooden surface.

There'd been a movement at an upstairs window; now the door swung open. Mike stood there, wearing an identical shirt to the sweat-soaked one Dave was wearing. He too seemed angry.

'Hey! What the fuck's the matter with you?'

'You bastard!'

Dave's fist connected square with Mike's face, sending him staggering back, a spray of blood flying from Mike's nose on to the hallway wall. Mike stumbled and fell in an undignified heap on to his arse.

Dave stepped forward, towering over him, menacing in his fury.

'Alright you bastard, where's my wife?'

Marie groaned inwardly as the door opened and another two punters entered, looking about them as they came. Dave had left her holding the fort, and as ever when that happened, there'd been a rush on. Suddenly, as if they'd all got a midday alarm call, the pub had filled, and she'd been run off her feet trying to cope.

As she pulled yet another pint, one of the two newcomers pushed through the crowd at the bar and, ignoring the venomous looks of the regulars, called out to her.

'Julie Harding?'

'Who wants to know?'

She should have known. The clothes, the hairstyle were a dead giveaway. Old Bill. As he flashed his badge, Marie wondered just what kind of trouble Julie had landed herself in now.

'She's not here,' she said, handing across the pint she'd just poured. 'One eighty-five, please, love.'

'So who are you?'

'She's Marie,' one of the regulars said, with a belligerence born of a lifelong suspicion of the police. 'You got a problem with that?'

The two detectives looked about them, seeing at a glance that they weren't welcome here. Not wanting to get in a ruck first day of the year, they turned back to Marie.

'So when d'you expect her back?'

'Difficult to say. Can I give her a message?'

The detective's lip curled into a smile. He knew they weren't going to get anything out of this lot. Turning away from the bar, they made their way towards the door.

'Fuck off!' someone said from the far end of the bar, to a murmur of agreement, but they just kept on walking.

Julie jumped down off the bus, cursing. She was late. Not only that, but she'd promised to see Charlotte at half two.

Not that that was a problem. It had frightened her at first, but now she was looking forward to it. All her adult life she'd half expected it – half hoped for it – but now that it had happened—

She stopped dead. With all that had been happening, she had tried to push it from her mind; tried to convince herself that it wasn't that big a deal, but it was. Charlotte was her blood – the only child she had or ever would have.

Only everything was happening too fast. She knew it had been a mistake to get back with Dave, but she'd not been able to help herself. She liked Dave. Liked the way he loved her, flaws and all, with that strange, puppy-like affection of his. And Mike – well, it wasn't just Mike she liked as what he brought her: Nancy and the sense of family she'd never had. But now Charlotte had come back into her life, and Marie was threatening to tell Dave about Mike and—

It was all too much. Time, then, to get out. To move on, like she'd always moved on. They'd get over her soon enough.

She almost smiled. Almost. Only it was too much to take at one go. Leaving one man was bad enough, but two . . . Julie shivered, then walked on, through the hospital gates and up the steps, hurrying now.

Chapter Twenty-Two

A Girl Like You

'Julie Harding,' the policeman said. 'That's right – mid-thirties, blonde hair . . .'

While the hospital receptionist began looking through her book for the name, the elder of the two detectives looked about him. It was quiet. One or two patients sat at tables in the nearby canteen. An old guy in a dressing gown was getting himself a cup of tea from the machine. Two nurses stood waiting by the lifts. He studied them a moment, but neither fitted the description.

'Ah, here we are,' the receptionist said finally. 'According to this, she's in the Anna Beaton Ward – that's up on the third floor. Take the lift and turn left when you exit.'

'Ta, love.' And, nodding to his partner, he walked over to join the nurses.

'Hiya, ladies. Happy New Year!'

They smiled guardedly, recognising him at once for what he was.

'Either of you know a Julie Harding?'

'Yeah,' the younger of the two said. 'Why? Is it about her mum?'

'Pardon?'

'Just that she's been sick. Near death's door. I thought—'

'Oh yeah yeah. No, it's not that. But it is to do with her family.'

Or families, he thought, resisting the urge to laugh.

'You work with her, then?'

'I did. But she's not on the wards today.'

'Oh, but I thought—'

'Try Accident and Emergency. They were short-handed, so she got sent down to help out . . .'

*

'Damn it! Can't you go some other way?'

The cab driver half turned to Karl and shrugged. 'Ain't my fault, mate. One of those big articulated's trying to back up, silly bugger—' he smiled stoically '—and as the traffic's backed up behind me, there's nowhere I can go, is there?'

Karl huffed impatiently. 'How far are we from the hospital?'

'It's that big building over there, mate. End of the street, just past the lorry!'

'Then why didn't you bloody say that!' And thrusting a fiver through the partition, Karl threw the door open and jumped out.

The driver of the articulated lorry was making a right pig's ear of backing into the side road, however, so for a moment Karl found himself trapped on the wrong side of the hospital. Nearby, two men and a woman, sitting in a car, were all yelling at the lorry driver impatiently, like they were in every bit as much a hurry as Karl. One of the men was holding an ice-pack over his badly swollen eye.

Winding the window down, the uninjured man leaned out and yelled at the driver: 'Come on, you pillock! Shift your fucking lorry!'

The lorry driver ignored him, grating his gears as he tried to put the big articulated into reverse again.

'Tosser!' the injured one yelled, wincing as he placed the ice-pack against the side of his face once more.

The two men, Karl noted, were wearing exactly the same dark blue shirt.

'Come on,' Karl hissed, between his clenched teeth. 'Move your lorry, you fucking arsehole.'

But after moving three or four feet backwards, the lorry driver stopped again and, grating his gears yet again, edged forward once more.

''Ere, Marie, take over!' one of the men in the car said. 'Mike and I can leg it from here.'

Gears grated, the lorry slowly edged back. Suddenly there was a bit of space between the lorry's cab and the wall. Hurrying – before the silly fucker changed his bloody mind again and shunted the lorry forward – Karl and the two men rushed for the gap.

As the ambulance backed into the bay, Julie stood there, wondering how she was going to get away to see Charlotte. If she'd been on the wards as usual, it wouldn't have been a problem, but down here was another matter. Still, she could hardly have said no when they asked her, and maybe things would ease off in a bit.

The driver jumped out and hastened round to the back of the ambulance, where he opened the door for his fellow paramedic. Julie stood back a little, letting them slide the trolley out. Another nurse, a ward orderly and a junior registrar stood close by, ready to take the patient off the paramedics' hands.

'He's a bit distressed', the driver said, speaking to them all. 'That's why we had to strap him down in the ambulance. Smells like he's had a few and seems he took a bit of a tumble. There's no sign of any obvious breaks, but it's probably best to get him X-rayed. He couldn't stand properly on his right leg.'

Just then the patient seemed to come to sudden life. He began struggling and shouting. Julie stepped forward to help them try to pacify him.

It was as this was happening that the hospital Tannoy – never at its clearest in A & E – announced: *Would Nurse Julie Harding please report to the General Manager's office. Nurse Julie Harding—*

Julie half turned, thinking vaguely that she'd heard her name. She turned back, giving her full attention to the patient, putting a gentle pressure on his shoulders so that he wouldn't sit up.

'It's alright, sweetheart,' she said soothingly. 'You'll be okay.'

It was only then, as he tilted his head back to give her a venomous look, that she saw who it was.

She jumped back. '*Oh Jesus Christ! Brian!*'

Brian's eyes flew open. His heavily-slurred voice filled the corridor.

'It's you! You bitch! You fucking bitch! What're you doing here?'

'Hey!' one of the paramedics said, pushing Brian back down. 'Watch your mouth. You don't threaten the nurses, okay? Or you'll have me to deal with.'

But Julie had backed away. In a complete panic now, she ran across and pushed through the transparent flap doors and out into the main reception area.

And stopped dead. Mike, Marie and Dave were standing there, as large as life. Seeing her, Mike threw aside the ice-pack and, letting out a howl of anger, took a step towards her. Dave saw her at the same time. He too looked angry, but also deeply hurt. Marie grabbed Mike's arm, pulling him back, then stepped forward to confront Julie.

'How could you do it?'

Julie's eyes flashed about her, seeking an escape route. 'This is none of your business, Marie. So just keep out of it, okay?'

She was about to flee, to make a break for the main doors, when a middle-aged man, a total stranger, gently but firmly took her arm.

'Julie Harding?'

She whirled around, tugging her arm free. 'What the—?'

At that moment, the trolley with Brian strapped to it came rattling through the flap doors.

'That's her, the bitch! She's the fucking one!'

Mike was standing next to her now, facing the stranger. 'Who the hell are you?' he asked.

'He's the Old Bill,' Marie said. 'He was round the pub earlier.'

The detective looked from Mike to Dave. 'And who might you two be?'

Both men stared hard at Julie as they said their names, Mike's face full of anger, Dave's wracked with misery.

'Michael James.'

'Dave Freeman.'

'And they're both married to her,' Marie chipped in.

The detective raised an eyebrow, then took out his notebook and looked down his list of names. He wrote down the two names, then looked to Julie.

'You *have* been a busy girl.'

But they weren't done. Just then Karl arrived. He'd been up to the wards, but had been re-directed down here. Seeing him, Julie gave a shriek. Seeing her, the anger and the hatred that had bubbled under the surface for the past months erupted and Karl bellowed and ran at her, as if he was going to kill her.

Mike, Dave and the policeman intervened.

The detective pushed Karl away and flashed his badge. 'Behave yourself.'

'Who the hell are you?' Dave asked, seeing the look in the newcomer's face.

'Karl,' Karl said, glaring at Julie. 'And I'm her fucking husband, that's who I am!'

'Her *husband*?' Mike and Dave said as one. The detective just laughed.

Julie swallowed, then looked down, as if genuinely ashamed. But just then Brian started up again:

'Where's the bitch gone? What've you done to me? You've given me something, ain't you? Where is she?'

The policeman turned, annoyed. 'Shut that bloody man up, will you?'

Dave reached out, touching Julie's arm, trying to get her attention.

'I don't understand. I don't know what . . .' His voice trailed away.

Julie looked up, meeting his eyes. She could see he'd been crying. 'Dave, I—'

Unable to bear it, Dave raised his hand to silence her, then turned and walked away. Mike stared a moment longer, then, bitterly: 'Why?'

Julie shook her head miserably. But Mike had no sympathy left in him. 'Come on,' he demanded. 'You were screwing me, screwing him . . . screwing every bastard in the south of England by the sound of it!'

Julie looked up at him through her tears. 'I'm sorry, Mike. I never meant to hurt anyone.'

'No?' he said bitterly. 'It really sounds like it.' And then he too turned on his heel and walked away.

Karl stood there, his arms crossed, a look of immense satisfaction on his face. 'So! How's my loving wife?'

'Oh, sod off!'

'Karl, you said,' the policeman interrupted, noting it down on his list. 'And what surname would that be?'

Julie waited while the detective – Melville – unlocked the police car's door, then ducked inside, the young WPC climbing in after her. Everyone was watching her, and for once Julie didn't like the attention. As the car made its way along the narrow drive towards the gates, Julie glimpsed Charlotte, sitting on the bench where they'd spoken last time. Her hand went to the window, meaning to wind it down and call out, but something stopped her. She didn't want Charlotte to see her in a police car.

Her hand fell away. Slowly, almost at a crawl, the car drove past the bench. Julie turned to watch her daughter through the back window, her heart torn from her, a single tear – the first she'd shed that day – rolling down her cheek.

Matthew Parker strolled through the front doors of Bow nick, pleased to see that the place was half-deserted, only a couple of placid-looking down-and-outs cluttering the bench to one side. Walking up to the desk, he gave his old friend Sergeant White a smile.

'Hi, Deek, what's up?'

'Slow day, is it?' the sergeant answered, looking up from his book, not overly pleased to see Parker there at his desk. The man was bad news. Literally.

'Come on, Deek. Favours I've done you.'

'Oh yeah?' The sergeant couldn't think of one, but he knew what a persistent pain in the arse Parker could be. If the past was anything to go on, he'd be hanging round all bloody afternoon if he didn't give him something. Even so, he wasn't going to make it easy for the creep.

'It's quiet,' he answered after a moment. 'Guess all the villains are on their winter break in Benidorm.'

'Yeah?' Parker laughed. 'So what about those who can't afford the airfare?'

'Sleeping off Christmas, I suppose.'

Parker leaned across the desk, trying to read the entries in the day book. The sergeant closed it; stared at Parker pointedly.

Parker looked round as the doors swung open and Julie was led into the station, a detective on one side and a pretty WPC on the other. The detective glanced up at the wipe-off board hanging on the wall behind the desk, then spoke to the WPC.

'Take her through to room five.'

For a brief moment Parker and Julie made eye contact before she was led away. As she disappeared along the corridor, he stared after her.

'You ain't going to believe this one,' the detective said, already imagining telling the story in the pub later that evening.

Alert at once, Parker jerked round to see Julie's name being written up on the board.

'I've got myself a serial bigamist here. We're up to five and still counting, I reckon. Get someone to bring some tea in, will you?'

The sergeant nodded, and as the detective made his way towards room five he glanced across at Parker.

Both men smiled. But Matthew Parker was already imagining the headline, the double-page spread on pages four and five, the wedding photos lined up one under another. His grin widened.

Julie Harding, eh?

Hunched over the steering wheel, Imogen looked up from her newspaper, surprised that Charlotte was back so soon. Then she saw her face:

'What is it? What's the matter?'

Charlotte climbed into the car. She shut the door then pulled on her safety belt, every action slow, deliberate. She had been crying.

'She didn't come.'

'Oh—' Imogen made to hold her, but something in Charlotte's manner stopped her. 'I'm sorry, sweetie, I—'

'I guess she didn't want to,' Charlotte said, a coldness in her voice. 'If it were me, I'd—' She stopped, then shook her head. A fresh tear slowly trickled down her cheek. 'I suppose I shouldn't have expected anything else. Seems like she's spent her life running away from her responsibilities. Why should she start behaving differently now?'

'You don't know that,' Imogen said, finding herself cast unexpectedly in the role of Julie's defender. 'Maybe she just couldn't get away from the ward.'

Charlotte turned to look at her. 'I went up there. She wasn't on the ward. I looked, but she wasn't there.'

'Then maybe she was sick.'

'But she had my number.' Charlotte sniffed, then wiped the tears away, hating herself for hurting so much.

'You want me to go in and ask? Maybe they know something. Maybe she left a message.'

Charlotte shook her head forlornly. 'Just take me home.'

D.I. Melville and a female colleague – a young WPC – sat on one side of the table, Julie on the other. Not three paces away, a uniformed officer stood with his back to the door. The tape was running.

'So,' Melville said, 'you married Ian in 1991 and were divorced in 1998.'

'If you say so.'

'But in 1994 you married Anthony Holloway.'

'Then the divorce must have come through earlier, mustn't it?'

Melville sat back a little, smiling now. 'According to Navy records, your husband moved out of married quarters in 1995, but again it was five years before that marriage could be dissolved.'

Julie shrugged. 'I don't know what all the fuss is about. Anyway, I don't know what they've told you, but neither of them treated me right. Months on end I was left on my own.'

'Maybe so,' D.I. Melville said patiently, 'but that's not the issue here, is it?' He looked down at his notes again. 'Now where were we? Ah yes – you weren't divorced from Tony until last year, yet in 1996 you walked up the aisle with our good friend Brian Carter.'

'I was never married to Brian,' Julie said, looking the detective square in the eye. 'We just lived together. He was more of a lodger really.'

'Then how do you account for your signing in as his wife on prison visiting forms?'

'Common-law. And that was only cos I felt sorry for him.'

D.I. Melville slowly shook his head. He'd been amused at first, but now this was getting tiresome. He took the copy of the wedding certificate from the file and, turning it about, put it down in front of Julie. Patiently, he read out the details, pointing them out with his finger.

'Julie Vera Harding – that's you – married Brian Peter Carter on the thirteenth of July, nineteen hundred and ninety-six.'

He sat back again.

'Stop pissing about, will you, love? We've got a few more to get through yet and I'd like to get home for my dinner.'

He sighed. 'Okay – Karl. Karl Mason, that is. You married him in 1997. Then we have Dave Freeman – you married him in 1999. And last, but not least, we have Michael James, whom you also married last year. And you know what—? Not a divorce in sight, my love. Now, either you've got an aversion to paperwork, or else you've got a bit of a problem. Either way, Julie, my sweet, you are in serious trouble, and if you want to avoid being in even deeper shit, then you'd better start filling in the gaps.'

Julie sat there, playing with her wedding ring, considering.

'Come on, sweetheart,' Melville said, giving her his best smile. 'In for a penny, in for a pound.'

Julie met his eyes. 'Will it work in my favour?'

Melville nodded. 'Who'd you think I'd rather be banging away – you or some bastard drug dealer?'

'Alright – there's two more, but they're both legal.'

Melville laughed.

'No. I mean it. There's Duncan, Duncan – Muir, that is. He was my first husband. We were together nearly five years, but he was killed in a car crash.' She looked from Melville to the

WPC and back. 'I'm tellin' the truth. He looked after me, Duncan. Only one who ever did, until Dave. And then there was Gary. I think I married him on the rebound. I was at college then. You know, nursing college. We'd only known each other a couple of weeks.' Julie smiled sadly. 'I can't even remember his surname.'

She was quiet a moment, thoughtful, then: 'Will you have to keep me here?'

Melville smiled sympathetically. 'I shouldn't think so. You ain't got any weddings planned this weekend, have you?'

Julie almost smiled. 'No.'

'Then I think that's it. Unless you fancy a cup of tea before you go?'

Julie nodded gratefully. Melville looked to the uniform at the door and nodded. Unlocking the door, the officer went out.

'Thanks for cooperating,' Melville said and, giving the date and time, he ended the tape, then rose from the table, along with his colleague, the already bulky file under one arm.

'Take care,' he said, looking back at her from the door. But Julie didn't seem to be listening. She just sat there, hunched forward now, a sad, pathetic-looking figure, more like a frightened child than the man-eater the police file suggested. Melville went to say something more, then, knowing he'd probably not get an answer, stepped out, closing the door behind him.

Maybe the old joke was true, after all. Maybe the poor woman did just love the taste of wedding cake.

Chapter Twenty-Three

The Crying Game

Jack woke in the dawn's first light. He was lying in a big double bed, in a room with yellow curtains. Beside him lay a woman, her naked back turned to him, her long blonde hair – dyed, the roots showing black – reminding him of where he was.

Donna's house. Or, at least, Donna's brother's place. He was away, so Donna was looking after it for him.

He studied her a moment, tracing the shape of her spine with his eyes, noting the faint mottling of the flesh at the top of her back, the tattoo – a spider, complete with web – on her right shoulder.

Though eight years older than him, Donna was a good-looking woman and made love like an angel; she was kind and made him laugh a lot; nor was she unintelligent, if it came to that, but she was not Charlotte, and though they'd spent a good New Year together, Jack knew he would have to leave, before they took this any further.

He put his hands behind his head and lay there a while, thinking. Maybe Charlotte really *didn't* want him. If so, there was nothing he could do about that; just grit his teeth and get on with his life. But he wasn't going to leave it. He'd made himself a resolution to try one last time; to go down on his hands and knees if need be and beg her to make a go of it.

Why? He didn't quite know why. Just that running away hadn't worked. That, though he'd fallen into Donna's arms – and others' very like her – they weren't enough for him. Nothing was enough if it wasn't Charlotte.

It was like there was a hollow inside him when she wasn't there. A space he couldn't fill – not with drink or drugs or other women. And though he tried to tell himself that it oughtn't to be so – that there would be others, and that in time he'd come to love them just as much – something perverse in him denied that.

Even last night, as Donna had made love to him, his mind had been elsewhere, and though his body had succumbed finally to her embraces, still some small part of him was forever held back, not given, *reserved* for Charlotte. Even when he betrayed her, he was still hers.

Careful not to wake her, Jack climbed from Donna's bed and, naked, went through into the living room, closing the door behind him.

He dialled the number without thinking, waiting, watching the door and listening, making sure Donna didn't wake and disturb him. Then, finally, an answer.

'Hello, Mum? Yes, it's me, Jack. I'm coming home.'

Karl had been at the police station most of the previous evening, giving his statement, but also trying to find out what he could about the situation. Now, as he sat on the early morning train, heading back to Portsmouth, he felt a small glow of satisfaction, remembering the brief telephone conversation he'd had with Anita late last night.

'*So how do you feel about it?*' she'd asked.

'*Apart from feeling a prat? Relieved, I s'pose. I mean, as things stand I was never legally married to her so . . .*'

He'd paused, sensing the expectant tension on the other end of the line, then:

'*Anita?*'

'*Yeah?*'

'*Will you marry me?*'

Karl grinned, oblivious of the other passengers looking at him. She said she'd be waiting for him at the station, and never – never, in his entire life – had he wanted to see someone more.

Yeah, he thought. *It's all worked out for the best.*

It was over now. He could get on with his life.

Julie put her overnight bag down, then, feeling a little sheepish, reached out and knocked. It was early yet, not even eight, but she could hear noises inside as Marie got Ellie ready for school.

Marie was smiling as she opened the door, saying something to Ellie, but the words died on her lips. A look of shock came into her face.

'You!'

'I'm sorry, I—'

'You've got a nerve! Turning up here?'

'Marie, please. You're my friend.'

But there was no kindness in Marie's face. 'Friend! You don't know the meaning of the word! Friends don't lie to you, for a start!'

'I didn't mean—'

Marie just shook her head in disgust. 'I took you in when you didn't have a place to stay. I—'

But Julie was looking past her at Ellie, who had come out into the hallway to see who it was. She smiled at the little girl.

'Hello, sweetheart.'

'Hi, Julie, do you want to see my new scooter. I—'

'Not now, Ellie!' Marie said harshly. 'Now go back in the kitchen and shut the door!' She rounded on Julie again. 'I don't know what you think you're doing here, but I don't want to see you.'

'But I've got nowhere else to go.'

'So where did you stay last night?'

'At a B and B.'

'Well, there you go!'

'But I haven't the money.'

'Well, you should have thought of that, shouldn't you?'

Marie went to shut the door, but Julie put her hand out, stopping her.

'Marie, wait!'

'*What?*'

'I've got a daughter.'

'A *what?*'

Julie looked on the verge of tears. 'She's eighteen. I had her adopted but she came and found me. I didn't want her to know about—' She swallowed. 'I thought, if I could start again then maybe we could, you know, get to know one another and she's the only thing in my life I've ever really cared about and—'

Julie stopped. Marie's face was hard. It was as if she hadn't been listening.

'How many lives have you ruined, eh? How many poor bastards have you left in tears? And you've the nerve to say you *care* about something! Don't you ever stop?'

She stared at Julie for a moment longer, a withering contempt in her eyes, then, knocking Julie's arm aside, she slammed the door shut in her face.

Charlotte lay on her bed, the curtains drawn, the daylight kept at bay, her music a faint murmur in the darkness. She was thinking of Julie, of reasons why she hadn't wanted to see her yesterday. Of reasons why . . .

Sitting up, she reached out for the bedside light and switched it on. In the sudden brightness, she caught a glimpse of herself in the wardrobe mirror, her hair lank, unbrushed, her face pale, the eyes red from lack of sleep.

And from crying.

Her handbag was on the floor where she'd dropped it on coming in last night. She leaned over and picked it up, then took out the tiny white envelope and removed the picture of the scan from it.

For a while she simply stared at it, taking in every detail of that tiny, blurred shape, then nodded to herself. Reaching beneath her clothes, her left hand gently stroked her slightly swollen belly.

She would not *be* her mother. Whatever else happened in this life, she was not going to let this tiny life be taken from her care. This tiny being, this small and helpless creature – it was *her* responsibility.

She slipped the image back into the envelope, then returned it to the bag. Yet even as she did, her eyes were caught and held by the photo propped up against the lamp – the three by three snap of Julie as a six-year-old.

A momentary bitterness made her reach out and grasp the photo. For a moment she felt the urge to take it and rip it into a thousand tiny pieces, but though she was angry and hurt, she had not entirely given up on Julie. Not yet.

She let the photo fall, then stood. It was time to get bathed and dressed and face the day. Time to get on with her life.

It was midday and Marie was on her own behind the bar. Dave had gone down to the police station again to see if he could find out what was happening, but she didn't mind being left. Not this time.

She felt sorry for Dave. More than that, she felt guilty – guilty because it had been she who'd introduced them; who'd brought Julie into his life, with such devastating results.

She'd never seen a man cry quite like Dave cried last night. Never seen anyone – not even a child – look so distraught. They'd closed the pub for the evening and – opening up a bottle of scotch and a half bottle of vodka – had drowned Dave's sorrows between them.

This morning he'd been a lot more together. Not that he wasn't still hurting – she could see he was – but some small core of self-respect had woken in him. Julie was in the past and he had to put her behind him – so he said, and she could see that part of him meant it. But she knew Dave well enough to know that this was a major, maybe even a terminal blow to him as a man. As he saw it, Julie had been his last chance at love, and now she was gone.

It had almost been enough to make her sleep with him. For comfort's sake. But that would have been a mistake – maybe a bigger mistake than introducing Julie in the first place – because though she liked Dave and felt really sorry for him, she wasn't in love with him, and the thought of a serious relationship just wasn't on.

In that way she was different from Julie. Radically different. Because she was conscious of the possible outcome of her actions, and not only conscious, but unwilling to hurt someone in the future for the sake of some smaller pleasure now.

As she pulled pints and cleared glasses, she found herself getting angrier and angrier with Julie. Julie was no better than a spoiled child, a petulant, thoughtless, self-centred little girl,

who'd never grown up. But now she was going to get her just
deserts, and about bloody time!

As for her calling round this morning—

Marie gave a little shiver of indignation, then turned to find
the eyes of a customer on her. Passing trade, not a regular.

'Can I help you?'

The guy was a little portly, in his late thirties, maybe even
forties, but he seemed pleasant enough, and he had a nice
smile.

'A double scotch and soda, ta, love. And no ice.' He paused.
'And one for yourself?'

Marie smiled but shook her head. 'It's kind of you, but I'd
better not. Gotta keep me wits about me.'

Again that smile. 'I saw you were on your own. Dave not
about then?'

'You know Dave?'

'Oh, from way back. Heard he'd had a bit of woman
trouble. Thought I'd come and cheer the poor bugger up.'

'Ah.' Marie studied him a moment, then: 'Any particular
scotch?'

'Whatever comes.'

She put the glass beneath the measure and poured two shots.
Turning back, she saw he was smiling still, as if amused by
something.

'What?' she asked, reaching down for a soda.

'I was just wondering why Dave should have been so hung up
on this other woman with you for company. You could be one
of those cocktail waitresses with those lovely long legs of yours.'

Marie almost blushed, enjoying the flattery. 'Nah – I like it
here.'

'Well.' He took the scotch from her, handed her a fiver.
'Cheers, love.'

As she handed him back his change, he asked casually, 'So
how did he find out in the end?'

'It was me, I guess. I saw her . . . with the other bloke. Then,
when Dave went round to sort him out, he and the other guy
put two and two together.'

'Blimey! Must have been a shock, eh?'

'You bet! You know, I still can't believe it, to tell you the truth. And you know what?'

'What?'

'She only turned up on my doorstep this morning. Looking for a place to say. What a nerve, eh? Bold as bleeding brass, she was. And as though that weren't enough, she tells me she's got this eighteen-year-old daughter. Just like that.'

'Bloody hell,' he said, looking surprised and concerned, but inside, Matthew Parker was exulting.

A love child, eh? Better and bloody better, my old son!

Ricky hadn't had to go in to work until midday, so Sonia had let the children stay up late to watch a film. She was just about to go upstairs and see if they were awake yet, when the doorbell rang. The radio was on, out in the kitchen. It was a Craig David song – one she really liked – and as she walked back down the hallway she sang along with it.

She pulled open the door, smiling, the tune still running through her head, then felt a tiny wave of shocked surprise wash over her.

'Oh my God.'

Julie stared back at her. 'Hello, Sonia.' Then she burst into tears.

Sonia noted the overnight bag, the look of desperation on her face and, beneath her breath, muttered, 'Oh shit.'

For a moment longer Julie stood there, sobbing, then Sonia took her arm and half led, half pulled her inside.

Sitting out in the kitchen, clutching a cup of tea, Julie told her the whole story. It was some tale, but Sonia, listening to it all, was a lot less prepared to take it all on face value than she might once have. The bits about Karl, for instance, worried her, and if Julie was lying about Karl, then why not about the other men?

Even so, Julie seemed genuinely distraught, and while Sonia knew what Ricky would have to say about it, she didn't have the heart to send Julie packing. Even so, she felt duty-bound to let Karl know that Julie had reappeared, and while Julie was in the bathroom, freshening up, she made the call.

Anita answered the phone.

'Hi, Neet. Is Karl there?'

'No. Not right now. But I'm meeting him up the station in half an hour. You'll never guess what—'

'She was married before. Several times.'

Anita sounded shocked. 'How d'you know that?'

Sonia hesitated, then, 'She's *here*.'

'*There?* But—' Anita was clearly at a loss for words. 'Why?' she asked finally.

'I dunno,' Sonia said, trying to keep her voice down. 'I don't think she had anywhere else to go.'

'Yeah, but what'll Ricky say? And it ain't very nice for Karl.'

'What could I do?' Sonia asked quietly. 'She was my friend.'

Ricky would murder her. She sighed. 'Look, Neet, I gotta go. She'll be back in a sec.'

Sonia hung up the phone. Poor old Karl. It must have been a real shock, finding out. But some small part of her was impressed. Eight husbands! I mean, one was bad enough at times, but eight!

As Julie emerged from the bathroom, more relaxed, her eyes no longer quite so haunted, she asked, 'Who was that?'

'Just a mate,' Sonia answered, surprised that Julie had heard. Then, more brightly: 'So? You fancy a fry-up, or what?'

Matthew Parker climbed down off the train and looked about him.

'What a shit-hole!' he said softly.

He was travelling light, just his notebook, a portable tape recorder and a half bottle of whisky. Skirting his way round a kissing couple – *too bloody old to be doing that*, he thought, checking the woman's arse anyway as he passed, impressed that a woman her age had kept herself so trim in the bum department – he made for the taxi rank and, jumping in the back of one of the cars, gave the driver the address he'd wheedled out of D.S. White the night before.

The latest husband – Mike – hadn't wanted to speak to him. He'd gone round there earlier on and nearly got a good kicking for his trouble. The man had told him to fuck off in no uncertain terms, but he'd change his mind, when he'd had time to calm down: when he came to realise that the best medicine was revenge – *his* story there in the press in black and white. No better feeling, he'd convince the man – no better way of getting back at the bitch.

Nor had he been able to speak to the other one – Dave – just yet, though his little chat with the barmaid had been more than productive. He didn't have a name for the kid yet, but he'd get it. No problem!

As the car pulled up outside the two-up, two-down little Wimpey house, Parker leaned forward between the seats and, giving the driver a twenty, said, 'Wait here. If I'm gonna be longer than half an hour, I'll come out and let you know, okay?'

The driver shrugged, then switched his engine off. As he did, another car from the same firm came up the curving drive and stopped directly behind them. A door opened and, to Parker's surprise, the man and the woman who'd been snogging at the station stepped out and proceeded to walk up the path to Karl's house.

Seeing that they were about to go inside, Parker hailed them, then hurried up the path.

They had turned, wondering who the hell he was.

'Are you Karl Mason?'

'Why? Who wants to know?'

'My name's Matthew Parker. I'm a reporter for the *National Star*, and I wondered—'

Karl took two steps towards him and grabbing his lapels, lifted him clear off his feet. Parker raised his arms, trying to break Karl's grip, and for the briefest moment it looked as if the two men would come to blows, but Parker took a step back, holding up his hands.

'Hold up, mate. I know how angry you must be, finding out about your wife and all that, but—'

'Just fuck off,' Karl said. 'D'you understand? I don't want to talk to you or any scum like you. So just fuck off back where you came from, unless you want my boot rammed up your arse!'

'But I only want to know—'

'You wanna know anything, you get it from the horse's mouth!'

Parker narrowed his eyes. 'What d'you mean?'

'I mean, you want to talk to the bitch, you go knock at number twenty-three.'

Parker laughed. 'You're kidding?'

'No, mate. You go and ask her what the fuck she thought she was playing at.'

Julie was unpacking her overnight bag in the spare room when there was a knock on the door.

'Come in,' she said brightly, and turned to find Sonia standing there, next to a man she'd never seen before.

'Julie, this is—'

The man stepped past Sonia, putting out his hand as he did. 'Hi, Julie. My name's Matthew Parker.'

'Hi,' she said, confused now. She looked to Sonia for an explanation, but Sonia just stood there.

'I'm sorry,' Julie began, looking back at the man, 'but—?'

'Oh.' Parker smiled reassuringly. 'It's okay – I'm not with the police. Actually I'm from the *National Star*. I just wondered if I might have a quick word with you. I know you must be tired, what with all that's happened, but it won't take long, and—'

'The *National Star*?'

'That's right, and I'd like to talk to you about getting an exclusive on your story.'

'An exclusive?' Julie looked stunned.

'You know the kind of thing,' Parker went on. 'We'd have a chat about all your husbands, take some nice pics of you – in a wedding dress, of course, cutting the cake, that sort of thing – and then a few anecdotes: what it's like to have eight different mothers-in-law; who was good at this, who was good at that—'

Julie stared at Sonia, not quite able to believe what was happening, while Parker carried on oblivious of her. But he was beginning to sense that she might not be as willing as he'd hoped.

'Oh, and I'm sure we could arrange some kind of fee. But obviously, that's only if we get the exclusive.' He paused, then positively beamed at her. 'It's a great story, Julie. Really great stuff.'

But Julie wasn't smiling. Scowling now, she pushed past Parker angrily and stormed out on to the landing. A moment later, the bathroom door slammed shut behind her, the bolt slotting into place with a resounding thud.

Parker turned, looking to Sonia, as if she might help resolve things, but she shook her head and smiled. 'I think that's a no.'

Jack set his bag down in the hallway, then turned, looking directly at his mother. He had changed. She could see just how much he'd changed – and not just physically. He'd cropped his hair and lost a bit of puppy fat, but the difference was his eyes. In the months he'd been away, he had grown up; had become an adult. She held out her arms, hoping he would come to her, as he'd used to as a younger boy and, after a moment's hesitation, he did, smiling now, holding her tight in an embrace of purest affection. It made her feel like crying. Made her so happy that it almost paid for all the days and nights of worrying she'd done. Jack was home. Life could carry on now. Jack was home.

But as he broke from the embrace, she saw something else in his eyes and frowned at him.

'What is it, Jack?'

Again, that slightest hesitation. Then, 'Come through to the kitchen, Mum. There's something I've got to tell you.'

She was shocked. No point disguising the fact, she hadn't expected Jack's news. Oh, it explained a lot, but—

'You're sure?' she asked. 'She wasn't just saying that to – you know . . .'

He shook his head, his eyes, his mind, elsewhere. 'No. She wouldn't do that. She was always very straight.'

'And you're sure it's yours?'

Jack simply looked at her, older than her at that moment. 'Mum—'

'Sorry. Only . . .'

But she didn't pursue the point. Besides, she didn't think Charlotte was the kind to sleep around. She seemed a nice girl.

'So what are you going to do?'

'See if she'll see me. Talk to her. Persuade her.'

'Persuade her what?'

'To marry me.'

Shock again. In those few words she saw all her hopes and dreams for her son evaporate. She'd wanted so much for him and now here he was talking of landing himself with a wife and baby before he was even twenty.

'I didn't think—' she began.

'You thought I'd go to university. Get a degree. Maybe meet a girl there. Yeah?'

She nodded, struggling to contain her anger. Young people thought they were so bloody smart, but they couldn't even have sex without getting pregnant.

'And if she says no?'

He looked away, and in that moment she realised he had not only thought of that, but had dwelled on it – maybe thought of nothing else these past few days. It made her heart bleed for him – to put so much hope into something. But didn't they all? Wasn't that the whole point about love? The risk of it?

'You hungry?'

He nodded, and then he smiled. 'Thanks, Mum.'

She smiled, knowing that the only thing she could do now was to be there for him.

The driver looked up, meeting Matthew Parker's eyes in the rear-view mirror.

'Listen, mate. You sure you don't want to find a hotel for the night? I don't reckon she wants to talk to you.'

'No?'

Well, that just shows how little you know, Parker thought. The curtains had twitched a couple of times, as one or other of them had checked to see if he was still there. Julie would no doubt be impressed by his persistence. She'd be thinking that he wasn't going to go away – not without a story – and that if not him, then someone else would latch on to it, so why not tell him and get it over with?

At least, he hoped that was what she was thinking. If not, he was out sixty quid in taxi fares.

He was about to say something more – to explain things to the guy – when the front door opened and the other one – Sonia – beckoned to him.

'There we are!' he said quietly, but triumphantly. 'What did I tell you?'

Parker peeled off another twenty and handed it across. 'Now stay right there. I'll be an hour at the most.'

Julie was waiting for him in the living room. Sonia ushered him in, then closed the door behind him. Julie had done her hair and made herself up, so that she looked attractive. A nice figure and a friendly smile. He could see why so many men had fallen for her.

'Julie, thanks – I appreciate this.'

She gestured toward the armchair. He sat, then smiled at her.

'Cup of tea?' she asked, indicating the pot that rested on the low table nearby. 'It's fresh.'

'Ta.'

He watched her pour, wondering where to start, what angle to adopt, when she began to talk.

'I didn't want to speak to you. I still don't really. But Sonia persuaded me. Said I might as well – get all the others off my back. And there will be others, won't there?'

Parker gave a little nod. 'Yeah. Look, we're talking an exclusive, right?'

Julie met his eyes. She seemed ashamed, like she knew she was doing something wrong, but she nodded anyway.

'You go speaking to anyone else and our agreement's off, alright?'

'And what is our agreement?'

'Three thousand for the complete story – you to pose for pictures.'

'Five.'

'Four.'

She nodded, then handed him his cup. 'So what do you want to know?'

Parker smiled. 'Everything, Julie. I want to know everything about you.'

After he'd gone, Julie sat there, staring at the wall, feeling empty, hollow. She hadn't told him everything – how could she? – yet even what she *had* said had upset her. It made her feel cheap, sordid somehow, even though the truth was far from sordid. It was like he'd been fishing for something, only she wasn't sure quite what. Some of his questions—

There was a knock on the door.

'Yeah?'

Sonia poked her head round, then stepped inside, holding out a glass of wine.

'Thought you'd like something a bit stronger.'

'Ta. Thanks, Sonia. You're an angel.'

'Ricky'll kill me.' Then, blurting it out. 'I meant to tell you, Karl took the furniture.'

'What?' Then she understood and laughed. 'Poor bastard. I bet he was pissed off, wasn't he?'

'You could say that.'

Julie's face changed. 'You didn't—?'

'The box?'

Julie nodded.

'I got it upstairs.'

'Ah. Did you look inside it?'

Sonia hesitated, then nodded.

'So you knew?'

'Sort of. I wasn't sure. Only it was odd – three lots of wedding photos.'

Julie smiled sadly. 'I've made a real balls-up of things, ain't I?'

The front door slammed. Ricky called out from the hallway. 'Son, I'm home!'

Sonia looked to Julie, then jumped to her feet, rushing out into the hallway to break the news.

*

Matthew Parker sat on the train, talking into his mobile as the countryside flashed by outside the rain-streaked window.

'Yeah yeah, no, that'd be great. I appreciate it, babe. Yeah, take care.'

He clicked the mobile off, then sat back, feeling an immense satisfaction. *A good day's work, Matthew, old son*, he told himself. Now he only had to hope things kept quiet for a day or two and bingo!

He grinned, then took his notebook out and looked through it once more. He had it all on tape, too, but it was his notes – his shorthand comments on further leads and questions to be asked – that were generally more important. He was an instinctive reporter, and his instinct right now was that there was a lot more dirt to be dug out of this one. The woman had held things back – the existence of her daughter for starters – and he was pretty damn sure that the bigamous marriages were just the tip of the proverbial iceberg, but you didn't ever get to see what was below the surface without a bit of digging.

Yeah, and a bit of cunning, too.

Our Julie hadn't been at all keen to talk about her upbringing. Even now he didn't know what town she'd been brought up in. But he would. Now that he'd got her date of birth – just for the record, he'd told her. From that he'd get her birth certificate, and from that he'd get the details of her mum and dad and where she was born.

But he wouldn't have that until tomorrow. *Fuck the New Year*, he thought to himself.

Word would get out, of course – a case like this, how couldn't it? – only he was well ahead of the pack, and he had the woman herself under contract.

Or as good as.

That was something he ought to deal with at once. He could get Harry to draw one up straight away. Get it all watertight.

Standing up, he wandered down the carriage until he came to the toilets. Locking himself in, he got out his mobile and tapped out Harry's number.

'Hello, Harry? Yeah, it's me, Matthew. Get your chequebook out, mate. Have I got a story for you!'

Chapter Twenty-Four

Always On My Mind

The old girl had tried to close the door on him, but he'd got his foot in – yes, and half his leg – and he wasn't going anywhere until she'd told him what he wanted to be told.

'I ain't got nothing to say,' she was saying, distressed now. 'You ain't got any right—'

'Come on, Vera,' he said, his voice all reasonable, even as he struggled to keep the door from closing on him. 'Just a few questions. Your Julie's going to be a bit of a celebrity, and I'm sure you'd rather tell your side of things than have it all made up by some toe-rag in the Sunday tabloids!'

As if that was just what she feared, Vera put up even more of a struggle, trying to squeeze him like a paste back out on to the landing, but Matthew Parker wasn't going anywhere, and with a final little push, Vera relented and, standing back, let him in.

She stood there, looking terrified, and, seeing it, Matthew Parker also relented. He smiled at her, then gently closed the door.

'There,' he said quietly. 'We don't want everyone in the block knowing your business, do we? See, the thing is, your Julie's in a spot of trouble . . .'

He got her to sit down in the old-fashioned living room and, while the tape ran, he made small talk. She looked upset, as if she already knew, yet when he told her exactly why he was there, she seemed astonished – indeed, the look of shock on her face was almost comical.

'Eight?' Vera repeated, as if he'd surely said something different. 'Isn't that illegal?'

'Yeah, but good luck to her, I say. I mean, it's not as if she's done anyone any harm.'

'So she's not really in trouble?'

'No. She'll be fine. A slapped wrist, I reckon.' He smiled. 'So, what do you reckon then, Mum, about being the butt of eight lots of mother-in-law jokes?'

Vera leaned towards him, her face anxious. 'Look, I ain't seen Julie since she was sixteen. I can't tell you anything about her since then. These men – well, I don't know about any of them.'

'Since she was sixteen? Why was that?'

Vera stood. 'I'm sorry but you're going to have to go. My husband'll be back any minute and he don't like people coming into the flat.'

'Yeah, of course.' Matthew made to get up, then collapsed back down. 'Actually, I couldn't have a glass of water and a biscuit or something, could I? Only I'm diabetic and I feel a bit—'

Agitated, Vera reluctantly went out into the kitchen. While she was gone, Parker hurriedly looked about him, opening drawers. Finding a number of family photos, he quickly pocketed them.

Calling out to her, he asked, 'So why did Julie leave home? Was it a family row? It's a difficult age, sixteen. Bit of a handful, I expect—'

He opened another drawer, began poking through the bits and pieces there.

'Or was it because of the baby?'

He closed the drawer and turned. An elderly man was standing there.

'Who the hell are you?'

Recovering quickly from his surprise, Parker took a step towards the old man, offering his hand.

'Matthew Parker, *National Star*. I'm just here to ask—'

'Get out.'

'Sorry?'

'You heard. Now piss off out of it. You're scum, the lot of you!'

Vera appeared now in the doorway. She looked afraid. 'He forced his way in, Ted. I couldn't—'

'You stupid cow.'

Parker looked from one of them to the other, noting the tension. 'Look,' he said, 'I just want a bit of background—'

Ted rounded on him. 'You still here?'

'Alright. I'm off. But if you want to talk—'

Ted glared, and Parker quickly left. Alone with his wife again, Ted turned on her angrily.

'What did you tell him?'

'Nothing, Ted. I promise.'

'You—'

His blow caught Vera square on the side of her face, just above her right cheekbone. It knocked her down, and as she struggled to get up, he reached down, his fingers gripping her short, grey, curly hair and tugging it viciously.

'You stupid cow!'

Matthew Parker didn't realise just what treasures he'd brought with him out of the flat until, tipping the photos out on to his desk that evening, he saw the tiny scrap of paper that had somehow piggy-backed its way south with him and, unfolding it, read the name and address on it.

Charlotte. Same name as the baby Julie Harding had given birth to eighteen years ago. Of course, it could have been anyone. A family friend, or an old acquaintance, only why keep it in with those photos unless it had some personal significance?

The address was in North London. He could get over there in an hour if the traffic wasn't too bad. Then again, he was tired. It wouldn't hurt if he left it until the morning.

As he was trying to make up his mind, the phone beside him rang.

'Hello? Matthew Parker.'

'Hi, babe. Got that information you wanted.'

He listened, making notes, and as he did, a smile slowly crept into his face, until he was grinning triumphantly. 'Great! You're a fucking star, Alice, my love! A fucking star!'

Putting the phone down, he clenched his fist and gave a little cheer, like he'd just scored a goal in a cup final. He'd known it.

His every instinct had told him that it had to be something like this, and what he'd glimpsed through Ted and Vera's letterbox had good enough as confirmed it for him, but here was the proof.

'Gotcha, you old bastard,' he said, and grinning, reached behind him and put on his jacket. It was time to fit the last few pieces into the puzzle.

'Lottie, sweetheart, there's someone here to see you.'

Charlotte looked up from the TV and saw, just behind Richard, a stranger – a middle-aged man with a pronounced beer belly.

'Dad?'

'He's from the press. He says he has news . . . about Julie.'

She came out, walked through into the kitchen. Richard made to go, to leave her alone, but she called him back.

'No, Daddy. I want you to stay.' Then, to the reporter, 'Well?'

The man looked at her awkwardly, apologetically. 'This isn't easy,' he said. 'Do you think—?' And he gestured towards a chair. But Charlotte didn't like the press. She made no concessions to the man. Whatever he was here for, it could not possibly be to her benefit – that much she knew in her eighteen-year-old way. She remained standing, obliging him also to stand.

'Alright,' he said, sighing heavily. 'It's like this. Your mother – your birth mother, that is – has been arrested.'

'*Arrested?*'

Parker nodded, his face all false sympathy. 'Yeah. Seems she's been marrying but forgetting that she was already married.'

'Bigamy, you mean?' Richard asked.

'Bigamy,' the reporter echoed. 'Six counts of it, as far as I can make out.'

'Six—' Charlotte looked to Richard, her eyes round with surprise. She shook her head. 'You're lying. She was divorced and widowed. She told me.'

But she knew even as she spoke that it was true. That he

wouldn't be here if he didn't have the facts. And she knew, too, that she was the colourful twist to the story – the daughter conceived out of wedlock and given away as a baby. She swallowed, angry and bitter suddenly, then took a step towards the man.

'Get out! Get out now, before I call the police!'

The man raised his hands defensively. 'Alright. I'm going. But if you want to talk about it then you can get me at the *National Star*. Matthew Parker.'

'Out,' she said again, in what was almost a feral growl.

Parker left.

She stood there, swaying slightly, appalled by what had just happened. Then she jerked upright as the doorbell rang again.

'It's okay,' Richard began. 'I'll sort it out.'

But Charlotte pushed past him and, rushing to the door, threw it open, yelling as she did.

'I thought I told you to— Oh, it's you.'

Jack stood there, looking very sheepish. It was cold out and he looked wet and miserable. 'I'm sorry, I— Can I come in?'

Matthew Parker was getting into his car when the boyfriend turned up. Quickly, he snatched the camera from the glove compartment and fired off a dozen shots. He didn't think he'd got a good one of the boy, but the last few had captured Charlotte perfectly.

It had begun to rain, and as he drove, he hummed to himself, replicating the rhythm of the windscreen wipers.

He was grinning now. Grinning fit to burst. This story had everything. Or almost everything. The girl, for instance – she'd tried to hide it from him, but he could see she was pregnant. And the young lad who'd called – that, doubtless, was the father.

Like mother, like daughter, he thought, and smiled to himself, the story already forming in his head.

Back in the office, he removed his jacket, rolled up his shirtsleeves and got down to work. Up until a year or so back he'd worked on an old Remington typewriter, ignoring the moans of the subs who had to type it all up again as well as correct his wayward grammar and punctuation. Now, however, he worked on a word processor and, though he'd argued otherwise in the past, it made his work a lot easier.

By six he had the first draft down, complete with straps and headers. Another hour saw it polished. Pleased with himself, he carried it through to Harry's office and slapped it down in front of him.

Harry read it through, blank-faced, then looked up. 'It's good, but what have we got in the way of pictures?'

'Bits and pieces. Her as a young girl with her parents. Her stepdad. The daughter. Oh, and Jimmy's down there right now getting a few shots of her in a bridal outfit.'

'The husbands?'

'We ought to be able to rustle up some snaps. She's got most of it in an old box she keeps. Wedding albums and that kind of thing.'

'Good,' Harry said, sitting back and smiling for the first time. 'Then all we've got to get is her story and we've got ourselves a feature, young Matthew. Good work! Bloody good work!'

Matthew grinned. 'Am I the bloody best or what?'

She had enjoyed it while they were there. Dressing up for the camera had been exciting; had given her a bit of a life. Now, however, she felt the emptiness flood back and, as she sat there, staring out into the night, all she could think of was her child – of Charlotte, and of how different it might all have been. She'd thought of phoning her, but she didn't know what she could say.

It was a bit late to be regretful. She knew that, yet part of her felt cheated, *denied*. If her dad hadn't died. If Ted hadn't come into her life. If she hadn't had Charlotte. Or, again, if she hadn't had to give her up. If her first husband hadn't died. So many ifs. But all of that had happened, and she'd had to get on with her life in spite everything, and if she'd tried to find a bit of happiness along the way, then who could blame her for it? Even so . . .

She couldn't face it, not even now – now that everything was out in the open. It was just too much to bear. But even when she tried not to think about it, she could still hear the old records, smell the old smells, as if she'd been transported back there. As if the days and years between had been but a waking dream.

Back to her childhood. Back, back to the darkness of her room and the creaking boards outside her door.

Julie shivered violently, then stood. Walking across the room, she paused at the doorway and, opening it a fraction, listened. Sonia and Ricky were talking. They were trying to keep it low, but Ricky was finding it hard keeping his voice down. Just the fact that Julie was there was winding him up something terrible. He was Karl's best mate, after all, and that woman . . .

Julie closed the door, then went across and slumped down on to the sofa. It was no good, she couldn't stay here. She'd have to go. But where?

Home, she thought. *It's time I went home.*

But was home really home any more? Was it the bright place of her early childhood? Or was it still the same place she'd fled from almost twenty years ago?

She let her head fall back and closed her eyes. Then, for the first time in a long, long while, she let go, the tears coursing down her face one after another, as if they'd never stop.

Chapter Twenty-Five

Who's Sorry Now

Sonia stirred the tea then carried it across, setting it down across from Julie.

'There you are. Look, you don't have to go, you know.'

'No, but I ought,' Julie said, smiling gratefully. 'I don't want to outstay my welcome. Ricky—'

'Sod Ricky. It's no skin off his nose. He's hardly here, is he?'

'No, but—'

Julie stopped. Ricky had appeared in the doorway. He had a strange look on his face. In his right hand was a copy of the *National Star*. That morning's edition.

Sonia turned in her chair and stared at him. 'What?' Then she noticed the paper and the picture on the front cover and put her hand up to her mouth. 'Christ! Already?'

While Julie went through the paper, Sonia sat there, looking on. They'd flagged the story on the cover and run it over four pages inside. From time to time Julie would groan, or give a tiny gasp of surprise, looking up to shake her head mutely, while Sonia looked on, concerned.

Ricky had gone out into the garden, supposedly to sort out something in the shed, but his look of smug satisfaction – that told-you-so certainty – had riled her, and as sure as eggs were eggs he'd sneaked off to avoid a row.

But that was fine. She didn't want a row right now. Julie looked hurt, bewildered. This wasn't the story she'd told that bastard of a reporter. This was much worse than just a few illegal marriages. This was her life – in its most intimate details – there for anyone to read.

'Is this true, Julie?'

Julie sniffed and nodded. 'Just goes to show, don't it? You can't trust anyone.' She gave a bitter little laugh. 'D'you think he got paid for giving 'em that photo? Bet he did.'

It wasn't Karl she was speaking about now, but her stepfather, Ted. And the picture – the one she had her finger on – was of her aged eleven, standing between her mother and her new stepdad; him grinning, them miserable as sin.

Sonia reached out and covered Julie's hand. 'There are people you can go and see. People you can talk to. You need help, Julie. Maybe that's why—'

'Nah,' Julie said, shrugging off her hand and folding up the paper. 'Not now. It's too late.'

Sonia stared at her beseechingly a moment longer, then dropped her eyes. It was clearly no use. *Poor cow*, she thought. *You poor, poor cow.*

Popping the paper into her bag, Julie finished her tea, then stood, smiling again. Her overnight bag stood in the corner by the door, already packed. She went across and hoisted it on to her shoulder, then turned, looking to Sonia again.

'Thanks for everything. You're an angel.'

Sonia stood, then went across and put her arms about her friend and hugged her. 'Take care, you.'

Julie smiled bravely. 'And you.'

After she'd gone, Ricky came back into the kitchen. He stood there, smirking, until she could bear it no longer.

'Ain't you got no feelings?'

'Look, as far as I'm concerned, she got what she deserved!'

'What she *deserved*!' Sonia stood, then threw the lukewarm contents of her teacup over him. 'You stupid bastard! Can't you sodding read, or what?'

Ricky glared back at her. 'What, all that bollocks about her stepdad?'

'Bollocks? What do you mean, bollocks? He was taken to court for assaulting a kid!'

'Yeah, but nothing was proved. Her word against his.'

Sonia shook her head in disbelief, then scowled as she pushed past him and left the room. *Men!* she thought to herself as she stormed up the stairs. *It's a wonder Julie married a single sodding one of them!*

*

Vera watched in silence as Ted, sitting close up to the fire, poked at the burning ashes of the newspaper with the poker, as if to ensure that not a single fragment of the paper survived. She had read it, all the same. Knew what it said, and knew the truth of it. Now, standing there with her winter coat on and her eye blacked, she stared holes in his back, a strange loathing of him awoken in her finally.

She hadn't known about the court case, but she had always known what he was. Known and gone on living with the fact of it. But suddenly it was out there, in the open, where all could see, and what she had allied herself to when she had married Ted Wright. And that fact changed everything. Everything. The girl had begun it all by coming here and awakening those memories in her. Things she'd forgotten, or had thrust deep down, into the darkest recesses of her memory. But now it was all different. There was no hiding now. A million eyes had peeked into that darkest of places and seen.

You bastard, she thought, her hatred for him pure suddenly. *You wicked fucking bastard.*

Ted gave a grunt as he poked once more at the last few blackened remnants in the grate, his broad shoulders hunched forward as if he were engaged in some much darker, fouler exploit.

And now she smiled; a savage smile of triumph over him. *You can burn all the copies you can find, Ted Wright, but your secret's out. They know now. Everybody knows.*

She turned away, leaving the flat, making her way down the concrete stairs, past the mess of graffiti on the walls and the smell of stale urine, aware that her neighbours were watching her, from their windows and doorways, or looking down at her from their balconies. It was hard to stand, that kind of scrutiny. But she could bear it. After all, she had borne far worse.

Imogen's face was ashen as she finished the article and looked up, meeting Richard's eyes. 'Oh my God!'

He reached out, took her hands.

'Has Charlotte read this?'

He nodded. 'One of her friends phoned.'

'Ah.' Which explained it. They didn't usually buy any of the tabloids. They were *Independent* readers or, at a stretch, the *Guardian*. The *National Star* they viewed on the same level as the *Sun* or the *Sport*. Celebrity trash, not news. Not real news, anyway.

'Oh God,' she said again, trying to imagine how Charlotte was feeling at that moment. 'That stuff about—' She swallowed, then shook her head. 'I'd better go see her.'

'No,' Richard said. 'Let her be. She needs time to think about all of this. To take it all in. Christ, it's—'

Imogen blinked, surprised to hear Richard say even that mild blasphemy. 'The poor woman,' he said. 'Imagine how she must have felt . . .'

But it couldn't be said. The awfulness of it was too much to contemplate.

'Yes, Mum – no, no, I hear what you're saying, Mum. I— look, I've got a pub full of customers right now – can we talk later? Bye.'

Dave put the phone back on the hook, then turned, looking to Marie. His face had a sour, almost pinched look to it this morning, like he'd swallowed a wasp. Beside themselves, the pub was empty. As soon as he'd heard what had happened, he'd put notices up at both doors – *Pub Closed For The Day. Temporary Repairs.* Then he'd gone out and bought all of the Sunday papers.

'Giving you grief, was she?' Marie asked, all sympathy.

Dave nodded. 'My mother likes nothing better than to say, *I told you so.* Mind you, it doesn't help that she was right.'

'She never did like Julie, did she?'

'Nah, well—' He seemed to give himself a little shake, as if he was trying to come awake. 'You know, if she'd only told me about – you know. Maybe we could have . . .'

Seeing how vulnerable he looked, how old and careworn, she stepped over to him and held him for a moment, hugging him, letting him put his head on her shoulder like he was a little boy.

'You'll be alright, Dave. You're like me . . . a survivor.'

'Yeah,' Dave groaned. 'But I miss her so much. Even after all she's done, I—' He caught his breath, then straightened a little. 'Ta,' he said, moving back and smiling at her. 'You're a real mate.'

She smiled, still tingling from the feel of his body against hers.

'What a bitch!' Mike exclaimed, positively glaring at the newspaper that lay beside his untouched breakfast.

I'll be a laughing stock, he thought. *How can I fucking well face them tomorrow after this?* The mere thought of it made him shake his head and groan aloud.

'You alright, Michael?'

Hearing his outburst, Nancy had got out of bed and was now standing in the door, in just her nightie. Mike got up quickly, moving his plate on to the paper to try to hide it.

'Yeah. Yeah, I'm fine.'

But Nancy must have glimpsed something, because she stepped past him and, pushing the plate back, pointed at one of the pictures. 'Is that our Julie?'

He was going to deny it, to make up some kind of story, but then he thought – what's the point? She's going to have to know some time. Only he was afraid. Afraid of what it might do to her. She'd really liked Julie, maybe even loved her – like a mother loves a daughter.

'You'd better sit down,' he said, pulling out a chair and helping her into it. 'It's a long story.'

Jack had pulled his mum's BMW into the garage to get petrol, and was walking across to pay, when he saw the headline on one of the tabloids – NAUGHTY NURSE JULIE WEDS EIGHT TIMES! It wasn't that so much as the fact that the picture underneath it reminded him a lot of Charlotte. He stopped and went over to the basket, picked up a copy of the paper, then opened it to the spread.

'Oh my God.'

The picture wasn't clear, and he had his back to the camera, but Jack had no doubt it was him, because that was Charlotte's house, and there, just to the right of him, was Charlotte herself.

He read the caption and groaned. *Like mother, like daughter*, it began, and went on to speak of Charlotte as Julie's illegitimate child. A few paragraphs later it told of Ted's past and, although it didn't spell it out, the inference was clear. The shock of it made him feel faint. Why hadn't Charlotte said? Why had she let him find out this way?

He threw the paper down, then ran back to the car, slamming it into gear and away, ignoring the shouts of the attendant as he squealed out into the busy main road.

'Why didn't you say?' he moaned, swerving the car past a bus and narrowly missing a cyclist. 'Why didn't you fucking tell me?'

Anita lay there in the new king-size they'd had delivered only last week, looking utterly gorgeous, her lovely, globe-like breasts visible above the fresh white sheets, and as Karl came back into the room, the breakfast tray in his hands, a newspaper under one arm, she smiled lasciviously at him.

He put the tray down on the bedside table, then handed her the paper. There was a moment's query in her eyes, and then a look of shocked surprise.

'Christ!'

'I was number six,' Karl said, shaking his head, still amazed by it all. 'Can you believe it, number fucking six!'

'Bloody hell,' Anita said, almost in a whisper, as she took in the array of wedding pictures. 'Mind you, you've got to hand it to her. It ain't easy finding eight blokes to marry you. And, I mean, they ain't bad-looking, are they?' She looked up at him, saw the momentary hurt in his face and, putting the paper aside, reached out for him. 'Hey, are you okay?'

But the look melted away, and seeing her looking up at him, that concern for him in her face, he smiled and nodded. 'Yeah. I'm fine.'

Matthew Parker unfolded a bright red fifty-pound note from the wad in his pocket and handed it over to the barman.

'Another round, young Robert, and make 'em doubles, will you?'

A copy of the *National Star* lay on the bar nearby, open at the story, while grouped around him were a dozen or more of his colleagues.

'We didn't just maul them, we fucking well blew them out of the water!' Harry, his editor, was saying loudly. He was pleased, very pleased, because not one of his rivals had even got a sniff. They'd had a clear run at the story, without a single spoiler, and though Monday's editions would doubtless follow up on it, today's sales were bound to soar, because – as Matthew himself had said several times – everybody loved a bigamist!

As for Matthew himself, he was feeling that smug sensation of well-being that only a scoop like this could give him. In terms of prose, it wasn't Addison or Steele, but he bet his bottom dollar that those two bastards had never written anything that had sold an extra two hundred thousand copies!

Smug. Yeah, he was smug, but then he deserved to be. He'd done a good, professional job. Gathered in his facts and made a coherent picture of them. A *tale*.

'Great job, Matthew,' Roy said for the hundredth time, putting his arm about his shoulder, like they were best buddies. 'Fucking brilliant, some of those little touches – I didn't know whether to cry or piss meself laughing!'

And on it went, with Matthew grinning and the beer and whiskies flowing, while throughout the country people read *his* story, in *his* words.

Fucking brilliant, he thought. Yeah, this was the best feeling in the world. This was the dog's bollocks.

Charlotte lay on her bed, cried out, the music blaring from the speakers, filling the darkened room. Jack had left an hour back, confused and in a rage. They'd yelled at one another, a mixture of hate and hurt that had got them nowhere – nowhere at all. Now she just felt hollow.

'Charlotte?'

She wasn't aware of Imogen standing there; not until,

reaching across, Imogen turned down that wall of sound.

'Charlotte? There's someone to see you.'

As Imogen stepped away, a second figure appeared in the doorway. Charlotte sat up partly, pulling a pillow across to support her back.

'How are you?'

Imogen had gone. Julie stood there now. She was peering down at Charlotte, her eyes, her whole face concerned.

Charlotte took a long breath. 'You.'

'I've been wanting to call you. I—'

Charlotte sat forward, a blaze of anger in her eyes. 'Yeah, but you were too busy calling the newspapers!'

'Charlotte, I—'

Charlotte winced. 'Don't use my name. It— I can't bear the thought that you gave it to me.'

Julie looked as though she had been slapped. When she spoke again, her voice was quiet, apologetic like a child's. 'You gotta let me explain.'

'What?' Charlotte said, sarcastically. 'Tell the truth, you mean?'

'I deserve a chance.'

'You deserve nothing! You're just a selfish bitch who's ruined my life!'

Julie looked in pain now. 'No—'

'Why?' Charlotte carried on, relentless now. 'Who else are you going to blame? You dumped me just like you dumped everyone else, and now I—'

Charlotte fell silent, then forced herself to ask the question, dreading the answer.

'Is that man my father?'

Julie swallowed. 'He's nothing. He's just—'

'Why can't you be honest?'

'Because it hurts.'

There was a brief silence between them, then Charlotte repeated her question. '*Is* he my father?'

Julie's eyes met hers. She was struggling now, trying to do the right thing for once in her miserable life. Tears were trickling from her eyes. Seeing that, knowing that the answer was yes, Charlotte's face crumpled.

'There's nothing of him in you,' Julie said. 'You're beautiful. You're a good—'

But Charlotte yelled at her. 'You know nothing about me. It's sick. *You're* sick. You should have had an abortion.'

'D'you think I didn't want to?'

'You should have told someone. You should have— Why didn't you run away?'

Julie looked away. She was quiet suddenly. 'I had nowhere to go. I—' She looked back. 'How do you think it's been for me? I've lived with this for eighteen years.'

'Yeah, well, you're lucky. I've got to live with it for the rest of my life.'

'Charlotte, I promise, I—'

Charlotte shook her head. 'Don't.'

'Please don't hate me.'

'I don't hate you. I don't feel anything. You're nothing to me.' And, turning away, she went over to the stereo. 'Now I want you to go.'

Julie struggled to speak. 'Not a day's gone by when I haven't thought of you.'

Music blared out from the speakers once again; a dark, relentless sound, like the sound of torment itself. For a moment longer, Julie stood there, looking longingly at her daughter – at the only child she had or would ever have. Then, with a look of pain, of utter desolation, she turned and left the room.

A minute passed and then the door downstairs slammed shut. And all the while Charlotte stood there facing the wall, as still as a waxwork, her expression implacable, her hands covering her swollen belly. Wondering.

Chapter Twenty-Six

Holding Back The Tears

Walking up the steps of the courthouse, Julie was conscious of eyes watching her, looking to see how she was dressed, what expression she wore, who she was with, and all the rest of it. Glancing to her side she saw that Sonia was keeping pace with her, her own face closed, like it was she who was about to be sentenced.

She had agreed to plead guilty six weeks back. There had been no point really doing otherwise, seeing as they had all the paperwork – the marriage certificates and everything! Only a fool would have tried to wheedle out of it, and she was no fool.

Closer to the front door, flashes went off as, recognising her, the little huddle of press photographers got in their shots. There were no TV cameras, but a couple of reporters pressed close as she approached the main entrance to the court, asking questions, their words a complete blur. She pushed through, firm yet silently apologetic, not a word escaping her lips, not even a 'no comment'.

Inside, a moment's relief. The main entrance hall was cool and hushed. Only very few people stood about. She looked to Sonia, received the tightest, most nervous of smiles, and reached out to take her hand.

'Thanks for coming.'

''S alright,' Sonia said, the smile becoming more natural.

The court they wanted was upstairs. With a nervous glance at each other, the two women began to climb. They had got halfway up the broad, plushly carpeted stairs when, looking to her right, Julie saw Karl, and next to Karl, Mike, and next to Mike—

'Oh, shit!' she hissed, grabbing Sonia's arm and at the same time turning her back so that she wouldn't be seen. 'I need to go to the loo.'

'Do you want me to come?'

'No! No, you listen out in case I'm called.'

Julie sat in one of the cubicles for a while, letting her pulse slow, her breathing normalise. She stubbed out the cigarette she was smoking, stood and flushed the loo, then stepped outside.

She was standing at the mirror, repairing her make-up, when a voice just behind her made her jump.

'Hello, Julie.'

She turned, facing Vera, astonished to see her there. An astonishment that turned, in an instant, to an uncompromising harshness.

'What are *you* doing here?'

'I wanted to see you.'

'Well, now you've seen me.'

Julie turned away, pointedly ignoring her.

'I read the papers,' Vera said quietly. 'I'm sorry – about everything.'

Julie gave her the barest glance in the mirror. 'Yeah? Well it's only taken you eighteen years to work your way round to that. You're turning soft, Vera.'

'I'm your mother.'

'Oh, per-lease!'

'What they said about Ted – I didn't know.'

Julie turned, her voice taking on a tone of incredulity. '*You didn't know?* Bollocks you didn't!'

'I swear—'

Julie stepped closer, almost in her face. 'Every nightmare I've ever had – and believe me, Vera, I've had a few – what do you think I saw, eh? I'll tell you. It wasn't his face above me as he raped me. It wasn't the pattern of the carpet he rubbed my face into every time he buggered me—'

Vera put her hands up to her ears, but Julie reached out to pull them away.

'Yeah, that's right. Pretend it never happened. But it did. And you know what I saw? Your face, through the crack in the door. You could see. You knew I needed you, but you never came. You never ever came.'

'That's not true.'

'Isn't it? Why can't you be honest, just for once in your rotten life? I might not be honest with other people, but at least I'm honest with myself. I know what *I* am.'

Vera had grown small. She shrank from her daughter now. Her voice was almost a whisper. 'You know what he was like. I was black and blue.'

'I don't care.' Julie took a heaving breath. Her face was dark now, unforgiving. 'I was your daughter. You were supposed to look after me. To protect me, I—' She hesitated, looked away. 'After a while I got used to him. I used to just blot it out, pretend it wasn't happening. Go through the motions just to get it over with.'

Julie turned, looking directly at Vera again. 'He took my innocence. But you – you destroyed my trust and every ounce of self-respect I had. You made me feel like nothing. It wasn't him. He's just an animal. It was you.'

'Please, Julie. I beg you.'

'Yeah, like I begged you.'

'But I prayed . . .'

'Oh well, that's alright then,' Julie spat. 'God forgives you.'

Just then the door at the end swung open. Sonia stood there. 'Julie. They're calling you.'

Turning back to the sink, Julie picked up her make-up bag and thrust it into her handbag. Walking past Vera, she totally ignored her. Outside, Sonia turned to her.

'Who was that?'

'Nobody.'

Her face set, she marched across to where her solicitor stood waiting and into the courtroom, the doors slowly closing behind her.

The hearing itself seemed dreamlike and unreal. Julie sat there, looking across at them, amazed to see them all there in the flesh and twice as lifelike. Mike looked angry, Dave sad, Karl smug and scornful. Brian just shook his head, like he'd known all along she was no good. He was enjoying this. Elsewhere in the court, Dave's mum shot her mean, vindictive looks, full of a petty triumph. She had been right! Oh, and how she gloated over it! But Julie was hardened to all of it. It washed over her. *You don't know the half of what I've had to put up with*, she thought to herself, and inwardly she laughed at them all.

As the judge read out his verdict, there was a strong murmur from the gallery – surprise, or was it disappointment? But Julie felt like whooping aloud and clapping her hands together with delight. Only she didn't. Her solicitor had warned her against any such show of high spirits, and so she sat there, a big beam of a smile on her face that seemed for once to put all of her enemies at naught.

As the doors to the courtroom opened and the people spilled out, there was a great eruption of noise. Embracing her solicitor, Julie allowed herself a little cry of delight.

Then, remembering herself, she reached across and held the woman's hand briefly. 'Thanks for all your help. You were fantastic!'

Eight months suspended, that was all she'd got. The judge could have sent her down for a year or more, but the suggestion of sexual abuse in her childhood and the fact of her natural daughter, lost to adoption at such a tender age, had both counted strongly in her favour. Neither were arguments she would have chosen to use, but the newspaper article had taken matters out of her hands. There were long faces from the abandoned husbands, but Sonia, at least, was delighted for her.

'What a result!'

'I know!' Julie answered. 'I've just gotta keep out of trouble now.'

Sonia gave her a hug. 'What are you doing? You coming back with me?'

'Nah. You go.'

Sonia stepped away, then, remembering something, fished in her shoulder bag and produced a tiny parcel. 'Some fella asked me to give you this.'

Julie took it and opened it. She stared, moved almost to tears. It was Nancy's necklace.

Sonia stared at it, amazed. 'Who's it belong to?'

'Someone – just someone I knew.'

She forced a smile, then squeezed Sonia's arm and leaned across to kiss her again. 'Go on now. Ricky'll be waiting for you.'

Julie turned, meaning to make a quick getaway, avoiding the press, when she saw Marie hovering nearby. She walked across.

'I wondered if you'd come.'

'Good result.'

Julie nodded. There was a moment's awkward silence and then they both went to speak at once. They laughed.

'I'm sorry, Marie. You were a good friend.'

Marie stared at her. There was compassion in her eyes – unexpected.

'I just wish you'd told me,' she said. 'It might have helped to talk. Ever since I found out about – you know – I just, well, I've imagined it happening to Ellie and . . . I'm so sorry, Julie.'

Julie smiled, more bravado than anything else. 'Hey, shit happens. How's Dave?'

Marie nodded towards where Dave was standing on his own. Julie squeezed Marie's hand, then walked across to him.

'Hi.'

'Hi.'

She took a deep breath. 'I wanted to phone you, but they said I shouldn't.'

Dave was struggling to hold himself together. Even so, what he said seemed cold, bitter almost.

'What's to say?'

'If I could have loved anyone, it would have been you, Dave. Any woman you fall in love with's going to be so lucky.'

He clearly didn't want to hear that. He made a tiny movement of his head, as if to physically avoid the words.

'Yeah,' he said, sadness replacing anger in his voice. 'Only I didn't want any woman.'

For a moment longer they stood there, staring at each other, both of them pained and hurt by the exchange. Then, almost afraid of what she felt, Julie jerked forward, kissed Dave on the cheek, and stumbled past him, heading towards the front doors of the courthouse.

*

Watching from the balcony above, Charlotte saw Julie kiss the man and then totter away on her heels. Considering it was such a solemn occasion, she'd been amazed by the outfit Julie had chosen to wear – it was bright to the point of being brassy. And that make-up! It had made Charlotte see another side of her: not Julie the nurse or Julie the betrayed child, but Julie the flirt, Julie the attention-seeker, dressed more for a Friday night out with the girls than for a serious court hearing.

'Is that her?' Jack asked.

Charlotte nodded, wondering if she would ever see her again.

'Yeah,' she said finally. 'That's her.'

Charlotte had chickened out at the last. Had sat outside while the hearing went on, Jack's hand in hers, strangely afraid for Julie. Now that it was over she found herself relieved. She had imagined a prison sentence, and no matter how much she had been hurt by this woman – her birth mother – she couldn't have wished that on her.

'What?' Jack asked, noting the strange smile on her lips.

'Nothing,' she said. Then, turning to face him, she smiled. 'I'm not like her. I know that now.'

'I could have told you that,' Jack said, and grinned. Then, his eyes changing, he took her in his arms and kissed her, conscious of the pronounced roundness of her belly there between them.

Julie waved farewell to the huddle of reporters and photographers, giving them one last posed grin, then slowly went down the steps, enjoying herself now that it was over. She was famous. She'd be in all the papers tomorrow morning.

There were taxis waiting at the foot of the steps. She went to the first and climbed into the back.

'Where to, love?'

She told him, then settled back. And as she did, so the feeling of excitement drained from her and her face changed, taking on a more sombre, reflective mood.

'Cheer up, love,' the taxi driver said, smiling at her in the rear-view mirror. 'It might never happen!'

Julie gave him a polite smile.

'I tell you who I picked up the other day,' the driver went on. 'He 'ad a right face on 'im an' all, and he's meant to be a bleedin' comedian! That one who's got all them plays on up the West End. I tell you what. If I had his money my bleedin' face'd be split in two I'd be laughin' so much!'

Julie grinned. He clocked her in the mirror again, smiled.

'That's more like it.'

Julie leaned towards him. 'I tell you what. If I'm going to cheer up, I'll need something a bloody sight livelier than that to listen to. Ain't you got Capital Radio?'

The driver fiddled with the radio controls. In a moment the sound of Capital filled the cab – Robbie Williams was singing. 'Angels'. One of Julie's favourites.

'Ah, I love Robbie. Who d'you like? I bet you're a bit of a Kylie man, ain't you?'

'I am as it goes.'

'Knew it! And – don't tell me – you're a Virgo.'

'Leo, I think—'

'Ah, yeah, but that'll mean you've got Virgo rising.'

'You an astrologer, then?'

'No. A nurse.'

'A *nurse*!'

And he grinned, looking at her in the mirror once again.